"I told Valerie I never loved her."

"How do you know?"

"I know what love feels like now." Ben bit down on his lip as a smile tried to spread across his face, and his head lolled over toward Kaysi. She was trying to stifle one of her own. *Geez, I probably should have kept that to myself at least a little longer. Oh well.* "You're really beautiful."

"You've said that."

"Because you are. My mom said anyone can be attractive with enough money, but beauty is a gift of the soul that shines outward. It's only given to a chosen few. You are here to bring beauty to the world."

Bring Me Back to Life

by

DeDe Ramey

Dalton Skies Series

Bring Me Back to Life

Cover Art by *Kristian Norris*

The Wild Rose Press, Inc.
PO Box 708
Adams Basin, NY 14410-0708
Visit us at www.thewildrosepress.com

Publishing History
First Edition, 2024
Trade Paperback ISBN 978-1-5092-5254-1
Digital ISBN 978-1-5092-5255-8

Dalton Skies Series
Published in the United States of America

Dedication

This book is dedicated to the wild horse rescues across the US.

Other Wild Rose Press Titles by DeDe Ramey:

24 to Life
A Life Unknown
Life in the Limelight
Flashes of Life

Chapter One

The hooves of the buckskin horse pounded against the hard dirt, running through the night with only the saddle lights to brighten the path. The chill of the January wind, and the icy moisture hanging within it, meant snow was on the way. Dead brush slapped against Ben Corbett's legs as he carefully guided his horse, Dash, down a steep embankment. A dilapidated rock house appeared in the shadows. He leaned down, bracing against the wind, heading to the corner of the land that backed up to highway fifty-one. His mind was reeling. *What the hell happened*? It hadn't been that long since he had checked that fenced area. Maybe a couple of hours.

Oren McIntyre, or Poppi, as Ben had called him since he was able to speak, owned the land. It butted up against his family's land. The two families had been close friends for generations, always there for each other when someone needed help. Poppi had been like a grandfather to Ben, since his grandpa had passed, and he had spent just as much time working on Poppi's land the past few years as he had his own family's.

They were kindred spirits. Neither was big on social gatherings, nor speaking just to hear themselves talk. They loved the land, and the work was satisfying. When Ben noticed Poppi starting to slow down, he figured it was time to step up his game. He had always helped when needed, but after a few unexplained incidents, Ben decided to help with the daily chores, even installing a gate between the two properties for easier access. Poppi welcomed the help, since he was approaching eighty.

He loved his ranch, and still worked hard to take care of it. It was all he had now, since his wife had passed away. The land was divided by the large farmhouse sitting on a ridge on the front half, while the back half dipped into a valley. A creek cut through the center of it, spilling down into the valley with some small waterfalls. It was beautiful. Pine trees covered a portion of the land, hay fields covered another. Crops took up a few acres, but most of it was open for his animals. He had a few cows, some goats, and chickens. But his true love was his wild horses.

Hearing that the gate to the back fence was open, and some of the horses had gotten out, had Ben confused. He knew the gate had been locked when he checked it. It was hardly ever used. After telling his dad to drive their trailer up the highway just in case the horses had ventured that far, he called Cody, his brother-in-law, to come help. It was all hands on deck.

Bright lights, shining up ahead, pointed him in the right direction. But he knew the land well and could probably ride it with his eyes shut. Poppi stood near his truck and was waving the remaining horses back away from the fence. Ben took off through the open gate to search for the ones that had escaped. Highway traffic illuminated the area, and he could see at least three horses heading in different directions. "Shit!" He dug his heels into the side of Dash hoping the horse had a little more in him. If the horses made it to the highway, it could be a disaster.

Scanning the highway, he spotted his dad's red dually truck fast approaching, pulling the trailer. As he eased off the side of the road, Ben steered Dash toward him.

"I've spotted three, but I have a feeling there's more," Ben said breathlessly. "Cody's on his way. I told him to grab Max and head out here."

"What do you need me to do?" his dad, Will, asked.

Car tires screeched, and Ben and his dad jerked their gaze toward the sound. A red sedan slid sideways in the road, narrowly missing a large black horse running in the median.

"Can you, maybe, put out some flares up the road, just to get the cars to slow down?"

"Yep."

Ben took off after the horse, which appeared spooked, but was only running at a slow gallop. It was easy for him and Dash to catch up.

Dash lived up to his name. The muscular buckskin horse had caught Ben's eye the day he appeared as part of a herd Poppi acquired. With his lightly speckled tan hair and blond mane, he almost shimmered when he ran. He was wild, but had taken a liking to Ben, so Poppi let Ben work with him, to see if he could break him. Ben started coaxing him with food, and after a couple of weeks, he had him taking carrots from his hand. Ben was rewarded for his hard work when Poppi surprised him with Dash for his birthday. Now, Dash and Ben were seldom separated.

Cars buzzed past Ben as he slipped a rope around the black horse's neck and drew it tight. Dash slowed his pace. One down.

They trotted back down the median and crossed

when there was an opening in the traffic. Will had set out some flares and traffic slowed to a crawl. He ushered the black horse through the gate, and Poppi patted him on the hind flank to get him to move toward the rest of the herd. A few flakes of snow started to fall. Ben turned his collar up to block the wind that had started to pick up.

"How many, Poppi?"

"I think we have three or maybe four more still loose."

"All right. Keep working the gate. I'll see if I can find them."

"Your buddy came through a little bit ago. I think he took off heading west."

"Perfect." Ben guided Dash out of the gate just in time to hear more screeching tires. He turned to see a black truck rear end a white SUV on the other side of the median. Whistling and clicking his tongue, he and Dash, took off after the chestnut-colored horse that had caused the accident.

"Call nine-one-one," he hollered at his dad as he passed him.

"Already on it."

Ben hadn't wanted to get the police involved. He worried it would get Poppi in trouble. But now that there was an accident, there was no way around it. Tossing the rope around the horse's neck, he tightened it, and Dash did the rest, coming to a slow halt. Two down.

Trotting back across the highway, he spotted Cody with a speckled white horse entering the gate. Cody had been a welcomed addition to the family a little more than a year ago. Ben's sister, Jenna, met Cody under terrible circumstances after Cody's dad had assaulted her. But Cody had protected her from him, and in the end, they had fallen hard for each other. And now, they were married and had a beautiful baby boy. Ben was happy for them, and enjoyed being the dutiful uncle, but he'd decided long ago he wasn't cut out for relationships.

Cody pulled his big black horse to a stop and eyed Ben. "How many more?"

"I think we have one or two still missing." A loud whistle got their attention. Ben immediately knew it came from his dad. He flipped Dash around and headed out the gate with Cody close behind. Although Cody had never ridden before meeting Jenna, he had picked it up quickly. Now, he was helping at the ranch in between his shifts as a paramedic and working at the gym he and his sister owned.

Ben followed his dad's pointed finger and saw two horses headed away from them in the ditch next to the highway. He gave Dash a kick and took off. Cody followed. Red flashing lights met them as a police car and ambulance headed to the scene of the accident. A firetruck lagged behind. One of the horses, a paint, was in a dead run and headed up onto the highway into oncoming traffic. The other peeled off down a dirt path. Ben pointed, motioning for Cody to follow the second horse.

Riding the shoulder, trying to catch up to the paint horse, Ben had Dash at a full run, but the other horse had a head start. Headlights pierced the darkness. Ben only had a matter of seconds to get the horse off the road before all hell would break loose. With his feet locked in the stirrups and his knees squeezed tight against Dash, he lifted the rope above his head and spun it; once, twice, three times, and then let it fly. The loop drifted in the wind and bounced over the horse's nose once before encircling his neck. Ben yanked tight and hurriedly drew the rope in while Dash slowed his pace to a stop. The horse narrowly escaped the wrath of an eighteen-wheeler as it barreled past them. Ben's heart skipped with the thunderous sound, realizing they were within inches of a horrible outcome.

He hauled the horse to his side and started back to the property, replaying the scene over in his head. A smirk crawled across his face as he thought about his talent with the rope. Cody appeared at the edge of the dirt road dragging a gray horse with a black mane. With its head hung low, the horse reminded him of a teenager who had just been caught sneaking out.

"Got him," Cody exclaimed gleefully holding up the rope.

"Yeah, and he doesn't seem very happy about it. I think you spoiled the fun he was about to have."

"He nearly went over the cliff on the far side, just past McIntyre's property. I saved his ass."

"Well, this one was just about to take on an eighteen-wheeler." They rode beside each other at a slow pace heading toward the property. Flashes of bright red and blue lights bounced off the low clouds. As they trotted through the gate, Ben overheard Poppi talking with one of the police officers.

"No. I checked the gates around seven and they were all locked up," Poppi said.

"Are you sure you checked this one? Maybe you forgot."

"No, no." Doubt crept over Poppi's face.

"It was locked," Ben confirmed. The officer turned to face him. "I checked it around eight."

The officer nodded at Ben then turned back to

Poppi. "And you didn't open the gate for any reason after that?"

"No. There's no need. I only use that gate when we are bringing in a trailer of horses or extra hay."

"Someone came and unlocked it," Ben chimed in again.

"Could have been some kids causing trouble," the officer suspected.

"But how did they get it unlocked?" Ben hopped off Dash and checked the lock. "The chain isn't busted, and the lock is intact."

The officer's eyes darted back to Poppi. "Are you sure you didn't open the gate for anything?"

"Positive."

"Does anyone else have access to your property?"

"Just the Corbetts." Poppi's eyes lifted to meet Ben's and the officer's eyes followed.

"I have keys. I help take care of the property. My dad has a set too, for emergencies."

"Any other family members have access?" The officer continued to press.

"No. My son had a set of keys, but he passed away two years ago."

"No one else?"

"No. Not that I know of."

"Well, without knowing how to pick a lock, I don't see how any kids would have been able to get this lock open."

"I don't either," Poppi said shaking his head.

"It's a good thing we only had a fender bender to deal with. It would have been a much different story if that car had hit the horse." The police officer shut his notepad. "Have you secured all of the horses?"

Ben eyed the herd. "I believe so."

"All right." He turned back to Poppi. "I would suggest getting new locks for the gates just to be on the safe side."

"I will do that first thing in the morning."

The officer shook Poppi's hand, then Ben's, and headed out the gate. Will passed him.

"I'm going back to the house unless you need anything else," he announced to Poppi, Ben, and Cody."

Poppi nodded his head and held out his hand. Will grasped it. "Thanks for your help. I really appreciate it."

"Hell, I didn't do much except keep an eye out for wayward horses. Ben and Cody did the hoof work." He slapped Poppi on the shoulder and turned and strolled through the gate.

"I'm headed out too," Cody added. "AJ hasn't been sleeping well, so we have been tag teaming him. I need to get back to the house."

"No problem. I'm just thankful you picked up and were able to come help. Give my nephew a hug from his Uncle Ben."

"Yeah, I appreciate the help," Poppi added, shaking Cody's hand.

"I'll get Max fed and put away before I go."

"Thanks Cody."

As Cody walked away, Ben turned his attention back to Poppi. "We had five, total. Are you sure we got them all?"

"Pretty sure. I was able to get most of them back inside the gate. There was only about a dozen on this end of the property anyway."

"And you can't think of anyone who might have done this on purpose?"

Ben detected a slight hesitation before Poppi answered. "No."

It gnawed at him, but it was late. He would broach the subject tomorrow.

"Maybe we just didn't notice that the lock was loose, and some kids came by and opened it."

"Maybe." Ben highly doubted it though. He was pretty good at making sure the locks were secured, and it wasn't like the land was in a heavily populated area. People just didn't stroll by at all odd hours of the night. No, unless Poppi had come out and opened the gate and forgot, someone had to have deliberately done it. But who?

In the past year, cattle had gone missing, several bags of feed disappeared, an expensive piece of equipment wound up at the bottom of a cliff, and now this. If the old man hadn't been so sharp, Ben would have wondered if he was just becoming forgetful. But every time he talked to Poppi, he never faltered. Something told him there was another reason.

He shook Poppi's hand. "I'm going to head out, but I'll check back with you tomorrow, and we can get the locks changed on the gates."

"Sounds good." Poppi patted him on the shoulder. "Thanks, Ben."

The look in Poppi's eyes gave Ben a sick feeling in his stomach. The old man was as strong as an ox and as stubborn as a mule, and he could count on one finger how many times he had seen it. Fear. It was there when his wife passed away. Even when his son died, he kept his composure. He didn't like seeing Poppi rattled. There was something he wasn't telling him, and he was determined to find out what it was.

9

After locking the gate and checking it, he swung himself back into the saddle. Giving a little nudge, he brought Dash to a slow gallop. The winter wind was biting against his skin, and he cinched in the collar on his jacket and brought the bandana he had tied around his neck over his nose. Even with his cowboy hat, thick jacket, and thermal shirt, his skin still prickled against the icy temperature. The snow was falling harder and would have the ground covered, he suspected, by dawn.

Dawn. That would come too soon. Cody and his buddy, Joe, who was a contractor, were supposed to be coming over to put the finishing touches on the bunkhouse. It was a remodeling project they had been working on for months. After it was the scene of a crime involving his sister being held hostage by Cody's dad, Cody getting shot, and his dad ultimately killed, Ben thought it would be best. Halfway into the project though, Ben decided he wanted to live in it. The changes they were making were extensive and gave Ben a nice studio for his projects.

Maybe, since Cody was out late too, they could start later. Or maybe he could just push them off for another day, so he could help Poppi get the gates taken care of. He would text them when he had Dash taken care of.

Once he arrived at the stable, he unbuckled Dash's saddle, yanked it off, and set it on the rack behind him. Steam filled the air from Dash's heated body. He bobbed his head and shook his mane like he was thanking Ben for the relief. Ben gave him a knowing pat. "I got you, Bud." Guiding the bridle from Dash's mouth, Ben wandered to the tack room, returning with a carrot and a brush. Running the brush along the horse's back and down his flank, Ben continued thinking about the events of the evening. Poppi was hiding something, and he needed to get to the bottom of it.

Chapter Two

Snowflakes drifted past the frosted picture window like a scene from a Christmas postcard. Kaysi Grayeagle sat on her sofa, curled her legs up under her fuzzy purple blanket, and tugged her laptop back into her lap. A cup of hot cocoa sat on her side table, complete with tiny, melted marshmallows. The yellow and orange flames of the fire in the fireplace mesmerized her for a moment.

"I can't believe you're still in your pajamas. It's two o'clock," Libby, her partner in crime said, as she sat in the chair across from her.

"Hey, it's Saturday and snowing. I'm not going anywhere, so why not stay comfy?" Kaysi tapped on her keypad. "I still can't believe you drove over here in the snow."

"I was *so* excited about my finds for your blog, I couldn't wait for it to melt." Her words were thick with sarcasm.

The blog, Kaysi's Kloset, started out as a hobby a couple of years ago. It was a way for Kaysi to share information about little hole-in-the-wall stores, where she found interesting pieces of artwork, fashion, and decor. She'd post a photo of the items with the artist's and store's information and would feature those artists whose work received the most attention, to help with their business.

Starting off, she didn't make much money, but since her primary job was working in marketing and promotion for her family's oil and gas company, it wasn't necessary for her to make a living at it. Although, if she had it her way, she would somehow turn her blog into her business. And with the recent increase in visits to the site, things had started moving in the right direction.

Over the summer, she brought Libby, a close friend from college, on board to help, after she'd commented that she needed a job while on summer break from teaching. When things took off, Libby continued to help on the weekends after she returned to teaching, but Kaysi knew it wasn't something she wanted to do long term. Libby made it clear, it wasn't exactly her cup of tea.

"Were the roads icy?" Kaysi asked, guilt tugging at her. Libby's comments were usually laced with sarcasm, followed by "just kidding."

They were an odd pair. Kaysi always considered herself easy-going. A peacemaker. Libby, on the other hand, had an edge. She said what was on her mind and fiercely protected Kaysi when she felt she was being taken advantage of. They had fun over the summer going to kitschy little shops, but Kaysi could tell Libby's heart wasn't into it.

"Actually, the roads weren't bad. The plows got them cleared."

"Good. I'm glad you didn't come all the way over here on slick roads."

Libby shrugged.

"So, what do you have for me."

Libby got her laptop out of her handmade muslin satchel. "Well, since you are trying to focus on

Arkansas-made art, I found this line of clothing that was kind of cool. This artist takes her watercolor artwork and transfers it onto items like scarves and bags. She even has some flip flops and earrings." Flipping the laptop around, Libby stood.

Kaysi pushed her laptop aside and focused on the photos on the screen. "These are beautiful."

"Decorate the house and decorate your body. Oh, and check out the bracelet I got." Libby jingled interwoven chains of silver flowers with a small, twisted piece of colorful fabric. "It's a little big but I liked it so much, I had to buy it."

"I love the colors she uses." Thumbing up the page on the laptop, she asked, "Where is her store?"

"It's part of a boutique in Rogers. I was going through there, coming back from Oklahoma, and decided to stop."

As Kaysi continued to scan the photos, her phone, that was sitting on the side table, chimed. She reached back and grabbed it. April. A smile spread across her face. "Hey, Chickie!"

April Westerman Grayeagle was one of Kaysi's closest friends, and now, her brother's wife. Their friendship had grown even closer, since April solved a family mystery, that was instrumental in bringing Kaysi's brother Joe, or Kameron, as his family called him, into their lives.

"Hey, Kaysi. Got a minute?"

"Sure. What's up?" Kaysi moved Libby's laptop to the table, then stood and walked into the kitchen.

"I was wondering if you would like to meet me for lunch tomorrow. I have something I need to talk to you about."

She grabbed two sodas and raised one to get Libby's attention. She nodded. "Oh? April, are you guys already talking babies?" Kaysi strolled back into the living room and handed Libby hers, then sat back down on the sofa.

"No. But it does involve my future."

"And let me guess, it's a surprise, and you aren't going to tell me." She took a swig of her soda and moved to set it down, then realized she still had hot cocoa on the table and pouted.

"My friend, you are very perceptive. Can you meet me at noon at Flame Masters, the new bar and grill, in Dalton? Do you know the one I'm talking about? It's on Main, downtown."

Dragging the blanket back into her lap, she smiled. "Oh. Yes. I've seen it. It's the wild west saloon."

"Yes."

"Yeah, I should be able to make it. I can't wait to hear what this is all about. Do I need to wear a dress? Are you proposing? No, wait. You're already married to my brother, so that would be weird. I mean you're basically my sister."

"Gah. You are such a nut. That is exactly why I love you."

"Love you too."

"Okay. So, are we good for noon?

"I will see you then."

"Oh, and no, no dress, but shirts and shoes are required."

Kaysi laughed. "Dang it. I guess I will put clothes on if I have to. It's cold outside anyway."

"Bye, Crazy."

"Bye." She set her phone back on the table.

"What was that all about?" Libby asked with a

sharpness in her voice.

"April wants to have lunch with me tomorrow."

"Oh? Why?"

"I'm not sure, she wouldn't tell me. I guess I will find out tomorrow." She glanced at the laptop which had timed out and gone black. Her finger brushed the pad and brought it back to life, then she stared at the photos again. "I'm not sure which photos I want to use, they are all so good. You did a great job. Did you talk to the store owner?"

"Thanks. No. She was busy," Libby said, sounding a bit insincere.

Kaysi met her eyes, wondering what was bringing on the attitude. "Everything okay with you?"

Libby's brows furrowed. "Fine. Why?"

"I don't know. you just seem a little miffed at me."

Her expression softened. "I'm sorry. You were all chummy chummy with April on the phone, and all you want to do is talk business with me. I miss just hanging out."

Kaysi was taken aback. She thought they spent plenty of downtime together. In fact, Libby took up quite a bit of her time when she wasn't with her boyfriend. *Maybe we do spend too much time discussing the blog.* "Well, let's make plans to just go out to dinner or something when the weather clears."

"That sounds great."

That got a smile out of her. Kaysi's phone chimed again, and she reached over and picked it up. Malcolm. "Hello?"

"Hey, what are you doing?"

Malcolm Blair was a dark-haired, brown-eyed yummy piece of male existence. He'd come into her life when her dad had hired him as one of their company's engineers. Her younger brother, Kaleb, and Malcolm had become office buddies. Like Libby and Kaysi, Kaleb and Malcolm's friendship was a bit odd since Kaleb was very outgoing and Malcolm was quiet and reserved.

She thought he was cute, but out of her league. Plus, since he and Kaleb were buddies, she figured she was off limits. The bro code and all. But evidently, she was wrong. He showed up at her apartment, with flowers in hand, and asked her out. That was six months ago.

"I am currently sitting here in my pajamas, covered in a snuggly blanket, working on my blog. What are you doing?"

"It's almost three."

"And your point is?" She rubbed her hand against the soft fibers of the blanket. "It's freezing outside, and the snow is falling so pretty. I'm not going anywhere. I have my hot chocolate, the fire, and I'm staying warm and cozy."

"Do you want me to come get you?" Although the idea of getting out and seeing the snow-covered neighborhoods sounded tempting, the idea of hanging out with Malcolm, didn't. She had felt that way for a while. "Not today. I'm working on my blog, and I think I want to just stay in."

"How about tomorrow?" She had to face facts. He was much more into the relationship than she was. He was completely charming and sweet, but she was realizing there was something that didn't feel right. Something was missing.

"I have a lunch date with April. Can I call you after that?" she asked, trying to get out of it as nicely as possible.

"Sure. But don't forget. I miss you."

Her stomach knotted. "Miss you too." She hadn't, if she was being honest. It had been five days since she had seen him. Now she was feeling guilty.

After she disconnected the call, she heard Libby's voice and glanced up knowing exactly what expression Libby was wearing. Bright eyes. Big smile.

"Malcolm?" Libby asked two octaves higher than her normal voice.

Kaysi took a deep breath and let it out knowing what was coming. "Yeah," she said with no enthusiasm.

"Trouble in paradise?" Libby mused. Kaysi knew not to say too much. Libby had had her eye on Malcolm since she'd introduced them. She was always playfully flirting.

"No. Everything's fine. We may go out tomorrow evening."

"Then why are you acting like your goldfish just died."

"I miss him," she lied again. Feeling guilty, she tried to balance it out with a truth. "I haven't seen him in a week."

"Ah," Libby said, giving her a sidelong glance. Kaysi could tell she didn't believe her. "Well, if you ever want to dump that delicious piece of man candy, I'd be happy to dry his tears."

Kaysi waved her hand in the air dismissing her comment. "Pffft. Don't get your claws out yet."

A smile curled the corner of Libby's lips. "I'm serious. He's gorgeous, and sweet. And if you don't want him, I damn sure do."

"You think I don't know that? You have made it abundantly clear on several occasions." She had. The sad truth was, not only was Malcolm not interested, but he also didn't like Libby. He had commented many times that he didn't trust her. Her somewhat hard, cynical personality didn't mesh well with Malcolm's proper raising.

His mom's British upbringing meant Malcolm lived by a certain standard. Kaysi found it refreshing at first. But the longer they dated, it grew rather restricting, and a bit boring. Although Malcolm treated her well, she knew their relationship was not meant to be and dreaded the inevitable. Libby, however, would be elated with the news. Unfortunately, her chances of walking down the aisle with Malcolm were slim to none. Telling Libby that though, would be an exercise in futility. Malcolm had tried to make it clear to her, on several occasions, sometimes even boldly, that he was not interested, but it never deterred her from flirting with him every chance she got.

"If Malcolm and I ever decide to split, you will be the first to know."

Libby winked and kissed the air as a thank you, then let out a giggle. "So, tell me the truth. You and Malcolm…"

Kaysi knew she should keep her mouth shut. Giving Libby any glimmer of hope would be almost cruel. But she desperately needed some advice, and Libby had given some solid advice in the past. She could also wait until tomorrow and ask April. She knew Malcolm too. But it was eating at her right now.

"I don't know. I feel a bit smothered. Don't get me wrong, he is very sweet and has always treated me like a queen, but—" she tried to figure out how to tell her without getting her hopes up; say something that might turn her away, "—he is so proper. I feel like I'm not good enough." Which was true. "From the way Malcolm talks, I get the feeling his mom doesn't think I'm good enough for her son either." She thought maybe that would dampen Libby's crush, but she underestimated her obsession.

"I could change his ways," she said with a sensual tone.

Chapter Three

After calling all morning while he, Cody, and Joe, worked on the house, Ben was starting to get worried when Poppi hadn't picked up. His concern only grew worse when he didn't answer the door just after lunch. Ben used his key and checked the house, but it was empty. As he turned to head back to his house, Poppi showed up in his beat-up farm truck. A scowl consumed his face as he slowly exited the truck.

"Poppi. Where the hell have you been? I was getting worried about you. I tried calling several times this morning."

"I was on the phone most of the morning with the police who called bright and early. And then I called my insurance company trying to figure out if I am going to have to pay for the accident last night. Once I finally got off the phone with them, Ricky called and wanted to have lunch."

"What did you find out?"

"Still trying to figure that out. I'm waiting for my insurance to call me back."

"Wait. Rick is in town? Why?"

"Said he was here for business but wanted to check on me." Poppi grabbed a bag from the seat before closing the door.

"What's that?"

"The new locks. After this morning, I'm surprised I remembered. I picked them up after lunch."

"So how is Rick? And why was he checking up on you?"

"Why don't you grab Dash and come help me get these locks changed out. I will fill you in then."

"Give me ten minutes."

Poppi nodded.

After returning to the stable, he saddled up Dash and replayed the conversation with Poppi. His gut clenched with each word. Rick is in town. Rick McIntyre was not his favorite person. In fact, he was at the bottom of the list. Ben had never liked Rick. Even when they were younger, they were more likely to get into a fight than get along. But the last straw was when he came to town for his dad's funeral and left with the woman Ben was supposed to marry. Just another shitty memory he had on replay in his thoughts.

When he headed out to Poppi's property, he found Poppi already changing out one of the locks. "I thought you were going to give me time to get back before you got started, old man."

"I was just getting things ready."

"What do you think? Should we go around together or divide and conquer?"

"I was thinking we could handle them together. That would give us time to talk."

The hair on his neck stood on end, and he rubbed at it beneath his coat collar. Poppi never said he wanted to talk. Neither of them had the gift of gab. Ben always said Jenna got his share of the chatterbox gene. For Poppi to want to talk, he had to have something weighing on him heavily. "Okay? Would this have anything to do with

Rick?" Ben took the new chain from Poppi's hand and wrapped it around the metal posts then picked up the lock. "What the hell is this thing?"

"It's a fingerprint activated lock, and I can program it through my phone. Once we get everything changed, we'll go back to the house and program them."

"How much did these suckers set you back?" He clamped the lock shut, then tugged on it to make sure it was secure.

"Don't ask. It's worth it, if it means not losing my horses again."

"True." Ben swung himself into the saddle and they slowly plodded up the fence line. "So, you didn't answer my question. Does this *talk* have something to do with your lunch with Rick?"

"Well, let me ask you something first. Do you like what you are doing?"

"You know the answer to that. I love what I do. There is nothing more satisfying than running the ranch with my dad and with you. I can't imagine that there is anything that I was cut out for more than this."

"So, if your dad turned the ranch over to you right now, what would you do different?"

"Wow! Okay. I didn't expect the conversation to go this direction." The question hit him out of nowhere. He had never really thought about it. Letting out a deep breath, he scratched at his beard, then responded, "Ummm…I really have never thought about it. But if I'm being honest, I would probably run it similar to how he runs it right now, with the exception of adding some more horses. Wild horses if possible. I don't think it will ever get old for me to watch your horses run along the ridge."

"That's exactly how I feel."

They stopped at the next gate and Ben took another lock from the bag. After removing the old lock, he wrapped the chain back around the gate post then added a lock. Shoving his foot in the stirrup, he got comfortable in the saddle again and prodded Dash to move.

Riding for a while without speaking, Poppi finally broke the silence. "Rick wants to take over some of the land. He thinks it's getting too much for me."

"He wants to buy some of the land from you?"

"Not exactly. He said, since it's part of his inheritance, he just wants to take over part of the land to help me out."

Ben could practically feel his blood begin to boil. "What exactly does he plan to do with it?"

Poppi squinted at the brightness of the sky, "He said he could take over the pine ridge area and the hay field, and harvest them," then returned his gaze to Ben. "But that would mean getting rid of some of the horses. I just wouldn't have the space or the money to take care of them." The sadness in Poppi's eyes nearly broke Ben.

"Why does he think you can't handle it anymore?"

"Read about the horses getting out in the newspaper this morning." Poppi tipped his hat back and scratched his head. "He's been talking to me about it for a while. I've always thought I could handle it. But last night made me wonder."

Ben sat back in his saddle and tugged on the reins bringing Dash to a stop. He took a deep breath trying to calm his temper that currently had him feeling like he was about to explode. Rick had no designs on being a farmer or rancher. Ben was sure of that. He hated spending time at the ranch when he was younger. There was another reason. He wanted to get his hands on the land, but it wasn't to help Poppi out, and Ben was damn sure going to find out why.

"Poppi, can I be honest with you? Man to man?"

"Sure. You've always been honest with me." A smirk ghosted his lips. "Still not sure you weren't lying about the missing lemon bar but—"

"I was ten. It was sitting out there begging to be eaten. Let it go."

"Ah, so you admit it now."

"I'm not admitting nothing. I'm merely stating a fact. If you leave something so delicious sitting out for everyone to see and smell, someone is bound to abscond with it." Poppi let out a low laugh, and Ben did the same, then shook his head remembering what they were discussing. "Anyway, hear me out." He adjusted himself in his saddle and leveled his eyes at Poppi. "You know I have no love lost with your grandson. I wish we could have been friends, but we were just born of two very different worlds, and too many wrongs have happened for that to ever change. That being said, I don't want you to think that has anything to do with this issue, and what I'm about to say.

"No, I don't like Rick, and I don't trust him. You can understand why. But beyond that, I seriously doubt Rick would have the time or patience to do any work on the ranch. He is a very busy man in his own right running his dad's business. Even if he had ideas to plant and harvest the pine trees and hay fields, I don't think he realizes how much work it takes. You would have to teach him, and it would just add to your work, not make it easier. He's probably figuring it would only take a few days, a couple of times a year, to take care of everything."

"You are probably right about that."

"I think he's been putting doubts in your head, Poppi. I know the police officer last night thought maybe you forgot to lock the gate, but I know it was locked and I haven't seen any signs of you being forgetful. It did cross my mind at first when the bags of feed went missing, but when the cattle disappeared, and the backhoe wound up at the bottom of the ravine, I knew something was up and went to Mitch. I have no doubt in my mind last night's incident had nothing to do with your memory. Someone is screwing with you, and I plan to get to the bottom of it."

"But why would they?"

"I'm not sure, but you can bet your ass I will find out. And as for Rick, don't let him have the land if you feel like you can handle it. Especially since it would mean losing some of your horses. I know how happy they make you."

"They do make me happy, but he was very convincing."

"Enough to give up your horses?"

Poppi slumped. "I really don't want to give up my horses."

"Then don't. Tell him no. If you are worried you can't handle it, tell me what you need help with. I'll make sure it gets done."

"You already help out, and you have your own property to worry about."

"I'm fine. I told you. I love doing this as much as you do. I can't think of anything I would rather be doing. And I damn sure don't want you making a bullshit decision, and losing your horses, if you don't want to."

"I really don't."

"You probably are going to think I'm an ass for saying this, but he has no right to this land. It's yours. You can keep it or give it to anyone you please. It doesn't have to be Rick. You know that, right? I mean, do with it what you think is best."

"But he's—"

"I get that he's your only heir, and I understand that you would probably like the land to stay in the family. Hell, your family has had this land for longer than we have had ours. In fact, I think someone in your family sold us ours, if I remember the story correctly. This is all your family's land if you get right down to it. Forgive me for saying this, but you aren't going to have a say when you are six feet under, and your grandson doesn't care about the land like you do. Once you die, I doubt seriously he is going to keep the land. He's never liked it here. He has his own life. So, if I were you, I'd hang onto it as long as possible, because once you're gone, the land will be too."

"This is true."

"Do with it what you think is best for now and later. If you want to keep it, keep it. I'll help you take care of it. And if you decide to divide it with Rick, let me know. I will take some of your horses, so you don't have to get rid of them. Just please don't give up your dream because it's his inheritance." Ben thought about Poppi's comments, and it suddenly made him curious. "Exactly how long has Rick been talking to you about the land?" They arrived at the next gate.

"It started after his dad passed."

Ben changed out the old lock with the new one, locked the chain and they moved on to the next. "What the hell, Poppi? And you're just now telling me?"

"We walked the property, and had a nice talk, not too long after Randy died. Then, a few months later, he asked what I thought about him taking over half. I told him I wasn't interested. He said I needed to think about it because I was getting up in age and wasn't always going to be able to work it. I told him I was just fine right now."

"Did he ever give you any indication he might want the land for something else? To sell it maybe?"

"No, he always said he wanted to help me."

"Did he care what chunk of land you gave him?"

"He's only talked about the pine ridge and the hay field."

"You're talking the ridge between our houses, right? Where the rock house sits?"

"Yeah."

"There aren't enough pine trees to even harvest and rotate. Why would he want that, other than it's pretty and has the spring running through it. He could split the hay field with you and harvest the hay, but he really wouldn't make that much money from it." Ben's mind was short circuiting trying to figure out what Rick's game was. He knew damn well that Rick had no intentions of helping Poppi. This was all a ploy. "And he is wanting you to just sign that land over to him?"

"Yeah. He said he would inherit it anyway."

"And there is no pirate booty, or hidden oil, or gold mine. Is there?"

"No," Poppi said snickering. "Not a real one anyway. There was an old story that diamonds once washed up in the creek. When Rick was little and would get under our feet, we'd tell him to go hunt for diamonds in the creek. He'd come back with all kinds of rocks. But I can't imagine he would seriously think that story was true and want to get the land for that."

"Well, is it?"

"Hell no. It's just an old story my great granddad told, and if it was, we'd all be rich by now after that flood a few years back."

After finishing with the last lock and chain, the men rode back up to Poppi's house.

"What else do you need me to do, Poppi?"

"Sit down, get warm, and have a beer with me before you head back to your house."

"I think I'll take you up on that. It's a bit cold out here. I hear we have another blizzard coming. Sounds bad. We are going to get buried."

The house was warm. Remains of several logs glowed in the fireplace. Ben removed his gloves just in time for Poppi to hand him a beer. He set it on the counter and shrugged his coat off, hanging it on the coatrack in the hallway. Poppi added some more logs to the fire, and the two men sat and watched the embers ignite the dry wood. Ben was still pondering everything that Poppi had shared with him when Poppi's phone chimed.

"Hello?"

Ben wondered who was on the other end of the call. It didn't take long to figure it out.

"No, Rick, I've decided to hang on to the land. I appreciate your concern, but you have enough to worry about with the company. Your daddy left you some big shoes to fill. I don't think you would have the time to invest in taking care of land that is seven hours away." He paused, and his face twitched with annoyance. "No. I didn't leave the gate open, I told you that. We think someone did it on purpose." He paused again.

"Ben, Will, and Will's son in law, Cody, came over to help get the horses back inside the fence." The expression crossed Poppi's face again, and Ben could tell Poppi was getting a bit frustrated with the conversation. "Rick, I'm just not ready. I will let you know if I need help. I appreciate your concern, but the answer right now is no." He disconnected the call and threw the phone on the coffee table in front of them, then cut his eyes to Ben.

"Sounded like he got a bit pushy."

"He talks a good talk. That's the salesman in him."

"He's like a financial broker or something, right?"

"Yeah. Randy taught him all the high-powered wheeling and dealing."

"I guess you can make some good money if you know what you are doing."

"Yeah. And lose it just the same. It's all just numbers on a piece of paper until you have it in your actual bank account. I'd much rather know exactly what I have and not worry that if the stock market crashed, I'd lose it all."

"More power to Rick, but I don't know anything about all that stuff, nor do I want to learn." Ben paused. "So, what did he say when you told him no?"

"Told me I was making a mistake. He said I was getting too old to be working that hard." Poppi took a swig of his beer and put his fist to his mouth letting out a satisfied burp. "I think his dad's death affected him more than I thought."

"How so?"

"When Randy died, Ricky showed up here acting all pissed. Maybe it was just his way of processing everything, but he seemed pissed at the world. Ever since his death, Ricky has come around more. Showed up on my doorstep unannounced, called me out of the blue. He never wanted to visit when he was a kid. Always pitched a fit the whole time Randy and Margo were here. Then after their divorce, when Ricky was eight or nine, he was living with Margo during the summers, so he didn't come around much. Randy got him during the school year, so we had a couple of holidays together, but that was it. Now, he shows up every couple of months. Says he has work in the area. Maybe it's just because he thinks I'm all he has now of his dad. He still has his mom and stepdad, of course. They live close to him."

Ben nodded, not knowing exactly what to say. He didn't trust Rick as far as he could throw him and wished it was as simple as that but had a sinking feeling it wasn't. He only hoped that Poppi's "no" was enough to get him off his back.

Poppi stared at the fire for a moment, took a swig of his beer, and stood. "Okay, let's program the locks. I have the instructions on the counter." Ben hopped up and grabbed the instructions. "When your dad has time, we can get him programmed into them too."

Chapter Four

Kaysi parked at the rustic restaurant on the corner. It resembled an old western saloon, complete with swinging saloon doors, which were currently pushed aside in lieu of a large pair of wooden and glass doors, due to the frigid temperatures.

She opened the door, and the delicious smell of flame-grilled food overtook her senses. Clanking forks and a low roar of voices had her head swiveling. Scraped hardwood floors and dark stained tables and chairs were scattered throughout the dining area that was split in half with a grand staircase leading to an upper level.

A long bar with a cement top and corrugated copper wrapped at the base took up the back on one side. Kaysi could picture summer days with the heavy wooden doors open and all that stood in the way to the outside were the saloon doors, with tables and chairs situated along the sidewalk, and people enjoying the warm weather.

But today, that was not the case. Piles of snow were drifted along the edges of the street. She barely could find a parking space that didn't have a three-foot mound.

Walking farther into the restaurant, she spotted April, smiling and waving from a corner table by the window, and hurried over.

"How were the roads coming in?" April asked as Kaysi slid into her chair.

"Not bad at all. I have to hand it to the street crew. They got out and got them cleared quickly. Libby even said they weren't bad yesterday when she dropped by."

April's smile faded. There was no love lost between April and Libby. Although they had similar snarky personalities, that's where it stopped. Where April's cynical take on the world made people laugh, Libby tended to take things a bit too far. April had even mentioned a few times that she thought Libby seemed to have a hard time with boundaries and filters.

"Libby was over?"

"Yeah. She dropped off information for some items she'd found for the blog. I still can't believe how it has blown up over the past few months."

"So, are you ready to quit your job at Grayeagle?"

"Oh, geez. I would love to. I love my family, don't get me wrong. But oil and gas is…boring. The people there are great, but it's just not what I want to do for the rest of my life."

"Technically, you don't *have* to work."

The oil and gas company, that had been part of her family since oil had been found on their land in Oklahoma, had afforded them a very comfortable lifestyle. However, her father was never one to rest on his laurels and taught his kids the same. Money was considered a blessing and never taken for granted. April's family had the same fortune and the two had practically grown up together.

"You don't either."

"Yeah. Speaking of that. I'm about done with working at the vet. Now that I have finished my design degree, I am thinking about branching out."

The waitress arrived, took their drink orders, then

disappeared. Kaysi hadn't even glanced at the menu sitting on the table in front of her, so she opened it up to check the offerings. "Wow! This place has everything."

"Yeah. Joe and I have been here a couple of times since it opened. Everything we've had has been crazy good. The lunch salads are huge. And by the way, this is my treat."

Her eyes scanned the salads, finding one that caught her interest. "You don't have to do that."

"I want to. It's kind of a bribe."

"A bribe?" Kaysi giggled, wondering what April was up to. She hadn't given her any indication of what the lunch meeting was about on the phone yesterday. "So why do you feel like you have to bribe me with food?"

April's face lit up, which made Kaysi immediately excited. April was not known for letting her unbridled happiness show very often. But it was showing a lot more since she married Kaysi's brother, Joe.

"You're pregnant, aren't you?"

April jerked back and rolled her eyes. "Oh, dear god, no. Why would I need to bribe you about that anyway?"

"I don't know, but I can tell you are excited."

"I think we will make beautiful babies at some point. And I enjoy practicing, *a lot*. I don't think either of us is quite ready for kids though. We are perfectly happy being Aunt April and Uncle Joe to AJ for now."

Kaysi giggled. "Okay? Then—"

"I will say, the surprise will kind of be like having a newborn."

Kaysi's curiosity was peaked. "How so?"

"You will need to quit your job to help me take care of it."

"You want me to quit my job?" Kaysi asked in a

slightly squeaky voice.

April bit her lower lip for a split second before responding, "Yes," she said slowly, and held up a finger before Kaysi could comment. "I want to open a store...with you as my partner." Kaysi's mouth dropped open, and she wanted to respond, but nothing seemed to be escaping in the form of words, just noises, so April continued. "You have the most amazing taste in art and style. And since I've gotten my degree, I want to start my own interior design company, so I can add my touches to the houses Joe builds. We both have a following on our blogs, so I thought maybe..."

Kaysi sat, blinking in stunned silence, trying to process what April had asked.

April tilted her head, obviously waiting for an answer.

"Oh my gosh, April. Yes! A thousand times yes. When do we start?"

"Wait I haven't finished my spiel," April said quickly. "I figure we can maybe combine the blogs and I can contribute stories to yours or maybe we can just post back and forth on each other's until we can combine. I haven't worked that part out quite yet, but it would be a good marketing—"

"Again, I'm in. When do we start?" Kaysi bounced in her chair wondering when she would explode from elation. The waitress appeared with two glasses of water and two teas and set them on the table.

"Are you guys ready to order?"

Kaysi was just slightly miffed about getting interrupted at possibly the best moment in her life and couldn't for the life of her remember what she had decided on. After scanning the menu again, she settled on a salad.

"I'll have the same," April added.

"Anything else?"

"No. Thanks," Kaysi said in a rush, hoping the waitress wouldn't take too long, so they could get back to the discussion at hand.

The waitress grabbed up the menus and scurried away.

"I was so nervous I forgot to actually decide on what to eat," April exclaimed.

"What? You didn't think I would want my dream job? Are you nuts?"

"I had no clue if you would want to go into business with me."

"Oh my gosh, April. Why? I love you. You are drop-dead hilarious. I can imagine what it would be like working with you. I might have to bring some changes of pants to work in case I pee myself from laughing so hard."

"Well, let me tell you what my thoughts are. You already have a good selection of artists and designers that we can start with. We will contact them and see if we can make some purchases. I scanned your blog and I think all we need are a few larger items; chairs, sofas, actual furniture, then we can do some groupings. You can be the primary buyer, and I can do the designs."

"That sounds perfect." The waitress dropped their food off, but Kaysi was too buzzed to notice until it was right in front of her. "Do you have a location in mind?"

April grabbed her heart pendant on her necklace and chewed on the corner of her lip. "I do," she said quietly. Concern splashed across April's face for just a second before she donned a cheery smile. But it didn't get by

Kaysi.

"You're going to make me move, aren't you?"

April's lips tucked into a straight line. "Is it a deal breaker?"

"Depends. Are you going to ask me to move to Chicago or Wyoming? I would say hell no to Chicago, but I hear Wyoming has some good snow skiing."

April laughed. "I really do love you."

"Joe has some stiff competition."

"That he does, my friend. But I wasn't thinking about going that far, at least not yet. I found a place…here. At the other end of the block."

"Here? As in Dalton? Do you think we would have enough foot traffic to maintain the business?"

"I think, combined with my interior design work for Joe's construction business, and our internet sales, we would definitely be able to turn a profit."

"But your design consultation would be your money alone."

"No. You are going to provide me with the awesome stuff, so everything is fifty-fifty. Well, for starters it might be nothing-nothing until we get it off the ground."

"And you said the building is up the street? Is it one of the historical buildings?"

"Yes. It's actually two."

"Two. Do you think that's a good plan? Shouldn't we start out small?"

"They're being sold by the same person, so we can get a good deal if we take them both. For the floor space, I think it's the best plan. We can do more groupings, and I can have a consultation area."

"You have really thought this through, haven't you?"

"I've been stewing on this for over a week, trying to put it all together to present to you."

Kaysi laughed. "So, can we go see our new store? Oh my gosh. We need a name."

"Yeah. When we get done, we can walk down there." She held up the key. "I've got it until five this evening."

"I can't believe this is happening." Kaysi took a deep breath, trying to clear her thoughts that were bombarding her. "When do you think we will be able to open?"

"Not sure. Joe doesn't have much work right now because of the cold weather, so any construction stuff we need done, he can do it."

"What's Joe think of all this?"

"He loves the idea. There is a developer he is talking to right now, about some land west of town. If they can work out a deal, he might be able to put some spec homes out there, and I would get to do the interior design for the open houses." She took a bite of her salad and continued. "So, do you think Malcolm would be okay with you making the move?"

Kaysi's chest tightened. She hadn't called him about getting together, but the more she thought about it the more she knew she needed to end the relationship before it went any further. "I don't think that's going to be a factor for much longer."

"Uh oh. What happened?"

"Nothing really. That's kind of the problem. We've dated for six months, and I'm just not feeling the chemistry. He is so sweet, and I hate feeling this way because it's obvious he cares about me. But if I'm being honest, he's a bit too sweet and too reserved. There's no spark. No passion. He never loses control."

"Awe. I really like Malcolm. He's such a cutie."

"He is. He's adorable, and I love his voice with that quirky British accent. But that is part of the problem. He's so proper, and I've caught him numerous times staring at me like I'm doing something wrong. Mind you, he's never called me out on anything, but I could tell by his expression, he was judging me. I can't get the idea out of my head that he doesn't think I'm good enough."

"That's a shame though, that someone would judge you on your eating without smacking your food skills." Kaysi had to laugh at that. "But seriously, any mother of your guy would be lucky to have you. You are the sweetest person I've ever met."

"I guess that's part of the problem. I do try to be nice, but I also like to go wild sometimes and be adventurous. And that doesn't seem to interest Malcolm."

"I've got the opposite problem. Joe is always wanting to go hiking or fishing or some other kind of sport where you sweat. And trust me, it's taken me a hot second to get used to all that." April's brows shot up. "I just had a brilliant idea. We'll trade. Only when Joe wants to go on one of his outdoorsy trips or whatever." She tapped her finger to her chin. "And no hanky panky allowed."

"To be honest, I think Malcolm would be too reserved, even for you."

April's lips pinched on one side in a slight grimace. "You really are done, aren't you?"

"Eh. It's for the best. If he's not the one, he's not the one. No use wasting the man's time."

"Yes. You definitely need to find your guy."

"I don't know." Kaysi winked. "Maybe I'll just fight Joe for you."

"Yeah. I'm a catch." April snickered. "So, are you ready to go?"

"Absolutely."

April dug in her purse for her wallet.

"Are you sure I can't help you pay?"

"No, Kaysi. This is my treat."

"But I don't need to be bribed, April. This is my dream come true."

"Good. But I'm still paying."

"Fine." She spotted some artwork on the walls around the restaurant and stood, still feeling a twinge of guilt. "I'm going to peruse the artwork while you pay the bill. If that's okay?"

"Yeah. I'll come find you."

Kaysi slid her bag off the back of her chair. Her eyes scanned the room and landed on a large framed western painting. She strolled over to it and took a moment to examine the colors. Two cowboys on horseback on a cattle drive. The artist had captured the evening sky in a perfect blend of pinks and grays and teal hues. Dragging her phone from her purse, she snapped a quick photo. To the side was the name of the artist, so she snapped a photo of that too, so she could search the name later for other pieces. Moving on, she saw another western painting, but it was more of a landscape. She tipped her head studying it, waiting to feel the familiar twinge of excitement, but it didn't come.

Twirling around quickly, taking in the other walls, she noticed a piece on the other side of the restaurant. The closer she got, the more intrigued she became. In a rustic wooden frame was an intricately designed artistic piece. Several strips of alternating stained wood pieces were joined together, then carved and etched, then finally burned for shading, to form a beautiful waving flag. She leaned in. Her breath stalled. There was so much detail. It was exquisite. Holding up her phone, she took a photo then flipped over to her blog. With the short comment, "You should see this in person," she uploaded the photo. Then, realizing she needed to add the artist's information, she captured the tag next to it. EtchedIn was the artist, and it listed the e-mail address. She heard April's voice and quickly edited her post. A smile crossed her face as she strolled over to the door where April was waiting.

"Find something?" April asked when she got close.

"Yes, I did. It would be perfect for our store. Something for maybe a mancave. I need to remember to send the artist an e-mail, because I have a feeling that piece is going to get a lot of attention."

As they walked up the sidewalk, a red brick two story building came into view. Large windows spanned the front with smaller windows above, framed in an ornately carved design. The second floor had a large spire that jutted out from the building with more windows that wrapped around it.

Pushing the door open, they were hit with a musty smell and dingy, water-stained walls. The wood floor had seen better days but appeared to be salvageable. Two glass front display cases sat at the back of the room, probably from the previous owner. The red brick was visible along one side with a fireplace in the center. Plaster had fallen from a couple of spots in the ceiling. Kaysi tried to stay positive. It did have potential, but it needed work. Lots of work. Overall, she loved its old charm but wondered if the long, narrow building would provide the room for the groupings that April had described. Then she remembered she had said there were two buildings.

"I know it's not great, but Joe and the inspector have already gone through it. There are a few items we need to take care of, plumbing, sprinklers, handicap access, and the a/c needs to be upgraded."

"Those sound like expensive issues."

"They are. But necessary. Other than that, Joe will blow out that wall," she pointed, "giving us all that space we need. On the backside of that building is our storage area."

"What about the upstairs?"

A sly smile crept across April's face. "Go look. The stairs are right around that corner. There are also exterior stairs out back" She handed Kaysi the key. Kaysi raised a brow in confusion but headed for the stairs.

Windows everywhere. Exposed beams and brick. A large open space, with a grand stone fireplace along one brick wall. A nice sized kitchen sat in the back of the room. Ornate columns flanked a brick arched wall with two pocket doors. Pushing the doors apart, Kaysi walked into another large room with windows at the front. Her heart was about to beat out of her chest. The place had so much character, and she could picture how she would decorate it with live plants, large graphic canvas paintings, dark wood and metal to complement the brick. She saw it all.

"What do you think?" came a voice behind her, causing her to jerk, then turn. April stood outside the pocket door.

Kaysi knew she probably had a goofy grin on her

face, but she didn't really care.

"Pretty amazing, isn't it?"

"I want this!"

"I knew when I saw this place, you were going to flip." She crooked her finger, and Kaysi stepped out of the bedroom and followed her. A bright red door off the kitchen led out to a massive deck with stairs leading down to a garage and covered carport.

"This is insane, April."

"Get you some comfy couches, a firepit, a little grill. You could have some awesome parties."

Kaysi's eyes met April's, and they both squealed. "Let's do this!"

April opened her arms and Kaysi wrapped her in a hug. They bounced together a couple of times, then Kaysi stepped back and screamed, "We're going into business together."

April nodded. "Friday."

Kaysi jerked. "What's Friday?"

"We're signing the papers at two."

"Wait. What? We're signing the papers this Friday? Don't I have to pitch in money and stuff, and send an application to get qualified or something?"

"Nope. It's all done. You just have to show up and sign on the dotted line."

"You already knew I would do this. Didn't you?"

"Well, I really hoped you would, and I figured if you didn't agree to it, I could beg and plead you into submission in the next few days."

"But this is still fifty-fifty. Right?"

"Right. We will work out the money later. I didn't want to lose this place, so I got the ball rolling. Joe said he would be happy to remodel your loft after we get the downstairs done. There's only a couple of minor fixes that need to be done for you to move in now. Can you make it at two on Friday?"

They headed down the stairs, and Kaysi took one more peek at the store. "I wouldn't miss it for the world. Where's it at."

"I will text you the address."

"I guess I'm going home to quit my job, find a renter for my place, and pack."

April opened the door.

"Oh my God, April. I can't believe we are doing this."

"I know." She turned off the light and walked out the door. They slowly strolled back up the sidewalk, giggling all the way.

Kaysi gave April another hug when they got to their cars. "Thank you."

"I can't think of anyone I would rather do this with. Oh, and Jenna said she would pitch in when needed."

"She knows?"

"Everyone knows. I wouldn't be surprised if Kaleb didn't know."

She rolled her eyes. The thought of having to tell Kaleb about her and Malcolm's relationship coming to an end suddenly made her stomach queasy. Him playing matchmaker was the main reason they had gotten together. She let out a long breath. One more item on the quickly growing list. Break up with Malcolm. It had to be done. And the sooner the better.

She lifted her gaze to April and waved. "I'll see you at two Friday."

Her hands shook as she opened the car door. *Oh my gosh, what did I just do?* A grin spread across her face with the thought of what was coming. She dug her phone out. Three missed calls. Two voicemails. One from Malcolm and the other from Libby. She punched the call button.

"Where have you been?" Libby blurted through the phone. "I was getting worried."

What was she, five? She didn't need a keeper. "Hello to you too. What's up?"

"Have you seen your blog? It's blowing up on the photo you posted from the artist, EtchedIn?"

"Isn't it awesome? And you should see it in person. It's beautiful."

"Eh. It's fine," Libby said without any enthusiasm. "A little rustic for my taste."

"I can't wait to see what else this person has to offer."

"Well, I've already found the website. There are several versions of the flag, plus some etched boxes, a few pieces in metal, and a really cool etched skull in a feather headdress."

"Send me the link, and I'll try to get in touch with the artist."

"I will. How did your lunch with April go?" Kaysi's chest suddenly tightened. She wasn't sure how Libby would take the news, and Kaysi wasn't ready to get into it with her.

"Fine."

"What did she want?"

The tone of her voice, even through the phone, let her know Libby was bothered with the fact she went to lunch with April. "I'll talk to you about it later. I need to call Malcolm. Is there anything else?"

"Oh. Letting him off the hook tonight?"

"Libby—"

"Fine, fine. Bye."

She opened her e-mail and typed up a short message to EtchedIn, asking for an interview. Then she called Malcolm.

Chapter Five

The high-pitched metal whine of the table saw cut through the thumping of the hammers in the large open room. Ben grabbed another piece of wood Joe had trimmed and carried it through the large opening leading from the outside. The bunkhouse was coming together nicely.

It had taken them a couple of months of working in between everyone's schedules to remodel it. Cody had hired more workers at the gym and was able to help when he wasn't on shift at the fire department. And with the colder weather, Joe's construction business had slowed down, so he had more time to devote to the project.

"That one is part of the trim for the barn door," Joe hollered to Ben as he carried the large piece of wood inside.

The interior was rustic. An open living area in the center of the house fed into the kitchen and dining room. Wood beams crossed twelve-foot, pitched ceilings.

One end of the house held a large master bedroom and en-suite. Two more bedrooms flanked another hallway on the other side of the house, with a bath on one side and a large barn door at the end that opened into Ben's studio. His place of solace.

One wall was filled with windows for optimum lighting. The adjoining wall held shelves and brackets for his supplies and pieces. The floor was cement but had brightly colored rubber mats at different tables making it easier to stand for long periods of time. A large blue table sat off to one side with a wooden flag and wine rack he was working on. At the far end was a plexiglass rolltop door that opened to a large deck.

Ben set the piece of wood against the wall. "It's nearly noon, why don't we take a break and grab a bite to eat?"

Cody stopped hammering. "Sure. I'm starving. I fed AJ before I came in and forgot to grab breakfast. I'll be glad when the little guy gets his sleep schedule worked out. I feel like I'm wandering around half asleep most of the time."

"And that's different—"

"Shut up, Joe."

Joe yanked down the rolltop door. "How many times have I found you kicked back in your chair; sound asleep at the gym?"

Cody backhanded him playfully as they walked through the sliding barn doors. "Did you not hear me? I said shut up. I'm telling you I'm sleep deprived."

"And what is your excuse for when I found you before you had a kid?"

A wolfish grin slowly curled on Cody's lips. He opened his mouth to answer but was interrupted.

"I'm going to save you on this one—" Joe said pointing at Ben, "—and add, before Jenna, since you obviously forgot her brother is standing right in front of you, throwing daggers with his eyes."

Cody opened his mouth again then shut it and pinched his lips together. "No comment."

Ben opened the refrigerator. "All I have over here is

some stew my dad made. You guys good with that?"

"Sounds good with me," Cody responded quickly.

Joe nodded. "That sounds great." Ben grabbed some beers and handed one each to Cody and Joe, and set one on the counter, then picked up the large glass container and shoved it in the microwave. "I haven't moved much stuff over here yet. I was kind of waiting until we got completely done, so it wouldn't get all dusty. I just brought the stew over last night when I was working on a couple of projects.

"The stuff on the table?"

"Yeah. I finally found someone to put together a website for me that didn't cost me a fortune. When there is a purchase, the money goes straight into an account. Each order comes through e-mail with all the information I need."

Cody took a swig of his beer. "Well, let us see." Ben gave him a "seriously" look but slid his laptop off the counter. He quickly loaded up the webpage and turned the screen around for Cody and Joe to see. As he pointed out all the features, he noticed the number eighteen up in the right corner of the screen.

"Eighteen?" He yanked the laptop back to him and clicked on the symbol of the envelope. When the screen loaded, his eyes widened at the list in his e-mail. "Shit!" He clicked through each e-mail completely dumbfounded by the continuous requests for his work.

"What's up?" Cody asked.

"Someone posted one of my flags on some website thing and I just got a bunch of orders."

"That's awesome!"

"Yeah. No. It takes some time to create a piece. I've been able to keep up with the orders so far but to get a bunch all at once is going to take me weeks to complete."

"Do you have any completed already?"

"Yeah, I do." He paused, thinking through his inventory. "I also have one at the new restaurant that I can use. I have a couple I have to drop off at the post office anyway, so I can run by and grab it." He continued to read through the e-mails. "But I will still have at least, one, two…" he continued to count, "twelve, that I am going to have to make."

"More money, more money," Joe chanted.

Ben had to concede. It would mean good money to a good cause. "That's true." The microwave dinged, and Ben grabbed the container. He found some paper bowls in the cabinet and plastic ware in the drawer. "It's not fancy, but it's pretty good." Both guys filled their bowls and sat back down at the table. Ben opened the last e-mail. It simply read, *"Your flag is exquisite. Would love to see more pieces you have created and interview you. Please let me know if you would be interested.*
K."

The return address read info@kaysiskloset.com.

He appreciated the free publicity, but he had no idea how long it would take him to complete all the pieces, so he just replied, "No," and slammed his laptop shut.

Cody's brow lifted in surprise. "What's all that about?"

"Apparently, the person who posted the photo and e-mail wants to interview me for their blog. I have more than enough work for me to handle right now. I told them no."

"Well, you shouldn't be pissed at them. They're getting your art out there. You got skills man."

"It's just coming at a bad time. I'm trying to get this

place done, and work on our ranch, and help with Poppi's."

Cody lifted a spoon full of stew and blew on it. "Did you figure out who could have opened the gate?"

"No. We went out and changed all the locks." He took a bite of his stew. "His grandson, Rick, is giving him shit about it though."

"About someone opening the gate?"

"He wants Poppi to turn over part of the land to him. Said he's getting too old to take care of it all. He thinks he left the gate open."

"What do you think?"

"The guy is sharp as a tack. I checked the gate after he did. That thing was locked up tight. I think someone did it on purpose, and I wouldn't put it past his grandson to do something like that."

"Why? You know him?"

"Oh yeah. Quite well, unfortunately. When he would come to visit, Poppi and Marie always tried to get us together to hang out. But he was a little shit, and we always got into fights. Then a couple of years ago his dad passed away, and the funeral was here. It was right after mom died. I was engaged, and about a month away from getting married to a girl I had dated for a couple of years. We went to the funeral, and Rick was being uncharacteristically nice, acting like we were old friends. He stuck around for a few days afterward, saying he was taking care of some business, and then low and behold, by the time he left, Valerie, my fiancée, had decided she didn't want to get married anymore. They got married a few months later."

Joe stopped mid bite. "No shit?"

"Jenna never told me that," Cody chimed in.

"She knows how much it pisses me off." He sat back and pushed his bowl away. "I'm more pissed right now though that he thinks he has a right to Poppi's land. That's all the man has. Those horses and land are his life. I think he plans to die there. That would make him happy.

"Rick hated Dalton when he was young, and I know he has absolutely no desire to do anything with that land but sell it. He told Poppi he wanted to help him, by taking the area on the ridge with the pines and the hay pasture, to cultivate and harvest, but I'm not buying it."

Cody wiped his mouth. "Did you talk to Poppi about what you thought?"

"Yeah. And he told Rick no deal. I have a feeling it's not over though. He's in town. Poppi said it was for business, but I can't imagine what he would be doing. He's some kind of broker. He took over his dad's business when he died."

"Is he in real estate?" Joe asked.

"No, stock market. His dad did well, I guess. Last time I saw him he was driving a Mercedes or one of those luxury cars and wearing a watch that probably cost as much as my truck. But I don't know how it's done since Rick took over."

"Maybe he lost it all," Joe said blandly.

"I wouldn't doubt it. And that's what I'm afraid this is all about."

"Speaking of real estate." Joe flexed his fingers and leaned back in his chair. "I know you just said you are up to your eyeballs in work, but I'm going to ask anyway. Would you guys want to help me with April and Kaysi's new project?"

"How big a project? What is it?"

"They are opening a home décor store. April is going to use it to get her interior design business going. Kaysi will run the shop; buying and selling the décor."

"So, April is getting out of the animal business?" Cody asked.

"Yeah. She's turning the reins over to Jenna. Did she not tell you? She likes animals fine, but she has been taking classes in this design stuff for a while and with this new project I am hoping to dip my fingers into, she would be a huge asset."

Ben spun his bottle of beer on the table before lifting it. "What project is that?"

"My old construction boss, Bill Becker, is in talks with a developer in Montclair on some land in between Montclair and Dalton. It's part of an estate. Right now, there is an old, abandoned house sitting on it with about a hundred acres. It's a beautiful piece of property and a developer is trying to see if the owner will sell it to them. They are wanting to put in a mixed housing development. Becker wants to include me on it doing some spec homes. If we get it, April will be my designer."

"That would be convenient." Ben paused continuing to process the conversation. "And so, she's opening an interior design business?"

"Yeah. She and Kaysi will be buying pieces to sell in the store and use in the spec homes, along with some other, one of a kind, items they find. Kaysi has a blog she does kind of showcasing stuff she finds on the internet and different places. She has developed quite a following."

Ben listened but a question kept crossing his mind. "Who's Kaysi?"

Joe snickered. "My sister?"

With Joe's words, Ben's entire body felt like it burst into flames.

"You met her. Light brown hair, blue eyes...nice boobs," Joe said, with a teasing tone.

He'd met her all right. The first time he had laid eyes on her, he couldn't stop staring. He felt an electric quake pulse through him the moment she slid in beside him at TopHops. She was beautiful but not just her features. Everything about her, the way she moved, the way she spoke, the way she laughed, everything.

That was the one thing his mom wanted for him, to find someone special, who was truly beautiful inside and out. Kaysi was beautiful, and of course, he embarrassed the hell out of himself when he met her. He was probably better off not having a chance with her anyway. She was Joe's little sister.

"That's just gross man. You don't talk about your sister like that," Cody admonished.

Joe turned to Cody. "You don't remember?"

Ben shot Joe a glare. "Seriously man?"

"Remember what? What am I missing?" Cody chimed in.

Joe chuckled. "Maybe you were already backstage." He sat back in his chair. "The night your band debuted at TopHops, Kaleb and I got into it about something, and one of our drinks went flying and spilled on Kaysi." Joe smirked and started laughing. "Ben helped clean her up."

Cody's mouth dropped open, and his eyes darted to Ben.

Ben rolled his eyes, feeling his neck heat up, and it continued into his cheeks, then his ears. He hated the feeling. "You're an ass, Joe," he said without any heat in the words. "You're the one who knocked over the drink."

"That was Kaleb."

"Bullshit. That was all you."

Cody's eyes darted between them. "You are so red, man. What happened?"

Ben wadded up his napkin and threw it at Joe, but he easily dodged it and kept his eyes glued on him. Ben huffed. "She had ice water spilled all over her. Her shirt was kind of thin and loose and ice went down it. She was gasping and reaching and grabbing, and I grabbed some napkins and started soaking up the water. Aw, hell. I was just trying to help." The memories played through his mind, flashing on every moment.

"He got a little handsy," Joe added.

"I didn't mean to."

"Sure, you didn't."

He knew Joe was just picking, but the memory of the night was so vivid. When she scooted into the booth next to him and he glanced at her for the first time, he could have sworn she spoke to him without saying a word. Her smile caressed his soul and filled him with a warmth that somehow shed light into the darkness he was feeling.

When she introduced herself and smiled, it was like the whole room lit up. And when she started chatting with him, the way she leaned in to listen to him, it ignited every fiber in his being. She seemed genuinely interested in him. And even though Ben hadn't wanted to talk to anyone of the opposite sex since his ex left him twisting in the wind, something about her made every reservation within him disappear. With her easy smile, her pretty blue eyes, and her sweet voice, he actually enjoyed it.

The moment she took the napkin away from him, he

realized his hand was practically down her shirt, and he lifted his gaze to see the shocked expression on her face. It still haunted him. He was surprised Joe and Kaleb hadn't beat him to death right there. The rest of the night he barely said a word to her and left right after Cody played his set. "Screw you, Joe," he growled.

"Hey, I'm just teasing. I know it was all innocent, and you know that."

Cody interrupted, "So what are you wanting us to help with?"

Ben appreciated that Joe understood the whole situation, even if he was the brunt of his jokes, but he was glad Cody changed the subject.

"Oh yeah, so like I said, April and Kaysi are starting a business together. They are signing papers on a building on Main on Friday. The place is pretty much already gutted. I need to blow out a wall and take care of a few electrical and plumbing issues that came up during inspection but overall, the building is in decent shape, so the build out should go pretty fast. I've already got some ideas on design that I need to go over with April and Kaysi, and I need to pull some permits with the city, but once that's done, we can get started with the actual remodel. I've got my guys lined up, but they have a couple of other jobs to finish up, so I could use some help."

Ben leaned back in his chair and crossed his arms. "I don't know if I will have time with these new orders. When are you wanting to get started?"

"They're signing papers at two Friday, so I'm planning on heading over around four if you guys want to come check it out. I'm hoping to get started with some light demo. The quicker I get it done, the quicker they can open and make me some money."

The thought of seeing Kaysi again caused Ben's pulse to race. On one hand, he was chomping at the bit to see her, but on the other, he would be mortified knowing she would probably remember him groping her. "I've gotta get the work done around the ranch and at Poppi's in the morning, and I will need to start working on the orders, but I might be able to give you a couple of hours. I need to go into town anyway and pick up my piece from the new restaurant, so I can run by after. Beyond that, I will have to see how much time these orders take. You said the building is on Main?"

"Yeah. It's on the other end of the block from the new restaurant. I noticed the pieces you were working on sitting on the table back there," Joe commented. "How long does one piece take you?"

"A piece, like the one hanging in the restaurant, takes at least a week."

Cody leaned forward, putting his elbows on the table. "What got you into it?"

"It's kind of my therapy. Between my mom's death and Valerie, and then everything that happened with Jenna, I kind of needed a way to deal with everything."

Cody nodded in agreement.

"Well, if you will help me get the store up and running, I will help you get your pieces out."

"I'll take that deal."

Chapter Six

Kaysi grabbed her purse and took a deep breath. Today was the day of change. She had already submitted her two-week notice to HR and was surprised she hadn't had a phone call from her dad. The plan to visit with him in person went out the window when she found out he was out of town for the day.

Figuring sooner was better for dropping the bomb on Libby, Kaysi asked her to meet her for lunch. She had no clue how she would take the news. Checking her phone, she had fifteen minutes to get to the deli up the street.

Her phone buzzed. Malcolm

—*Just thinking about you. Can't wait for tonight. I've missed you. I have so much to tell you*—

And there was the other change she was going to make. This would be, by far, the hardest of the discussions she would have to have. *Might as well rip off the Band-Aid all at once and get everything taken care of in one fell swoop.* She really didn't plan on it all happening in one day, but if everything went well, she would be all set up for her new life by nine tonight.

—*I've been thinking about you too. Sounds like we have a lot to talk about*—

She had three e-mails of interest on her townhouse within two hours of when she posted the ad. One had already offered to pay a full month of rent and deposit if they could move in a week. Their application was stellar, so she accepted. Now Kaysi was praying all would go well with the closing. She'd already started loading her car with boxes, ready to move.

As she made her way up the street, she went over the conversation she planned to have with Libby. Would she be happy that she was finally off the hook, or upset that she wasn't included? Kaysi was sure one would happen. This was the part of her dreams coming true that she hated. Confrontation. Kaysi avoided confrontation like the plague. She didn't want to hurt Libby, although she had a feeling she was about to.

Dishing it Deli came into view and she did a little shoulder wiggle when she found a parking space in front. The scent of roast beef filled her nose as she stepped inside. Removing her gloves, she searched the room to see if Libby had already arrived but didn't see her. A seat by the picture window was available so she removed her coat and slid into the booth and waited. Libby appeared in the doorway, and she waved her over.

"Right on time." Kaysi gave her a bright smile, hoping it would set the mood. By the scowl on Libby's face, she wasn't buying it.

"Have you ordered yet?" Libby asked as she slid into the booth.

"No, I just got here." The waitress stopped by the table and quickly took their orders, placed a bowl of pickles on the table, then disappeared.

It didn't take long for Libby to pick up on Kaysi's nervousness. "What's going on?"

"That obvious?" Kaysi asked with a sigh.

"You've never been good at hiding things from me."

Libby shoved a pickle in her mouth. "Let me guess. It has to do with your date with April. Doesn't it?"

Just the way she said April's name ramped up her nerves and told her this was going to go downhill fast. Kaysi took a drink of her water and tried to collect her thoughts. Libby had stated on several occasions that she was only helping temporarily because she needed some summer cash. When everything blew up on her blog as the summer ended, Libby agreed to stay on as a favor to Kaysi while she navigated the sudden increase in interest.

It should be an easy conversation. It should make Libby happy to know she wouldn't have to be Kaysi's "glorified gopher," as Libby put it.

The waitress returned with their food and drinks and Kaysi wondered if she was even going to be able to eat her lunch. She locked eyes with Libby and let out a breath. There was no turning back. "Yes, this has to do with April." Her words stuck in her throat as she tried to find the best way to deliver the news.

"And?" Libby prodded with an edge in her tone. "What's going on, Kaysi? I only have thirty minutes before I have to be back at school."

"And…I'm going into business with her and moving to Dalton," she said, spilling everything at once. Probably not the best option, but Libby's comment flustered her.

Libby's eyes widened with disbelief, then her face filled with confusion. "Doing what?"

Kaysi was surprised at her question. Maybe things wouldn't be so bad. She tried to keep her voice upbeat. "We're opening a store."

Libby bit into her sandwich. "When?"

"We sign the papers Friday."

With a head jerk, Libby peered up at Kaysi and dropped her sandwich. "Friday? Like as in this Friday?"

"Yes." Kaysi said slowly.

"Wow. Okay. She didn't give you a lot of time to think about it. Did she?"

"She didn't have to. It's my dream. I finally get to do, in real life, what I've been doing online for the past two years."

"What *we've* been doing." The irritation thickened in Libby's tone.

Kaysi sighed realizing she wasn't going to avoid the confrontation. "Libby I—"

"Don't. I knew something was up when you wouldn't talk to me yesterday. I can't believe you are doing this to me."

"Doing this to you? I asked you to help me over the summer when you said you were needing money. You made it clear to me it was only temporary. Then things got busy."

"And I thought when you asked me to stay on, that it was something more permanent. That we were partners."

"You told me you weren't interested when I asked you. Remember?"

"I meant, I couldn't until I could make a living at it."

"You still wouldn't be able to make a living at it right now, but I could still use you."

"Don't do me any favors, Kaysi. You know April and I don't get along. You have obviously made up your mind as to who you would rather work with, and it isn't me."

"Libby don't do this. I had no idea you felt this

way." Tears brimmed in Libby's eyes. "It was just a misunderstanding."

"How could you not know, Kaysi? I spent all my spare time checking out the internet and wandering around Arkansas, Oklahoma and Missouri hunting for stuff for you, instead of doing stuff I enjoyed."

Kaysi felt guilty. But this move was her dream, and she knew April was going to be an amazing partner. "The reason I didn't know, Libby, is that comment right there. You always made me feel guilty every time you brought me information for a new piece, like I was making you do it against your will. Like you hated working for me."

"I'm sorry if I came off as being ungrateful. I know you didn't necessarily need me."

"Oh, I absolutely needed you."

"Not at first. I knew you just hired me to help me with my bills at the time. Thinking back, I guess I did come off a bit inconvenienced by it. I'm sorry."

"I didn't do this to hurt you, Libby. I had no idea April was going to offer this to me until we went to lunch. But this *is* my dream. I couldn't pass it up."

"I get it, and I don't blame you. You deserve this, and I am happy for you, honestly. I just wish it was me."

"You can still work with me. It's going to be the same thing just on a grander scale."

"You don't have—"

"I want you to. If *you* really want to. But only if you want to. I have to admit I don't know what it will be like to start off with. We have some work to do on the store before we can open."

Libby sat back in her seat; her focus drifted out the window. "I'll think about it. Going into February and March we are going to have tests and end of the year stuff."

"No problem. Just let me know. The job is there. We can work around your schedule."

"Thanks. I do appreciate you letting me work with you. The extra money has been a huge help. I hope you know that…at least now."

"I do. I couldn't have made it through this summer without you." Silence fell between them again and Libby lifted her phone.

"I'm going to have to get back." She shifted in her seat to slide out of the booth. "When will you be moving?"

Kaysi again hesitated with her answer. "This weekend."

Libby sighed. "Okay. Well, if you need help, call me." She stood and shouldered her purse, giving Kaysi a dejected sigh.

"You okay? I really am sorry about springing it on you."

"Yeah. I'm good. You're right. It wasn't like you and April had been planning this all along. And this is your dream. I'm happy for you." She leaned over and gave Kaysi a hug and then walked away. Kaysi still wasn't sure how she felt about how things ended. Libby was so hard to read.

****

A knock at the door sent tingles through Kaysi's body. *This is not going to be fun.* She took a deep breath and dug her fingers into her long brown hair as she walked to the door and opened it. Malcolm smiled and leaned in for a hug.

"Are you ready? What smells so good?" he asked; confusion spreading across his face.

She hadn't dressed up or fixed her make up, thinking it would be better to get it over with. He would probably wonder what all the boxes were for anyway. But she thought if she cooked, maybe, it would soften the blow. "Come in." Malcolm stepped inside and Kaysi could tell he suspected nothing. He was so nice and had been so good to her. It was going to be hard to walk away. However, it was the right thing to do. This new opportunity in her life opened her eyes to what she wanted. No more settling. No more second guessing her abilities. She was going for her dreams. "I cooked tonight. You want something to drink?"

Malcolm tilted his head and his lips pursed, cluing her in that he now knew something was up. "Am I going to need one?"

"Have a seat. Dinner will be ready in about ten minutes." Kaysi walked into the kitchen and poured a couple of glasses of tea. She handed him a glass, then sat on the sofa next to him. Taking a deep breath, she licked her lips, trying to put together the words to start. Her mouth suddenly felt like the Sahara Desert.

"What's up? I don't think you have ever cooked for me."

She kicked her slip-ons off and tucked her feet under her on the sofa. "I was offered a chance to go into business with April Westerman."

His brows drew together. He knew April vaguely. They had all run in the same social circles the past few months since they had been dating. "That's great," he said with genuine enthusiasm.

"It's a dream job for me. I'll be turning my blog into a business and helping April start her interior design career." She paused as Malcolm shifted on the sofa to face her more.

"I'm so happy for you. But why do I get the feeling this isn't all good news?"

"Malcolm, the job is in Dalton. I will be moving."

"When? I'm guessing soon by the looks of all the boxes." His voice now sounded a bit raw. She knew he was preparing himself for the incoming bomb.

"I'm getting the key Friday."

"Friday? Seriously?"

"The store has a loft above it that I'm moving into. It needs some work, but it's livable, and it would be best for me to get moved in, so we can get the business up and running quickly. I already have someone to rent this place."

"Wow. You really did have a lot to tell me. I was just going to tell you that I got a promotion. Kaleb is putting together an environmental and safety team. With my background in biological engineering, it all fit."

"That's awesome. You deserve it." She meant every word. He was one of Grayeagle's best employees. She hated the fact that she was ruining a good day for him, but she couldn't keep stringing him along when she couldn't see a future.

"I got a nice raise and an extra week of vacation." He paused for a beat. "I will have to travel a bit more checking out equipment and facilities."

"Oh, what do you think about that?"

"The great thing is, I can be flexible with my hours in the office. I can work remotely if I need to. I'll be working with Kaleb on environmental projects at different facilities. So, as long as I stay on schedule, they couldn't care less really whether I'm there or not unless I'm needed in a meeting."

"That sounds amazing. You can work in your jammies—"

"Or nothing at all," his eyes narrowed, and a wolfish grin slid over his mouth. "See, your little news doesn't bother me. It's only a thirty-minute drive, and I can work from your place if I need to." He reached down and played with Kaysi's fingers, rubbing his thumb along the back of her hand. Every muscle in her body tensed and she jerked her hand away.

Her eyes lifted to his. "Malcolm, you are so sweet, and you have treated me with such respect, but I just don't think this is going to work. I'm going to be busy getting the business up and running, and you're going to be getting used to your new job—"

"No. I suspect this job is going to be easier to manage, because I can make my own hours. You don't have to worry with that. I may even be able to help you out some with the store."

He wasn't going to make it easy for her, and she hated, more than anything, hurting people. It was inevitable in life, but she tried to avoid it if possible. "I think it's better if we part and just be friends. Its more than just not having time. We have been dating for a few months and, I'm sorry, but I don't see it progressing. I need more."

Sadness swept across his face, and Kaysi knew she had broken through. It gutted her. "I guess I don't understand exactly. What *more* are you talking about? What did I do wrong?"

"Nothing. You are the sweetest man I ever met, and you treated me like a princess."

"Then what is it, because you are everything to me, Kaysi. I am head over heels in love with you."

"I'm not in love with you though. I don't want—"

"How can you say that? We get along so well. We have so much fun together. We are able to talk so easily."

"But what you just said is more of a friendship, and I do adore our friendship, but I'm not in love with you."

"Well, we have only been dating for six months. It takes time for love to grow."

"I have tried to make this work, Malcolm. I have tried to tell myself that it takes time, but it's time to accept the fact that it's just not there. And what we have is not going to grow into love for me. I can't just make myself fall in love. It doesn't work that way."

"I must disagree. I think you are trying to deny something that is obviously there. I feel it, and I know you do too. You are scared of making a commitment. We just need to nurture the relationship, make more of an effort."

Kaysi was backed into a corner. She was wanting to run away, and he was wanting to step up the chase. "It's not going to work, Malcolm."

"Yes, it will, love. You are scared because of the distance that will be added, but I'm telling you, it's not going to affect anything."

"Malcolm, there is someone else." Her breath caught as the words spilled from her lips. She never wanted to lie to him. She had always been truthful, and lying always seemed to turn out bad, but the words flew from her mouth before she could think better of it.

His head jerked toward her. "I'm sorry. What?"

"There is someone else," she said barely audible.

His eyes leveled with hers and he searched her face for a long moment. "I don't believe you, Kaysi. You would never do something like that to me."

The words caught her off guard. But why should he? She was telling him a bald-faced lie. "You don't believe me?"

"No. I don't," he said. "I've been around you long enough to know your little quirks. You're a terrible liar. You, my dear, are lying. And if you were dating someone else, I don't think he would take too kindly of you cooking dinner for another man."

"I'm not lying. He knows about you. He knows we were dating." Her pulse increased. She was digging a hole for herself, deeper and deeper.

"And he didn't care? Doesn't sound like much of a man to me, to steal someone else's lady." He paused. "How did you meet?"

She closed her eyes. She was in this far, might as well jump in with both feet. "He's a friend of my brother."

"What friend? Do I know him?"

Kaysi suddenly realized her slip. "Not Kaleb. Kameron. Joe. April's husband."

Malcolm smiled, and she knew he could see through her lie, but she had to go with it, because he wasn't accepting that she just wasn't that into him. "So, how long have you guys been together?"

"It was just over the past week."

"Oh, so a new love." He continued to smile at her. "So, I still have a chance."

"What do you mean?"

"Well, my darling, Kaysi, if you are dating a guy, who stole you away from me, which I am still inclined to believe you aren't, then I plan to steal you back, and show you who is the better man."

Oh geez, what is it going to take to make him realize.

68

"I don't want to start a competition."

"I am willing to fight for you; to show you how much I love you."

"Malcolm, I just don't feel the same way."

"And I think you do. Why don't we have dinner and let me start showing you how you're lying to yourself."

"You know Malcolm, I am kind of thinking you were right. It probably isn't a good idea to have you stay for dinner since I'm dating someone else. I am going to need you to leave."

"Kaysi, you're not serious."

"I am."

The somewhat playful tone in his voice had been replaced with one laced with irritation. "Fine. I'll leave. We aren't done though, Kaysi. Far from it." He rose and grabbed his coat on the way out.

Kaysi removed the casserole from the oven. Serving herself a good portion, she sat down at the table, opened her laptop and scanned her blog. An e-mail from the EtchedIn address caught her eye. She clicked on it and immediately felt annoyed, when the only response was "no." There was no name attached. Just "no."

Skimming the rest of the comments, she stopped on a post from the Charity Donation page for an event coming up that she and her family had put together. In the body of the post it simply said, "I'm watching you." A chill went through her. She had trolls on her blog before, but the charity page? The event was a little more than a week away. Another chill went through her. Malcolm would be there. He probably expected them to go together. "Shit. I need to find a boyfriend."

Chapter Seven

Flame Masters Bar and Grill was busy for a Friday afternoon. Ben scanned the area as he headed to the back. Stopping at the bar, he caught the attention of the bartender.

"Hey, what can I get you?" The bearded guy, in a colorful vest and white shirt with cuffed sleeves, asked.

"I'm trading out one of my pieces. Just wanted to let you know." His eyes tracked to his flag, and he hooked his thumb in the direction.

"Oh. Yeah. No problem." Ben walked over to the wall and lifted the framed wooden flag off the hangers. Setting it on the floor, he then replaced it with an etched and burned piece with a skull in a feather headdress in a similar size. Stepping back, he eyeballed it to make sure it was centered. Next to it, he traded out the price tags, then grabbed the flag preparing to leave. A blonde woman, staring at him, from the booth across from him, stopped him dead in his tracks. His chest tightened, and it immediately stirred a hornet's nest inside of him.

She seemed different. She wasn't in her trademark blue jeans and ruffled shirt. Her hair had gotten longer, and she was wearing more makeup, but there was still no mistaking her. Valerie. He hadn't seen her since she broke their engagement two years ago and hated that it still hurt so bad. Something in her eyes pleaded with him.

It wasn't like she hadn't seen him. She hadn't taken her eyes off him. He knew he should just walk away, but he was drawn to her.

He took a step closer. Her eyes finally darted away. She swallowed and gently tucked her hair behind her ear. God, she was still pretty. Confusion filled him. He took another step.

"Hi, Ben," she said quietly.

Hearing his name from her lips stirred up every memory he had of them together, and the pain in his chest increased. He let out a long sigh. "Valerie." *I should have walked away.* He really didn't want to talk to her, but it was too late. "What are you doing here?" His harsh tone surprised him, and Valerie turned away.

Without turning back, she responded, "Waiting for Rick."

Was that regret he saw in her expression? Or was she just playing one of her mind games. Waiting to twist the knife. He didn't want to wait around to find out. "Then I should go." He clutched the art piece and spun around.

Her hand reached out, but he was already too far away. "Ben, wait."

She stepped closer and wrapped her fingers around his wrist before he could move farther away. His gaze lifted to the ceiling, then he closed his eyes. Pinching his fingers across the bridge of his nose, he let out another sigh. "Valerie, whatever you are going to say, I—"

"I'm sorry."

His eyes slowly opened and dropped to hers to see them glistening.

"I'm so sorry, Ben."

Is she kidding me, right now? He moved his hand

and unwrapped her fingers from his wrist. "Whatever," he said, shrugging, then turned again to leave.

"Please, Ben. Forgive me," she cried and wrapped her hand around his arm.

His eyes darted to the grip she held on to his arm, and he yanked it away. "Valerie," he growled, "you made it very clear, when you left, who you wanted. It wasn't me. My mom was barely cold in the ground, and you couldn't wait to add insult to injury by telling me, in no uncertain terms, that I wasn't good enough for you; that I couldn't give you what you wanted for your life." Taking a step away from her, his posture deflated as the memories of that horrible day flooded back like it happened yesterday. Things hadn't been that great between them. But he had attributed it to his mom being sick and then dying, and then the stress of planning a wedding.

It completely gutted him though, when she showed up at his house just days after Rick's dad's funeral spouting that she wanted more than a farm boy and that she didn't love him. She acted like the two years they had spent together was merely a fling, a one-night stand, that meant nothing more than a booty call, and it was time for them to go their separate ways. "I'm sorry if you are regretting your decision, but I hope you understand why it's a little hard for me to forgive you."

Valerie's eyes scanned the restaurant. Then, barely above a whisper, she confessed, "Rick and I are separated. I've been at my parent's house for over a month. I'm meeting him here to talk."

"I'm sorry to hear that, but it's not my problem."

"Things were doomed from the start. He changed the minute we got back to St. Louis." She peered at him through her long lashes. "He's evil, Ben."

His fingers curled into a fist at his side. As much as he hurt from what she did, he still somehow cared about what happened to her. "He didn't hurt you, did he?"

"No. Not physically. But he's a liar and a manipulator. And he's controlling."

"Again, not my problem. You made your decision. I am not, and do not want to be, a part of your life anymore." As he turned to leave, he heard a voice call him. Rage exploded within him.

"Corbett. What the hell are you doing talking to *my wife*?"

My wife. Now, more than ever, he wondered if Rick married Valerie just to piss him off. Everything was a competition to him. He didn't seem to have a conscience. He always did things just to get a rise out of people, but somehow found a way to charm them and manipulate them to where he came off as a decent person. Even when he and Rick got into a fight when they were little, or got in trouble because Rick did something stupid, others always made excuses for him. Even Poppi.

His jaw clenched. "Just leaving. She spoke, so I thought the polite thing to do would be to respond."

Rick glared at Valerie then turned back to Ben. "You been talking to Oren?"

Ben hated the fact that Rick called his grandfather by his first name. It was the height of disrespect and showed just how cold he was. He was an arrogant, heartless, soulless bastard and Ben knew, early on, how manipulative he was, and he didn't fall for his bullshit. But seeing fear spark in Valerie's eyes, Ben felt like dancing with the devil. "I talk to him every day when we do chores. Why?"

"Did you tell him not to give me the land?"

"What land?"

The veins in Rick's neck thickened. Rage filled his face, and Ben held back a snicker. "His land, you moron."

"Why would he give you his land? And why would you want it? You live seven hours away. You always hated going to the ranch."

"He can't handle it anymore. He's losing it. Becoming forgetful. You saw it. He forgot to lock the gate, and his horses nearly caused a catastrophe on fifty-one. He said you helped round them up."

Ben roughly rubbed his beard, trying to keep the rage building inside of him, at bay. "I checked that gate myself." His eyes bore into Rick. "I think we both know he didn't leave that gate open. Someone did it to cause him trouble."

Was there a flinch in Rick's stony expression?

"That's crap. The old man is just getting forgetful. He can't handle the work anymore."

"What? And you think you can? You have no idea what it takes to run that ranch. How do you think that would help him?"

"Oh, I can handle it. I've got plans."

"I'm sure you do. And none of them have anything to do with helping Poppi."

"Poppi? You still call him that? Isn't that a bit childish, Corbett?"

"At least he knows someone cares about him like he's family. Unlike you, who can't even muster up the decency to call him, Grandpa." Ben could tell by his demeanor that Rick was up to something, so he decided to test the waters to see if Rick might expose any of his plans. "Is there a reason you have your heart set on the ridge and hay field?"

"Oh, so you did talk to him."

"He might have told me that you talked."

"Well, not that it's any of your business, but the land has productive soil. I can make money off the crops, and I can harvest the trees and sell them to the mill, then put it back into the ranch."

"Have you researched that? Do you have any idea how much it would cost to harvest those trees, or the type of equipment you would need? Do you even know the growth cycle of pine trees?" Rick's expression told Ben the answer. "Yeah, I didn't think so." He pushed him a little further. "You're after the diamonds, aren't you? You seriously believe all those fairy tales of the land being littered with diamonds?" Again, his expression gave him away, and Ben laughed. "You know I would love to play poker with you sometime, because you definitely are an easy read."

"What do you mean?"

"I mean, I know what you are thinking, and you're calling me childish? You're an idiot if you believe any of that bullshit about the diamonds. That was probably some story cooked up to help sell the land."

Rick crossed his arms and narrowed his eyes, and Ben saw how serious he was about getting his hands on the land. Pain pierced his chest. The last thing he wanted to see was Poppi lose his land for something so stupid. His mind filled with thoughts of Rick destroying the land searching for something that wasn't there.

"Look, his ranch, and those horses, are his life. If you take the land, he will have to give up some of his horses, and if you take that away from him, to search for some lie you were told as a kid, you will kill him."

Rick blinked, and for a moment Ben thought his words might have made an impact. Then he took a step closer and squared his shoulders. *So, this is how it's going to be.* Ben set the piece of art down next to the booth and turned. They were nose to nose. He wasn't going to be intimidated. Rage vibrated between them.

"You know nothing about what I'm after, or what's best for my family, so stay out of our damn business. I am his family. Not you."

"You could've fooled me. I don't think you know what's good for anyone but yourself. Hell, you don't even know how to keep your wife happy, which doesn't surprise me one bit." Ben's eyes darted to Valerie's when she gasped, and a sudden flash of fear crossed her face. He wiped his mouth with his hand, questioning the reaction, but continued. "Sounds like you wouldn't know what a family was if it jumped up and bit you in the ass."

"You stay away from my wife, or I'll make sure you disappear. You got that?"

"Oh, trust me, that's not a problem. But I better never hear about you laying a hand on her, because I will come after you, and we will settle this once and for all." Confusion filled Rick's face and Ben again wondered why.

"Is there a problem here?" A deep voice interrupted from behind them. Ben turned to see the bartender, standing behind him.

His eyes darted to Rick. "No. I was just leaving." Bending down to pick up his artwork, he glanced at Valerie who sat stunned, and considered her earlier expression again. She was scared. But was she scared because she had lied to him, or scared Rick would punish her for talking to him?

He strolled to the door and pushed it opened. The cold January wind burned his already chapped skin, even with his thick beard. The confrontation with Rick still filled his thoughts as he wrenched open the door to his truck and dropped off the art. He needed to talk to Poppi and let him know what Rick was up to. Peering back into the restaurant, he caught a glimpse of Valerie and remembered her words. "We're separated." He couldn't help but feel a bit of sweet revenge that her lust for the finer things in life, she thought Ben couldn't give her, got her where she was. He was glad though that she finally saw Rick for who he was. Nothing but a manipulative ass.

He headed down the sidewalk, turning up the collar of his coat, as memories of their time together spun within his thoughts, and he realized he wouldn't have been able to make her happy any more than Rick. He could remember her talking about wanting to travel to Europe, and live in a fancy house with a pool, and eat at the fancy restaurants. Her pipe dreams. Everyone had them. He realized now, she would do anything to make it happen, even if it meant giving up what they had, and selling her soul to the devil. The stab to his chest made him take a deep burning breath of the cold winter air.

He spied Cody's jeep in front of the building. It was always easy to spot. Metallic ruby red. He treated it like a pet, going as far as to even name it. Rubi. Ben smiled. Cody had become one of Ben's closest friends. He trusted him, and Joe, and would do just about anything for them. This new project though, had him a bit nervous. Not that he couldn't handle the work. He had learned quite a bit about construction from remodeling the bunkhouse. No. It was that blue-eyed woman that he would have to be around.

Kaysi. Just thinking about her had his cheeks heating up. How in the world could one thought of a woman he barely knew send a flood of heat throughout his body so quickly? He had to figure out a way around her invading all his thoughts. There was no way anything could happen between them. She was Joe's little sister. Off limits. He really didn't have time for a relationship with anyone anyway. Especially not her. Regardless how his brain told him she was a no no, his body wasn't listening.

An echo of voices hit him as he pushed the door open to the old building. One glance, and he knew there was much more to be done than Joe let on. His mind raced with thoughts of how he would fit it in his schedule with all the new orders. For Joe, he would try to make it work. As he took in the intricate architecture, he knew he wanted to work on the project. It was like one of his pieces. He wanted to see what they could create from the old worn-out shell of the building. That was the only reason he wanted to be there, at least that's what he kept telling himself. Then he caught himself listening for her voice, hoping he would hear her. The entire week was spent replaying that night at TopHops. There was something about her, and how easy it was for him to talk to her.

His eyes searched the room briefly. She wasn't there. Joe and Cody were standing around a folding table with blueprints spread across it. Cody glanced up. "It's about damn time."

"Hey, some of us have important jobs that take precedence." Both stared at him with a "seriously?"

expression on their faces. They all had other jobs. Cody owned 24 to Life gym and was nearing the end of his training to become a paramedic, and Joe worked at the gym, and recently had become a licensed contractor. This project was a labor of love. There was very little if any money that would wind up in their pockets. Ben was fine with it. He didn't mind helping.

"I was able to get the blueprints from the city. The wall we are taking out is load bearing so we will need a support beam. We will work that out after we tackle the plumbing, electrical, and other fixes. Let me take you up to Kaysi's loft and show you what we are dealing with."

Joe started heading to the stairwell on one side of the building, and Ben wondered if he had heard Joe correctly. "Kaysi's moving above the store?"

Jogging up the stairs, Joe answered without turning around. "Yeah. You should see this place. It's pretty sweet. Once we get the store done, I'm going to do some work up here." He unlocked the door and stepped inside.

Ben took in the open space, and his mind ran wild picturing Kaysi curled up in a blanket on a leather sofa in front of a roaring fire in the fireplace. The warmth returned to his cheeks.

"The bedroom and bath are back there." Joe's voice brought Ben back to reality. "The fuse box for the store and for the loft are both up here, so we need to separate them, and we have a leak up here in the kitchen that we need to figure out. I've got my plumber and electrician coming first thing tomorrow."

The door opened in the back of the loft and Ben heard a female voice. His heart stumbled anticipating seeing Kaysi for the first time since he met her at TopHops. April came through the door instead, with a couple of pizza boxes, some drinks, and her phone pressed to her ear. Joe quickly made his way to her to help. She pulled the phone away and smiled. "I brought dinner."

Chapter Eight

Kaysi carried a laundry basket full of cleaning supplies up the stairs and unlocked the door. She stared at the open space and smiled. Today was the day her dream would begin. She tried to prop the door open with the basket, but it wasn't heavy enough, and the door started to shut. It quickly pushed opened again, and Libby stepped through the door. "Libby? What are you doing here?"

"I was going to stop by your apartment to see if you needed help, but you were leaving. I figured you might be moving, so I followed you. You didn't think I would let you move by yourself, did you? I brought you a latte and Kolache. It might be a little cold."

"Aw. You didn't have to do that." Kaysi wrapped Libby up in a hug. "I'm getting the small stuff today." She backed away and smiled. "The movers are moving the big stuff Monday. I have to get everything cleared out and cleaned by Wednesday. I have a guy moving in."

"Well, let's get this party started. What do you need me to do?"

"I'm going to wipe things down first and then I have a carload full to bring in."

"Why didn't you have cleaners come in? It's not like you can't afford it."

"I have a crew that's cleaning my place in

Fayetteville when I am done moving. This place is going to get dusty once they start working downstairs, so I'm going to just do a light cleaning. Maybe after everything is done, I will have someone come in and do a deep cleaning. I don't mind cleaning though. It's my mess. I can clean it."

"So, where do you want me to start?"

Kaysi scanned the area. "I'll start cleaning. Can you start unloading the car?"

"Sure. Is the car unlocked?" Libby asked, moving toward the door.

Kaysi grabbed a couple of rags out of the basket and a bottle of cleaner. "Yeah." Her eyes darted around as she searched for anything that would prop the door open. In one of the cabinets, she found an old phone book. "This will never be used again." The old, yellow book, with a thick layer of dust and grime, told her it hadn't been touched in years. Kaysi grabbed it and wedged it under the door just as Libby plodded up the stairs with a couple of boxes. Behind her, Kaysi watched a bright blue, four-wheel-drive pickup pull up. From the splatters of mud sprayed across it, it was obvious it hadn't missed too many puddles.

A guy in a cowboy hat with a thick red beard stepped out. He glanced her way, and she backed away quickly not wanting him to see her staring. Her heart skipped. *What is he doing here?* Ben. She hadn't seen him since they met at TopHops. The minute he introduced himself to her, she felt like her body was going to ignite all on its own. There was something so unique about his somewhat disheveled, take me as I am, appearance. And the storm that brewed behind his deep blue eyes had her wanting to know what caused it.

His voice was deep and rich and after they started chatting, she was even more drawn in, feeling like she'd known him for years. He was so down to earth. She loved how passionate he was talking about his work at the ranch. It gave her butterflies.

When Joe spilled her water on her, Ben was quick to help. The touch of his hands against her cold skin set off a firestorm that had her fighting for every breath. But from the humiliation that filled his face when she yanked the napkin from his hand, she didn't convey that fact very well. He had no idea what he'd done to her, and he was obviously mortified. She tried to reassure him it was okay. But the damage was done, and he quickly scooted away and barely talked to her, then left after Cody's band was done.

"Kaysi?"

She blinked and realized Libby was standing in front of her with her arms full of boxes. "Oh, sorry."

Libby eyed her quizzically. "Everything okay?"

"Yeah, fine. Just thought I saw something," Kaysi said hesitantly. She stepped aside letting Libby in.

"Where do you want these?"

Kaysi read the writing on the boxes. "Just put them up against the wall in there." She pointed toward the living room, then took her rags and cleaner and headed to the kitchen hoping her flushed cheeks didn't betray her.

The coffee Libby brought her still sat on the counter. She took a drink and a bite of Kolache hoping it would settle the butterflies that had taken flight in her stomach, but just as she felt like her nerves were settling, she heard deep voices from the stairwell on the other side of the room. Her eyes locked on the door as it pushed open. Joe,

Cody, April, Jenna, Kaleb, and two other guys she didn't recognize, all entered. No Ben. That was him, wasn't it?

"Hey, Kaysi. We came by to get you for breakfast, but looks like you already got something yummy," April said as she traipsed across the room.

"Libby came by to help and brought me some coffee and a Kolache."

Jenna stepped up to the counter while the guys took off into the bedroom and bath area. "Is there anything we can do to help?"

"I'm just cleaning and moving some of the little stuff over. The movers are going to take care of the furniture Monday."

"Well, put us to work. Hillary and Jack have AJ for a few hours, so I'm all yours."

Libby appeared in the doorway with another two boxes stacked in front of her. "These say pillows." Kaysi turned to respond. Libby's face filled with annoyance as her eyes darted between April and Jenna who were standing at the counter. She dropped the boxes against the wall.

"Hey, Libby have you met…" Kaysi began, but Libby darted out the door.

"I better go find out what's going on," she sighed. "If you guys want to help, I have a car full of boxes and cleaning supplies. Make yourself at home."

Joe came out of the bedroom with the guys trailing behind him. "Kaysi, can we get in the kitchen for a little bit? Wayne needs to find out where the leak is coming from."

"Yeah. Sure. Are we going to be in your way if we are cleaning and moving boxes in?"

"No, just don't put any boxes in the kitchen for right

now. I don't think we will be up here too long. Jerry is going to be working on moving the fuse box in the utility room while the electricity is off, and if I'm right, the leak should be an easy fix."

Kaysi traded places with Wayne behind the kitchen counter. "Okay. I'm going to run downstairs for a minute." She hurried down the steps. Libby was getting into her car.

"Libby," she hollered. "Wait." Kaysi ran up to the car just as Libby was about to close the door. "What's wrong?"

"You don't need me. You have plenty of help, now that April is here."

Kaysi took a deep breath. She loved Libby to death, but her jealousy was exhausting. "I need all the help I can get, and I'm glad you came. I don't understand why April is such a threat to you."

"You don't?" Libby screamed. "She took you from me. Once you are moved, I will never see you."

"Libby, I told you, if you want to work with me, you have a job. I've already talked to April. She thinks it's a great idea. We need help building our inventory and clientele getting started."

"And once you have that in place, you will kick me to the curb."

Kaysi let out a heavy sigh, feeling the frustration building. "Libby," she started, but the frustration and irritation took over her ability to stay level-headed, "you know what? I'm tired of battling with you over this. It's your call. I'm not your only friend, and I don't tell you who you should be friends with, so you shouldn't get to call the shots of who I can be friends with, and how I want to live my life. April and I have been friends for years and this business is my dream, and if you can't handle it, then I'm sorry, but that's not on me, that's on you. April has been nothing but nice to you, and you have constantly put me in the middle with your jealousy. I've done everything I can to make you happy, but I'm not willing to give up my dream."

Kaysi turned and walked to the back of her car, grabbing a couple boxes out. She lifted her eyes to see Libby still sitting in her car, and she wondered what her decision would be. In a way, she was hoping Libby would just leave. She was tired of fighting the same battle over and over again. But the memories of the times when Libby stood up for her, when someone was taking advantage of her, sent guilt flooding through her.

Her eyes shifted when the back door to the store opened. Ben appeared, dropping a box outside the door. She ducked behind the boxes she had in her arms. His eyes lifted, glancing her way. She froze. After a moment, he turned and went inside, shutting the door. Closing the hatch to her SUV, she climbed the stairs, and heard a car door slam behind her.

"I'm sorry." She heard Libby say behind her. "I can't help being possessive. You mean so much to me, and you are such a good person. I just don't want you to get hurt."

"But it's okay when you hurt me?" she responded, turning to see Libby standing at the bottom of the landing.

"I'll leave if you want me to."

"I gave you your options. You decide. But I'm not doing this again. This jealousy has to stop. I love you to death, but honestly, you are making it hard for me not to be frustrated." She walked through the door and dropped the boxes in the living room. Libby appeared in the doorway a minute later. A man's torso and legs were sticking out from under the kitchen sink when Kaysi walked over to grab her coffee from the counter. Libby held her arms open, and Kaysi gave her a hug.

"I'll try to be less protective," she said, releasing Kaysi from the hug. Kaysi wanted to forgive her, but as time wore on, it was becoming harder and harder. Since she had given her the news of the business venture, her face had been in a constant scowl. And even now, something in her voice made Kaysi wonder how truthful she was being. Libby gave her a questioning glance, but Kaysi didn't say anything. She took a step back and searched for Jenna and April. A scuffing sound came from below her, and she caught sight of the plumber scooting out from under the sink. The tall, lanky, slightly balding guy, sat up with a groan.

"I think we got the leak taken care of. I just need to get back under there and clean up a little bit of a mess I made." He dusted his hands and stood. "I'll be back up later. I need to check downstairs and make sure there are no leaks."

"That's fine. Take your time." Kaysi took another sip of her coffee and turned to Libby. "Libby, I guess, if you are sticking around, just continue to help me get the car unloaded." She strolled toward the bedroom. "I need to find April and Jenna, and then I will be down to help."

Libby nodded. "Sure." Turning, she stepped out onto the balcony.

Kaysi headed into the bedroom and found Jenna and April standing in the middle of the room holding cleaning supplies.

"What are you guys doing?"

"I was just giving Jenna my vision of what you should do with your space."

"You started to tell me the other day what you were thinking, but we got distracted. So, what's your idea."

"Brushed brass fixtures and jewel tones. Set your bed against the brick just past those windows. Hang fairy lights from the ceiling, and drape them with some soft cream-colored chiffon, to create a canopy. Set a chest at the end of the bed for blankets, and put a tufted cushion in gold, on top. Oh, and I saw the perfect velvet, tufted, round love seat in a sapphire blue that would fit in your turret window. Add a soft blanket, and a cool brass chandelier floor lamp with a small table, and you have the perfect reading nook."

"You've really put some thought into this." Kaysi said, surveying the empty room. "I don't know how you come up with all your ideas, but I love what you're thinking."

"I just see it. When I walk into an empty room, my brain sees it furnished. This room, with the exposed brick, needs some soft fabrics, and I think the canopy adds a romantic feel."

They strolled out of the bedroom into the kitchen area. "I don't know that I will need the romantic feel though."

"Oh? You and Malcolm having problems?" Jenna asked.

"I broke it off with him."

"What? Why? He seemed nice."

"He is, and he is attractive. And to find that is very rare. But there just wasn't the…spark. I mean, I like him. I just thought my feelings for him would have grown by now, and they haven't."

Libby walked through the door with a couple of boxes. She dropped the boxes on the floor and turned. "Feelings for who?"

April quickly responded. "She was just telling us about her break-up with Malcolm."

Kaysi felt every bit of Libby's glare. "Oh. When did this happen?"

"A few days ago."

April rubbed her arms. "You know, it's getting kind of chilly in here. I think Joe has some heaters downstairs. I'm going to run downstairs and grab a couple." She turned to Jenna. "Wanna help me?"

"Sure."

Silence fell over the room until they were gone, and Kaysi knew Libby's fuse had yet again been lit. "When were you going to tell me? I've talked to you how many times this week?" She walked toward the door. "Never mind. I know the answer. You weren't. You didn't want me to go after him. You don't think I'm good enough for him."

Kaysi followed her out the door. "No, Libby. That's not it at all."

"Oh, it's not?" She turned and faced her. "Then enlighten me."

She followed Libby down the stairs. "The subject never came up. I was busy this week, and all I was focused on was my job, and the business, and the move. There was no underlying reason. I was just busy. If you want to go after him, be my guest."

"Seriously? You wouldn't care?"

"No. Have at him. Good luck."

"What's that supposed to mean?"

Reaching into the car, she closed her eyes trying to

stifle the scream threatening to escape. "Geez, Libby, give it a rest. Do whatever. I'm done." Grabbing two boxes, she headed back up the stairs.

As she entered, she heard voices. April and Jenna held two large black boxes in their arms. Libby came through the door with two more boxes.

"What are those?" Kaysi raised a brow.

April smiled. "Heaters."

"Oh. Right."

"We were getting cold with the door open, so I grabbed them. They're battery powered. The guys use them when they are working in the cold."

"Awesome! I was thinking about putting a fire in the fireplace, but I figured I needed to get it checked out first."

"Joe said he thinks they should have the fuse box hooked up in a few hours, then they will be able to get the electricity turned on, so you can use the heater."

"Great."

"We are going to run and grab some breakfast tacos from Tia Luna's for everyone and give the loft some time to warm up. Want to go?"

"Sure. Let me get the heaters going, and I'll be right down." April and Jenna headed downstairs. Kaysi set up one heater in the middle of the living room, then took the other heater into the bedroom, closed the door and turned it on. Noticing some of the cleaning supplies in the bathroom, she gathered them up, wiped up a couple of places that had been missed, and headed into the bedroom again. The sound of the outside door slamming startled her. Sliding open the door, she yelled, "Libby?" Immediately she was engulfed by a wall of smoke. "Oh, crap!" Her lungs seized up, and her eyes burned as the acrid haze surrounded her. Gagging and coughing, she ran for the stairs, screaming, "Fire! Fire!

Joe's eyes widened. "Cody, get your guys from the fire department over here, now. I've got an extinguisher in my truck." He turned to Kaysi, "You okay?"

Jenna and April wrapped their arms around her. Still coughing, she only managed to nod at Joe.

"Get out of here. We'll take care of this." The girls headed for the front door while Joe went out the back. Kaysi stood on the sidewalk watching as the upstairs windows lit up with flickering flames. Libby came around the corner of the building.

"What's going on? I was grabbing some boxes from the back of your car, and Joe came barreling out the door."

"The loft is on fire."

****

"It's primarily smoke and water damage," Joe explained as he led Kaysi, Jenna, April, and Libby up the stairs after the fire department left. "I'm going to need to do some work on the kitchen. It sustained the most damage." He opened the door, and Kaysi could feel her eyes stinging with tears.

"It's going to take me at least a couple of weeks to get it livable, so it's a good thing you didn't have your stuff moved today, because you are going to have to stay at your place a little longer."

"I can't. I have a guy moving in Wednesday." April, Jenna, and Libby wandered around the soot covered room.

"Tell him he has to wait."

"I can't. He's moving here for a job. He's from out of state."

Joe took a deep breath and ran his hand over his mouth. "Call Kaleb. He's just up the road. It will at least keep you in Dalton."

"But what will I do with all my stuff?"

"Store it."

"No. I have a better idea," Jenna suddenly interrupted. "Joe, aren't you guys almost done with the bunkhouse?"

"Yeah, we have a few more finishes to take care of, but it's pretty close."

"Kaysi can move out there. Ben hasn't moved in there yet."

"Don't you think you need to ask Ben about that first?" Cody chimed in.

"Where is he? He was here earlier."

"I sent him to Fayetteville to pick up some supplies."

Jenna slid her phone from her pocket and called him. "It went to voicemail. It will be fine," she said a little tentatively, pushing the phone back in her pocket. "He wasn't planning on moving over there for a couple of weeks anyway. You will have her back in here by then."

"I don't know, Jenna. Ben—"

"He will just have to deal. Kaysi needs a place to go. This is the perfect option. I'll try him again on the way over." Jenna grabbed up one of the salvageable boxes. "Kaysi, did they tell you what caused the fire?"

"Yeah. One of the guys said it was probably electrical because of the building being so old. They're pretty sure it started in the kitchen."

Joe stopped in his tracks. "Wait, what? Who told you that?"

"One of the firemen. He said it probably started in

one of the outlets on the wall."

"Well, I'm no fireman but I know it wasn't electrical." Kaysi raised her brow in question. "There's no electricity."

"Oh crap. You're right.

Chapter Nine

Ben set the bags of supplies down on the soot covered bar and dug in his pocket for his phone, scrolling to Joe's number. He picked up on the second ring. "Just got back with the stuff. What the hell happened? Where is everybody?"

"Had an issue with a small fire. Lock the door, we're done for today. We're helping Kaysi get her stuff moved."

"A *small* fire?"

"Yeah. We got lucky. It could have been worse. Anyway, we gotta shift gears. I need to work out the logistics, and we will get together tomorrow if you have time. Good news is, we have the leak fixed and the fuse box is moved, so I should be able to get the electricity on tomorrow if the wiring isn't damaged."

Locking the door behind him, Ben hopped in his truck and continued the conversation. "I'll be there after I get the ranch squared and Poppi taken care of."

"Behave tonight."

"What the hell is that supposed to mean?"

"Just keep your hands to yourself."

"From what?"

"It was Jenna's idea." The click on the line told Ben he wasn't getting any more information.

Driving away from the store, frustration filled him

as he continued to mull over what Joe could have been alluding to. His mind flipped through all the conversations they had had throughout the day, but nothing got him any closer to a possible answer. He spent the better part of the morning cleaning up the trash left behind in the store, then Joe sent him on a run to Fayetteville for parts and equipment. He picked up more supplies for his flags and other projects, since he had more orders coming in.

As he merged onto the highway heading to the ranch, his mind started playing through everything he needed to get done. Talk to Poppi about Rick. It bugged him that he didn't get to talk to him this morning when he showed up to tend to the horses.

But first, he needed to drop off the wood for the flags and check the studio for pieces he needed to finish and others that were ready to mail.

He remained irritated at whoever it was that posted his site to their blog, because he still hadn't figured out how to get all the flags done quickly. It did mean more money for Poppi's horses, but with orders pouring in, it would take him a year to get them done by himself, and he really didn't want other people messing with his artwork.

Turning up the dirt road, a calm came over him. Nothing calmed his soul like the ranch. He loved every aspect of it, especially Dash. Stopping at the stable, he grabbed a bag from the passenger seat and hopped out. The ground was icy in spots, and the sky hinted at more snow to come.

Horses whinnied and snorted as Ben strolled into the stables. The scent of fresh hay filled his nose. A black nose surrounded by golden hair appeared over the stall door. Dash. "Hey, buddy." Ben rubbed the satin softness of the horse's nose. "Did you have a good day?" Dash bobbed his head under Ben's hand, coaxing him to pat him more. He dug his fingers into his hair, running them down his neck to his mane. "I brought you a snack." He opened the bag and brought out a bright red apple. Digging his knife from its holder, he cut the apple in quarters then, holding a chunk in his palm, he let Dash take the sweet snack. Once the apple was gone, Ben ran his fingers through Dash's mane and scratched him between the ears. Then he headed out of the stable and crawled back into his truck. The gravel crunched beneath his tires as he continued down the dirt path. His heart stopped when he noticed a white SUV parked in front of the bunkhouse. He knew whose car it was. Every chance he got, he peeked out the back door to try to catch a glimpse of her. *What is she doing here?* Stopping next to her car, he put his truck in park and stared at the bunkhouse. Suddenly Joe's comments made perfect sense. He picked up his phone to call Joe and noticed a message from Jenna.

— *Hey, I tried calling you a couple of times, but you didn't pick up. Kaysi had a small fire in her loft, so I offered the bunkhouse until Joe could get her place fixed. I figured you wouldn't mind since you guys still have some work to do before you move in—*

"Shit." Pinching the bridge of his nose, he closed his eyes and bounced his head against the headrest. "This is not what I need right now." His lips drew into an irritated line, and his fingers brushed over the screen of the phone, dialing Jenna.

"Hello?"

"You figured wrong, Jenna. I've got a ton of shit to

do, and I can't be babysitting your friend."

"Don't yell at me. She was desperate and had nowhere else to go. Would it kill you to be nice for once? You aren't going to be moving in for a couple of weeks anyway."

"Just because I'm not living there doesn't mean I don't need to be there. We can't finish until she leaves. How long did Joe say it would take?"

Jenna's voice quieted. "A few days."

"How many days?"

Silence filled the other end of the line and Ben dreaded what was coming.

"Maybe a couple of weeks," Jenna said, weakly.

Ben's stomach dropped. "Weeks? Damn it, Jenna," he roared, and rubbed his hand over his forehead and down his face.

"I'm sorry if I am imposing on your precious privacy, but I was trying to help her out."

"She has money. She could have stayed at the hotel. Or hell, what about Brant's grandma's bed and breakfast?"

"Ben, sometimes I really don't like the fact that you are my brother. Grow a heart for once. She needed a place, and you have one you aren't using." With the click of the phone, he was back to staring into the windows of the bunkhouse.

Jenna didn't have a clue how the woman effortlessly upended him. Without even seeing her, his heart was already beating out of his chest. The night he met her kept replaying in his head, and humiliation washed over him again as the memory of the panic in her eyes, resurfaced. Yeah. She was the last thing he needed in his life right now. But it was too late for him to put his foot down. She was already moved in.

Rubbing his hands up and down his face in frustration, he let out a low growl, shut the engine off, gathered the materials for his artwork, and pushed open the truck door. He wandered up to the garage door on the studio and opened it. His eyes immediately landed on her beautiful face. Her eyes were filled with surprise like the night at TopHops, and his emotions went to war. Resentment battled with compassion and desire. He bit into his cheek, trying to keep the bitter words swirling in his head at bay. The bashful smile, that slowly captured her full pink lips, made the harsh words evaporate, and completely stopped him in his tracks. "How'd you get in here?" he asked calmly, surprising himself.

"The doors were open. I hope you don't mind."

Just seeing her up close again made his insides feel like they were short circuiting. Heat rushed up his neck into his cheeks so fast, his hand flew into his beard trying to stifle the tingling feeling. "It's a mess in here right now. I have a huge order to fill, and it seems to be growing by the day."

Her smile grew. "You're EtchedIn Designs." The way she said it confused him. He closed the exterior door, shutting out the frigid wind.

"Yeah. You didn't know? I figured Joe would have told you, since he's been remodeling this place."

"No. I hadn't been able to talk to him much until April and I decided to go into business together. We have both been busy, so…" She let the words fall away when her eyes drifted to one of his pieces. "I knew he was helping you remodel and may have mentioned you had a studio. But he didn't tell me what you did."

"So, I'm guessing you saw one of my pieces

before?"

Her attention moved to a flag sitting on a long table up against the wall. "Yeah, at Flame Masters. I couldn't quit staring at it. It's absolutely mesmerizing. It's so intricate." Her fingers gently brushed over the carved wood. "There's so much…emotion."

Ben watched her delicate fingers dance over the wood, surprised by her comment, that she understood what he felt creating each piece. Stepping closer, he let his hand follow hers across the folds of the flag. "Each piece is unique. I let the natural colors of the wood direct how I carve the folds of the flag."

"I just can't take my eyes off it. It's just exquisite."

"I'm glad you like it." Her hand brushed against his, and a surge of electricity shot through him. The stunned look her eyes held, told him she felt it too. A rosiness filled her tanned cheeks, and she gave him another shy smile before backing away.

"I-I'm sorry. I probably shouldn't have come in here. But when I saw the flag…" the irritation he had felt minutes before, from the invasion, was quickly dissipating with each gentle word she spoke, and the overwhelming feeling he had when he met her at TopHops replaced it.

Like his art, there was something about the way she spoke, and the way she gazed at him, that eased his anxiety. She did seem more timid, and shyer than he remembered, but he thought it might have something to do with her having to be in his space.

"It's okay. I normally don't like random people roaming around my studio, but Jenna told me what happened with the loft." He dropped his jacket and bags of supplies, and passed in front of her, moving through the barn doors, up the hallway, to the kitchen. She followed behind him.

Opening the refrigerator, he reached for a beer, and held it up to her. Initially, she acted like she was going to pass, but then took it from him. "Did you find out what caused it?" Confusion filled her face as he slid out a chair at the small dining table and nodded for her to have a seat, so he explained. "The fire, I mean."

"They were thinking it was an electrical fire, but Joe pointed out—"

"The electricity isn't on."

"Exactly."

"So, what? Do they think someone set it?"

"I have no idea."

He lifted his beer to his lips. "Well, I'm sure you have a ton of enemies," he said sarcastically, and smirked.

Kaysi's mouth dropped open, and she playfully swatted him. "Most people love me."

A laugh stuck in his throat when something in her tone made him wonder if there was more to what she said than he considered, and a sudden wave of concern filled him. She seemed so carefree and had an easy laugh at the bar, but something or someone had stolen some of her joy.

"Seriously. Do you think someone is after you?"

A flash of fear skirted her face, but she quickly tried to hide it with a wrinkle of her nose and a wave of her hand. "Nah."

"You don't know how to lie very well, do you?" He took another swig of his beer then set it down. "Now why don't you level with me. Why would anyone want to hurt someone as nice as you? I mean, I could see it with me.

I'm an ass most of the time. Ask Jenna. But everyone I've talked to that knows you says you are the nicest person they've met."

"Oh, you'd be surprised."

He lifted a brow, and she turned away and took a drink of her beer. Her eyes met his again, and she took a deep breath.

"I have been getting some threats on my blog."

He leaned forward on his elbows, concern rising in his gut. "What blog? Why would someone be threatening you? What are they saying?"

"My family and I put together a charity dinner to raise money for the National Center for Missing and Exploited Children, in honor of finding Joe. I posted a link for the event and donations on my blog. A few days ago, I started getting some comments telling me to stop. I got one that said I didn't know what was good for me. Then the last one I got was yesterday, and it said I'm sleeping with the enemy, and to watch my back."

Ben's cheeks puffed as he let out a long slow breath. The last thing he wanted to do was get in the middle of her problems. He had plenty of his own. His mind flashed on Poppi. He needed to let him know what Rick was up to. But something was compelling him to delve deeper. "So, you think it is someone who doesn't want you to do the charity event?"

"I honestly don't know. So much has happened with the finalization of the event, and the new business, and the move. The first negative post was a couple of days ago when I posted the information for the charity dinner and the link for the donations, so I associated it with the event. But then they kept coming."

"Could it be anyone else?" Ben rubbed the

condensation from the bottle and studied her face. Full lips in the perfect shade of pink. Eyes the shade of a clear sky at dawn. Cheeks that held hints of dimples and gave her the perfect "girl next door" natural beauty. And she had a certain smile. He remembered it from TopHops. It was bright and wide, and made her eyes light up, like she was seeing the world for the first time. But she had yet to show it to him today. Today, the only thing her face held was sadness and defeat.

"Let's see, I have a boyfriend I just broke up with who refuses to believe it's over. And then there's my friend who is pissed that I moved from Fayetteville to start a new business, even though I told her she could work with me," she huffed. "So, I have that going for me."

"Geez, okay. I thought I had it bad." He chuckled. "Let me see the comments you've gotten."

"You don't have to do that. I'm sure there are simple explanations for the comments and fire."

"Just let me see your damn blog," he growled. Then seeing her eyes go wide, he added, "Please."

She gave him a hesitant nod, then rose slowly from the table and walked into the guest bedroom. When she returned, she had an open laptop in her hands. Setting it in front of him on the table, Ben's eyes rested on the words on the screen, and his whole body tightened. Kaysi's Kloset. He closed his eyes slowly trying to still the anger growing again in his gut. *Why didn't I put two and two together? Of course, she's the one responsible for the hordes of people wanting my flags.* His lips pursed, and he scratched his beard.

Her brows pinched together. She'd obviously noticed his change in demeanor. "Something wrong?"

"Just show me the posts."

Her voice weakened. "You don't need…" his eyes narrowed and landed on her. "Oh. Okay." She leaned over him. Her breast brushed against his shoulder, and he caught a whiff of her floral scent.

The energy vibrating between them nearly had him lifting right out of his chair. His heart pounded so hard he figured she could hear it. Curling his fingers into a fist, he pressed them against his mouth to stave off the pressure building within him. *What is she doing to me?* He was pissed as hell at her for posting his artwork and causing his orders to blow up, but also worried that she had someone after her.

That all paled though at the problem his body was currently posing with her hovering over him, and it was growing worse by the millisecond. Gently brushing her finger against the pad on her keyboard, she finally came to the first derogatory post.

He peeked up at her, and his eyes met hers for a split second before they returned to the screen. There was no mistaking what her eyes held. She felt it too.

Tapping the pad, she backed away. He returned his gaze to the screen and read the entry, then scrolled through post after post of comments, praising the different items she had listed. Another negative post, then pages of posts that again praised another item.

"Have you said anything to the police about these negative posts?"

"No."

"Why?" he chided, his tone harsher than he expected since his guts were basically turning inside out.

"Because I figured it was just a troll. There's always those who want to stir up trouble just to see what kind of response they will get. Anyway, there aren't that many posts."

"And I would agree, except for the fact that someone tried to set your loft on fire."

"We don't know that for sure or whether the two are connected."

He grunted in frustration. "Well, what the hell do you think happened? It is impossible to have an electrical fire when there is no electricity."

"I don't know."

"Exactly. You need to tell someone in case there is a problem." He paused. "How many people know that you were moving, and where you were moving?"

She stared at him for a long moment and swallowed. He could see the fear she was trying to tamp down. Her eyes began to shimmer. "I-I…don't know," she said, shaking her head slowly.

Meeting her gaze, he stayed silent.

She inhaled and rolled her eyes. "Fine." Glancing back at the screen, she let out the breath. "I'll go to the police tomorrow."

He sat back in his chair, continuing to keep his eyes locked on her.

"Do you really think someone might have set the fire?"

"I have no idea. But let the police at least know about it. Don't brush it off." His finger pushed at the pad on the keyboard, and he searched for the post she made of his flag. When he came to it, he read her comment "You should see this in person." His finger brushed the pad, and he scrolled through comment after comment, admiring the piece, and complimenting the talent of the artist. As he continued to scroll, he found pages of comments. People left comments on his website, but they were few and far between. Nothing close to what he was seeing on hers. Were all these comments real? Was his art really affecting so many?

"I've never had so many people respond to anything like they did to your flag."

"Did you ever think to ask first, before posting the piece?"

"Honestly? I figured if you had it hanging in a public place, you wanted people to see it and contact you. So, no. I just thought I was helping boost your visibility. I mean, why have a website and hang your art in public places, if you don't want people to see it, and order your stuff?"

"I've only hung a few of my pieces around town because I wanted to limit my audience."

"But that's not the case on your website. Anyone could have done what I did."

"I don't advertise. It's basically an art gallery to display all the work I've completed. I'd gotten minimal amounts of viewings, until you made that post. Your site is followed by millions."

"Okay, say I did ask your permission, you would have told me no, just like you did when I asked for an interview."

"But you should have given me the courtesy. I've got forty plus orders from your post. And that's the last count from this morning." Frustration rose in his voice as he thought about what it was going to take to get all the orders filled.

She plopped down in the chair next to him. "Most people would be ecstatic to have so many orders."

"Not me. I mean, it's flattering. But do you know

how long it takes to make one flag?"

"No," she said quietly.

"At least a week. It's several steps, down days to let the glue dry, then the stain, and then the poly, and you can't fudge that. Forty flags would take almost a year."

She blinked slowly, as distress washed over her face, and her eyes lowered. "I'm sorry. It was just so breathtaking, so intricate, so unique. I just wanted to share it. It was one of those pieces that I seldom come across, and when I do, it's like I've found a buried treasure."

Why was it he couldn't stay mad at this woman. She had royally screwed up his life, and he saw no good way out. But he still felt ashamed of himself for being mean to her. "They *are* intricate, and the way I create them, there are no two pieces alike. I can't mass produce them."

"Is there something I can do to help you? I'm going to be here for a while."

"No, damn it. Don't you think you've helped enough?" he barked, and immediately regretted it, when she flinched and turned away.

She pushed her chair out. "Great. Now I have you mad at me too. Her hand pressed the laptop closed. "I'm so sorry, Ben," she said on a sigh. "I really was trying to help."

Hearing her soft voice say his name, felt like her lips were pressed against him, whispering it in his ear. His body felt like every hair had been electrified. Then, seeing the tears, about to spill down her cheek, gutted him. *What the hell am I doing? She has enough going on without me yelling at her.* His fingers dug in his hair as he tried to come up with an apology. "I'm not mad at you. I just don't know how I'm going to get all these orders filled. I'm busy with the ranch, remodeling this place, and helping Joe get the building done. This is supposed to be how I unwind and relax. Now it's taking priority."

Chunking her bottle in the garbage, she came to an abrupt stop in front of a picture of a horse, hanging on the wall in the living room. "That's my horse, Bandit," Ben said.

Kaysi turned quickly with an odd look of confusion, then stared at him.

"What?"

Like she was awakened from a dream, her eyes fluttered, and she turned back to the photo. "Nothing. He's a beautiful horse."

Ben stood and closed the distance between them, wondering why she seemed so startled. "Had him since I was old enough to ride."

"What happened to him?"

"Got old. Got sick. Wound up having to put him down a few years ago."

"Aw. He was so sweet." Her words caught him off guard, and his eyes locked on her. This was getting weirder by the second. How did she know Bandit?

Obviously realizing he was staring at her, she nervously backtracked. "I-I mean, he looks sweet."

He knew something was up. But how would she know Bandit? She probably hadn't been around horses much, living in the city. Glancing back at her, he caught her staring again. Those hypnotic eyes searched his face, and he couldn't turn away. They were sucking him under like a riptide. What would it feel like to have her lips pressed to his; have her body pressed to his?

Darting her eyes away, she broke the trance. Reality came crashing back. She was Joe's little sister. Regardless of the fact that Joe had only known her for a little over a year, she was still his sister. He needed to keep his distance. But telling himself that, and actually being able to accept it, was yet to be seen. His body sure wasn't jumping on the bandwagon.

Backing away, he turned and headed through the barn doors to the studio with Kaysi hot on his heels. "He was a good horse. Really gentle." His fingers brushed over several pieces of stained wood until he came to one that he stopped to study.

"What made you start doing all this?"

Glancing back over his shoulder, he saw her staring at another piece of his. The outline of a skull was stained to resemble the flag. "Wood working class in high school. Did a couple of pieces that I thought were horrible, but my mom ranted and raved about them and entered them into the county fair. They won first place. I piddled with it here and there after that. Then, when my mom got sick, the hospital bills started piling up. Money was starting to get tight, and everything was spiraling out of control. Dad had to sell off a bunch of cattle, but it still wasn't enough. I made a few pieces then, partly to keep from thinking about what my mom was going through, but also hoping to help with the finances. I hung them in a few local businesses, and they started selling. It wasn't much, but it got us through."

"What did she die from?" she asked, studying another piece hanging on the wall. Her arms were crossed, and she chewed on her bottom lip as her eyes squinted like she was taking in every nuance.

He suddenly realized he had forgotten to breathe

when she spoke again.

"It's okay."

His mind went back to the question she asked. The subject was hard for him, but the gentleness of her voice seemed to lessen the sting.

She turned and stepped closer to him. "You don't have to answer."

He realized, in that moment, a long silence had fallen between them.

"I'm sorry. I just remembered Jenna saying something about her passing away."

"Cancer." He hated the word; hated the disease and hated that it took his mom. But he hated himself even more for not being there for her.

Kaysi's eyes bore into him, and he suddenly felt like she could see his thoughts. "It really affected you," she said softly. "You've changed."

His head jerked up, confused by the comment. It wasn't said like she was asking a question, but like she somehow knew him. Her eyes were following her finger that was brushing against a piece of the stained wood on the table.

"What do you mean, I've changed?"

The twitch of her head, and the panic on her face, told him she was hiding something. "That...her death had to have affected you," she said quickly. "How long has it been?"

He knew she was trying to steer the conversation away from the comment. "Three and a half years," he said, but his mind was now searching his memory for how they might have met in the past. He knew her family was very well off. Her dad ran a successful oil and gas company. Their lives were so different. He couldn't see how they would have crossed paths. His eyes followed her as she slowly meandered across the room to a bench that held wooden keepsake boxes. He studied her face trying to find a memory from his past. *No. I would have remembered if I met her before. But why did she say I had changed? How did she know Bandit?* He took a deep breath. *Damn it, I don't have time for this right now.* "I need to grab some more supplies out of my truck and head to my neighbor's house. Is there anything you need?"

"Where do you keep the wood for the fireplace?"

"It's around the corner, on the side of the house. I'll grab you some before I go to Poppi's."

"No need. I don't mind getting it." She walked back toward him. "Who's Poppi?"

"Mr. McIntyre. Our neighbor. I help him with some of the work on his ranch. He runs a rescue for wild horses."

Ben watched, as that bright smile that made her eyes light up, engulfed her face. "Oh, I hope I get to see them while I'm here." The twinkling of her eyes was back and took another stab at Ben's resolve. He flexed his shoulders trying to release the tightness in his chest. *How does she do that?*

Forcing himself to avert his eyes, he picked up his jacket and asked, "Do you need anything else?"

"Um…" She tapped her lips, thinking. "Oh, do you have any sheets for the bed in the extra bedroom? I have some, but I really need to wash them. They smell like smoke, and the rest of my linens are packed. I won't get them until the movers get here on Monday."

Ben's head jerked. "Movers?" His blood instantly became molten lava. "Why the hell are you having the movers bring your stuff here?"

"Jenna said it would save me from having to pay for storage. It's not much. I'm leaving most of my stuff at my place in Fayetteville for the guy moving in. But the movers had already loaded the truck, and I needed a place for them to take it."

"Why didn't you just have them deliver to the store, and put it downstairs?"

"Well, one..." she paused, "...I honestly didn't think of that, and I'm guessing no one else did either. But the boxes would be in the way while you guys are working."

Rolling his eyes and shaking his head, he rubbed his hand down his face. "This just keeps getting better."

"I'm sorry, Ben."

He stormed out of the studio and up the hallway, with Kaysi hesitantly following. Yanking open a closet, he grabbed a set of sheets and chunked them at her.

"Please don't be mad. Jenna was only trying to help."

"I wish to god people would just stop trying to help."

Chapter Ten

She had to admit, there was a lot more stuff than she remembered packing, once the movers finished unloading all her belongings. The living room was stacked with boxes, shelves, tables, and other pieces of furniture, to the point she could barely get around. Ben was going to have a conniption.

She heard him rummaging around in the studio Sunday, but she stayed away from him. After their encounter of mixed messages, she felt it best to leave him alone. One minute he was livid, the next he was worried about her. The next minute, he was devastated by his mom's death. And, at one point, she could swear he wanted to kiss her. Then he was back to being livid again. By the end of the night, she had lost count of the different emotions she had witnessed from him. His mood swings were worse than hers, when she was PMSing, and had her head spinning in confusion. But one thing she wasn't confused about, was the electricity that shot through her body every time they were close. She had felt it at TopHops when he had his hands on her, and again, even stronger, when they were scrolling through her website. And the minute she made the connection of who he was, it was nearly unbearable. She wasn't imagining it. It was a palpable charge. And she could swear Ben felt it too.

What was it about him? It couldn't have been just the memories. She didn't even realize who he was until their encounter was ending.

When he appeared in the doorway of the studio, he was in a heavy suede, Sherpa coat, a pair of blue jeans, and a cowboy hat. He smelled of sawdust, and leather and the scent had her wanting to lean in and breathe deep. His strawberry blond beard was full and a bit shaggy, but she figured, as hard as he worked, he just didn't make time for himself.

The minute he spoke, with that deep angry growl, she melted. Even though he was a bit unwelcoming, her body obviously didn't care. And it continued not to care as she tried to sleep that night, but couldn't, because her mind was racing with fantasies of him.

Sunday was spent on the internet searching for inventory for the store. But not much was accomplished, because she kept thinking about Ben, and wondering what he had been doing all these years.

Her focus landed on a tower of boxes in the corner. Reading the writing on the outside of each box, she found the one she was after...on the bottom. Of course. Making quick work of restacking the boxes, she slid the box to an open spot on the floor and ripped the tape off. Small plastic frames filled one side of the box, while photo albums filled the other. A red binder, with gold piping, and labeled "Summer Camp," sat in between one labeled Events, and another labeled School. Lifting the binder from the box, she sat cross legged in the open space, and flipped through the photos until she landed on Sterling Springs Dude Ranch.

For most of the year, the ranch was a high-end resort on the border between Arkansas and Missouri. But every summer, the resort set a couple of weeks aside to become a true dude ranch for kids. For the young campers, the weeks were filled with riding horses along the trails, playing in the river, hiking, and eating smores around the campfire. For the teens, they too rode horses and played in the river, but they also found out what it was like to work on a ranch, complete with tending to the horses and washing the dishes after dinner was served in the dining hall.

After a particularly hard year in junior high, which included hitting puberty with a vengeance, and getting braces, Kaysi asked her mom if she could learn how to ride a horse. It was something different from her usual summer art camp. Searching the internet for just the right camp, she fell in love with the photos of Sterling Springs. The ranch was within driving distance from Fayetteville, which was also a plus. She normally had to fly, and the previous summer the airlines had lost her luggage for nearly a week.

She'd never been to a real ranch, and she was excited about learning to ride. However, she had no idea how to clean out horse stalls, or how to care for the horse for that matter. That part scared her. That was, until she saw who was going to be teaching her and training her how to ride. A boy with sun kissed skin and strawberry blond hair. His name was Ben. Every morning when she had to clean the stables, he would be there with Bandit.

Kaysi stared at the photos in the album. A photo of a boy with big blue eyes, wearing a straw cowboy hat, a button-down checked shirt, and faded blue jeans, stared back at her. She had immediately fallen hard for him, along with fifty other girls ranging in age from eight to eighteen. Unfortunately for her, she'd entered that stage that was just past cute kid, but not quite hot teen girl, where she was still a bit chubby, with a haircut that resembled more of a bird's nest than hair, a pair of indestructible glasses, and braces.

Kaysi chewed on her lip as she rubbed her finger over the photo of her sitting on a horse for the first time, remembering that young girl and how lost she was. She hated herself. At the time, she felt like an absolute failure and disappointment to her family. It wasn't that her parents didn't love her or encourage her in everything she did. She just didn't believe them and didn't feel like she belonged.

The first day of camp was filled with anticipation. Walking to the stables, she could feel her stomach tingling with the excitement of seeing Ben. Robin, a girl who'd attended Sterling Springs for several years, joined her. She had Down Syndrome. Kaysi enjoyed talking to her. She seemed to take life in stride, something Kaysi needed to learn to do.

After being taught how to muck out the stalls from one of the other workers, she wandered out to the corral and waited on the fence with Robin and a few other students. Out of the corner of her eye, she saw Ben leading a dark brown spotted horse, with a white nose, and a dark brown band across his eyes. The tingles filled her body, and a smile spread across her face. He smiled back when he saw her. He was always nice to her while she was learning to ride, even agreeing to take a photo of her with her phone, the first time she got in the saddle.

A flood of emotions filled her recalling that summer, and how it changed her life. Banging at the front door made her jump. She didn't figure she would see anyone but the movers, and planned on working her way through the boxes, so she put on her comfy jeans and an old sweatshirt. Her hair was up in a messy bun, and she had her glasses perched on her nose. *Did I even wash my face this morning?* Rubbing the possible mascara from under her eyes, she dodged boxes while making her way to the door and opened it.

The sting of the icy breeze immediately cut through her sweatshirt, and she folded her arms against herself, trying to ward off the chill bumps erupting on her skin. It only took a second for the chill to disappear though, and be replaced by a flood of heat, when she saw Ben standing at the door with his arms loaded with firewood.

"What are you doing?" she asked, fighting the smile trying to spread across her face as Ben made his way into the house.

"There's a storm coming. You asked about the firewood the other day. I wasn't sure if you got any, and I figured you would want a fire when the storm hits. I wanted to get the rack loaded, so you had some dry wood." His eyes darted around the room at the stacks of boxes. "Geez, I thought you said you didn't have a lot of stuff. We aren't going to be able to do any of the trim work with all the boxes stacked against the walls."

"I thought you were going to focus on your orders and the loft while I was here."

The heavy sigh he gave her told her he might have forgotten everything he was involved in.

"I guess that's what's going to happen, because I damn sure won't be able to do anything in here."

"I'll try to get as many boxes unpacked as possible, so there is more room."

"Don't do it on my account. You aren't going to be here long enough." He loaded the firewood rack and moved toward the door. Kaysi's phone chimed. She slid it from her back pocket, immediately rolled her eyes, and headed into the living room.

"Hey, Malcolm. I can't talk right now."

"I just wanted to see if you could have dinner with me tonight."

"No. I don't think that would be a good idea. And anyway, I wanted to get as much unpacking done as possible before tomorrow."

"Do you need help? I can come by and help if you need me to."

"No. I'm not at the loft. There was a bit of a problem, so I'm staying at a friend's place until it gets fixed."

"A problem?"

"Yeah." She thought about telling him about the fire but decided against it. It would only make him more adamant about seeing her. "I appreciate the offer. I just don't think it would be a good idea. I'd rather unpack myself, so I know where everything is."

"Well, I wanted to talk to you about the charity dinner."

"Malcolm, I—"

"I know you don't have a boyfriend, Kaysi, and you need an escort. So, why don't we go together. No strings attached."

Her heart pounded as she tried to come up with the right words to let him off easy, but she remembered it didn't seem to work the last time. "Actually, I have someone to go with to the charity ball."

"Really? Okay then. I guess I will see you there."

"Okay. Bye."

Kaysi stared at her phone for a moment, then turned

around to find Ben standing in the doorway with a scowl on his face. "Everything okay?"

"Yeah. My ex. He has been texting me. I guess I haven't responded fast enough, so he called."

"Is he harassing you?" Ben growled.

"Well, yes. But not in a bad way. He's harmless. Sweet even."

Ben relaxed his stance and uncrossed his arms. "So, why'd you break up?"

Kaysi studied his face, wondering why he was even interested. "We had dated for a little over six months, and there was just something missing. Don't get me wrong, he was the perfect gentleman. He doted on me, sent me flowers, took me out to fancy places. I just didn't want to lead him on.

Ben's expression filled with irritation, "You women…" and he turned and walked away. Yanking open the door, he headed down the steps.

Kaysi stood in the door letting the cold air cool the anger heating her core. "What's that supposed to mean?" Disappearing around the corner, he said nothing. When he returned with another armload of firewood, she asked the question again, "What do you mean?"

"What?"

"You women."

"We can take you out, shower you with presents, try to do all that we can to please you, and it's still not enough. It's never enough."

His comment caught her off guard, but the fact that he included himself in the comment, and the harshness of his tone, told her he'd probably been hurt in a relationship. "Maybe if I were materialistic, it would be. But I believe in love. And I don't think two people should be together unless both love each other. I don't think you should settle."

"So, you broke it off because you didn't love him?"

"I loved him. I mean, he's a good guy. But I wasn't in love with him, and he deserves someone who is."

"But he is in love with you?"

"Honestly, I don't think he is. I think he is in love with the idea of being in a relationship. I think his family has expectations of him. But we are too different in the wrong ways."

"How so?"

"Why are you asking me all these questions?"

"I don't know. Never mind." He knelt to load the wood in the rack.

With his back to her, she answered. "I wasn't good enough for him."

Shooting her a side glance, he called back over his shoulder. "I doubt that very seriously."

"He's British…and rich. He was raised very proper. That appealed to me at first. I was curious…infatuated even, but…" she huffed and flopped onto the sofa, "I quickly realized being raised with manners was not enough to date him.

"It wore me out constantly being on edge, wondering whether I was holding my fork right, or talking with my mouth full. He would kind of glare at me, and I knew I was embarrassing him. I started picturing what my life might be like if we married. I just couldn't see us being happy."

Ben pushed a few boxes out of the way and sat on the floor, stretching his legs out, crossing them at the ankles. Tilting his head, he asked, "So, what kind of guy are you searching for?"

She studied his expression, continuing to wonder where all the questions were coming from. "I guess just someone I can be myself with." She examined herself. "Someone who thinks I'm as irresistible in a sweatshirt, torn jeans, and bare feet as I am in a little black dress and heels. Someone who doesn't play games, who speaks his mind. I can't stand when it's obvious something is wrong, but he just plays it off as nothing, then sulks for days.

"You have to talk it out. Lay your cards on the table, even if it is painful at first."

Ben bobbed his head.

"So, I'm guessing you get it." She sat up and crossed her legs in front of her and played with the fringe at the hole in her jeans. "Did you have a bad breakup?"

"You could say that." He sat up, and his eyes moved to the open photo album. Kaysi's eyes tracked where he was focused and quickly shut the album, tucking it next to her. He turned to her with a curious gaze, and the side of his mouth lifted. "What'cha hidin?" he asked in a sing song voice.

Shaking her head, she responded, "No. You tell me about your ex, since I played twenty questions with you."

He slumped back and sighed. "Not much to say. We dated for two years, got engaged, and a month before we were supposed to get married, she decided I wasn't the one and ran off with someone else." His eyes drifted. "Didn't have enough money to meet her needs."

Kaysi wrinkled her nose, and a pain settled in her chest. She couldn't even imagine how hurt he must have been. "That's harsh. I understand why you are a little wary of the opposite sex."

"More than a little."

Her eyes met his. "How long ago?"

"Couple of years. I saw her for the first time a couple of days ago."

"How'd it go?"

"She apologized. Told me he wasn't being good to her."

The twenty questions were starting to make sense. A sick feeling stirred in her gut. Was he thinking about going back to her?

"What's that look for?"

"What?" she quickly answered.

He raised a brow. "Who's playing games?"

She huffed, knowing he was referring to her earlier comment. "I just hope you aren't going to jump—"

"Aw, hell no. She had her chance. She's not getting another." He sat up with his ankles still crossed and wrapped his arms around his knees. "I don't think I'm cut out for relationships anyway."

"Why do you say that?"

"I've tried it. I'd rather not go through that again."

"Don't let the unfortunate things that happened in your past, make you forfeit your happiness forever."

He gave her a "where did that come from" expression, opened his mouth and paused. "That's very profound, but I'll take my chances."

"Don't you want to be happy?"

"I'm happy."

"You could've fooled me."

"Happiness is overrated."

"It's better than being angry at everybody."

"I'm not angry at *everybody*, just those who annoy me."

She giggled. "Everybody."

That got a chuckle out of him.

"Touché." He studied her for a long minute, then added, "You seem a lot happier today."

"As opposed to…"

"The other day when you arrived on my doorstep."

"Oh, you mean the day you yelled at me when I was just trying to help?"

"Fine. I'm sorry I yelled. I'm just a wee bit stressed about getting all those orders out, and I'm up to fifty-two by the way."

"I'm sorry too. Things didn't quite go as planned, and I hate when I feel like I am causing problems."

Ben stood. "Eh. Don't worry about it. We'll get it figured out."

Excitement bubbled inside her. "You mean you will let me help you?"

Ben rested his hands on his hips. "God help me, as much as I don't want to, I might have to take you up on the offer."

Kaysi jumped up and clapped her hands. "Yay!" She couldn't hold back the smile that filled her face, and before she thought about it, she slammed into him, wrapping her arms around his waist. He let out an "oof," but his arms slowly moved from his hips and snaked around her. The tingle of her body from their connection made her quickly realize what she had done. She slowly released her hands, but his arms remained tightly wrapped around her. She lifted her eyes to his. The smolder in his eyes immediately sucked the air from the room. But just as quickly as it hit, the spell was broken. He cleared his throat, dropped his hands, and looked away.

"I better go get the rest of the wood."

Chapter Eleven

Ben was up early. He had slept hardly at all after his brief encounter with Kaysi. When she wrapped her arms around him, her warmth did something to him. It wasn't so much a physical heat. Her eyes. Her smile. Her words. Everything about her had a warmth that penetrated the thick icy wall his heart was encased in. It bugged him. And something else bugged him. Something about her appearance, with her glasses and hair tied up on her head, felt familiar to him. After the strange comments she made about him and Bandit, he realized, he had to have met her. But where? How long ago? Bandit had been gone for a few years. And then her statement "you've changed." What did she mean?

From that first night in the studio, she drew him in. And the more he tried to fight it, the more enticing she seemed. Every moment with her stirred up the myriad of emotions within him. She irritated the hell out of him and yet, he wanted to grab her and kiss the life out of her. And nothing he did took his mind off her.

Sunday, he worked in the studio and found himself hoping she would come in. But she didn't. So, he planned on stopping by the next day to help unload the moving truck after he got done with his chores, but the truck was gone when he arrived. The firewood was the best excuse he could come up with to see her.

He hadn't meant to stay. He was just going to fill the firewood rack, check on her, and leave. But after hearing the panic in her voice when her ex called, something inside him wanted to protect her; wanted to make sure the guy wasn't harassing her. Then he couldn't keep his mouth from spewing out questions. One question he didn't have the guts to ask, was who she was going with to the charity ball. When she mentioned she had a date during the call, the way she chewed on her lip made him think she was hiding something from her ex.

Finished with most of the chores, he was heading out to the pasture to check on the cows, when he saw Kaysi coming out of the bunkhouse with an armload of flattened boxes.

"Do you need help with that?"

She jumped at his voice, and then a huge smile engulfed her face as she laid eyes on Dash. "Oh my gosh, Ben, who is this?" She immediately dropped the boxes on the ground, walked up to the horse, and rubbed her hand up and down the horse's nose.

"This is Dash."

"He's beautiful. I love his color," she said, letting her fingers dig into the hair under his chin.

Ben unbuckled a bag on his saddle and dug out a carrot. "Here. He's probably wondering where his snack is."

She took it from him and held it up in front of Dash's mouth. The horse gently grabbed it from her. "Good stuff. Isn't it, buddy?" Her hand rubbed along his neck digging into his soft winter coat.

"Do you need help?"

She raised a brow in confusion, so he pointed to the boxes on the ground.

"Oh. No. I'm going to take them to the store later. We can use them for mail orders. I've got to meet April this afternoon." She continued to rub Dash's nose as he chewed his carrot. "So, what are you guys doing?"

"Gonna go check on the cows, then head next door to talk to the neighbor." He had been by Poppi's several times, and tried to call him, but he hadn't been able to get ahold of him, and he was getting worried. He wasn't the greatest at picking up the phone, but he usually let Ben know if he was going to be away for a few days, so he could make sure the animals were taken care of.

"Would you care if I came along?"

The question caught him by surprise. "Do you even know how to ride?" Somehow, he knew what the answer was going to be.

"Uh, yeah. I was taught by the best," she said, with a playful smile creeping across her face making him wonder what she meant.

"Oh really?" A smirk threatened, and he tried to fight it. "Was it one of those polo club places where they wear the weird pants? Because I only have these types of saddles." He patted the saddle horn and Dash bobbed his head.

"No. I ride western." On one hand, he wanted to see how she did, but on the other, he really didn't have time to babysit her while he was working.

"As much as I would love to put your riding skills to the test, I don't think it would be a good idea. It's cold, and I'm going to be out for a while."

"I don't mind. I have some thermals I can put on."

"You would need a whole lot more than that."

"I've got a good coat." He rolled his eyes and she continued, "And a hat…" He knew this battle was a lost cause and shook his head. "…And gloves. And I can he—"

His hand flew up stopping her. "Please don't tell me you can help me, because we all know what happens when you help." He meant it to annoy her, but there was a little bit of humor in his voice that he hadn't intended, and her smile put the nail in the coffin.

"Please?" She even folded her hands together for good measure, and he was done.

Glaring at her from the corner of his eye didn't faze her. Thick, long lashes batted over wide sky-blue eyes, filled with hope. A twinge shot through him. Shaking his head again, he shooed her off. "Go get your clothes on. I will saddle up Dusty and be back in ten." Dash snorted as he gently tugged on the reins. Kaysi clapped, and that beautiful smile filled her face. It was going to be the death of him, and he couldn't help but smile as he rode away. He'd never met anyone with so much life in them. So much pure joy. Except his mom.

Ten minutes later he rode up, towing a chestnut-colored horse. Ben was about to get off Dash when the door opened. The moment his eyes landed on her his entire body tensed. He committed every part of her to memory. Skintight blue jeans were tucked into a pair of intricately scrolled, black cowboy boots with insets of red. A fur vest covered an open leather jacket that topped a thick, brightly printed, button-up sweater, and a red scarf was wrapped around her neck. She had tied back her hair in a low ponytail, and a wide brimmed, tan cowboy hat sat low on her head.

He knew his mouth was gaped open, because it had gone bone dry. But no matter how hard he tried he couldn't seem to shut it. He was kind of worried what she would think was appropriate to wear. But she dressed like it was just another day on the ranch for her. She reached up, without a word, and scrubbed her hand against the horse's nose, then gave her a kiss. After sliding on a pair of gloves, she gracefully swung herself into the saddle, and grabbed the reins. An overwhelming need for her, shot through him.

"Are you just going to sit there with your mouth hanging open, or are we going to ride?"

Her comment shook him out of his daze, and he was ready to see what she could do. "Are the stirrups a good length for you?"

She nodded. "Yeah." She rubbed her hand along the horse's neck. "What did you say her name was?"

"Dusty. She's Jenna's horse." His gaze locked on her again, and her head tilted.

"*What?*"

"Just surprised is all." He *was* surprised. Surprised he could talk coherently. "I wasn't expecting a little city girl to be so comfortable in the saddle." He tugged the reins and Dash turned. Dusty followed, and Kaysi rode up to his side. "Where'd you learn to ride?"

Kaysi stiffened, and her eyes darted away. "Camp."

"Camp?" He still pictured her riding English style with all the jumps.

"Yeah. I went for several years during the summer while I was in school."

"I worked at a ranch up on the Missouri border one summer teaching horseback riding. Hated every minute of it. The managers were horrible, and the kids were a bunch of spoiled brats. I wouldn't have done it except I was trying to buy a truck, and it paid well."

"Oh, I bet it wasn't so bad," Kaysi said, but Ben

noticed a shakiness in her voice.

"It pretty much sucked the whole time."

"Did you work the entire summer?"

"Hell no. Two weeks was plenty for me. Sterling Springs only has the dude ranch for a couple of weeks during the summer. The rest of the time it's a western resort and spa for the hoity toity."

"Were you able to get your truck?"

"Yeah."

"So, it was worth it?"

"Well, that's debatable. Those two weeks were soul sucking."

"Aw. I'm sure it had some redeeming qualities."

"Wanna bet?"

Kaysi rolled her eyes. "Are you always so grumpy?"

"When do you have to be back to meet April?"

"Later this afternoon. We are meeting to discuss the name of the store. Kind of an important item when you have a business."

Ben nodded in rhythm with the clop of Dash's hooves. "It would probably be a good idea."

"Oh my gosh, Ben," Kaysi blurted. "Why didn't I think of this before?" She turned in her saddle. "You have to make our sign."

"No. I—"

"I'm not taking no for an answer. It would be perfect."

"You do realize, I'm the one who has to make it, and if I decide I can't, it won't happen."

"Please, Ben. You have to. Your artwork is so unique. It's so…rare for me to find something that speaks to me on so many levels. It's gritty and rugged, and yet so beautiful and emotional all at the same time."

"You don't understand. I'm not saying I won't do it. I'm saying I can't just be given something to do, and do it. I have to be inspired."

The glow from her smile nearly blinded him. He loved when her eyes sparkled with excitement. It was like standing in the sunlight on a snowy day.

"But you would do it?"

"Geez, woman. Are you always this giddy? This, this smiley?" Truth be told, he loved that about her. It made him feel a little less empty, especially when he knew he put that smile on her face.

"When I get my way." She swayed in her saddle. "So, you'll do it. Right?"

"I didn't say that. But give me the name and I'll think about it."

She bounced in her saddle and giggled.

"I'm not promising anything."

"I can't wait to tell April. She is going to lose her mind."

"You need to come up with a name first."

"I know. I've been wracking my brain, and that's what the meeting is about. April is having a hard time too. We thought if we got together, we might be able to bounce stuff off each other until something sticks."

They approached a small herd of cattle around a full hay feeder, and Ben halted Dash. "What is it that you do exactly on your blog?" he asked as he lowered himself to the ground.

"I find unique pieces of art, or furniture, or clothing, and I share them with the world. Most of the time, I try to contact the artist to get their story. Unless, of course, they are grumpy, temperamental artists, who can't be bothered with that kind of nonsense, because it messes with their creativity."

Ben walked away quickly, brushing his hand in the air, hoping she wouldn't see him laughing at her comment. He checked the hay feeder to insure there was extra hay for the cattle, since there was snow in the forecast, and the pasture most likely would be covered in the white stuff for a few days. To make sure they were sheltered for the inclement weather, he'd brought them to the lower pasture recently. After assessing the herd and the feeder, he swung himself back into the saddle. "Remind me to add some hay to the feeder."

"Okay. How many do you have?"

"Several, but I'll know which ones need it."

"Okay," she said, and smiled broadly.

He got comfortable in the saddle, adjusted the reins, then lifted his eyes to her, questioning. "What the hell are you so happy about?"

"That you let me come with you. I *love* horses. There is just something so amazing about them. I haven't gotten to ride in such a long time, and I swear it does something to my soul when I ride. Doesn't it you?"

He had to agree. "Yeah. It does, I guess." He wondered what she would think about seeing the wild horses on Poppi's land. "You ready to dig in? I want to show you something."

"Let's go."

He kicked his heels and chirped his lips and Dash took off. Dusty followed stride for stride. Ben glanced at Kaysi and was mesmerized by how her body moved so effortlessly in the saddle. She really did know how to ride. They stopped at the gate to Poppi's land just long enough for Ben to unlock it, and then rode along the ridge. Passing the dilapidated rock house covered in brush and trees, Ben glanced back to see Kaysi slowing to a stop.

"Wow! This place is awesome. Have you ever gone inside?"

Ben trotted Dash back to her. "No. It's too dangerous. The roof is about to cave in."

"Nah. It would be great to explore. You never know what you might find. You wouldn't believe some of the places I've explored, and the things I've found."

"Well, if you want me to ask Poppi if you can explore it, I can. But I don't think it's a good idea for you to go alone. You could get hurt."

"I would love to. Abandoned places, like this, hold some of the coolest treasures.

"And snakes, and rats, and spiders, and tetanus."

"Worth it for the rare finds."

He thought about what she said. "You should use that."

"Use what?"

"Rare finds. For your business. It's what you're after. Isn't it?"

There was that grin again, that absolutely mutilated any negative thought he harbored. It was like she was slowly chipping away at the darkness that had consumed him for the past few years and was replacing it with little shards of flickering light. They were tiny pin pricks. But her light was breaking through none the less. He knew he needed to keep his distance, but her infectious personality was too damn irresistible.

"That's it! Holy cow, Ben. It's perfect. Rare Finds Designs. It is exactly what I was searching for. And for April, she goes for different, cutting-edge designs. So, it fits what she is after, too." He couldn't keep the smile from spreading across his face. And damn if it didn't feel good.

A low rumble had Ben tugging on the reins as the ground began to quake. Scanning the land, he pointed to more than a dozen horses running across an open field and glanced at Kaysi. Her lips parted and tears shimmered in her eyes. Seeing her so awestruck had Ben fighting a lump growing in his throat. Her eyes darted to him, but she didn't say a word. She didn't have to. He knew. He felt it every time he saw them run. They were so powerful and so majestic. It took his breath away. Poppi had taken in countless horses over the years. Some were just being relocated. Some were rescues from bad situations. He would nurse them back to health, and release them, to run free on his land.

"Ben," she said, her voice trembling as tears streamed down her face. "They're amazing." They watched the horses run wild until they disappeared into the pine trees. Ben chirped his lips and tugged the reins, guiding Dash down into the valley from the ridge. When they reached the open land, he took off and Kaysi followed.

Within a short time, a modest two-story house, with a large wrap-around porch, came into view. Tightening the reins, Ben slowed Dash when he noticed a strange car outside the house and saw Poppi talking with Rick. The closer they got, the more obvious it was that it wasn't a friendly discussion. He tapped Dash, and they took off. Just as they approached the house, Rick grabbed Poppi's arm and spun him around causing him to spill the container of feed he had in his hand. Ben leaped from his horse before he was fully stopped. Rage pulsed through his body. Approaching the confrontation, his hands landed on Rick's shoulders, and he jerked him so hard that it yanked Poppi off balance, nearly sending him to the ground. "Lay another hand on him you son of a bitch. I dare you."

Rick let go of Poppi and wrenched away from Ben's grasp. "This doesn't concern you, Corbett. I told you to stay out of my family's business. Get the hell out of here."

"Like hell it doesn't. I'm not going to stand by and let you attack Poppi. You wanna beat on someone, come on. Give me your best shot. I've been wanting to put your ass on the ground for a long time anyway."

"Don't tempt me," Rick seethed.

"I thought you were here to help your grandpa, not rough him up."

"Shut up. Like I said, this doesn't concern you." His attention moved over Ben's shoulder. "It's obvious you have better things to do than to meddle in our lives, so get the hell out of here."

"Not on your life. I'm not leaving you alone with him. Poppi has made it clear that he wants to keep the land. That's where it ends. It's his land to do with what he wants."

"He can't maintain it anymore. He's losing horses and cows. He needs help."

"And I told you, that wasn't his fault, and that's not why you want the land. You want it, so you can rip it up for some crazy ass story about diamonds."

"Bullshit."

"Don't deny it, Rick. I can see it plain as day on your face. You want to get your hands on the ridge, so you can dig up the creek to find the diamonds that aren't even there. It's a stupid story someone made up, and I can't believe someone as smart as you," he said thick with sarcasm, "would ever fall for it."

"Ricky is that true?" Poppi interrupted.

Rick's eyes darted to Poppi. "I told you I wanted to help, Oren, that's all," then returned to Ben. "I said nothing about the damn diamonds. That was you. But you can't seem to stay out of my business. Doesn't matter anyway, because I've made up my mind. If he doesn't sign over the ridge to me, I will petition for guardianship, on the grounds of diminished mental capacity, and take the whole damn thing."

Ben's gut tightened. Rick wouldn't stop until he got his hands on the land. "You go ahead and try, and I will have the entire town lined up to back up Poppi. There is nothing wrong with his mental capacity. But there is something certainly wrong with yours. So, you go ahead and file all the paperwork you want, because I will fight for him with every dime I got. You can bet your life on that."

"And you will lose."

"I'll take my chances. Now, get out of here before I call the law on you for assault."

"I didn't assault anyone. If anybody assaulted anyone, it was you."

"You sure about that? I think I was defending a friend, and I got witnesses that will back me up." A cold wind whipped through the trees as Rick's narrowed eyes searched the faces around him.

"This isn't over," he growled, and gave Poppi one last glare before stomping away. They watched as he crawled into his car and backed out onto the road.

Ben's gaze returned to Poppi. "Geez, I'm glad we came to check on you. Are you okay? Where have you been? I've been by here a dozen times and called you even more."

"I'm fine. I've been busy taking care of some long overdue business."

"Would it kill you to pick up the phone once in a while, just so I know you aren't dead in a ditch somewhere?"

Poppi huffed. "You sound like my wife, Ben." His eyes lifted to meet Kaysi's. "Who's this pretty young lady?"

"This is Kaysi." Poppi walked over to her and lifted his hand. Dusty danced a bit then settled. She grasped his hand and smiled.

"It's a pleasure to meet you, Kaysi." He nodded his head to Ben. "Is he treatin you okay?"

"Yes." Her nose wrinkled. "He's a bit grouchy. But I think I'm wearing him down."

"You let me know if he steps out of line. I've known him since he was in diapers, I'll put him in his place."

Ben felt fingers of heat crawling up his neck. "Poppi, I—"

"And you." Poppi's eyes landed on him, and he could hear the irritation in his voice. "Don't be gettin into dustups with Ricky. I can handle him. I appreciate you standing up for me, but I need to take care of my family matters. I'll let you know if I need your help. It's best you keep your hands clean of this whole mess."

"I'm not going to stand back and let him assault you, Poppi. I was—"

"Trying to help. I know. And I appreciate the help, Ben. But you are getting yourself in too deep. I need to handle this myself."

Ben's eyes darted to Kaysi at Poppi's comment, then

focused back on Poppi, and he nodded. "Okay." He respected Poppi. And if Rick really was going to the courts to file a petition for mental competency, it might be better for him if he didn't hover.

Truth be told, he enjoyed helping Poppi. Enjoyed his company, and the conversations they had. Or didn't have. He appreciated Poppi's wisdom, especially when he and his dad weren't seeing eye to eye. But the last thing he wanted was for Poppi to be seen as incompetent or unable to handle his ranch.

He scratched at his beard and glanced at Kaysi. Her expression told him she knew how concerned he was. Then he remembered why they were there. "Kaysi here," he forced his eyes back to Poppi, "was wondering if she could snoop around the old rock house. She is opening a decorating business downtown. She buys and sells unique pieces, and she thought there might be something interesting left behind in there." A flash of uneasiness passed over Poppi's face, and he tried to cover it, but Ben caught it. "If you are concerned about it being dangerous—"

Poppi's eyes drifted to Kaysi. "Young lady. What you wanna go snooping around in that old nasty place for?"

"Oh, well, like Ben said, I am starting a new business, and I am always on the hunt for unique pieces, and rare finds." Ben smiled at her trying out the idea for the store name.

"Unique pieces? If you call a foot of dirt and spiders unique, I guess you might find something. Honestly, I don't know what you might find. A bunch of rotting wood, I suspect. I have no idea when the last time someone was in there. It could be dangerous. You really want to go crawl around in there?"

"Would you mind? I don't care if there is a little dirt. You should see some of the places I've been in."

Poppi shook his head. "Go ahead. I don't think you will find much. Just be careful." His eyes lifted to Ben, and he pointed at Kaysi. "Where'd you find this girl?"

Ben snickered. "She was kind of dropped in my lap."

"Well, you ought to thank whoever did it. She is a hell of a lot better than Valerie. Sounds like she don't mind getting dirty." Poppi side eyed Kaysi. "I get fifty percent of any treasures you find."

"Oh, okay," Kaysi said with a nod.

He chuckled, and returned his attention to Ben saying, "I really like her," then turned to walk away, calling over his shoulder, "little lady, you keep anything you find in there. It's all yours." Ben swung himself back up in the saddle. Poppi turned around and leveled his eyes at him. "Ben, if you're smart, you'd wrap her up and never let her go."

Chapter Twelve

Clouds were rolling in, and Kaysi could feel the temperature dropping. Her cheeks were starting to feel the prickles of being chapped from the brisk wind. But she didn't care. Today had been perfect, except for the little "dustup" as Poppi called it.

"So, I'm guessing Rick is Poppi's grandson?"

"Yeah. I never have liked the guy, and it turned to something much worse when my fiancée decided to run off with him. He doesn't have an honest bone in his body. Yet for some reason, people just fall at his feet."

Ben's confession stabbed at Kaysi's heart. She could hear the despair in his voice but couldn't tell if it was regarding what Rick was doing to Poppi, or the loss of his fiancée, or maybe a little of both.

"I thought what you did for Poppi was admirable."

"I just don't know how I'm going to protect him without making him seem like he needs help. And I know Rick isn't doing this to help him."

"Do you really think it has to do with the diamond story?"

"Honestly, I wouldn't doubt it. But I think there is more to it. I think this is just a ploy. I need to figure out what Rick is up to."

Heading back from Poppi's house, they spotted the wild horses again. "I would love to have a huge photo of them running, to hang in my loft," Kaysi said as she watched them. "How are you with a camera?"

Ben eyed her and smirked. "I'm great at taking blurry photos," he said sarcastically. Kaysi giggled at his attempt at making a joke. The smile he was trying so hard to hide, looked good on him. Much better than the scowl that seemed to be permanently imprinted. Kaysi wondered what happened to put him in, what seemed like, a perpetual state of anger. She knew his ex had something to do with it, but there had to have been more. The boy she remembered smiled easily.

"April has a good eye when it comes to photographs. I might get her out here to see if she can get some shots."

Ben snorted, and then broke into a deep laugh.

"What?"

"I was just picturing you trying to talk April into getting on a horse. She and Jenna have been friends for years, and she avoided this place like the plague. Too much dirt."

"I'll get her out here. Maybe not on the back of a horse. But where there's a will, there's a way."

"Yeah, I'm not holding my breath." He turned Dash. A glint sparked in his narrowed eyes, and she thought she could see a bit of a mischievous smile forming. He gave Dash a good kick and Dash took off. A challenge.

Dusty took off in a dead run like she knew exactly what was happening. Kaysi dug her knees in, and the chase was on. They headed through the gate barely a length apart, then past the bunkhouse, running full speed down into the valley by the creek. Kaysi's heart thrummed, feeling the icy mist against her face. Ben had gotten a good distance ahead as they approached the stables but slowed Dash some. She figured he was letting her catch up, so she gave Dusty a kick and ran past him, then stopped just short of the stables and hopped off. Throwing her arms in the air, she danced around and screamed, "And the crowd goes wild."

Ben slowly rode up with a goofy grin on his face, slow clapping. "I have to hand it to whoever taught you how to ride. They did a damn good job. I concede the win."

Kaysi tried desperately not to grin from ear to ear, possibly causing him to become suspicious. "I told you. I was taught by the best." She figured she would tell him at some point, but right now she was having too much fun dangling the carrot to see if he would catch on.

"I wouldn't think anything else. Probably one of those snooty places, like the one I worked at."

"You could say that."

"Did *you* enjoy it? I mean, it's obvious you at least learned how to ride."

"The first year had its highs and lows." She cut her eyes to him. "I met some very interesting people, to say the least."

"I did too. Most made me never want to go back."

"Most? So, I'm guessing there were a few with some redeeming qualities?"

"A very few."

"Like whom?" She doubted very seriously that he would ever make the connection. She had changed so much. Tamed her hair. Gotten rid of the glasses and braces. And developed…well, made it through puberty in a much better state. Not that she was bone thin by any stretch of the imagination, but even she was okay with how she developed.

"There was a girl with Down Syndrome. Riley…

Reagan..." he paused, clearly trying to remember the name. "Robin," he said triumphantly with a smile. "She would come to the stables every morning, all smiles. She never failed to say hi, and no matter how bad my day was, she made me smile. Did all her chores with a smile and never once complained. There was a young girl that always came with her. I don't know if I ever knew her name, but I called her Ray, because she was my ray of sunshine. Just like Robin, she never complained, always smiled no matter what. They'd come in early, and get my day started off right."

Kaysi's body filled with goosebumps. Desperately trying to hide the smile that was forcing its way to her mouth, she feigned a yawn. "Well, that doesn't sound so bad."

"No. They were fun. They made the two weeks almost bearable. Unfortunately, there were many others that were thorns in my side."

Kaysi turned away, dragging her saddle off Dusty. "Where do you want this?" Ben turned and gave her a glance.

"Oh, set it on the stand in the tack room."

She set the saddle down and grabbed a couple of brushes, handing one off to Ben, who stood with his mouth gaped open.

"You really surprise me, you know."

"How so?"

"You have never had horses of your own?"

"No. Why?"

"Just how well you rode today. And how comfortable you are in here. You know what you are doing."

"I went to camp every summer for five years and

worked there for two. By the time I stopped, I *was* fairly comfortable."

He studied her for a long minute, and she nearly gave in and confessed. The chime of her phone stopped her. She let out a groan when she saw who was calling. Malcolm. Squeezing her eyes shut, she seriously thought about not answering, except she hated being mean.

With one hand perched on her hip, she turned away from Ben. "Hello?"

"Kaysi, we need to talk. I'm in town. Can you meet me at the Arnie's Deli?"

"You're in Dalton? Right now?"

"Yeah."

"Malcolm, I'm busy."

"How about in thirty minutes? I really need to talk to you."

"I don't know what more there is to say."

"Just meet me, please?"

The pain in his voice pierced her resolve, and guilt reared its ugly head. "Fine. Give me half an hour. You said Arnie's?"

"Yes. I'll see you then."

Kaysi disconnected and tapped the phone against her forehead. "He knows," she said under her breath.

"Knows what?"

Kaysi jumped at the low rumble of Ben's voice. "Nothing." She let out a breath. "I just did something I shouldn't have."

"Lied to the ex about having a date to that charity thing?"

Stunned, she let out an audible gasp. "How'd...I didn't—"

"I was there when he called, remember?"

"Oh. Right." She leaned up against one of the stalls, closed her eyes, and crossed her arms. "It's a little more than that though."

"Meaning?"

Her eyes cut to his. "Remember me telling you he wasn't taking no for an answer when I tried to break it off with him?"

"Vaguely."

Her stomach flopped around like a fish out of water. "I might have implied that I was breaking up with him because of someone else."

"Implied?"

"Okay, fine. I told him I was seeing someone else." She let out a long breath. "I don't know what to do. He knows I'm lying. I know he wants to see me to call me out on it." Tipping her head against the stall post, she stared up at the ceiling. "He won't let go." Her eyes dropped to Ben, who was brushing Dash. "You wouldn't want to be my boyfriend for a few weeks, would you? No strings attached?"

"No," he said abruptly, then continued. "No offense. I am just not good at..." his eyes scanned her, "...women."

"No. Don't worry. I get it. I'm beginning to think I'm not so good at..." she raked him with her eyes, "...men." She let out another long breath, walked over to Dusty and started brushing her again. "I could use some of your mom's sage advice right now." She could remember Ben talking about his mom's advice when they were at camp.

Ben slowly turned. "What?"

Kaysi realized what she had said and panicked. "What?"

"What did you say about my mom?"

It was a good thing that Dusty had moved between her and Ben. Kaysi knew if he could see her face completely, he would know something was up. Keeping up this game was going to kill her, but she didn't want to share her secret just yet. "I just meant, I'm needing a mom's advice, and since we are at your house..." It felt like quicksand shifting beneath her feet as she continued to lie. She knew he was starting to get suspicious, and she was horrible with quick comebacks. She peeked around Dusty to see if she could get a glimpse of his expression and sure enough, his eyes were locked on her with one brow raised.

"Well, I know what my mom would say."

"And that would be?"

"Lying always comes back to bite you. Tell the truth. It may hurt at first, but in the end, you have a clear conscience."

"See. Sage advice. The only problem is, I did tell him the truth, and he didn't accept it. He said I was denying my feelings."

"Are you?"

"No. I'm more certain now than ever. Having to take these drastic measures to make him let go, and then he still doesn't? It's nerve wracking."

"I still say it's best to own up to him. Then you have a clear conscience. And if he still won't leave you alone...get a restraining order."

Her eyes darted to his, and she snickered. "I can't do that. He's a nice guy."

"Not if he won't leave you alone."

She finished brushing Dusty and set the brush down. "Which stall?

He cut his eyes to her, "Oh, two," and pointed.

"What are your plans?"

"Why? Do you need a bodyguard?"

"No. Like I said, he's nice, just persistent as hell."

"I might make a stop at the police station, then head over to work on the store."

"I'll probably see you over there later." She dropped off the brush in the tack room.

"Do you want me to take you back to the bunkhouse?"

"Would you mind?"

"No. Give me a minute." He put away the brush, removed Dash's bridal, and put him in his stall. After giving him and Dusty some food, he twitched his head at Kaysi as he yanked his keys from his pocket.

****

Kaysi parked at Arnie's and wondered if she should have taken Ben up on his offer to come. Not so much as a bodyguard, but moral support. The more time she spent away from Malcolm, the more she realized how much he had smothered her. And spending time with Ben today made her realize that the life Malcolm would provide was far from what she wanted. Although she dreaded what was ahead, she still couldn't keep the smile from her face, thinking about spending time with Ben. The only thing that could have been better, was if it didn't end.

She stared into the restaurant window to see if she could see Malcolm, but he was nowhere in sight. The sign on the sidewalk outside the shop, stopped her in her tracks. ''Sweet dreams are made of cheese. Who am I to dis a Brie?' Arnie's restaurant made a name for itself because of their unique menu offerings and their sidewalk signs. It was one of the hotspots in town. She laughed out loud as she opened the door and stepped inside. The delicious smells immediately enveloped her as she scanned the sea of people enjoying their meals.

Walking toward the back, she spotted Malcolm sitting in a booth tucked away. He evidently wanted privacy. His eyes lit up when he noticed her, but then tracked down her body, noticeably scrutinizing her outfit. "What are you wearing, my love?" It was already starting. Her stomach churned at the criticizing tone of his voice.

"I was out riding horses, helping get the feeders ready for the storm coming in, when you called. I didn't have time to change." *And I didn't want to.* The look on Ben's face when she stepped out the door left no question about what he thought. He approved.

"I thought you were only staying there for a couple of weeks. I didn't realize work was part of the living arrangements." he said, with a sarcastic laugh.

It wasn't. She practically forced Ben to take her.

A waitress walked up, thankfully putting the conversation to rest. She set a couple of glasses of water on the table, then turned to Kaysi. "Would you like a menu?"

"No thank you, just a glass of unsweetened tea, if you don't mind?"

"Go ahead and order something. I'm sure you're hungry."

"No, I won't have time."

"Come on, Kaysi, it will be my treat."

"I told you, I'm busy. I have a meeting with April in a little bit at the shop. I will grab something then." She was thankful she had an excuse.

"Oh," he said dejected. "All right then."

The waitress turned to Malcolm. "What would you like?"

"I guess I won't be eating either. I think I will have tea, hot, with a slice of lemon."

"Got it. My name is Liz." As she spoke, she wrote on a smaller version of the sidewalk sign. "If you need anything, put the sign out, and I will be right over."

Kaysi smiled and nodded, and when the waitress walked away, she turned to find Malcolm's gaze squarely on her. She knew he was about to unload, and figured might as well get it over with. "Malcolm, I—"

"Let me start, Love. I drove to Dalton today, just to see how far the distance is from Fayetteville. I've never been here. It's not that far. Quite a nice drive honestly, and the town is very quaint. I even thought about finding a place here." He took a sip of water and continued. "I thought maybe you were worried it would be too much of a hassle to drive back and forth, but it's not bad at all."

"That's not it, though."

"Then what is it, Sweetheart? I just don't understand. What we have is good."

"But it's not great, Malcolm. All we are, are friends with benefits. Admit it. You don't love me. I embarrass you. I see it in your eyes. I saw it when I arrived today. I don't fit your criteria. You want someone to go with to the dinners and benefits. I'm a convenience relationship, not love."

The waitress returned with their teas, and they both glanced up as she placed them on the table and left without saying a word.

Malcolm returned his attention to Kaysi. "You are crazy, Kaysi. This is not just a convenience for me. Yes,

I love having you there with me for dinners and gatherings, but it's because I am proud of you. I'm not embarrassed of you."

"Yes, you are. You need to find someone that measures up to your standards. I don't."

"Where is this coming from?" He reached across the table and grabbed her hand. She tried to wrench it away, but he gripped it harder. "I've never said I was embarrassed of you."

"No. You have never said a cross word to me. But you don't have to. I can see it on your face, and it drives me nuts. Even when you are mad at me, you never say anything. Instead, you just shut me out. Half the time I have no idea what I've done, because you just tell me "no worries." I can't live like that. It kills me when I know I've upset you. And I can't correct what I've done if I don't know what it is."

"I can't believe you haven't told me this before."

"That's just it. I have. I've told you that I wanted you to be honest with me, to open up, but you continue to shut down when we disagree."

"Then let's start over. Wipe the slate clean. I will be better. I promise. We can have a nice night out at the charity dinner to celebrate a fresh start."

"No."

"No? But why?"

"I told you. What we had is not what I want. It was a relationship of convenience. It was comfortable. It wasn't love. I don't love you and I-I—"

"Please don't give me that preposterous story that you have found someone else, because I am not buying it."

"Well, maybe you should." The deep, booming,

velvety voice behind her made her heart skip. She turned to see Ben standing at the corner of the booth. He had removed his cowboy hat, and it looked like he had tried to tame his unruly hair a bit. "Hey, baby." He smiled and winked. "Did you need me to give you a few more minutes? I know I said I would leave you alone to handle it, but it sounds to me like he isn't respecting your wishes." He nodded at Malcolm. "Ben Corbett, by the way." He held his hand out across the table, offering a handshake. Malcolm hesitantly let go of Kaysi's hand and complied; his eyes filled with confusion, darting from Ben to Kaysi.

"No, that's okay," Kaysi said softly, wondering what made him change his mind. She knew, by his response to her earlier, that he had no desire to be dragged into her lie, yet here he was, offering her an out. One which she would gladly take, if it meant putting the relationship between her and Malcolm to rest.

He dropped into the booth with her, and immediately put his arm around her, sliding her close to him, and brushing a soft kiss to her temple. She wasn't sure if her heart would ever start back up on its own. Her hand found his thigh, and she waited to see if he would shy away, but instead, he scooted even closer.

The waitress stopped by and smiled at Kaysi, then winked at Ben, obviously approving of the two of them together. "Can I get you something to drink?"

"I'll take a sweet tea, if you don't mind?"

"Not a bit. I'll have it right out for you." She turned and walked away, and Kaysi felt her whole body tighten when Ben moved his arm, dropped his hand to her leg, and let his fingers play with the inner seam of her jeans. She rubbed her lips together trying to stay focused, but he was making it extremely hard.

Malcolm's face had gone noticeably pale when Kaysi's attention finally returned to him. "Malcolm, I'm sorry. I know you thought—"

"No, no. It's quite all right," he said, clearing his throat, "I'm the one who's sorry, Kaysi. I should have believed you. You have always been honest with me. I meant no disrespect. I just thought…maybe…you were stressed over the business deal." His confident tone was gone and replaced with a tinge of humiliation. "I guess I will need to find another date for the charity dinner," he said with a weak chuckle. He scooted out of the booth, grabbed his overcoat, and slipped it on. "It was a pleasure to meet you, Ben. And again, I hope you accept my apology." He held his hand out, and Ben grasped it.

"It's all good."

Malcolm disappeared, and Kaysi let out an audible sigh. "I'm so sorry. I didn't mean to drag you into this."

"You didn't do anything. After you left, I really started wondering what he was up to, so I came by to check on you and heard a bit of the conversation. The guy wasn't going to take no for an answer. You were clear with your intentions. He just wasn't listening. Poor fella had it bad for you."

"I wasn't good enough for him, and he's probably already realizing that as we speak."

"I don't see how you can say that. Any guy would be lucky to have you. I think he knows what he is going to be missing."

"Aw. That's sweet of you to say." Her mind went back to what he had said before. "So, you came in here to protect me?"

He picked up his tea, that the waitress had dropped

off, and took a drink. "Maybe." Setting it down, he spun the glass with his fingers, wiping away the condensation. "Guys can be irrational when it comes to women. I just wanted to make sure you weren't misreading him and his intentions."

Even though Malcolm had left several minutes before, Kaysi was highly aware that Ben hadn't moved. He hadn't taken his hand from her leg either. Just the warmth his hand was putting off made her body erupt in goosebumps. Ben's brows knitted together. He stared across the nearly full restaurant, and Kaysi tried to figure out what he was looking at.

"Didn't you say you had to meet with April at the store?" he said, bringing his attention back to her.

Excitement filled her thinking about their meeting. "Yeah. I do. I have to share your idea about the name."

Ben glanced away again, and then quickly returned his attention back to her, still with a bit of a scowl. "Why don't we head over there. I've gotta help Joe with some stuff anyway."

"Sure." Noticing his tea was almost full, she questioned, "Do you want to get a to-go cup for your tea?"

"No, that's okay." His hand squeezed her thigh, then patted it as he slid out, allowing her to do the same. She turned to grab her coat, when his sudden jerk had her eyes darting up to see why. A tall, thin, blonde woman had her hand on Ben's shoulder, and the mere sight caused a stabbing pang of jealousy in her chest. She could feel the heat instantaneously fill her face. *What the hell? He's a fake boyfriend for heaven's sake. I can't be doing this for something that's fake. He didn't even come out and say it exactly, just implied it.*

"Hey, Ben," the woman said, with an unmistakable sultry tone.

Kaysi didn't know if she should stay, or head for the door. Her eyes were beginning to burn with the thought that Ben might have another woman in his life. But then why did he tell her he swore off women.

"Valerie."

Valerie. That name sounded familiar, and the expression on his face left no question that he wasn't as happy to see her, as she was him. Kaysi took a chance and stepped closer, touching the back of his hand with hers. He immediately laced his fingers within hers.

"I didn't expect to see you in here. I thought you didn't like this place."

Ben glanced at Kaysi. "We just stopped in for a glass of tea. The place has stepped up its game in the past couple of years."

Kaysi felt Valerie's eyes on her, so she decided to put the question to bed. "I'm Kaysi Grayeagle." She held out her free hand, and Valerie hesitantly took it.

"Valerie McIntyre. Me and Ben go way back."

"She's my ex," Ben filled in, with a bit of a bite in his tone. "I thought you and Rick would have headed back to Missouri by now."

"I told you. We're separated," she responded coldly.

"Seems to me he was still laying claim on you the other day when I saw you."

"That's his problem. I told him I'm done." Her eyes glanced up and down at Ben, and another sultry smile crossed her face. *Does the woman have no shame?*

Without saying a word, Ben released his hand and wrapped his arm around Kaysi, squeezing her into him. She played into his game, dipping her hand under his jacket, and snaking her arm around him.

"Well, when you see him again, tell him to give up on whatever game he's playing, trying to steal Poppi's land. It's not going to work."

Valerie's eyes widened, and Kaysi could tell she knew exactly what Ben was talking about.

"What did he tell you?"

"He said he's just trying to help. You and I both know that is complete bullshit. So, tell me what he's planning."

"Ben, don't get involved. Rick's—"

"I'm not going to let Rick strongarm Poppi, Valerie. If Poppi doesn't want to release part of his land, he shouldn't have to. I know Rick is up to something, and I will figure it out whether you tell me or not."

"I don't want you getting hurt." Kaysi looked at Valerie and saw something flash in her eyes. Something wasn't adding up.

"Hurt? You said Rick hasn't laid a hand on you. Were you lying to me?" Ben's voice had dropped to a growl.

"No, I didn't lie. He hasn't hurt me, but…" Her voice trailed off, and again Kaysi got the feeling Valerie was hiding something. Rick wasn't the only one playing games.

After a long silence, it was obvious she had shut down, and Ben had had enough of her evasive tactics when he said, "We need to get going. We have places we need to be." His eyes landed on Kaysi. "Don't we, babe?" Another sexy wink, and a smile bloomed on her face.

"I think they are waiting for us, actually." She knew good and well he was just playing a part, but a small part of her had waited for this moment for a long time.

"Ben…"

The wrinkle between his brows deepened as he glared back at his ex. Kaysi knew the woman was harboring some old feelings, but she had a hard time mustering up sympathy after what Ben told her.

"I hope everything works out for you, Valerie."

Chapter Thirteen

Ben was, again, feeling like his emotions were being jerked in a thousand different directions. He hadn't planned on interrupting Kaysi's meeting with Malcolm, but after eavesdropping on their conversation, it was obvious Malcolm was going to force her into something she didn't want, and he didn't want to see Kaysi giving into his manipulative tactics. He figured, if he played along with the scheme just this once, Malcolm would leave her alone.

It bothered him though, that Kaysi felt like she wasn't good enough for him. There was something so delicate about her that made him want to wrap her up and protect her from the world. But he couldn't. He'd play the boyfriend just to get the exes to leave them alone, but there was no way anything could happen. She was Joe's sister. The big no no. He knew Joe wouldn't approve. And if he kept telling himself that, maybe, just maybe, his body would take notice.

Valerie had made it clear, by the way she touched him, and the fire in her eyes, she wanted him. He knew, all too well, what that look meant. But the more he was around Kaysi, the more he realized the relationship he had with Valerie was probably similar to the one Kaysi had with Malcolm. It was one of convenience. He liked being in a relationship and having someone there to talk to and hang out with. But was it love? Was he really heartbroken that she left him? Or was he just humiliated that she picked his mortal enemy over him?

He liked having Kaysi there to show Valerie that he'd moved on. Even if it was a fake relationship, Kaysi helped him see that he really was over Valerie. The only problem was, he couldn't keep the heat from coursing through his body, just thinking of how Kaysi felt in his arms. All he wanted to do when they left, was take her back home with him.

It was a good thing they both needed to be somewhere, but unfortunate that it was the same place, where he was going to be forced to be around her. The way she smelled, when he pulled her close for the first time, had his body humming. A little bit of leather with a hint of honeysuckle and lemon. It was bottled sunshine. Perfect for her. There was so much about her that drew him in.

He parked in front of the store, and Kaysi eased her SUV in next to him. His eyes went straight to her when she got out. She was gorgeous, dressed in her leather jacket with her hair in a ponytail. Then the familiarity struck him again.

"What are you staring at?" she asked, as he stepped up next to her.

"You. There is something about you that reminds me of someone, but I can't figure out who."

She pursed her mouth mischievously. "Oh really?"

"It really hit me last night when you were wearing your glasses. But for the life of me, I can't figure out who you look like."

"I'm sure it's some beautiful actress."

"Probably not."

Kaysi feigned offense and swatted him.

"I didn't mean you aren't pretty enough to be an actress. I don't watch a lot of TV or movies. It's boring when you have no one to discuss them with."

She tipped her head back and forth, then finally said, "Okay. I guess I'll let you slide, since you said I was pretty."

Ben shook his head and chuckled as they walked in the back door to the shop. Joe, April, Cody, Jenna, and Kaleb, Kaysi's other brother, were standing around the counter with three large pizza boxes in front of them. They each had a slice, in various stages of being eaten, in their hands. Cody grunted with a mouth full of pizza and pointed to the boxes. Kaysi's brows raised in confusion.

Jenna piped up, "He is wanting you to join us in our fancy dinner."

"I'm glad you were here to interpret, because I wasn't sure."

"Been with him more than a year."

"She's fluent in baby grunts too," Cody added after swallowing his mouthful. The room echoed with the sound of laughter at the comment. Ben reached around Kaleb to see what each box held, and he settled on a supreme.

"Ewww. You like pizza with olives?" Kaleb whined.

"Don't listen to him," Kaysi huffed, "he likes pineapple on his pizza."

Kaysi eyed Kaleb and curled her lip in a playful snarl, then reached for a slice, too.

"Oh good. I thought I remembered you liking supreme," Jenna said, and Ben nodded.

"I do too. It's my favorite," Kaysi said around a bite. "This is either really delicious or I was hungrier than I thought."

April moved beside Kaysi. "You look so cute. I think the ranch is rubbing off on you."

"Thanks."

"So, how did it go with Malcolm?" Kaysi's eyes shot to Ben, and she clamped her lips together trying not to smile. Ben turned away wiping his smile from his mouth.

"Umm…I think okay. I think he finally got the message."

"Finally. Maybe he'll leave you alone now."

"What's this with Malcolm?" Kaleb questioned.

"He's having a bit of trouble with me breaking up with him."

"You broke up with him? When did this happen?"

"Right before I moved to Dalton."

"And he's giving you trouble? Do you need me to talk to him? We're working together now."

"No. I think he finally realized I was being serious."

"Good. I wasn't too excited that you two were dating anyway. It was awkward having to listen to him talk about his love life, knowing he was talking about my sister."

"Aw, you were jealous that he wasn't talking about your bromance," Kaysi teased and put her arm around Kaleb.

"Shut up. That's not it at all."

"Ya sure?"

Ben loved the fact that Kaysi could go toe to toe with Kaleb. He was the comedian of the group and purposely annoyed the hell out of everyone most of the time.

"You do realize you were the one trying to get us together. Right?" Kaysi continued to tease. Kaleb shrugged. "Aw. Are you upset because you failed at something?"

"Kaysi, geez."

Kaysi widened her eyes and smirked.

"Listen, Malcolm is a great guy, and you…"

His words dropped and Kaysi patted Kaleb's pink tinged cheeks. "Were you going to say I needed a good guy because I am so sweet and pretty?" She wrapped her arms around his neck. "And the best sister in the world."

"No. And get off me." He pushed away from her trying to extricate himself. "That was the furthest thing from my mind." Kaleb shoved his pineapple pizza in his mouth and strolled away.

"Fine. Geez, what crawled up your shorts and died?"

"Nothing." Kaleb plopped down on a stack of lumber and finished his slice of pizza.

The room quieted, and Joe finally spoke. "You okay?"

Kaleb brushed his hand through the air. "Yeah, fine," he said around the mouthful of pizza. "Sorry, Kaysi. I didn't mean to bite your head off. I just have a lot on my plate right now."

"If you don't have time to do this, it's not a big deal. I know you have classes and—"

"No. it's fine."

"Okay. Suit yourself."

April turned to Kaysi and smiled. "So, are you going to just stand there, or are you going to tell me this magnificent name you came up with."

"First, I didn't come up with it, Ben did. I was following him around today while he did his chores, and we were discussing the issue. We passed by this abandoned house, and I told him I wanted to snoop around in it to see what rare things I could find. And he came up with the name from that. He gets all the credit, and I want him to make the sign for us."

April's and Jenna's faces lit up. "That's a fantastic idea." April paused. "It would be so cool to have a double-sided sign hanging on the corner under the turret. Don't you think? Then everyone on either street could see it."

Kaysi peered up at Ben. "You tell them. It's your idea." Fingers of heat crawled up his neck to his cheeks. He eyed Kaysi and shook his head adamantly, but the plea in her eyes wreaked havoc on his defenses. *How the hell does she keep doing that?*

He rolled his eyes and let out a breath. "I suggested Rare Finds Designs because Kaysi said—"

"Oh my gosh!" April's eyes darted between Ben and Kaysi. She grabbed Kaysi by the arms and a grin spread across her face. "That's perfect."

The way Kaysi grinned and danced in April's grasp completely obliterated any chance of Ben being able to concentrate on anything other than her while they were together. "I know. That's exactly what I thought when he said it."

Kaysi grinned back at Ben, and he couldn't keep the smile from playing on his lips. "You said it, I just suggested you use it for your business."

"Whatever." Kaysi swatted him on the arm, and April raised a brow in a questioning expression, again darting her eyes back and forth for a different reason. Ben knew what she was thinking, and if she said something to Joe, he would be toast.

Joe was a beast. He stood at least five inches above him, and every inch of him was lean muscle. Ben had been working out at the gym since Cody joined the family, and was happy with the results, but he was no match for Joe, and never would be. Not that he had ever seen Joe in a fight with anyone, other than a sparring partner in his martial arts classes. Even there, his moves were impressive.

"Have you talked him into displaying any of his work?" April asked. Kaysi's face transformed from happy to scared, and she quickly pinched her thumb and forefinger together across her lips motioning April to zip her mouth, then shook her head. Ben turned away, so she wouldn't see another smile that surprised him.

"So, are you guys getting along now?" came a voice over his shoulder. He turned to see Jenna with a half-eaten slice of pizza in her hand.

"We are tolerating each other."

"Ben Corbett, don't you dare make her cry, or you will rue the day I was born."

"I already do," Ben huffed.

Jenna swatted him on the arm. "She is the sweetest person I've ever met."

"Hey, what about me," April chimed in, joining the conversation. Jenna snickered then let out a bark of laughter. April stuck her lip out pretending to pout, and Jenna wrapped her arms around her.

"Sweet is not a word I would use to describe you, and you know you wouldn't either, but you are the funniest person I've ever met, and I wouldn't trade you for the world. You fill my life with excitement and laughter every single day, because I never know what is going to come out of your mouth."

"Okay. I guess I will take that as a compliment."

"But I'm serious, Ben. Don't you dare be mean to Kaysi."

"Geez, you make me out to be a monster, biting the heads off the people I meet."

"Well, you gotta admit, you can be a bit harsh sometimes."

"I wouldn't worry about that. I think Kaysi's got him right where she wants him," April said, butting into the conversation again.

"What's that supposed to mean." Ben shot back and glanced over his shoulder wondering where Kaysi had run off to, and if she was in earshot of the conversation. Joe had her cornered, discussing something in the blueprints.

"Oh nothing." The curl of April's lips, transforming into a playful smile as she strolled off, told Ben it was a whole lot more than nothing.

Ben turned back to Jenna, who was now studying his face. "Is there something going on between you and Kaysi?" Her voice was barely above a whisper. "What is April talking about?"

"I have no idea. And no. There is absolutely nothing going on between me and Kaysi." Jenna leveled her eyes with him, and his chest tightened with the thought of what she could see. He darted his eyes away, but they landed on Kaysi, so he quickly changed course and brought his focus back to Jenna who was now smiling.

"Oh my gosh, Ben. You like her. What happened?"

"No, I don't." His eyes slammed shut, then he started again. "I mean. She's fine. But nothing happened between us." He fought like hell trying to keep a smile at bay and managed to pull off a somewhat neutral expression. He thought.

"Yes, it did," Jenna accused. "Tell me. Ben, she is super sweet, and I think you guys would be awesome together. If anyone could get you to smile, she could."

And she had. He had to admit. Riding with her earlier in the day had been fun. Most of the time he was alone doing his morning chores, and although he enjoyed the peacefulness, having her there was a nice change of pace. She was easy to talk to and didn't try to make conversation just for the hell of it. They had ridden in silence for long periods, and when he would glance at her, she always had a smile on her face as she stared out at the land. And watching her face light up when she saw the wild horses would be something he would never forget. Complete and utter elation.

But he couldn't like her. She was Joe's sister, and he had to keep telling himself that. "Trust me Jenna, there is nothing going on between us. We've barely seen each other since she moved in," he lied. His mind flipped through the moments they spent with each other, and he stopped as he pictured her with her sweatshirt, and glasses, and messy hair. "But I do have a question."

"What's that?"

"Have we met their family before?"

"Well yeah, at TopHops, remem—"

"No. I mean like before that, maybe even years ago. Can you think of anywhere that I may have met Kaysi? An auction or something?"

"No, not that I can think of. I mean, April and Kaysi have been friends for several years, so it's possible, but they hung out in Fayetteville mostly, so I doubt it. Why?"

"I don't know. There is something about her that seems familiar, and she keeps making comments that make me wonder if we have met."

"Like what?"

He peeked over his shoulder again, and didn't see Kaysi anywhere, so he turned his attention back to Jenna. "When I went to my studio the other day, she was there. She spotted the picture of Bandit, and she said he was so sweet, like she had met him before."

"She probably just meant he looked sweet."

"No. I'm telling you; it was like she knew him. And then right after that, she made a comment that I had changed, like she had met me before."

"I don't know, Ben. It's possible I guess, but I don't remember meeting her. And if she met you when you still had Bandit, then that would have been at least, what, six or seven years ago." She paused for a beat. "If it's bothering you, why don't you ask her?"

"Yeah."

"But you're serious? There is nothing going on between you two?"

"No. I mean, we don't hate each other. She asked if she could ride with me while I finished the chores, so I let her ride Dusty. Oh, and that reminds me. Did you know Rick and Valerie are back in town?"

"I thought I saw Valerie the other day."

"Yeah. Rick is trying to take Poppi's land away from him. Says he is too old to take care of it, and he wants to help. But I think he's trying to get his hands on it, because he thinks there is an old diamond mine on it, or something."

"A diamond mine? Where did he get that idea?"

"Poppi said the story has been around since he could remember. But it was probably something someone made up to sell the land."

"Oh my gosh. And he believes it?"

"I think he does. I sure as hell know he isn't trying to get the land just because he wants to help Poppi, like he says he is."

"He can't just take the land from him. Can he?"

"He's trying. He said he is going to petition the courts for guardianship due to diminished mental capacity."

"You gotta be kidding me."

"No. I went over to Poppi's today, and he was there. He had Poppi by the arm. I stopped whatever it was he was about to do, and he said he was going to file the petition." His fingers threaded through his beard. "I don't know. He's got me worried."

"That he might be right about Poppi?"

"Hell no. There's nothing wrong with Poppi."

"But then why did you start helping him?"

"I've been helping out for years, because I love taking care of the horses. I mean, yeah, maybe a small part of me is helping him out just because he is getting up there in years, but trust me, Poppi is as strong as an ox, and there is nothing wrong with him mentally."

"And Valerie?"

"Um." Immediately, his entire body recalled the feeling of having Kaysi pressed up against him.

"What's that look for? Please tell me you aren't still fawning over her."

Her voice jerked him back from the thought. "What? No. Maybe on her part, but I'm not interested. Not anymore."

"What happened?"

"I ran into her, and she said she and Rick were separated."

"Already?"

"She asked me to forgive her. Said Rick is very controlling, and she made a mistake leaving me." He flashed on the way it felt when Valerie put her hand on him, and the desire in her eyes. "But I'm realizing it wasn't a mistake at all. She did me a favor. Marrying her would have been the mistake."

"Finally. I was wondering when you would come to your senses." She grinned. "Say it."

"Say what?" he questioned with a growl.

"That your baby sister was right."

"No."

"But I was. I told you from the get-go she wasn't right for you. She wanted a much different life than you did as evidenced by what she did to you. I always thought she was using you." Jenna's eyes drifted. "Kaysi, on the other hand…"

Kaysi appeared at his side, and he flinched as a bolt of electricity shot through him. "I'm heading out," she said to the two of them. "I've got some work to do at the house." Ben detected a bit of sadness in her voice and wondered why. She had been so excited about talking to April.

"Everything okay?" he asked before he could stop himself.

"Yeah, it's just been a busy day." He didn't buy it. Something had her upset. It was so easy to tell. That sparkle in her eyes disappeared.

Ben noticed Jenna stifling a smirk as she turned to Kaysi. "Have you gotten all unpacked?"

"As much as I'm going to. I don't want to have to repack in a week. I've pushed everything off in the corners though, so it's at least somewhat out of the way."

He finally caught her attention, but she quickly darted her eyes away, which bothered him even more. "Anyway, I just wanted to tell you bye." She reached out and hugged Jenna and gave him a quick glance, before turning and walking out the door. His eyes remained on the door after she left.

"You like her," Jenna said, recapturing his attention.

"I've sworn off women. Remember? They're trouble. She's already proven that."

"How so?"

"She posted my flag I had hanging at Flame Masters, and now I have fifty some odd orders that I don't know how I'm going to fill." Which was true to an extent, but he had come up with a plan he hoped would work, giving him the help he needed without losing the creative aspect.

"If you didn't want people ordering, why did you hang the flag up there with your e-mail on it?"

"It's not that I didn't want orders, it's just the amount that her post generated."

"She had no control over how others were going to react. For all she knew, no one would respond."

As much as he hated to admit it, she had a point. "I just wish she would have asked me, before she posted it on her blog."

"If you have your art hanging in a public place, with a way to get in contact with you, it means you are good with your art being publicly displayed."

And another good point. Kaysi hadn't done anything wrong. He had just panicked from the enormous order. And ultimately, it would bring in money that he could use to help Poppi feed the horses. He needed to apologize. Jenna was right.

"Hey, Ben?" *That might have been why she was upset since April brought it up. Shit. She thought I was going to get mad.* "Ben?" He jerked when a hand landed on his shoulder. *Dammit I wish people would stop doing that.*

"Yeah?" He turned to see Joe.

"Sorry didn't mean to startle you. I was just going to see if you, would help me for a minute to get the support beam in place. I need you and Kaleb on one end, and Cody and I will be on the other, while we lift it."

Jenna was right. She was sweet, and he wasn't. He needed to apologize and then stay far far away from her.

Chapter Fourteen

Darkness had taken over the sky by the time he was headed home. He was cold and tired, and his head was swimming. He could barely focus on the road as he turned down the gravel trail headed to his house. Passing the bunkhouse, Ben noticed the light on, and he thought about stopping, but he was grimy and needed a bath, and he figured it might help him gather his thoughts.

His place was dark and quiet, and for the first time in a long time, he felt lonely. The day's events bombarded him. Riding with Kaysi made the day so much more exciting. Experiencing everything with her made him love the ranch even more.

Tossing his keys and phone on the nightstand, he shucked his clothes and stepped into the shower. His body ached, and the hot beads of water prickled his skin. Closing his eyes, he let the steaming suds drizzle over his torso. The jets of water pulsated against his back, and he hoped it would relieve some of the ache.

A thumping noise outside the door, had him quickly turning the water off and grabbing a towel. Who was knocking? It was already past eight. Maybe something happened at Poppi's, or his dad needed something. He stepped out of the shower and wrapped the towel around his waist. No calls or texts on his phone when he checked, so he wandered out to the living room tucking his towel to secure it. Through the window, he found the culprit. Kaysi stood on his porch in a long, thick, white robe, with her hair wadded on top of her head, resembling a cute little snowman.

"Can I help you?" he said jerking open the door. The frosty air sent chill bumps over his wet skin, and he shivered. Her eyes immediately went to the towel around his waist, and pink filled her cheeks.

"Oh God." Her hand flew to her face covering her eyes. "I-I'm so sorry. Never mind. I'll talk to you later." She turned to walk away. He shook his head, trying to fight a smile, because she was just that cute, and grabbed her arm.

"Get in here." Dragging her inside with her hand still covering her eyes, he chuckled. "You know, I can see you peeking through your fingers."

"No, I'm not." She lowered her hand and Ben noticed her cheeks were now the color of ripe cherries. "I'm sorry. I saw the lights from your truck when you came by, and I-I-I don't know. I know it's late, and I'm sure you were wanting to relax, but I needed to talk to you. But it can wait." She was talking so fast Ben barely caught a word she was saying. He was too mesmerized by her eyes and the movement of her lips. She broke the connection when she turned away to leave. He grabbed her again.

"It's okay. I need to talk to you too. Let me throw some clothes on." He pinched his lips together when he noticed her eyes tracking down his body, and she let out a sigh. He wondered if he should rethink getting dressed. She nodded, and he glanced to the kitchen. "There's some tea in the fridge." She nodded again.

Her rapid-fire word dump came to an abrupt halt,

and she was now just giving him head gestures. She moved toward the kitchen and opened the fridge. He hurried to his bedroom and threw on a T-shirt and a pair of fuzzy pajama bottoms.

When he returned to the living room, he found Kaysi sitting on his sofa with a pair of snow boots sitting on the floor next to her. Her feet were tucked up under her, and he had to fight back a smile again when he realized she still seemed a bit flustered.

A glass of tea sat on the counter, so he grabbed it and sat on the opposite end of the sofa, propping a pillow behind him, and extending his legs. Bringing his glass of tea to his lips, he took a sip, then set it on the beat-up coffee table in front of him.

Most of his furniture, as well as the furniture in the bunkhouse, was hand me downs, or stuff friends had given him. He even had some stuff Poppi had given him after his wife passed away. He had planned to slowly replace some of the worn-out items once he got moved into the bunkhouse.

His eyes lifted to find panic taking over Kaysi's beautiful features. "So, what's got you so stirred up?"

She let out a long breath and the panic suddenly turned to sadness. His heart squeezed cutting off his breath. "Ben, I am so sorry." Guilt flooded him thinking she was apologizing about posting his work. "I should have never—"

"No. I'm the one who should be apologizing. I had a talk with Jenna when you left, and I shouldn't have blamed you for all the orders. You had no way of knowing what would happen. The same thing could have happened on my webpage. You just have a lot more friends on your blog. So, I'm sorry for getting mad at you."

"Oh. Okay. I appreciate that—"

"I noticed you had gotten quiet at the store, and Jenna kind of griped me out for the way I reacted when I told her what happened. I panicked from the flood of orders, but I think I've come up with a way to get them out faster."

"That's great. And if I can help in any way, just tell me what I need to do." A brief smile passed over her face, then the sadness returned, and he wondered if that's what was bothering her after all.

"That's not what's got you bugged. Is it?"

Her teeth skimmed her bottom lip causing a shudder to shoot through his body.

"I just wanted to apologize for dragging you into my problems. I should have never asked you to lie to Malcolm and pretend to be my boyfriend. I am so sorry you got roped into this."

"Actually, I'm kind glad you did." Her eyebrows shot up in surprise.

"You are?" Her feet uncurled from under her and inched closer to his legs, and suddenly, he became hyper aware of her every movement.

"You helped me out when Valerie damn near accosted me. Having you there kept me from going off on her."

"I don't think she's completely gotten over you."

"She doesn't want me. She might think she does right now, maybe because she's having issues with Rick, but it was clear when she dumped me what she wanted, and I didn't have it. She wanted someone with an unlimited credit card.

"But now that she's separated, and she's back in her

old stomping grounds, she's searching for something familiar, and who could be more familiar than an ex that you jilted. I'm thinking, since I didn't quite respond the way she had hoped when she saw me the first time, she decided to step up her game, but you kind of put a stop to that."

"Well, I'm glad you aren't mad at me." Her foot tapped his calf, then rubbed up against it. She slowly leaned forward and lightly brushed her fingers against the material. "Oh my gosh, your pants are so soft. Where did you get them?"

"Jenna gives me a pair every Christmas. You would have to ask her."

She continued to rub the material, completely oblivious of what she was doing to him. Before it became obvious how his body was responding, he slid his leg away from her hand.

She sat back, color filling her cheeks. "Sorry."

He let out a breath, trying to steady his pulse that she had caused to ramp up. "Was that all you wanted to talk about?"

"Well, no. I mean, now that you have been kind of shoved into my lie, I need to know how you want to play this."

"What do you mean?"

"At the charity dinner."

Shit. I completely forgot about that. "Look. I was fine with helping you get your ex off your back, but I'm not going to the dinner. I'm not cut out for that kind of stuff."

Disappointment spread across her face. "He's going to be there, though."

"Tell him I'm busy, or I'm sick."

"I'm scared he'll start hitting on me. You saw him today. He told me, when I first said I found someone else, that he would fight for me."

Just the thought of him having his hands on her had Ben's blood boiling. But the whole idea of him going to the dinner was nonsense. Leaning his head against the sofa, he pinched the bridge of his nose, annoyed with the fact that his seemingly simple gesture to help her had exploded into something much larger. He was surprised her ex even believed him since he and Kaysi were such an odd pair. "Kaysi, I'm not the type of person that goes to those kinds of things. I mean, look at me." He ran his hand through his long damp hair. "I'm not your typical suit and tie kind of guy."

"Joe's not either. Plus, a bunch of people from the gym are going, so there will be a bunch of familiar faces."

"And there's the other elephant in the room."

"What?"

"Don't you think it would be a problem for me to have my hands on you, with your brothers there?"

"Well, I wasn't expecting you to grope me...again...but I don't really think they would have a problem with it. They like you. If you are worried, we could tell them it's just for show."

She was giving him no out. Every time he brought up a possible problem, she had an answer. And did she really think her brothers would be okay with having him dating their sister?

"I don't know that they would be okay with it. Joe told me to keep my hands to myself when you moved in."

She tilted her head. "He did? Was he serious?"

174

"Well, no, not exactly. But I'm sure there was an inkling of truth to it."

"He was just picking on you because of the incident at TopHops. He knows you were just trying to help me after he spilled water all over me."

And…he was done. He had no other excuse he could come up with. "Do I have to wear a tux?"

"No. Do you have suit?"

Hope bloomed on her face, and he hated to admit that he did have a suit.

He had bought a nice one for Jenna's wedding. "Yes. I have a suit," he said on a heavy sigh of defeat.

"So, you're set."

"You wouldn't be embarrassed to be seen with me?"

Her brows furrowed. "Why in the world would you ask that?"

"Look at me, Kaysi. I'm one step shy of modeling as a homeless dude, and you're…you."

"You can't be serious. Ben, you're handsome. I love your smile, when it shows up. And I kind of like your scruffy style. You're genuine. You don't put on airs."

His disheveled appearance kept most people away. Except, obviously, her. He hadn't had a haircut since Jenna and Cody's wedding, which was just a trim, and with his beard, he resembled a mountain man who hadn't come out of his hideout in years. And that was how he liked it.

"Maybe I can go get a haircut before then. When is it?"

Kaysi grimaced. "Saturday."

He huffed a breath at the thought of even considering the idea, but it did make him feel better that there would be people there he knew.

"I can clean you up, if you want?"

"What do you mean?"

"My aunt is a barber, and she taught me how to do a few things. I have clippers, and sheers, and everything, if I can find them in all my boxes."

His fingers dug into his hair. "Do you think you could handle this?"

"I don't know. We shall see. You'll have to trust me." The glint in her eyes made him wonder if he should.

"Oh. Now you're asking a lot of me. I won't be bald when you're done. Will I?"

He could tell she knew she had him. "No. I'm not that bad actually. My dad and brother both let me cut their hair. I've even given my mom a trim a few times."

His eyes met hers. She laced her fingers and brought her hands to her chest, pleading.

"Fine. We'll get together later, and I will let you have your way with me." Her brows wiggled at his inuendo, and he couldn't help but laugh. The touch of her foot against his leg again, and her tongue peeking out of her lips, ignited a spark in him. "So, if we are going to keep up this charade, what were you thinking you would feel comfortable with. I promise I won't grope you…unless, of course, you want me to."

"Well, I just said I didn't expect you to. I didn't say you couldn't." Just the thoughts she was putting in his head had him sitting back farther into the pillow and crossing his legs. She was so bubbly, and seemed so innocent, but she was now making him wonder if there was another side to her.

"I'll try to control myself."

"I trust you. Whatever you feel comfortable with."

"Kissing?"

"Sure."

"Friendly, polite? Or a little more?"

She slowly tilted her head back and forth with a scrutinizing eye. "Depends."

The look on her face made him laugh. It was an odd combination of bashful yet sultry.

"On what?"

"If you are a good kisser. I mean, if you are going to lick my face like a Labrador, just keep it chaste, but otherwise I would be fine if you went a little further."

She obviously didn't know what naughty thoughts her innocent words were conjuring. The whole "I will try to control myself" was quickly going out the window, and they had barely touched tonight. She had the perfect kissable lips, and they had invaded his fantasies since the night he groped her at TopHops.

His eyes followed her as she slowly rose from her seat and crawled over him. The weight of her body on top of him made his entire body burst into flames. Her eyes held a mischievous sparkle as she stared into his, while she hovered over him, and then the little minx whispered, "Kiss me." Oh. Yep. There definitely was another side to her.

The rapid pounding of his heart made him lightheaded. *What the hell is this woman doing to me?* That was the last thing he expected her to do. He swallowed hard. "How do you want me to kiss you?" His deep breathy tone surprised him.

Pulling the band from her hair, she let her sable locks fall around her shoulders. Then, she sat up and shrugged her robe off, revealing a lowcut pink tank, with "give sleep a chance" on the front, and a pair of low slung, candy-cane striped cotton pants. Her perfectly curved body was on full display and his body took notice. "Kiss me like *you* want to kiss me."

Strangely, he felt his nerves kick up, wondering if she would think he was a good kisser. "But what if I don't want—"

Her hand gripped his shirt, and with a hard tug, her lips pressed against his. A thousand fantasies raced through his mind all at once as his breath abandoned him. She slowly released him and backed away. Her eyes remained on him, searching. He figured the look in his eyes easily gave him away. She said nothing, but her tongue darted out just enough to wet her lips. Those plump, rose colored lips felt exactly as he'd thought they would; soft and pliant. His body was shaking in desperate need for her lips to be pressed against his again. He knew even before their lips collided again, that she had the power to destroy him. Her fingers reached up and lightly touched his beard and her lips curled into a faint smile.

Cupping his hand behind her neck, he drew her to him. The thought crossed his mind to keep it fairly innocent, although he didn't know if his body would listen. His nose brushed lightly against hers, and he paused, then gently pressed his lips to hers, once, then again, nibbling her bottom lip. Tingles scattered through him like a cold chill, but there was nothing cold about him. He could feel her smile against him, and he couldn't stop himself. She said kiss her like he wanted to.

He tilted his head and pulled her in, deepening the kiss. As her lips parted, he heard her sigh softly, and he swept his tongue against hers, tasting her for the first time. Sweet honey. Immediately, he became lost in her, never wanting the kiss to end. Those perfectly formed lips kissed him like he had never been kissed before. They were magic. They had to have been.

Everything around him disappeared. All he could feel was Kaysi's mouth pressed against his. All he could smell was the lemony honeysuckle scent of her hair. All he could hear were her soft whimpers. And God, did they sound like the music of angels to him.

Lacing his fingers in her hair, he tugged her closer, breaking the kiss just for a breath, and then pressing his lips to hers again, hungry for more. All thoughts that it was just for show, and more importantly, that she was off limits, evaporated. His hand traveled down her side resting on her butt. Her skin was satiny soft, and she felt so amazing against him. She moved, slowly trailing her lips down his neck. He pressed his hands to her hips, letting the sensation of her body against his sink in.

The chime from her phone caused them both to jump, bringing them back to reality. She quickly sat up. Her hair fell into her face, and she brushed it back. His eyes connected with hers, and for a split second, he thought he saw something, but he wasn't sure what. Regret? Confusion? Her breast, at eye level, moved with her heavy breaths. He wondered if she had ever kissed Malcolm like that. All he knew for sure, was he was already missing her soft lips on his.

He needed to get away from her before he did something he shouldn't. Pushing himself up, he let her move off him. She reached for her robe, and retrieved the phone from one of the pockets, and answered it.

"Hey Joe…No it's fine…I just couldn't find my phone, and I was getting a bit panicked…What?…No, I haven't…Okay…When?…" He could hear a sadness creep back into her voice the longer she stayed on her phone. "Yeah...No. I'm good. Thanks...Okay...bye." She put her phone on the table and stood, shrugging her robe back on, but leaving it hanging open.

"What was that about?"

"Joe was giving me an update." Collapsing onto the sofa, she dug her fingers into her hair. "I'm sure you will probably be happy to hear it. He took me up to the loft earlier and kind of gave me a rundown of what was left to be done. He said if everything goes well, he should have it finished next week. The call, was him telling me he might be able to push it up even more and asked if I had ordered the furniture yet."

By the expression she held, he knew the news didn't make her happy, but he was curious as to why. "And you're *not* happy about that?"

Playing with the belt of her robe, she let out a long breath. "I am."

"You could have fooled me."

"It's just..." a hint of a smile crept across her face, "today was...perfect. I haven't ridden in so long, and it felt so good to be in the saddle again. I miss riding with you and was hoping I would have a little more time to talk you into letting me do it again."

"Well, just because you move to the loft doesn't mean you can't come out and ride," he responded quickly, then replayed her comment in his head and sat up. "Kaysi, can I ask you something?"

"Sure." She folded her feet up onto the sofa.

"Have we met before?" Her brows shot up, and she pursed her lips like she was stifling a smile.

"What makes you ask that?"

"You said you missed riding with me."

"I did? I misspoke. I meant I missed riding?"

"I don't think so. You really aren't good at lying. And you didn't answer my question." To be honest, I've wondered for a while. You acted like you knew Bandit when you saw the photo on the wall, and at one point you said I had changed, like you knew me. And the other day when I came by, and you were unpacking, there was something about you that was familiar." Her teeth grazed her bottom lip and left him wondering what her answer would be.

"I don't know. Maybe I just resemble someone you know. And as for my comments, I just get flustered around you and say things wrong."

"No. I think you know."

She turned away with his comment.

"I have been wracking my brain for the past few days trying to figure out when it would have been. Bandit has been gone for I think close to seven years. Was it at an auction? Or livestock show?"

Her eyes drifted, and she pinched her lips together.

"You aren't going to tell me. Are you?"

"I didn't say I met you. I said, I don't know." She didn't sound convincing at all.

"So, you're just going to leave me wondering whether I should know you or not?"

She leaned over and picked up her phone. "Whoa, look at the time. I think it's about time for me to go to bed."

"Well, I think I'll just be riding by myself then."

"You wouldn't do that to me. Would you? I told you I don't know."

He raised a brow, and Kaysi's mouth dropped open.

"And I told you, you are a horrible liar." He narrowed his eyes. "I *will* figure it out whether you tell me or not."

She crawled over to him like before, then reached down, grabbed his phone, and sat back on his legs. "What's your passcode?"

"Why?"

"I'm going to put my number in here, so you can text me when you are free, so I can cut your hair."

"Why don't I just come by?"

"Because I may not be there. I don't just stay holed up there."

"Twenty-eight thirteen."

She tapped on his phone, and he heard a ding and noticed her phone light up.

"What did you do?"

"I sent your number to me. I don't answer strange numbers, so I don't want to miss your call."

"Well, don't be sending me stupid texts with those kitty memes and crap like Jenna does."

"Why does she do that?"

"She says I'm always grumpy, so when she finds something cute, she sends it to me."

"You do seem to be a little unhappy most of the time, Eeyore."

The comment made a snicker escape before he could stifle it.

"I was thinking about going to the rock house tomorrow to see if there was anything there. Wanna come?"

"No, I have a full day. But let me know, and I will open the gate, and tell Poppi you are there."

"Shoot. I was hoping you would go with me. I don't know if I can get there alone."

"It's not hard. You can see the roofline of the house

from the bunkhouse. Just head down the trail from the back of the bunkhouse, and after you go through the gate, head right."

"All right. I think I can find it."

"But promise me you won't go there alone. I don't want you over there by yourself. You could get hurt."

"Aw, you worried about me?"

He wasn't going to admit it, but he was, and he needed to quit. He needed to get his head together. "Just take someone with you."

"I will. I promise." She leaned forward and shoved her feet in her boots. "And by the way, I'm really good with you kissing me the way you want to, any time you want to." Standing, she cinched her robe closed and tied it.

He stood and stretched, now remembering the kiss. "Well, I have to admit, I now have a good idea why Malcolm doesn't want to let you go."

She tipped up on her toes and planted a soft kiss on his lips, then opened the door and disappeared in the darkness. How in the hell did she make him lose his mind so fast?

Chapter Fifteen

She was on her second cup of coffee and still waiting for it to kick in. Sleep? Who needs sleep? She was too excited about what she might find in the house to sleep, and that wasn't the only reason. She kept revisiting that kiss. Oh, he had kissed her all right. Their tongues had gotten to know each other very well.

Malcolm had never even come close to kissing her like that. He was not a fan of French kissing. Ben was. And she couldn't have been happier. He took possession of her entire being with just his lips. Just thinking about it made her whole body shudder. She could almost feel his lips on hers again. She would gladly let him kiss her like that any time he wanted and hoped it would be soon. She wondered what he thought. His comment about Malcolm made her wonder if he felt it too.

It was all supposed to be fake, but lord, there was nothing fake about that kiss in her mind. She knew he wasn't seeking a relationship. Heck, he made it clear that was the last thing he wanted. So, when he suddenly showed up, pretending to be her boyfriend, to continue her lie to Malcolm, it made her wonder why. Ben was a walking contradiction. He always carried a chip on his shoulder, acting all angry, but then he would suddenly soften, wafting from broody recluse to fierce protector.

One thing she was sure of, he was all man. Hard

working, hard talking, hard body, man. One look at him turned her brain to mush. Every time she was around him felt like an out of body experience. And the more she was around him, the more she wanted to be around him. And him agreeing to the haircut gave her that opportunity.

Beyond the physical attraction, she was excited to have a chance to dig deeper, get to know him better, and maybe find out what changed him. No doubt Valerie had something to do with it, but she felt like there was more.

Although he was somewhat of a loner at camp, he was always one to help. He never missed a chance to work with Robin and her on their riding technique. Always seemed happy to talk to them, and acted like he enjoyed taking them on the trails. A hint of a smile played at the corners of her mouth. *I wonder if he will find my hidden answer to his question?* It was fun leaving him hanging, wondering if they had met.

Her phone buzzed. A text from April.

— *Not on your life*—

She had texted her about going to the rock house and snooping around. Figuring it was a longshot with April, she texted Libby too, but knew she wouldn't be able to go in the middle of the week. When her phone buzzed again, it was Libby.

— *Sure. I have teacher in service conferences this week, so I can come later this morning*—

— *Great. I will let Ben know. What time can you be here?* —

— *Around eleven. Who's Ben?* —

— *We'll talk when you get here. Wear your grubbies. I have gloves.*

Kaysi did the happy dance. Now she just needed to let Ben know. She knew she wanted to explore the old

185

house the minute she laid eyes on it. It wasn't uncommon for her to veer off the highway at a random house, if it appeared to have been left to decay. She had found several pieces of furniture and other items sifting through the rubble of old abandoned houses. Although, her trespassing moments she kept to herself.

— *Hey. It's Kaysi. But I guess you know that, since I put my name in your phone. Libby is coming at eleven, and we are going to the rock house. Would you mind opening the gate?* —

She stared at her phone, trying to send her best telepathic message to him to text her back, but it didn't come. So, she set the phone on the counter and opened the refrigerator. Luckily, she had remembered that all he had in the house was beer and water when she arrived, so she had stopped and gotten a few things for quick meals. Grabbing some yogurt and blueberries from the fridge, and some bananas from the counter, she set them all down, and retrieved her blender from the cabinet. Within a couple of minutes, she had whipped up an icy smoothy. Savoring the flavor, she sat down at the table and opened her computer. Scrolling through the comments, she realized she'd gotten several new responses. There had been a few who had signed up to attend the dinner, but one comment caught her eye. "Quit, or you will pay." Her phone buzzed. Ben.

—*I let Poppi know. I'll probably be at the store by then, but I'll make sure the gate is open*—

—*Are you having a good day?* —

—*It's fine. And you?* —

—*I was*—

—*?*—

—*Got another one of those comments on my blog*—

— *What did it say?* —

— *Quit, or you will pay*—

— *You need to talk to the sergeant*—

—*What can he do? They are all posted anonymously*—

—*He might have access to someone who can trace it back to the location of the posts*—

— *Maybe. I'll try to go by later*—

— *I need to talk to the sergeant also, so I'll come by and get you*—

—*Okay. Text me when you're free*—

****

Kaysi drove as close as she could to the old rock house. After following Ben's directions, she realized just how close the house was to the bunkhouse. Covered in brush and sticks, it had an eerie feel to it. But she was hoping, once inside, it would hold more treasures than ghosts.

Libby didn't share her excitement. The minute she laid eyes on the house, she was ready to turn back. Kaysi took one step at a time, making sure each would hold her. The porch, at one time, had been painted blue. But now, all that was left was its remnants, and rust stains on the old worn wood. The front door was closed, and it suddenly occurred to her they might not be able to get in. Not relishing the idea of having to possibly climb through the busted window, she was relieved when the door opened with a little coaxing.

Dust particles, glistened in the air like fairy dust from the disturbance, as Kaysi and Libby took in the first sight of the inside. The living room was mostly empty. Windows covered the walls, with shutters, that were pushed back, to reveal the sunlight. Several were busted.

An old, upholstered chair sat next to a deteriorating fireplace. The material was mostly gone, and it appeared a family of squirrels might have taken up residence.

"Why has Ben's family kept this place? It's on the verge of caving in."

"This isn't on Ben's land. When we came through the gate by the bunkhouse, it became Poppi McIntyre's land. Poppi told me I could rummage through the house and take anything I wanted."

"Poppi is a he?"

"It's what Ben has called him since he was little. His name is Oren."

Kaysi stared at the beautiful intricate molding along the wall and fireplace and could almost picture the room in its heyday. A wave of sadness hit her, realizing the place would probably never be restored. Her eyes went to the ceiling where she noticed several areas that had caved in.

In the next room, which she deemed the library due to the old bookcase that stood on one end, stained wallpaper drooped, revealing shiplap walls. In one corner sat an old upright piano. It wasn't salvageable. A dusty, stained rug filled the center of the floor.

Carefully making her way into the next room, she turned, and realized Libby was no longer with her. "Libby?"

"Yeah?"

"Where are you?"

"In here?"

"Where's here?"

"The kitchen."

Kaysi followed her voice, and a smile curled on her lips, when she took in the sight before her. "Jackpot." On one wall sat an old, dark-stained, hardwood hutch. Though covered in dust, it was still in decent condition. One door stood open revealing a few old glasses inside. An iron stove sat next to it, with a teapot sitting on it like it was just about ready to whistle. Along another wall, were shelves filled with different shaped bottles and cans. Some had different kitchen utensils stowed in them. The cast iron sink sat under a dingy window with a pot in it. On the far wall was a wooden buffet in the same stain as the hutch, with plates sitting in the center of it. A small table sat in the middle of the room, with four chairs pushed in, waiting for the next meal to be served. Kaysi wondered what happened. Why was the place left this way?

Libby turned and pointed. "I'm going to explore some more." Without waiting for a response, she headed up the stairs.

"Watch out for rotted wood," Kaysi called out, hoping she heard her. Her phone chimed in her pocket. When she withdrew it, she let out an exasperated breath. Malcolm. *Why is he calling?*

"Hello?" Kaysi continued to walk around the room and wrenched open a door. Shelves lined the walls.

"Hey, Love. How are you?"

"I'm fine, but I'm a bit busy at the moment. Do you need something?" She smiled, seeing bowls and old decanters perched on nearly every shelf.

"I wanted to apologize. I felt bad about the other day. I'm truly sorry I didn't take you at your word when you said you had found someone else. You have never lied to me, and I should have believed you."

Her gut tightened hearing his confession, and knowing she, in fact, was lying to him. "It's okay. I know it was kind of sudden." Glancing at the floor, she noticed a cut-out piece, that was askew. Sticking her finger in the crack, she lifted it to find stairs descending into the darkness.

"How did you guys meet again?" The sound of his voice brought her back to the conversation, and she had to replay his words in her head.

"Oh. Um. He and my brother are friends. They are working on some construction projects together." Staring into the darkness, she wondered what was down there.

"So, he's the guy you are taking to the dinner?"

She hated the tone he used when he was being judgmental with her, and even more, knowing he was judging Ben. It sent a rush of anger through her.

"Yes, Malcolm, he's the guy. Why?" This was going to be way out of his comfort zone, remembering what Ben had said, yet he was still willing to do it for her. She knew he didn't feel like he fit in, but maybe, with a little cut and shave, he would be more comfortable. After silence continued on the other end, she was ready to end the call. Lifting the piece of wood more, a black widow spider crawled up from the underside. Kaysi screamed and dropped the board.

"What happened, Kaysi? Are you okay, Love?"

Kaysi shuddered and dusted her arms and chest, hoping no eight-legged creatures were crawling on her.

"Kaysi?"

"Yes, Malcolm. I'm fine. I just saw a spider." Quickly shutting the door, she returned her focus to the kitchen, scanning the rest of the area, and taking inventory of the items she wanted to take with her, and what she would need to come back for. "Was that all you needed? Have you found anyone to go with?" It occurred to her that if she could get him to pair up with Libby, she could get back into Libby's good graces, and keep him occupied where he wouldn't be bothering her. Though the thought was fleeting, since Malcolm wasn't a fan of Libby's. Wouldn't hurt to try though.

"I haven't."

"You know, Libby was already planning on going. Why don't you guys go together?"

"Kaysi. You know Libby's not exactly my type, and I don't trust—"

"I know she can be a little intense—"

"And moody," he added.

"And sometimes moody," she corrected, then heard a gasp behind her. Knowing she just set the match to the dynamite, she slowly turned. Lowering her head to her hand, she rubbed her temples when she saw Libby with fire shooting from her eyes. Kaysi ended the call, and followed Libby, who was quickly heading out the door. "Libby, wait. You are taking the conversation out of context. I was suggesting he take you to the dinner."

"Sure, you were. It sounded like you were steering him clear of your intense, moody servant. I don't know why I even agreed to come today. No telling what kind of diseases are in this place. You do realize those are blood stains on the porch. Right?"

Kaysi glanced at the large, rust stain. "How do you know that?"

How do you not?" Libby said, lifting her arms in the air. What did Malcolm call for anyway?"

"I'm not sure. He said he was apologizing."

"For what?"

"For not believing I have a boyfriend."

"Boyfriend? This Ben guy is your boyfriend?"

"Kind of," she said, hoping that Libby would accept the answer and move on.

"So, Malcolm met Ben?"

"Yes." A cagey grin slowly spread across her face. Kaysi knew exactly what it was about too. "And that was why I was trying to encourage Malcolm to take you to the dinner."

"By telling him I was moody?"

"He called you moody. I was about to tell him your good qualities when you walked up on me and pitched a fit."

"I didn't pitch a fit."

"Okay, a tantrum."

"Not a tantrum either."

Kaysi rolled her eyes and huffed. "Then what would you call it?"

Libby shifted her posture and continued to scowl.

"Face it, Libby. You *are* kind of moody. That's just who you are, but you wouldn't hurt a fly."

"Why do you say that? You think I would—"

"No. God, Libby. Stop. I was trying to help you, not hurt you."

"Right."

"Can we just finish up here...please? It's getting cold." She glanced back at the door. "Did you find anything upstairs?"

"Yeah."

"Show me."

Libby narrowed her eyes and pressed her lips together in a thin line. For a moment, Kaysi wasn't sure Libby would stay, but she slowly turned and headed back into the house.

Ascending the stairs, Kaysi was again hit with the despair of knowing, that under all the dirt was a beautiful house, with intricate woodwork, and probably so many stories, that no one would ever be able to appreciate again. Her hand glossed over the wood railing, brushing more dust into the air. Even though there was no electricity, and the cold wind, from the impending storm, blew through the cracks in the house, there was something warm about it. She could feel the love that permeated the walls. It was almost like she could hear the house laughing.

As they hit the top of the stairs, her eyes locked on a small doll carriage, and a grin spread across her face. This house had kids. Entering the first bedroom, her heart skipped. Against one wall, sat a beautiful dresser with a hutch. The glass was busted, and all the drawers were missing except for one, but she could see it sitting in the store, displaying items. Against another wall, was a bed, with a hardwood headboard and footboard. A rocking chair, with a solid, intricately carved, curved back, sat next to a window. She could picture a young mom sitting there rocking her baby and staring out at the landscape.

"And I saved the best for last," Libby sang, as she ushered Kaysi into a large bedroom with two beds. A huge red brick fireplace sat on one end with porcelain figurines still perched on the mantle. To one side, was a small child sized rocking chair, and next to it was a wooden pull toy, with the rope still attached. To the other side, was a small child sized table, with two chairs. She had hoped to find some things she could bring back to the store, and this was far more than she expected. But she almost felt sad, contemplating why everything was left behind, like they hurried away.

After searching through the rest of the house, she and Libby gathered a few of the smaller items, that they could load into the SUV, and left. Libby was still acting a bit irritated and didn't stay after dropping off their finds at the bunkhouse. Kaysi had hoped to breathe life back into her friendship with Libby by getting Malcolm to take her to the dinner, but she was pretty sure it was now gasping its last breath.

After grabbing a shower and a late lunch, she sat on the sofa in the living room and examined her treasures. Everything needed a good scrubbing. Years of dirt had rendered some of the objects to a lifeless form. But she could see past the dull pasty covering, and knew she had some great pieces. Although they were unable to get the larger items, she was hoping Ben would help her move those later. Furniture was just not built with the same creative eye anymore. And if it was, it had a hefty price tag to go with it.

Her hand brushed against the red photo album, stuffed between the cushion and the arm of the sofa, and she was brought back to when she was thirteen. Opening the album, she turned to the photos of the summer that changed her life. Snapshots, of people playing in the river and sitting around the campfire, filled the pages. One page was filled with photos from inside her cabin.

A particular photo caught her eye. Julie and Cheryl. Funny how you tend to remember the names of the people who truly bless your life, along with those who leave scars. The two junior counselors were supposed to be the ones the campers, and ranch hands, would go to if they had a problem, the ones to go to if you needed help. But instead, they were the ones who instigated the trouble, especially for Robin. They had been to the camp before and knew Robin.

When they first met Kaysi, they were nice. She was the newcomer, and they acted like they wanted to get to know her. But it didn't take long for her to suspect that there was something up by the way Robin steered clear of them. She finally confided to Kaysi that the girls were not nice, and Kaysi found out soon enough what their true colors were. It was obvious they came from affluent families from the way they constantly threw their travel experiences, and expensive clothes and toys, in everyone's faces. Although Kaysi was aware of her family's wealth, she was raised not to flaunt it.

The derogatory comments started the first week for Kaysi, when the two noticed her hanging out with Robin. Just what she didn't need with her already fragile self-esteem. There were comments about her hair, and her glasses, how they were too big for her face. Then there were comments about her braces. And let's face it, braces are just awkward, but in the end deliver great results. Everything that she was most self-conscious about, they zeroed in on. The worst were the comments about her weight.

Skimming the photos now, Kaysi realized just how off she was about her body image at the time. She wasn't skinny, but she wasn't over-weight either. Her tummy wasn't flat. But she wasn't the size she pictured herself as, or the size that Julie and Cheryl wanted her to believe.

Their constant taunts against her were nothing though, compared to the all-out bullying they did to Robin. The first week was little things, like purposefully bumping her, causing her to drop her tray in the dining hall, or knocking her suitcase over.

Early on, Kaysi had decided to stick to Robin's side, trying to stave off the incidents. When she realized no one paid attention to what was happening, she wanted to help. But one day, as Kaysi was returning from the nurse's office after getting a cut at the stables, she heard a loud banging, then Robin's distressed cry.

Picking up her pace, knowing Cheryl and Julie had probably pulled another prank, she was horrified to find Robin, standing outside the cabin, wearing pants but no shirt, frantically banging on the door, hoping someone would let her in. Kaysi quickly wrapped her arms around her to cover her bare chest and offer her comfort. Fury rose inside her, and she banged on the door, screaming to let them in.

Her head was spinning, trying to come up with an alternative plan, since they refused to open the door. Then, Ben appeared. Kaysi squeezed Robin tighter, knowing how humiliated she must feel, and stared into Ben's eyes with angry tears streaming down her face. She could see the mix of compassion and rage warring within him.

He stalked to the door, banged on it with his fist, and called out, for them to "open up." With the sound of a male voice, Cheryl quickly opened the door and smiled. Kaysi pushed past her, and ushered Robin inside, but heard Ben say behind her, "You and Robin meet me out here when you get her dressed."

After getting Robin calmed down and dressed, they found Ben and walked to the office to talk to the camp director. Unfortunately, there was no punishment handed down. The director informed them that, although they would like to send Cheryl and Julie home, their hands were tied. Julie was the granddaughter of one of the owners of the resort, and Robin was the daughter of another owner. Since there were only three days left of the camp, they asked Robin if she would rather leave now, but she refused.

The director said he would inform Julie's family of the incident, however, neither she nor Cheryl would be asked to leave. Kaysi felt defeated and angry, but Robin had already put a smile back on her face and was happy to be able to ride horses a few more days. Ben said he would keep an eye out, and he did.

Kaysi's phone chimed. "Speak of the devil." Closing the album, she set it next to the sofa and answered the call.

Chapter Sixteen

Ben rapped on the door and adjusted the collar of his coat against the icy wind that had increased throughout the day. Gray clouds were rolling in. The storm was coming. The door opened, and Ben's heart fluttered. Dressed in faded ripped jeans tucked into her fuzzy boots, and a soft burgundy V necked sweater under her leather fringed coat, Kaysi looked like she was going on a date, not to the police station. Her hair was down with long layers of dark brown locks brushing against her face. Her eyes had a bright twinkle in the sea of blue, and her lips…damn, those lips. Visions whipped though his mind of their kiss. He would love nothing more than to have those lips pressed against his again.

"Hey," she said, gesturing for him to come in. "Let me get my purse." That sweet voice had him blinking the fantasy away, and he stepped inside. Her honeysuckle scent was left behind as she disappeared up the hallway. Every time he was around her, his insides clamped down so hard he struggled to breathe.

Rubbing his hands together, he tried to dispel the tension building up inside him. It ticked him off the way she was starting to get under his skin. He didn't want to like her. He really couldn't like her…if he wanted to live. But it was already too late. It drove him crazy the way she was always so cheerful and had some strange ability to make him smile no matter how hard he tried not to. She was absolutely beautiful inside and out. Ben remembered his mom telling him, "Appearances can be bought, but true beauty is a gift." She had that gift.

Kaysi appeared with that bright smile on her face that he couldn't get enough of. "Okay, I'm ready." They headed out the door and climbed into his pickup. "You smell nice, what are you wearing?"

He had run home to grab a shower, after helping Joe stain the floors at the store. "I don't know, it's probably eau de floor stain."

She swatted his arm. "I'm serious."

"I have no idea. Something in a glass bottle that Jenna probably gave me for Christmas."

"I'm going to have to ask Jenna where she shops for your Christmas presents, especially for those fuzzy pajama pants you had on last night. I want some."

His mind immediately went back to her crawling all over those fuzzy pants, and he choked. Needing to change the subject quick, he asked, "Did you find anything at the house? I noticed some stuff on the table."

"Yes!" she said enthusiastically. "There are some big pieces, that I was hoping you, and maybe Cody, might help me move." She tucked her hair behind her ear. "Also, I needed to ask you something. And please, just tell me no if this would be a problem. I can figure something else out. I just thought it wouldn't hurt—"

"Just ask the damn question."

"*Okay*. Your studio, I noticed, has some extra space—"

"And you need to use it."

"Just for a little bit," she said, hesitantly, "to clean up a few pieces. I mean, I could move them straight into the store and work on them there. But we are going to be bringing in inventory, and some of the stuff may need to be re-stained, and—"

Even when she rambled, she was beautiful. Ben shook his head. "It's fine. And I have stain if you need it."

They parked outside the police station and were greeted by an older lady with plump cheeks. "We are here to see Mitch...Sergeant Gallagher," Ben said through the hole in the glass.

The lady pointed. "Let me buzz you through."

A loud buzzer sounded, releasing a heavy metal door. They headed down the musty hallway. Through the open door, Ben noticed Mitch on his computer, his usual spot, so he tapped on the door frame.

Mitch motioned them to come in. "How are you guys today? What can I do for you?" He turned in his seat to face them.

Ben scooted his chair closer to the desk. "Well, we're here on two separate issues. But they're kind of intertwined."

Raising a questioning eyebrow, Mitch slowly responded, "Okay." His eyes shifted to Kaysi. "Why don't you go first, young lady." Mitch picked up a yellow notepad and pen. "What's your name?"

Ben bobbled his head. "Right. I need to introduce you guys. Mitch, this is Kaysi Grayeagle."

"Joe and Kaleb's sister. Right?"

"Yes."

Ben pointed. "Sergeant Mitch Gallagher."

Mitch reached across the desk, and Kaysi shook his hand. "Like I said, I know your brother, Joe, as well as April, and this guy's sister, Jenna, and her husband,

Cody. Please, call me Mitch." He pointed his finger at Kaysi. "I have something I need to discuss with you later." Confusion filled Kaysi's face as she glanced at Ben, then back to Mitch.

"What about Kaleb," Ben piped up, wondering what he would say about Kaysi's younger brother.

"Let's just leave that one out of this."

"Ah. So, you do know Kaleb?"

"Unfortunately."

"Yeah. I'm right there with you, buddy. Try growing up with him."

Mitch let out a hearty laugh, and his eyes met Ben's. "I like this girl."

"Apparently, everyone does."

"With a few exceptions." The tone of Kaysi's voice got Mitch's attention.

"Oh? What's going on?"

"Well…" She cut her eyes to Ben, and he slowly placed his hand on her leg, hoping it would calm her. "I write a blog. It's primarily used to market interesting items I find, talk about little, out of the way stores, and sometimes help artists who create the pieces. Anyway, I've also been posting about the charity dinner this Saturday, which I think you might be coming to, if I remember correctly." Mitch nodded. "When I started posting about the dinner, I started getting some negative, almost threatening, posts." She leaned over and retrieved her laptop from her bag. After popping it open, she brushed her finger over the pad then spun the computer around. "This was the first one. They came about every day or two after that."

Mitch leaned forward and gazed at the screen with his brows knitted together, saying nothing. Finally, he pushed the computer back.

"It's nothing right? Just some troll trying to scare me?"

"I'm not sure, but it's not something to blow off. I think we need to dig a little deeper."

"Who do you think could be doing this?"

"It could be anybody. Do you have any ideas?"

"Tell him what you told me," Ben added.

Kaysi huffed. "Well, I first thought it was someone who didn't want us doing the charity dinner, because the threat was posted on the announcement. But some of the threats were on random photos that had nothing to do with the charity dinner.

"Ben asked if I had pissed anyone off lately. I recently broke up with a boyfriend of six months, and he kind of took it hard, and has been calling me. But I swear he is sweet and harmless. Seriously. The only other person is my friend, Libby. She wasn't happy with the fact that I was starting a business with April. Apparently, she thought I would go into business with her. Unfortunately, she never shared that bit of information with me, so I had no clue."

Mitch opened the drawer of his desk and retrieved something. "Would this be hers?" He laid a soot covered bracelet in a small plastic bag on the desk.

Kaysi's face paled. "Where'd you find it?"

"The fire investigator found it where the fire ignited. Is it hers?"

"Yes. It is. She was helping me move. It had to have fallen off when she put down a box."

"Was she always with you?"

"We were both running up and down the stairs, but if she wasn't with me, April and Jenna were both there too."

"The whole time?"

Kaysi sat back in her chair. "I can't remember. There were all kinds of people running in and out."

"This bracelet has traces of the accelerant on it."

"You think she started the fire?"

"We aren't ruling her out."

"But, Sergeant, she couldn't have done it. It must be just a coincidence. Couldn't it have just fallen off, and whoever started it poured the stuff on top of it?"

"Possibly." He paused. "But you are sure this is your friend's bracelet?"

"Yes." Ben could see the apprehension on Kaysi's face.

"And what's her name?"

"Elizabeth Janaway. She goes by Libby."

He jotted down the name and retrieved the bag. "With the threatening comments, and the fact that there was definite evidence that a fire was set in the loft, I have to take those threats seriously. Is there anything else going on?"

"No. I can't think of anything." Kaysi nervously threaded her fingers between each other, so Ben rubbed his hand on her leg, to give her some reassurance.

Mitch glanced up at him from scribbling something on the legal pad. "Now, what can I do for you?"

"Poppi." He paused. "I mean Oren, is being harassed by his grandson, Rick. I caught him manhandling him the other day. Rick said he can't handle the ranch anymore. Thinks Poppi left the gate open on those horses. I know he didn't. You know what's been happening on his land. I told you something strange was going on."

"I know. I've already spoken to Oren. He has it

handled."

"Are you sure? I think Rick has been behind some of these incidents."

"Like what?"

"Might have been the one who opened that gate and let the horses get out on the highway. He also could have been behind the missing cows and the damaged equipment too." Ben thought about what Mitch said. "So, Poppi spoke to you?"

"Yeah. He's been in contact with me. You may not be giving him enough credit. He's a very smart man."

"Oh, trust me. I know the man is smart. I'm just worried about what Rick might be capable of."

"The best thing for you to do is keep an eye on him...from a distance. You don't want to get mixed up in their business right now."

"Poppi said the same thing. What exactly is he doing? He's not putting himself in danger, is he?"

"Again, I know what he's got going on, and I'm keeping an eye on things. You just keep doing what you're doing. Keep your nose clean and stay out of his business for right now."

"You're being awfully cryptic, Mitch."

"I have to be until Oren gets things figured out. You will understand at some point."

Ben knew it was pointless to push Mitch on the subject, but he also knew he would have Poppi's back. He just had to figure out how.

****

Sitting in the living room, with a fire in the fireplace, and plates of burgers in their laps, Ben felt strangely...comfortable. He scanned the piles of boxes around him, wondering what each box contained. The thought of Kaysi's words about not wanting to leave, crept in. He had to make sure he took her for another ride before she had to move out, but tonight called for a winter storm, so it probably wouldn't be for the next couple of days. He knew they were closing in on having her loft finished. There were only a few more projects they needed to complete.

His eyes drifted to a flash of red next to the sofa. Spying the red photo album Kaysi had open on the table days before, Ben tried to figure out how to sneak a peek without her seeing him. From the way she reacted, after he noticed it days before, he knew there was something in it that she didn't want him seeing. If he could just push it open, he might be able to get a clue to when they met. Bringing his arm up, he casually scratched the back of his head, then lowered it over the arm of the sofa. His fingers skimmed the edge of it, but the album was just out of reach. *Damn it.* He tried to discreetly lean over, to see if it would give him the added inches he needed, without being too obvious.

"What are you doing?" The sound of her voice made him jump.

"Me? Nothing why? I was just stretching my back," he lied. She narrowed her eyes and stood. Ben thought she caught him when she walked over to him, but instead she motioned for his empty plate. He handed it off and let out a nervous breath.

"Are you ready to get your makeover?"

His eyes widened. "Here? Now?"

"I found my clippers and cape. So, why not?"

His gut tightened. He agreed to it when she first brought it up, because he was game for a free haircut, but now that she wanted to do it, he was having major second thoughts. Not that anything wouldn't probably be an improvement to his current appearance."

"Fine."

She set a chair out on the hardwood. "Great! Let me go get my stuff."

He stood and rubbed his hands down his thighs.

"Do you want me to wash your hair?" she hollered from up the hall.

"Whatever. This is your deal. I just washed it before I came though."

Appearing in the hallway carrying a bag, she grinned and said, "Park your butt in the chair, and let's get this party started then." He moved to the chair and sat down, releasing a deep breath. She set the bag on the table, shook out the cape, and wrapped it around him.

"All right. What will you allow me to do?"

"All I ask is that I'm not bald when you're done."

"And beard?"

"I'd like to keep at least some of it. It keeps my face warm."

"Got it."

The buzz of the clippers made him stiffen, and he sat still, feeling his hair fall away piece by piece. After a moment he asked, "Do you have a mirror?"

"No peeks until I'm done." Minutes past in silence, before Kaysi asked, "So, how long has it been since you had a haircut?"

"Since Jenna and Cody's wedding. Like a year and a half, I guess. The girl looked all of twelve, so I only got it trimmed then. My mom…" His gut soured as his thoughts took hold.

"Your mom what?"

"Never mind."

"No. Tell me."

He didn't want to get into it, but something about the gentleness of her voice, and the kindness that played in her eyes, had him relenting. "My mom used to cut my hair."

Kaysi was silent momentarily. "You were close to her, weren't you?"

The question surprised him, and another sting pierced his chest. "Eh. I guess not as close as I thought."

Her voice softened, and she paused what she was doing. "Why do you say that?"

"I was the only family member who wasn't there when she died."

"That doesn't mean anything."

"Yeah, well." He shrugged.

"I wouldn't do that if I were you, unless you want a bald spot." She gently put her hand on his head to steady it and continued drawing the clippers up the back of his head. "So why do you think you weren't close to her?"

Feeling the familiar pain, he thought about changing the subject, then Kaysi's face came into view. Her bright blue eyes stared into his, and something about her expression, allowed the pain to dissipate. He took a deep breath and let it out. "The ranch was hemorrhaging money, because of the medical bills. We were needing to sell a few of our herd to cover some of the costs, so we needed to go to auction.

"She was getting weak, and the hospice care giver said she could go at any time. I didn't want to leave, but she told me she would be fine. Dad said he needed to stay with her, so I finally gave in. She died before I got to the auction. She didn't wait."

"Didn't wait?"

The sound of her voice brought him back from the dark hole, he didn't even realize he had traveled down. It happened every time he thought about that day. Most of the time he just chose to hang out there, but her voice did something to him. "Never mind."

"Stop saying that. Tell me."

"I don't want to talk about it anymore." The tone in his voice was harsher than he intended.

"Fair enough. But if you need—"

"I won't."

The buzz of the clippers disappeared. "Close your eyes." Surprised by her demand, he glanced at her, then reluctantly did as she said. A mist of water hit his skin, and he flinched the first couple of times, making her giggle. "It's not acid. It's just water with a little conditioner. It won't hurt you."

"But it's cold."

She ran a comb through his hair and continued spraying until it was sufficiently wet. "So, do you always get so angry talking about your mom?"

"God, Kaysi. You drive me crazy. I told you; I don't want to talk about it."

"You gotta believe she had no control of when she took her last breath."

Ben grabbed the comb. "Kaysi, leave it alone."

"I just hate seeing you angry about something that should bring you joy."

She tried to comb his hair, but he jerked away, confused. "I should be happy about my mom's death?"

"No, of course not. That's not what I meant. Remembering her should make you happy. From what you've told me about her, she sounds like a wonderful lady. It just seems like you are focused on the wrong things."

She threaded her fingers through a pair of shears and began combing and cutting. "How would you know?"

Kaysi went silent for a moment. "Well, she cut your hair, didn't she?"

The comment she made kept playing over in Ben's head. You are just focusing on the wrong things. She was right. Every time he thought of his mom, all he could see was the last day, and it immediately made him mad.

She had been his confidant. The person who could talk him down from the ledge his whole life. He knew his dad loved him, but he expected a lot from him at an early age, and they butted heads. When he got overwhelmed, it was like his mom sensed it, and she would step in. With just a few words, she would set everything right. And she left him without saying goodbye. "Please, let's just drop it," he said, his voice now full of sadness.

Kaysi moved around in front of him. "Spread your legs apart." She leaned in and combed his hair, then began snipping it with the shears. Her hair fell in his face, and her finger brushed it behind her ear. The way she moved had his mind drifting to other thoughts. He again became hyper aware of every touch, every movement. His eyes dipped to the V in her sweater, that was now at eye level, and he found himself gripping the arms of the chair, just to keep from reaching up to touch her. She was, evidently, unaware where her cleavage was. "Getting an eye full?" Or maybe not. "Sorry, I'll be done in a second."

"By all means, take your time. I'm kind of enjoying the view."

"Oh yeah?" she said with a slight giggle, and he

added that to the growing list of things that he couldn't resist about her.

Slamming his eyes shut, trying to ward off the rising heat pulsating through him, he decided to make her as uncomfortable as she had him. And he knew just how to do it. "So, do you want to tell me the story of the little red photo album?" Her body immediately stilled, and he knew he had hit his mark.

Kaysi peered down at him. "Did you see any of the photos?"

"What do you think?" he said, tipping the side of his mouth up in a slightly wolfish grin.

She leaned back, still holding the sharp scissors in her hand, and gave him a sidelong glance, which suddenly made him wonder if he thought the plan through far enough. "Where did you find it?"

He was still so close to her that he could see the pulse in her neck. "Next to the sofa."

And boom. The smile that crossed her face told him he had been caught. "So that's what you were reaching for. You didn't get it," she sang teasingly.

Damn it. This woman. He had no comeback. "So, tell me what's in it."

"I already have."

"What do you mean you already have? When?" Had she really? He normally hated when people played games with him, but this was almost like a treasure hunt.

"Earlier."

"Earlier, when?"

"Uh uh," she said and shook her head. "That's all you get. You have it with you most of the time." *What the hell did that mean?* Kaysi lifted his chin and ran her fingers through his hair, then did it again, taking with them any memory of the previous conversation. And when she smiled, tiny pin pricks danced all over his body. Reaching over him, she pressed her body against his. Was she completely oblivious as to what she was doing to him? Flashes of her crawling up him, with a mischievous grin on her face, played through his mind.

Ben could feel his restraint begin to crack like a piece of broken glass. Hearing the buzz of the clippers again was just enough to draw him from his thoughts, and he stilled. Her fingers gently caressed his face, as she tilted his head from one side to the other, running the clippers through his beard. He watched as she concentrated, noticing her tongue playing on her lip occasionally. After a few minutes, she flipped the clippers off, and he let out the breath he didn't even realize he was holding. It was taking everything in his power to stay in the chair and keep his hands to himself.

She stared at his face, tilting it from one side to the other again. "Okay, close your eyes." *Damn. Is this torture ever going to end?* Not that everything didn't feel amazing, but there is a limit to what a man can handle before spontaneously combusting.

"Why?"

"Don't ask questions. Just do it."

Drawing his brows together, he stared at her for moment, before he let his eyes drift shut. He immediately felt it when she left. It was like the sunlight went behind the clouds. That gravitational pull had disconnected. He opened one eye, and took in his surroundings, to see where she was, and then heard the water running in the sink in the kitchen. "Lean your head back and keep your eyes closed." Lacing his fingers over his stomach, he slowly tilted his head back. The tingle of electricity returned as she applied hot towels to his face, and he jerked. "Is it too hot?"

"No. It just surprised me. It feels good." Pushing her knees in between his again, he felt her hands on his neck, gently massaging the muscles. She made her way down to his shoulders, then back up, running her fingers over his scalp, around his ears, and over his temples under the towels. As much as he fought his body in its response to her closeness, it fought back with a vengeance, and his laced fingers moved down to his lap. The longer she stood in between his knees, rubbing her fingers over his face and neck, the harder it was to maintain control.

"Okay, one more thing," he heard her say, but his mind had completely drifted into fantasies of what he wanted to do to her. "Keep your eyes closed." At this point, he had to. Opening them, would put him in danger of losing any self-control he had left, and acting on his fantasies. He felt the towels lift off his face, and they were replaced with a cold goo, slathered against his neck and face, and it made him jump again, but still didn't drag him from his dreamlike state. "Okay, be still." The sound of her soft voice so close, pushed him further into a fog, where he couldn't think. A twinge shot down his spine and he let out a groan. "You okay?" Kaysi questioned as her hands touched his cheek along with the cold steel of a blade.

"Yeah," he managed, but he really wasn't. Her body rubbed against him as her hands stroked his face, and he continued to try to resist his urges. Finally, she grabbed the wet towel again, gently wiping his face and neck. Then nothing. She was gone. He didn't know if he was supposed to remain still or not, although his body was so charged, he fought to stay in the chair. He heard her moving, then felt her hands on him once again. Against his better judgement, he popped open one eye, and watched a sultry grin spread across her beautiful face as she threaded her fingers through his hair once again, then brushed them gently against his beard. Every touch of her fingers left his skin smoldering and brought a flicker to something inside him that he thought had been snuffed out long ago, and any remaining restraint he had crumbled to ash.

Chapter Seventeen

Grabbing her wrist as she attempted to run her fingers through his hair again, Ben pulled her to him and pressed his lips to hers. Her body stiffened, and he was worried she would back away. She needed to. She needed to stop him. There was no question as to what he wanted. Primal desire had taken hold. Instead of pushing away though, she melted into him.

Straddling him, her arms snaked around his neck, and he continued his frenzied attack. Unlike their first kiss, that started out to prove to her that he had skills, this kiss was completely driven by the intense need to devour her. As much as he knew he was treading into dangerous territory, and probably making a huge mistake, he wanted nothing more than to claim every part of her...now.

Her lips parted, and his tongue invaded, tasting her sweet flavor. It was like a drug, intensifying his hunger. She whimpered as his tongue brushed against hers, and his hands traced down her soft curves. She backed away, dragging in a ragged breath, a smile tugging at the corners of her mouth, then her lips were against his again. Her delicate fingers caressed his face, and she was kissing him just as fiercely as he was her. She had reeled him in like a fish on a line, and all his fight was gone. He couldn't stop himself. His need for her, to hold her in his arms, to feel her skin against his, her lips pressed to his, was too much. He had to have her. His fingers laced in her hair, and the chair creaked as he wrapped his arm around her and pushed himself up.

Breaking the kiss as her feet touched the floor, he caught a glimpse of her eyes, the color deepening to a sapphire with the unmistakable fire that had taken hold. His mouth brushed a kiss against her jaw, then trailed them down her neck to the soft hollow when she tipped her head. Her eyes were now closed. Her dark lashes pressed to her golden cheeks. Her swollen, cherry red lips barely parted. Pushing her shirt over her shoulder, he continued his trail of kisses and nips, while her fingers dug into his neck, and her breath escaped in a tortured moan. The soft cry added fuel to the need to taste every part of her.

Slowly making his way to her mouth again, he captured it, hungrily attacking it before backing away, his hands cupping her face, his forehead pressed against hers. "You are going to have to stop me, if you don't want this, because I can't stop myself. Tell me no, Kaysi."

"No," she said breathlessly. The word sucked the air from his lungs, and his hands dropped. He stepped back, breathing so hard he was becoming dizzy. His eyes closed, and his hands covered his face as he tried to regain control. Disappointment coursed through his body. He knew it was better that they stopped. He wanted her, but knew it was wrong for so many reasons.

But she'd awakened something within him, and he couldn't stop thinking about her. Couldn't stop fantasizing about her. Couldn't stop craving her. In his mind, he knew this was the last thing he should be doing.

But his mind wasn't in control, and his heart, body, and soul wanted her.

Her hand grabbed his shirt, tugging him to her, and he opened his eyes. "I mean," her eyes lifted to his, "no, I don't want to make you stop." Her lips crashed into his, and her hands tugged at the hem of his shirt until they were touching his skin, causing a lightning storm that consumed him. Lifting her into his arms, still locked in a kiss, he carried her up the hallway to the bedroom.

"We shouldn't be doing this," he said, his voice as coarse as gravel. Setting her gently on the bed, he moved on top of her, dusting kisses over the soft swells of her breast, while she continued to tug at his shirt. He finally grabbed hold of it and yanked it over his head.

"Why?" The hunger in her eyes as she took in his body, and the way she bit her lip, caused a crooked smile to form on his lips. He leaned down and captured her mouth again. Nothing in the world tasted sweeter. Pulling away, she brushed her nose against his and smiled.

"So many reasons," he said. "Your brothers are going to kill me if they find out."

Slowly rubbing her fingers against his ribs, she responded, "I'm a grown woman, Ben. I can make my own decisions." Her eyes tipped up, and she brushed her fingers through his hair again. "Do you want to see what I did, before I mess it up? You might not like it."

"Do you like it?" he asked, his mouth hovering over hers.

"God yes. It's the best work I've ever done."

"Then that's all that matters." A smile bloomed on her lips, and when it sparked in her eyes, every sliver of control he had disappeared. His lips met hers, devouring her mouth. Her lips were so soft, and she tasted like honey and vanilla, and he couldn't get enough. She moaned, as he brushed kisses down her neck, while his hand tugged at her sweater. Pushing it down her shoulder along with her bra strap, he continued with his feather light kisses, until he revealed the soft breast that teased him earlier. Her cry as his lips nibbled at her velvety skin made him shudder.

"We really need to stop," he whispered, sucking on her neck and earlobe, as his hands dove under her sweater, pushing it up.

She raised up and lifted her hands, allowing him to drag it over her head. "You want to?"

His rough hand traced a line down the center of her stomach, over the top of her jeans, causing Kaysi's breath to hitch. Dusting kisses between her breast, he paused with his lips still hovering over her chest. "Hell no." His lips found hers again, and his hand reached behind her back to unclasp her bra. With his hand cupped around her cheek, he locked eyes with her. "Are you sure you want to?"

"Yes." She nodded.

He moved off the bed, keeping his eyes on her. His belt slid from the loops with a whack. His fingers worked his button and zipper, and in one smooth motion his pants dropped to the floor. Kaysi sat up on her knees, letting her bra drop, and began to unbutton her pants, but he moved her hand. "Let me do it." She slowly stood from the bed, letting his hands work the button and zipper, before sliding her pants down.

His hand traced the lace seam of her panties, and a slow grin spread across his face, with the knowledge that it was the only piece of clothing standing between them.

Kissing the dip in her neck, he gradually pushed her panties down her legs, laying tender kisses in a trail to her belly.

With one knee bent on the floor, looking like he was about to propose naked, he stared for a moment, before his eyes drifted to hers, and he stood. His hands cupped her cheeks and he gazed at her. His eyes again skimmed her body. She was soft and curvy, and strong, if by the way she handled the horse was any indication. But she was also delicate. He wanted to grab her and have his way with her, but he couldn't. She needed to be caressed, like the petal of a rose. She was doing things to him he didn't understand. "Do you know how beautiful you are? I mean, has anyone told you recently?"

Her hair fell over one shoulder, and it complimented her slightly tanned skin, which made her blue eyes pop. But when his eyes met hers again, he noticed a hint of sadness and wondered why. But then her smile returned. "Only one, that mattered."

He pushed her down on the bed, and dropped hot wet kisses along her stomach, to her breast, then her mouth. "Who was that?" he asked with his lips still against her mouth.

Her fingers grazed his side and lightly scraped against his back. "A friend. It was a long time ago."

"Seriously? No one recently? Not your ex?"

"Malcolm said it all the time, but I didn't believe him. There was only one who said it, and I knew, beyond a shadow of a doubt, that he meant it."

"A boy?" He raised up and focused on her face.

"Yes." Her playful expression as she answered, sent a jolt of jealousy through him, and made him wonder if there was more to her short answer than she was revealing. He cocked a brow, but she didn't speak, just started to giggle, and ran her fingers through his hair. The vibration ramped up his hunger even more.

He brought his forehead to hers and placed his hand on her cheek. "You, are absolutely beautiful inside and out."

She continued to giggle.

"Do you believe me?"

She put her finger to her mouth and tapped it like she was thinking, then slowly shook her head.

His mouth crushed hers, with a need to show her his truth. With his lips hovering over hers, he whispered, "Oh, but you are, Kaysi. Everything about you is perfect." His lips pressed against hers again, in another soul stealing kiss that threatened to incinerate them both, then he moved down her neck, to her breast taking one nipple into his mouth and gently sucking. Kaysi shuddered beneath him, and let out a strained moan, that added fuel to the fire.

Her fingers gently explored the hard muscles of his back, and danced over his shoulders, while her lips caressed his neck, leaving a trail of goosebumps behind.

"Stay right there," he said breathing heavily as he reached for his pants. Removing a foil packet, he ripped it open, and laid the empty wrapper on the nightstand.

Slowly, he slid into the bed, completely enchanted by this creature who had invaded his home, and now his entire being. Moving her on top of him, her fingers curled in his chest hair, then slid up the sides of his neck as she leaned in to kiss him. Pushing her dark silky hair over one shoulder, she gave him a mischievous smile before pressing her lips to his. The kiss was slow and passionate. She was taking her time to savor every moment. She lightly nibbled, and let her tongue brush against his lips, before slipping into his mouth. A low growl escaped as he fought his animal need.

Rolling her over, he settled between her legs, then stared into her eyes for a moment, before gently capturing her mouth, slowly sucking in one lip then both, deepening the kiss. His mouth dusted kisses across her cheek to her ear. "You tell me when." His voice was a low rumble in his chest. Not being with a woman for so long had him already hanging by a thread, so he hoped she wouldn't wait long.

Propping himself on his forearms, he watched as her breast lifted with each breath. His lips brushed against her skin, down her neck, until he took her soft peak in his mouth, while his hand explored her body. A smile crept across his face when she moaned. With every sound she made, every jerk of her body, he fought the urge to ravage her. She felt so good, so soft, so perfect, and he couldn't believe she wanted him.

Writhing beneath him, she finally cried out, "Now. Oh please, now." He kissed her neck, then lifted his eyes to meet hers, and warmth shot through his chest, radiating through his entire body, from the need that filled her eyes.

Wrapping his hand around her hip, he slowly pushed inside her. The minute they were joined, his body shuddered at the way she felt wrapped around him. Her eyes closed, and she let out a soft whimper, and just the sweet sound of her pleasure had him stopping for a moment, trying to stave off the intensity of his need. He desperately wanted to take his time with her.

Her fingers skimmed his ribs, sending electric pings down his sides, and her eyes opened. Gazing directly into his, she chewed on her bottom lip and smiled, and he knew he was in trouble. There was something so different about her. An innocence in its purest form, yet she was sensual.

Capturing her mouth again, he knew, no matter how fake their relationship was, this would not be a one-time thing if he had a say in it. It couldn't. Once would never be enough.

He glanced at her. Her eyes had closed again, her cherry red lips were parted, and a rosiness filled her cheeks as her breaths came in short bursts. She was truly beautiful. He leaned down, placing gentle kisses on her cheek and in her hair, and rocked slowly, hoping to hold on for a little longer. His lips found hers once more, but Kaysi broke the kiss as her body went rigid, and then began to tremble. "Ben!" she cried out. Her back arched as her fingers dug into his sides, and he let her draw him over the edge.

****

Kaysi felt like her heart was going to beat out of her chest, as she played the previous night through her mind. This growly bear of a man had made love to her, over and over, until she was completely wrung out from exhaustion. It was early morning, and she knew Ben was going to have to leave in a little while to start his chores, but she just wanted a little while longer with him. Even though they had been up most of the night, she couldn't get enough of him.

After finally falling asleep in the wee hours of the morning she had awakened cold, from the winter wind that was seeping into the house. The fire in the fireplace, that had been adding a layer of warmth, had gone out hours ago, and the down comforter on the bed, was just not enough.

All she wanted to do was snuggle in his arms. She hesitated though, suddenly wondering what he thought of their night together. Their relationship was just supposed to be for show. Could he have been acting on impulse and nothing else? Nothing about last night felt fake to her. And when she gazed in his eyes while they were making love, she thought she saw something more. But right now, all she knew was, she was cold.

Testing the waters, she pressed her body to his. He jerked, obviously awakened from her movement, then wrapped his arms around her. "You're cold," he said in a low, gravelly voice, and brought the covers around them. His fingers softly grazed her back, warming her, lulling her nearly back to sleep. Then she felt his lips on her. First on her forehead, then neck, and shoulder. "Are you getting warm now?"

She could barely make out his silhouette, but she thought she saw a smile on his face. "Mm…yes." Lying there for a little while, she dozed in his arms, completely warm, but completely unsettled. What was really going on? Was this still just a charade to him, with a few added benefits?

It was probably obvious that she was attracted to him. She had been since the night at TopHops. She thought he might have felt the same way, but he threw her off when he was so rude to her the day she moved in. Since then, though, his antisocial shell had begun to crack. And the more it revealed, the more she was drawn to him.

She knew it was probably wrong to see what would happen if she accidentally, on purpose, had to get a little close to him while cutting his hair. But when he finally grabbed and kissed her, like a hungry wolf capturing its prey, it was not a game anymore, and sure as hell didn't feel fake. But was it out of a desperate need to satisfy a lust filled craving? If it was, he would have made quick work of their moment. Wouldn't he? He might have been a little rough and would have taken what he wanted without regard to her, just to let her know what her little game did to him.

But what he did was neither quick, nor rough. Every word, every touch, every kiss, was filled with a reverence that Malcolm never conveyed. It was a side of him that was so gentle, so vulnerable, it took her breath away. And he stayed. He could have gone home, but he didn't. What did it mean? Was he as drawn to her as she was to him?

Ben groaned and stirred, snuggling her in closer. "I need to get moving."

"It's barely five."

"I need to see how much snow we got and check on the livestock."

"Do you have time for me to make you some breakfast? I have an awesome recipe for waffles."

"Do you have all the stuff you need?"

"Actually, I picked some groceries up at the store the other day, so I'm pretty sure I do."

"Well, sure. I'll grab a quick shower. You do your thing."

"Okay." Kaysi started to move off the bed, but Ben grabbed her wrist and pulled her back down to him.

"I really enjoyed last night," he said, as his fingers gently brushed her cheek.

"Me too." That little flicker of hope, sparked. There was something more than a fling there. So much more.

His hand wrapped her neck, and his lips captured hers. His tongue slowly brushed hers in long languid strokes. *Lord I could stay here all day doing this and die a happy woman.* She slowly backed away and ran her fingers through his messy but awesome hair. It was her new favorite thing to do.

Hopping up, she threw on some leggings and a sweater, and traipsed up the hall into the kitchen. Grabbing bowls from the shelves, and ingredients from the pantry, she set everything on the counter, and dug through the cabinet for the waffle maker.

"Shit!"

Ben's booming voice, along with a loud thump, made Kaysi jump, then a smile bloomed on her face knowing he had finally seen her handywork. Sneaking down the hallway, she heard his laughter echoing from the bathroom. That was a good sign. She peeked through the door. His fingers were threading through his hair as he stared at himself in the mirror. After a moment his eyes found hers, and a smile filled his face.

Nervously chewing on her fingernail, she asked, "Do you like it?"

He turned facing her. "I honestly forgot, and I scared the shit out of myself when I flipped on the light and saw myself in the mirror. I thought there was someone else in here." Staring into the mirror again, he continued, "But, yeah, I do. I like it a lot."

"Really?" Her anxiety was replaced with excitement.

"Really." He reached up and rubbed his much shorter beard. "I mean, I have never…I look…"

"Hot," Kaysi finished.

Ben chuckled and brushed his hand in the air.

"Don't give me that."

"You do. I mean you've always been hot. I just enhanced it."

He reached out and grabbed her. "Thank you. This is seriously, the best haircut I've ever gotten." He planted a gentle kiss on her lips that had her insides melting.

"You're welcome." She gave him a wink. "I better go back and get your waffles going." She wandered back up the hallway and threw the ingredients together. Within minutes the house was filled with the smells of vanilla and coffee and Kaysi's stomach growled.

Ben appeared from around the corner, smelling of sweet cedar and leather, and had something gracing his face that was new. A big grin. Not just a courteous smile. A cheesy grin. She had forgotten, until then, that he had dimples. "How did I do with my hair?"

She couldn't resist running her fingers through it. "It seriously looks amazing. But hang on." She ran down the hall and grabbed one of the bags in the bathroom and dug through it. Finding a small purple container, she ran back up the hallway. "Take just a little bit of this and rub it in your hands until its warm, then just run your hands through your hair. It will help it stay in place a little better." She rubbed her hands together, then played in his hair for a minute. "Perfect."

"Oh. That smells good too."

"Yeah, it does." She paused a beat, wiping her hands on a towel. "Okay. I decided to make some sausage to go with your waffles."

"You're going to eat too, aren't you?" he questioned as he sat down.

"I wouldn't miss it. They're my favorite too."

"Good. I was worried you were going to feed me,

and not eat. Or drink some shake or something."

"Joe has gotten me to eat a little better, but I don't deny myself much. Been there done that. Got the T-shirt."

Ben's face filled with confusion, but it didn't last long when he shoved a pile of waffles in his mouth. "Oh. This is delicious," he said around his mouthful. "I haven't had pecan waffles in years. I would guess the last time I had them was when my mom made them."

It was obvious how much Ben's mom meant to him, and it broke Kaysi's heart, thinking about their conversation the night before. "You loved her a lot, didn't you?"

Ben's body immediately stiffened, and he leveled his eyes with her. "Kaysi, can this be something off limits? I just—"

"Sure." She knew it was a hard subject for him, so she was going to respect his wishes, but then he continued.

"But yes, I did," He started, and Kaysi was hopeful he would continue. "It just hurt that I wasn't there. That she didn't hang on until I could get back. She had held on for so long. It was just one more day. I felt like she was getting rid of me. Like she didn't love me enough to want me there."

Kaysi wasn't sure if she should say anything but the thought of his words, and the pain in his voice, left her no choice. "But you seriously can't believe she could make herself die at will."

He sighed as his eyes drifted.

"It just breaks my heart that you are hurting because of this." Kaysi stared at him, but he didn't make eye contact. "Ben. I have two brothers. I know what moms think of their sons. There is a special bond between them. Moms are the protector, while the dad is the one who makes them into a man. I watched it happen with Kaleb.

"My mom protected him from all his crazy antics when he was little, then protected him from my dad when he pushed too far. And I'm pretty sure your mom did the same. There is a special love there." She paused. "Have you ever thought, that, maybe, it wasn't that she didn't love you enough for you to be there, it was that she loved you too much, and didn't want you to go through watching her die?"

Ben stabbed his waffle, but then turned and stared out at the darkness through the window for a long moment. She had struck a chord. She could tell by the softening of his eyes. But she didn't know if he was about to throw her out or give her a hug. He slowly turned back to her, dredged his waffle in the syrup, and piled it in his mouth.

Tipping his cup of coffee up, he drained it, picked up his plate and cup, and set them in the sink. His silence worried her, but he didn't exactly seem angry like he did the night before, so she was hopeful. She picked her plate up, and walked behind him, to set it in the sink. He turned and wrapped his arms around her and pressed her into him.

"Thank you," he said, placing a peck on her forehead.

"Did you like it?"

"The waffles were the best I've had. But Kaysi, what you said…"

She prepared herself for the tongue lashing she figured was coming. "I'm sorry, I know you said leave it alone. I just—"

"Will you be quiet for one minute?" She could see a shimmer in his eyes and worried she had pushed him too far. "I was going to say, what you said about my mom was true. She was always there to protect me, and you are a lot like her. She never let things go if she thought I was upset. So, I appreciate that you care." With another peck to the top of her head, he released her, and she began to rinse the dishes.

Ben's response surprised Kaysi, and gave her goosebumps, just replaying the words "you are a lot like her" in her head, but she could see the sadness in his eyes. She figured she had broached the subject enough for the day, but hoped she had clawed her way into his trust enough that he would open up more later.

The creak of the door as Ben opened it, caught Kaysi's attention. "Well, that was unexpected," Ben said with humor lacing his words. "I was wondering why it was so dark." Kaysi couldn't quite see what he was talking about, so she shut off the water, and walked around the counter, to see him standing in front of a wall of snow.

"Oh my gosh." She had completely forgotten about the snowstorm that they had last night. "Are we snowed in?"

"I don't know. It's probably just drifted up against the front, since it faces north. I need to check the door out back." He disappeared up the hallway. She started rinsing the dishes again and putting them in the dishwasher. She didn't think anything of it when she heard the back door shut, until she felt the icy cold snow on her neck. Kaysi screamed and flipped around. Although she wanted to be mad, the playful boyish grin, and fits of laughter he couldn't contain, immediately dispelled any annoyance she had.

Chapter Eighteen

Ben had a sickening feeling in his gut, thinking about the charity dinner this evening. The whole event was not something he was accustomed to. All the fancy clothes, people putting on airs, and money being thrown around like it grew on trees, was way outside his wheelhouse. He was working class. His hands showed it, and he was proud of the hard work he had put in. He didn't relish the idea of people looking down their noses at him.

There was also the real danger, that someone didn't want them to be holding the charity dinner at all, since Kaysi had received several threatening comments on her blog. Sergeant Gallagher had recommended beefing up security for added safety. And on top of everything, Kaysi's brothers would be there. He hadn't had the guts to tell them that he was taking her. They were both well over six feet tall. Both worked out, and it showed. Not only was he taking their sister to the event, but he was going to be pretending he was her boyfriend. That part wasn't so bad. In fact, it was not bad at all, as long as the brothers didn't beat him to a bloody pulp.

The past couple of days had been...indescribable...and confusing. His days had suddenly become filled with added jobs. If he wasn't helping Joe with the construction at the store, he was trying to set up an assembly line for his artwork. That alone could have filled his day but didn't even take into account the addition of the extra work on the ranch because of the snowstorm. Kaysi had helped. She didn't bat an eye when he gave her directions on what needed to be done. It made the morning go by quickly and ended in a snowball fight...that he lost...on purpose. The afternoon was spent relaxing by the fire and revisiting the night before. When she curled up next to him on the sofa and nuzzled her face in his neck, he knew he didn't want to be anywhere else.

Kaysi had flipped his world upside down. The fake relationship should have never happened, because now his head was swimming with questions. Being with her had awakened something within him, and the relationship felt anything but fake to him. And he got the feeling Kaysi felt the same way. But he wasn't sure. He had only agreed to be her fake boyfriend through tonight, and he had no idea what would happen after the dinner was over.

He was so busy with his artwork, and working his ranch, and Poppi's, he really didn't have time to be in a real relationship, nor did he think he wanted one, but now it was hard for him to imagine going back to the way it was before Kaysi blew into his life. The more he was around her, the more he found himself smiling and laughing, especially when he surprised her with a snowball to the chest that literally knocked her over. With snow in her hair and stuck to her lashes, he couldn't stop himself from kissing her.

That was another problem. Every ounce of control he had went out the door when it came to her. No matter how hard he tried to keep his distance, he couldn't.

Something happened to him when he kissed her, touched her, and held her in his arms. She was a walking bottle of sunshine, and she beat back the darkness inside him. He let out a heavy breath and tried to wipe the smile from his face.

Heading up to the store, to help Joe install some baseboards in the loft, Ben thought about mentioning the fact that he would be taking Kaysi to the dinner. He hadn't found the right time to talk to him before, since Cody or Kaleb were usually working with them.

Even though Joe was intimidating, he was very laid back. Ben had never seen him lose his temper, except when it came to April. He was fiercely protective of her. But Ben hadn't been around Kaysi and Joe together enough to know how Joe would react, and that's what had him a little on edge.

Because Cody had some business to take care of at the gym, he and Joe would be the only ones working today, unless Kaleb showed up.

As Ben approached the store, he saw Joe retrieving some baseboards from his truck. Ben pushed his door open and hopped out. "Got anything else you need me to grab?" Ben hollered, trying to catch Joe before he entered the building.

"Nail gun. Passenger seat. Nails are next to it."

"Got it." Dropping his cowboy hat in his truck, he jogged over to Joe's, reached in, grabbed the supplies, and followed Joe inside. The building no longer had the stench of smoke lingering in the air. It was replaced with the overpowering scent of wood stain and new construction. Things were looking good. Joe started laying out the different pieces around the room while Ben watched.

"Damn. What the hell happened to you?" Ben studied himself, confused at Joe's comment, until he pointed at his hair.

"Kaysi gave me a haircut."

"Ah. For the charity dinner? You're taking Kaysi. Right?"

Ben's stomach dropped. *How the hell does he know.*

Like Joe heard his thought, or more likely saw his stunned expression, he said, "Girls talk, man."

"Yeah, they do."

"Thanks for the help by the way. I just wanted to get this finished up quickly, so I can go get ready."

"Nervous?"

"God yes. I think the last time I had to stand up in front of a group of people, and give a speech, was eighth grade history class." He let out a long sigh. "I'm glad April will be there. I can at least focus on her." Lifting a piece into place, he glanced back at Ben.

"Are..." Ben rubbed the back of his neck as he tried to push the words out of his mouth. "Are you okay with me taking your sister?"

"Yeah. I just thought she was dating Kaleb's buddy. The British guy."

"Malcolm?" Joe nodded. "She broke up with him and he's been kind of pestering her. So, I told her I would go with her to maybe get him to back off."

"Good. I mean, the guy is nice enough, I guess. He's just not right for her. There was something about the way Kaysi acted around him, that made me wonder if he was treating her well. She always seemed nervous." Motioning for Ben to grab a nail gun nearby, Joe pointed to locations he needed Ben to nail. "So, you are *just* her escort?"

Ben thought about how much he should say to Joe.

"The other night it seemed like you guys might be heating things up a little."

It suddenly felt like a furnace had lit under him. Heat shot through his body, and he could feel his cheeks catch fire.

A smirk engulfed Joe's face.

"Well, I was going—"

"Dude, it's fine. She's a grown woman. She can date whoever she wants. Kaleb might feel differently, but I doubt it. Yes, she is my sister. But honestly, I'm still getting to know her. I'm fine with you dating her. Why wouldn't I be? Just be good to her."

"Well, we aren't technically dating. I'm not quite sure what to call it. It was just supposed to be a way for her to get Malcolm to back off, but—"

"Whoa." Joe quickly put his hand up. "Just say you like her. I Don't need the sordid details. Don't really want that mental picture, since she *is* my sister."

"Got it." Ben let out an audible breath.

Joe furrowed his brow and shook his head. "Were you worried?"

"Hell yeah, I was worried. She's your sister and you have a good half a foot on me, and a black belt. Who wouldn't be worried?"

"Well, just know, if you break her heart, we might be revisiting this subject with a very different outcome."

"Duly noted."

****

Ben stepped through the door of the bunkhouse, unable to form words. Kaysi stood before him in a long sleeved, off the shoulder, ruby red embroidered gown, that accentuated every one of her curves. Her hair lay in

234

soft waves down her back. A slit on one side, showcased her tanned leg, that looked a million miles long in the red high heels she wore. After a minute, he realized Kaysi was staring at him, with the same staggered expression he imagined he had. "You look incredible."

"So do you," she said breathlessly. "Oh my gosh, Ben…"

Still unsure, he rubbed his beard and asked, "So, do you think the suit is okay? Will I stick out like a sore thumb?"

"Oh, you will. You will a lot. You're gorgeous. I'm not sure I want to take you anymore. Someone might steal you."

Ben laughed. "I was thinking the same thing about you in that dress. You could be Jessica Rabbit's twin."

"Oh. No way."

He curved one brow and nodded.

She giggled. "Then I guess we will be the hot couple tonight."

He chuckled. "So, Jessica, are you ready to go?"

She gathered the bottom of her dress in one hand, and her clutch in the other. Ben grabbed the coat she had set out, and after watching her nearly slip on her first step on the icy ground, he hoisted her into his arms, and carefully made his way to his truck. He had shoveled the snow earlier but with the cooler evening temperatures, it had become a solid sheet of ice. She slid into the passenger side, and he wondered how she was actually keeping that dress on, then fantasized about how easy it would be to get her out of it. *This is going to be a long night, if I have to stare at her in that dress the entire time.*

Climbing in, he paused for a moment, then turned to her. "I just realized I have no idea where I am going."

"Oh, yeah. That would be helpful. Wouldn't it? The Ballinger Hotel in Fayetteville. I have the address. Hang on."

"Is that the one downtown that they restored?"

"Yeah."

"I know where it is."

****

Entering the hotel, Ben felt like he stepped back in time. Everything spoke of days gone by. Grand staircases, rising left and right, stood before him, and added to the grandeur of the room. The nineteen twenties hotel had been restored to its former glory. No detail was left out. Even the dials above the elevator, moved with precision, as the cart arrived at the different floors.

Stepping off the elevator into the sea of high society, Kaysi squeezed Ben's hand and smiled. "Are you ready?"

"We're here, so it's a little late for me to back out now." But noticing all the tuxes and gowns, the thought of stepping back into the elevator, crossed his mind. Even though he knew several of his friends would be there, since Joe was well known in Dalton, he still felt out of place. Spying a bar in the corner, he leaned into Kaysi. "I'm going to get a drink. Do you want one?"

"Amaretto sour?"

"Remind me not to drink too much."

"Okay? Is it a problem?"

"I've been told I get kind of chatty. I don't want to embarrass myself, or you." He strolled to the bar and ordered their drinks. Scanning the crowd for a familiar face, his attention was drawn back to Kaysi and that dress, and fire smoldered in his gut. But the feeling was quickly extinguished, and replace with irritation, when he saw who was standing with her. Malcolm. *He couldn't even wait five minutes?* Joe's comment rang in his head. He wasn't right for her. Her arms were crossed as she faced him, and the sweet smile was absent from her lips. Ben agreed with Joe, but Ben wasn't sure he was right for her either. She was so…beautiful. In the truest sense of the word.

He strolled back in Kaysi's direction, trying to act nonchalant. His eyes locked with hers, and the smile reappeared. He liked that he had that effect on her. Handing her the drink, he then turned to Malcolm. The guy was tall but had a thin frame. Ben figured he could take him in a fight. He nodded, "Malcolm," then snaked his arm around Kaysi's back.

"Ben. You cleaned up nicely. I barely recognized you," Malcolm stated, in his thick British accent that added to the condescending tone of his remark and made Ben stiffen. Malcolm turned back to Kaysi, and the polite tone disappeared. "I can't believe you said something to her." Ben realized, in that moment, Malcolm was pissed about something.

"Malcolm, I'm sorry," Kaysi replied. "She said she was going to talk to you about going together, after we broke up. I simply told her I didn't have a problem with it."

"She has been annoying the hell out of me. I don't like her, Kaysi. I wouldn't agree to go with her if she were the last woman on earth."

"She likes you."

"You think?" Malcolm's voice rose an octave. "She is a ticking time bomb."

"She's not that bad, Malcolm. Yes, she can be a little high strung—"

"I see I am the subject of your discussion again." Ben turned at the sound of a nasally female voice. "Kaysi, when are you going to let Malcolm go. He can make his own decisions about me."

"Libby, I didn't—"

"Shut. Up. Kaysi. I'm done. You've been a pain in my ass since we met. All I ever did was try to protect you. I even helped you with your stupid blog, and what did you do to me? Stabbed me in the back. I don't know why I ever wanted to be your friend. You've done nothing but sabotaged me at every turn." Heads turned. Libby threw her drink on Kaysi and stormed away. Malcolm raised one brow with an "I told you so," and Ben could see the horror spreading over her sweet face when she noticed all the attention was on her. He wrapped her into his arms as tears began to glisten in her eyes.

A thought crossed his mind to go after Libby, and set her straight about what happened, but he wasn't sure that was what Kaysi wanted, and knew it wasn't what she needed. He stroked her hair and kissed the top of her head, then lifted his eyes to see a perplexed look on Malcolm's face. He gave him a half-hearted smile. Glancing back down at Kaysi, he noticed tears still wetting her cheeks. As he wiped them away, he asked, "What do you need me to do, babe?"

"Nothing. I'm done." She stepped back and dabbed at her cheeks. Noticing Malcolm still standing next to them she turned to him. "I'm truly sorry, Malcolm."

"It wasn't your fault, Kaysi." He picked up the empty glass on the floor, shoved a hand in his trousers, and walked away.

"I'm going to go to the restroom and clean up."

Ben nodded and let her leave.

Glancing around the room at all the silent auction items, he strolled closer, curious as to how much money the charity dinner brought in. He thought about Poppi and the wild horses and how much, even an event on a smaller scale, would help.

Out of the corner of his eye, he saw someone approaching quickly, and he turned. Jenna stopped dead in her tracks, her eyes widened to the size of saucers. "Ben. Oh my gosh. You look amazing."

One corner of his mouth lifted. "Thanks," he offered, embarrassed by the production she was making. Cody strolled up and gave him an approving once over. Holding out his hand to Cody's, Ben said, "I didn't know if you were going to make it. I thought you were on call this weekend?"

Cody had been working toward getting his Paramedic Certification for over a year, after deciding against the police academy, which his dad had suggested. "I am. But since I'm still finishing up my classes, I haven't been put on full rotations, so I have a little more flexibility with my schedule."

The doors to the ballroom opened. Champagne colored tablecloths covered the tables with black napkins sitting on gold plates. Small flower arrangements, in assorted pink colors, were in glass vases as the centerpieces. A band played as people milled around, finding their seats.

Ben noticed Kaysi as she approached, still appearing a bit shaken. He hated when she didn't have the light in her eyes. Leaning over, he put his lips to her ear. "You okay?

"I'm fine." But he knew, by her tone, she wasn't.

"You didn't do anything wrong, sweetheart."

Tears glistened in her eyes.

"Do you want to leave?"

She paused, for a moment, then pushed her shoulders back. "No. I'm not going to let her tantrum ruin our evening."

Ben draped his arm around her shoulder and pinned her to his side. Leaning down, he drank in her scent and pressed a kiss into her hair. "That's my girl."

Strolling into the ballroom, Ben was introduced to Kaysi's parents, and a few others whose names didn't stick. Scanning the room, he located Joe and April, Cody and Jenna, Brant and his wife Bekah, and Mitch and his new girlfriend, Jessi. Kaleb passed them, heading for the bar, and Ben again noticed something off about his demeanor. He had known Kaleb for a little over a year, and he always had a goofy, life of the party, attitude. He was high energy and walked around with his head in the clouds most of the time. But for the last month, something seemed off about him. He barely spoke when he passed.

Kaysi laced her fingers with Ben's, and tugged him toward their table, but Ben turned his head when he heard a familiar laugh. A slender blond was walking away from him, with a guy with dark hair and a beard. *It can't be*. His gut soured when he confirmed who it was. Valerie. But the guy with the beard definitely wasn't Rick. He slid out Kaysi's chair and then unbuttoned his jacket before sitting down. Kaysi glanced at him, confused.

"What's wrong?"

"Valerie is here."

Kaysi's eyes widened. "Seems we are in the same

boat."

"At least yours is fairly open about his intentions."

"Oh, I think Valerie was pretty obvious about what she wanted."

"True. But from what I just witnessed; I think she found someone else. Maybe she'll leave us alone."

The microphone gave an ear-piercing squeal, and all eyes went to the stage. The band had ended their set, and Joe stood front and center, with panic etched across his face. His eyes scanned the crowd of people as they continued to quickly take their seats. April smiled up at him, and he took a deep breath then addressed the crowd. "Hello." His smooth voice rang loudly through the sound system, and he backed away, rubbing his hands together. "Thank you all for coming tonight."

Ben adjusted his chair, feeling the nervous energy Joe was emitting.

"This dinner, as you know, was organized to raise money and awareness for the National Center for Missing and Exploited Children. A staggering, eight hundred thousand children, under the age of twenty-one, go missing in the US every year. That's over two thousand a day. And as many as one hundred fifteen are considered "stranger abductions." The Grayeagle family has supported this organization for many years.

"My name is Kameron Joseph Cortez-Grayeagle. A little over a year ago, I was only known as Joe Cortez, the son of Tony and Gloria Cortez. I had no idea that I was adopted. I admit, I was a little taken aback to find that information out. But thousands of kids are adopted every day. There was only one problem with mine. It was a fraud. My parents were scammed. You see, I was one of those one hundred fifteen. I was kidnapped. Held for a ransom. And when things didn't go as planned, Charlie and Tamara Grayeagle were told their newborn son had been killed. I hadn't been killed. I had been sold.

"I can't imagine what they went through, or what anyone, who has had their child taken, goes through. For me, I was lucky. I was sold to a family that couldn't have loved me more, and about a year ago, when my true identity was discovered, I gained a second set of parents, who love me just as much, along with two siblings that drive me absolutely crazy."

"Yeah, right back at'cha, buddy," Kaleb shouted, and the crowd burst into laughter.

"That would be my little brother, Kaleb. He's a special kind of annoying." The crowd laughed again, and Joe glanced at Ben and Kaysi, and then Kaleb, and chuckled. "But I wouldn't have it any other way. The truth is, though, for many families, they won't have a happy ending like mine. The number of kids who are lost to human traffickers is going up. Tonight, is your chance to help us take steps to combat this horrible crime, so no family has to feel the crushing pain of losing a child. Your donations will go to state-of-the-art technology to help find missing children, take down human trafficking rings, and child predators, and implement programs to protect our kids." The crowd erupted in applause, and one by one stood. Joe returned a bashful smile. April clutched her chest when his eyes found her. "Thank you again for coming and donating, I hope you enjoy your evening."

Joe made his way off the stage as the applause continued. Soft music played through the speakers and Joe joined Ben, Kaysi, April, Kaleb, Mr. and Mrs. Grayeagle, Mr. and Mrs. Cortez, Cody, and Jenna.

"You did a great job," Kaysi piped up with a smile, as Joe sat down.

"Geez, I felt like I stumbled through every word."

Dinner was served, and the conversation flowed. Ben was surprised at how comfortable he felt. Making eye contact with Kaleb, he knew, by the smirk on his face, he was okay seeing him with Kaysi, and from the comments made from her parents, he felt fairly confident they were too. Kaysi excused herself, and took the stage, auctioning off several larger items that had been donated, and Ben was astonished at the amount of money being offered. After the rest of the Grayeagle family joined Kaysi on stage for a few photos, she made it back to her seat, and Ben whispered in her ear. "You did great." The way she smiled, with her bright blue eyes glittering, put a sting in his chest, and immediately made his whole body warm.

"I was so surprised at the bids," she said with such excitement, he couldn't hold back his smile.

"Do you want something to drink? I'm running to the restroom and then making a stop by the bar."

"A sparkling water with lime?"

"Got it." He excused himself from the table and headed to the restroom.

As he stood in line for the drinks, he felt a hand on his shoulder, and instinctively knew it wasn't Kaysi. Immediately jerking away, he turned. Valerie. "What the hell are you doing here?"

"Well, hello to you too. Having a good time?" Valerie purred.

"I was. I see you found another man you can sink your claws into?" he said, noticing the man from earlier disappearing around the corner.

"Geez, Ben. You don't have to be rude. He's just a friend I ran into."

"I'm sure Rick would love to meet him."

"It's completely innocent. He showed up alone, and so did I. We're just catching up. Anyway, I don't care how Rick feels."

"He's not here?"

"He hates charity events."

"Did you tell him where you were going?"

"No. I told you we're separated."

"Not sure he got that memo yet. But you know what? Not my problem. Now, if you don't mind—"

He turned to leave and heard her voice from behind him. "God, Ben. You've changed."

"It's just a haircut."

"No. I mean, you've changed. You 're so angry."

He turned again to face her. "Oh, I'm sorry. Maybe I should have smiled and waved as you left with that asshole, when you were engaged to me."

Valerie's head swiveled. Ben couldn't care less who heard him.

"I told you I was sorry."

Ben rolled his eyes and began to walk away.

"So, is it serious…between you and *her*?"

"It's none of your damn business, Valerie."

"You do know who she is, right?"

Again, he turned back to her. "What do you think? Now, again, if you don't mind, I would like to get back to *her*, not stand here making chitchat with you."

"No. I mean, do you really know her? Her family owns Grayeagle Oil and Gas. They are mega rich."

He let out an audible sigh, trying to stave off the anger boiling in his gut. "Yeah. I know. Just because

244

they're rich, doesn't mean they aren't nice people. What did you do, stalk Kaysi on her social media?" He paused. "Is that why you came? To spy on the family."

"I had to make sure she was good for you."

Ben's thread of self-control was quickly unraveling. "Bullshit, Valerie."

"Whatever you think, Ben. I just want you to be happy."

"If that were true, you would leave me alone and go back to your rich husband or that play toy you brought."

"I made a mistake."

"I tried to tell you that when you left me. It didn't seem to make a difference though. All you saw were dollar signs."

"He lost the money."

"Your problem, not mine. All I know is, whatever game he is playing with Poppi and his land, needs to stop."

"I know exactly what he's doing. He needs the money he can get out of the land. He got caught with his hand in the cookie jar, and his dad found out. His dad was in the process of trying to fix it when the accident happened."

Ben stopped dead in his tracks. Was she telling the truth? "You don't think Rick had anything to do with the accident, do you?"

"That was part of the reason I left and came back to Dalton."

"What do you mean?"

"Once we were back in St. Louis, he immediately started talking about how great things were going to be, now that he had his dad's company and the inheritance. He said we were going to travel and buy a big house, and yeah, I guess I got caught up in all of it. When we got married though, I noticed things were obviously not going well with the company. Rick was always on edge, and I was beginning to wonder if he had a drug problem, from the way he was acting. Then one morning I saw his computer sitting on the bar, where he had been working the night before. I glanced at what he was working on, and it was obvious the company was in trouble. And, of course, he caught me.

"He said he had made a mistake and was trying to fix it. He told me the whole sob story, that his dad found a financial discrepancy in one of the big companies Rick was working with and called him on it. He said it was a rookie mistake and after they'd talked, his dad offered to help him fix it, but then he had the accident.

"Ben, he's already blown through his inheritance trying to 'fix' the problem. I think he's hiding the money and using the 'mistake' as an excuse. The money should be there, but it's not. He said there wasn't as much of the inheritance money as he thought, and the company isn't even his. His dad gave the company to his partner.

"He's going after Poppi's land now. Banking on that land to get us out of the hole he's dug. He thinks the land is very valuable."

"Yeah. It is to Poppi. And Rick is trying to rip it out from under him." He paused. He hated to say it, but she had his attention. "Do you really think Rick had something to do with his dad's death?" She darted her eyes away, and her silence spoke volumes. "Valerie, if you know something you better damn well tell me. I don't want Poppi getting hurt."

"I can't prove anything. He's been quiet about it, like he's hiding something. And it has him panicked. The way he spoke about his dad, and the inheritance, and now Poppi's land; it's all about the money.

"Like someone else I know."

Valerie's eyes narrowed. The glare she gave Ben let him know his remark hit its target. "You know, Ben, she is just playing house with you. You can't think this is going to last. She is worth millions. She will lose interest in playing on your ranch soon enough. Everybody likes what money can buy and will do just about anything to keep it when they have it."

"Like you did?"

"God, Ben. I made a mistake. Let it go." She stepped up to him, to where her toes were nearly touching his shoes. "You know I'm better for you. We were made for each other."

"And that's why you dumped me, at the first opportunity, for someone with money. What kind of game are you playing, Valerie?"

"It's not a game. Rick's evil and will stop at nothing to get what he wants. I'm sorry I hurt you. I realize now I walked away from the only man I've ever loved."

"Bullshit. You don't love me. The only thing you love is the almighty dollar. You want me, because now you can't have me. Newsflash, Valerie. You didn't make a mistake. As much as it hurt, you did me a huge favor by leaving me. We didn't love each other. We never did. I see that plain as day, now."

"How can you say that, Ben?"

"If you loved me, it wouldn't have been so easy for you to leave me. You treated me like I was a one-night stand. Think about it, Valerie. I was never what you wanted. We were just meeting each other's lust filled needs."

"So, you didn't love me?"

"No. I didn't."

"How do you know?"

"Because I know what it is...now." As the words left his mouth, he was in disbelief that they came out so easily. Kaysi had shown him what love truly was, in everything she did. Every time she was with him, it was like nothing else mattered to her, except making him happy. And now, all he wanted to do was make her happy. But could he really be falling for her so quickly?

Valerie's lips pursed, and her eyes darkened. "Mark my words. She is just playing you. There is no way you are what she really wants. She is a city girl. A socialite. Plus, this would become your life, the charity dinners and social gatherings. Would you be good with that?"

"Well, I guess I will find out, won't I." Valerie opened her mouth but before she could speak, Ben finished with, "I am done with this conversation."

He turned and locked eyes with the bartender. "Sparkling water with lime and a gin and tonic...make it a double." Valerie's words took over his thoughts. Could Rick have had something to do with his dad's accident? Was Poppi in danger? And as much as he wanted to brush the rest away, Valerie's other comment haunted him. Was Kaysi just playing him? He returned to the table, but the questions kept coming, to the point he wanted to scream. He had no idea how to solve any of them. After he finished the first drink, he ordered another, and then another, trying to get her out of his head, and enjoy the night. By the time the evening was over, and goodbyes were said, the alcohol hit him.

"I'm thinking you are going to need to drive. My head is a little swimmy." He dug the keys from his pocket and swayed as he handed them to Kaysi. She grabbed his arm to steady him, and they headed to the elevator.

"Are you okay?"

"Yeah. Just a bit tipsy."

"No. I mean, you seemed…I don't know…preoccupied when you came back from the bar."

He hadn't wanted to tell her about Valerie, but for some reason the words started spilling out. "Valerie caught me at the bar." He grabbed on tight to the railing as the elevator started to move. "Sssshhee said Rick might have had something to do with his dad's death. I'm really worried about Poppi. I knew Rick was dangerous."

"What are you going to do?"

The questions kept rolling around in his head and he couldn't focus. "I don't know. I got to protect him."

"What else did she say?"

His eyes darted to Kaysi, and he swayed as the alcohol's effects continued to set in. "Geez. I didn't think I drank that much. That bartender must have made them extra strong." Kaysi stared at him. Her face filled with concern, and his chest tightened. "She said you would leave me. I don't want that to happen."

"I don't want it either. Why would she say that?"

"She said you…" his thoughts trailed off as the elevator doors opened. "…she said you…" he stopped in the middle of the lobby and put his hands on his hips. "I don't know what I was saying."

"You said Valerie said I would leave you."

"I don't want that."

"Why did she say that though?"

"She said…oh yeah, that's what I was saying. She said you would get tired of me, and life on the ranch, because you are a soci…soshhh…lite. You're rich. She said I wouldn't be able to keep you happy, and you would leave, like she did." His jaw clenched with the words.

"You've made me happy so far."

"I have? Even when I yelled at you?"

"Well, maybe not then so much, but I did cause you to panic, so I understand. But I had fun riding horses with you and playing in the snow."

"You didn't act like you were having fun when that snowball knocked you down."

"You threw that one a little hard."

"I'm sorry. I didn't mean to."

"I know." She paused. "But you do make me happy. Especially when I know you are happy. I've seen you smile so many times these past couple of days, and that makes me happy."

"You make me happy, Kaysi."

They got in the truck and Ben grabbed the seat belt but couldn't seem to get it snapped. Kaysi giggled at his exasperated expression and reached over to help.

"You are pretty cute when you're drunk."

"I'm not drunk."

"Uh huh." She shifted into reverse and started backing out.

"I told Valerie I never loved her."

"How do you know?"

"I know what love feels like now." Ben bit down on his lip as a smile tried to spread across his face, and his head lolled over toward Kaysi. She was trying to stifle one of her own. *Geez, I probably should have kept that to myself at least a little longer. Oh well.* "You're really beautiful."

"You've said that."

"Because you are. My mom said anyone can be attractive with enough money, but beauty is a gift of the soul that shines outward. It's only given to a chosen few. You are here to bring beauty to the world." His head felt heavy as he turned to watch the road. "My mom said a lot of good stuff."

"Yes, she did, and thank you." Her hand patted his leg. "That's very sweet."

He picked her hand up and brought it to his lips. "There's never a time I don't notice you. It's imposssssible." His head leaned against the seat and turned to her. "Especially tonight. Everybody noticed you. Hell, it's hard for me to think of anything but you. You've even invaded my dreams."

"I dream about you too."

"You do?" He let go of her hand and reached up to run his finger along her cheek. "You are like a work of art. Perfectly placed colors and pieces that come together to create a masterpiece."

"Wow. Coming from you, that is a big compliment."

Kaysi stopped in front of the house. Ben threw open the door and swayed as he tried to get out, but the seatbelt was holding him in.

"Need some help?"

"Nope." He wrestled with the seatbelt and finally got it unbuckled. "I got it." Slowly sliding out of the seat, he stood for a minute before closing the door. "Just a little dizzy." Kaysi chirped the fob and met him at the front of the truck. He draped his arm over her shoulder and stumbled up the steps. Plunging his hand into his coat pocket to retrieve his keys and unlock the door, he came up empty. He patted his pockets on his coat, then his pants, and panic tore through him.

"What are you hunting for?"

"My keys," he said desperately.

She held them up and smiled.

"Oh yeah."

Once inside, he kicked his shoes off at the door and shucked his jacket. Kaysi grabbed a glass of water and handed it to him.

"Drink this."

"Why?"

"It will help clear your head."

Ben was confused, but he took the glass and chugged half, before falling backward onto the sofa, and spilled the rest onto himself. "Shit!" Standing quickly, he swayed as he brushed the water and ice off. Kaysi came with a towel and started toweling him off. He wheezed a laugh and said, "This seems vaguely familiar," then grabbed ahold of her arms and leaned in for a kiss. "That's what I wanted to do to you that night at TopHops. I didn't even know you, but the minute I touched your skin, I wanted to kiss you."

"I wanted you too."

Valerie's words echoed in his head. "She's going to get tired of you. She's going to leave." A sudden ache slammed into his chest with the thought of her leaving. "Stay with me tonight."

"I don't know if that would be—"

"Please. I'll be a good boy. I promise. We don't have to do anything if you don't want to. Just stay with me."

"I'll need to go get me some pajamas."

"I've got something you can wear." Tears burned his eyes as desperation set in. "Just…please…don't leave. Everybody leaves me."

"Okay, Ben. I won't leave you." The ache subsided, and he tightened his arms around her. "I love you, Kaysi."

"Let me get you some more water." She patted his chest and wandered off to the kitchen.

He plopped on the sofa only to feel the wet cushion under him. "I'm going to go change."

Ben felt Kaysi yanking at his pants and it caused a snort to escape, wondering what she was doing. Then he realized he was lying on the bed. Desire filled him and he pulled her down on top of him. They were nose to nose, and he smiled. "You make me happy." His chin tipped up, and he got just a taste of her before she backed away.

"Ben. No. I'm just getting you ready for bed, sweetie. Maybe later when your head is a little clearer." She shimmied his pants off him, draped them over a chair, then took his socks off. He liked having her hands on him, so he threw his arms over his head. "Have your way, my lady." She unbuttoned the rest of the buttons he missed on his shirt, slid it off, then shoved his legs under the covers.

After a few minutes, he felt the bed give and knew she was there. Reaching out, he grabbed her and snuggled her close. "Thanks for staying." He kissed her forehead, and she settled in his arms.

Chapter Nineteen

Kaysi woke to Ben's warm calloused hand gently stroking her belly and then moving higher to her breast. It took everything within her not to let him have his way with her last night, when he grabbed her, and now he was fanning the flame that didn't go out. She rolled over to face him and opened her eyes. Still dark, it took a moment for her eyes to adjust, to see him staring at her. "What time is it?" Her voice was hoarse from the cold night air, and she cleared it. His fingers threaded through her hair.

"Early," Ben said, dragging her closer and kissing her on the forehead. Her hand skimmed his side, and he flinched. "Tickles."

Wondering if he was still a little drunk, she asked, "How's your head? I put some aspirin and water on the table if you need it."

"It's fine. Sorry about last night. Valerie just—"

She scooted up and flipped on the side lamp, so she could see his face. He flinched, and squinted his eyes, but then sat up. "Why are you sorry? I found drunk Ben to be rather adorable. Does he come out to play very often?"

"No. I try to keep him locked in the deep dark recesses of my dungeon. Drunk Ben shares entirely too much information, and I'm not sure I remember everything Drunk Ben shared last night."

Kaysi's thoughts drifted back to the conversation they had, and a smile played on her lips. "What do you remember?"

"I don't know. What did I say?"

"You said Valerie told you I would get tired of you."

"Yeah. She was trying to get in my head." All his comments replayed loudly in her thoughts. She knew he was drunk. But how much of it was the alcohol making him drop his guard and speak what was in his heart? There was no doubt about her feelings for him. Her soul had a history with Ben. A life changing moment in time that it never forgot. The minute she recognized who he was, her heart remembered. She knew she was falling for him but, with his issue with women, she didn't know where she stood with him. "She said you would leave me just like she did."

"What did you say to her?"

"I told her that leaving me was the right thing for her to do, because I never loved her."

Kaysi's body started to tingle. "And then?"

Ben smirked. "Didn't I tell you all this last night."

"Yeah. I just wondered if you remembered everything." From the expression on his face, he knew what she was doing. She could tell he remembered, but she wanted him to say it.

He quickly slid her under him, then his legs rubbed against hers. Lifting the covers, he searched under them, then peered up at her and the corner of his mouth lifted. "You are wearing my pajama bottoms.

She pinched back a giggle. "You said you had something I could wear. I told you I wanted some of the fuzzy pajama bottoms, and I found them on the floor and thought, why not wear them when I have the chance." Ben's face went to her neck, and he chuckled. "This is your T-shirt too. I like it because it smells like you."

"Doesn't it stink?"

"No. I got it out of the drawer. It's clean, but it still smells like you." His lips pressed against her neck. "So, what did you tell Valerie?"

Ben raised up on his elbows. "I wasn't drunk when I talked to her, you know. I started drinking after that, because she pissed me off."

"I know."

Placing a light kiss to her lips, he said, "I told her we were never in love, because I now know what love is." A rush of electricity spread through Kaysi's body. *Did he mean it? Or was he just saying it because he knew it would piss Valerie off?*

"Can I ask you something?"

"Sure." He kissed her neck again.

"Did you say it to just piss her off? Because…" her chest tightened, and her eyes began to sting just thinking about how she would feel if he said yes.

"What do you think?"

"I'm not sure. You said you swore off women, and that is a very big problem for me."

"Why is that?"

She felt a tear wet her cheek and a knot form in her throat. Would she be able to say it? *God, what if he doesn't feel the same way.* "Because…I think I'm falling in love with you." It came out almost a whisper, but she said it.

His blue eyes studied her for a minute, and her breath stalled. Then a smile spread across his face, and he laughed. "Oh yeah?" She nodded hesitantly. He moved up and pressed his lips to hers. "Kaysi, I said it, because I've never met anyone like you. You are so selfless. So genuine. You are kind to everyone. It's like you see into people's souls and know what they need to make them smile, and you provide it. All you want is to make others happy. You make me happy."

"I do?"

Ben slowly nodded, then leaned down and kissed her. "I remember something else I said in my drunken state," he said with his lips still pressed to hers.

"Oh yeah? What's that?"

"That I love you." She opened her mouth to respond but he continued. "And yes, I was drunk, but in that moment, I knew exactly what I was saying. And I meant it." Everything disappeared except him. Her lips parted and she slowly wrapped her legs around his back and crushed his body to hers as their tongues waged war against each other.

It was like a dam broke. His hands and mouth were everywhere, pushing at her shirt, kissing her neck, caressing her soft skin and sending sparks everywhere he touched.

Her fingers threaded through his hair as her body trembled from his onslaught of hungry kisses. Ben nipped and sucked his way down her belly, his hands pushing at her pants until she could kick them off. Giving her one quick kiss to her hip, he lifted her up just enough to remove the T-shirt and toss it to the floor. His blue eyes met hers, and a boyish grin spread across his face. That smile was her kryptonite. She was powerless against it. He might be thirty now, but in that moment, he was that eighteen-year-old boy who saved her life.

Lying there, with his body keeping her warm, she

was desperate for him. She needed the connection. Her hands skimmed the top of his underwear. His hand met hers and he took over, quickly removing them. Before she could take a breath, his naked body was pressed against hers, and the onslaught of kisses resumed. Kaysi closed her eyes, drinking in the feel of his lips on her. Wrapping her fingers in his hair, she let him drive her wild for a moment, then it was her turn.

She rolled him off her and crawled on top. His eyes grew big, and he let out a strained groan as her mouth traveled down his chest to his stomach. His body twitched beneath her with every kiss. Her fingers danced over his skin until his hand gripped her bicep and yanked her to him. Digging his fingers into her hair, he pushed it out of her face as he brought her mouth to his in a hungry kiss. "I need you, now," he growled and rolled her over, dragging her beneath him again. His eyes connected with hers. She searched his now deep, blue gaze. There was something there, more than desire, more than hunger. He needed her, but it was more than just now. Despite the physical craving they had for each other, his expression said more. It was the same one he had the night before, when he begged her to stay.

He moved off her and searched for his pants. Digging in his pocket, he removed his wallet.

"You don't have to use that if you don't want to."

His eyes widened with surprise.

"I'm on the pill."

"I haven't been with anyone without protection."

"Not even Valerie?"

"No."

"I trust you, Ben."

He pinched back a smile as the packet fell from his

fingers to the floor, and he slid back under the blankets. Her arms wrapped his neck, and her lips found his. She wanted him. Needed him, like she needed her next breath. God, she would never get enough of him. This. This was what she had dreamed of. She dusted kisses down his jaw to his ear, and she whispered, "I love you, Ben."

He leaned back and gave her that perfect dimpled smile, then pressed his lips to hers as he sank into her. Kaysi broke the kiss with a gasp. Her fingertips dug into his skin in response to the electric charges sparking throughout her body.

His movements were slow, deliberately drawing out every ounce of torturous pleasure. With each motion her breaths came quicker. Cries and moans escaped unexpectedly.

Ben propped himself on one elbow and moved her hair out of her eyes. "Say it again, Kaysi." His eyes begged her.

A smile played on her lips. "I love you," she said breathlessly.

Letting out a growl, his hand wrapped her cheek, and his lips captured hers, as he plunged deeper, claiming her, once and for all, as his.

She had to be, because no one would be able to love her like him. No one would ever be able to make her feel the way he made her feel. Every piece of the puzzle had finally fallen into place.

His hand moved down her body gently stroking her smooth skin, touching her in places that sent her into a frenzy, and bringing her closer to the release she was desperate for. Her breaths came in short staccato bursts. She could feel her body begin to surrender, then a blinding strike ripped through her. Her head slammed into the pillow, and she let out a primal scream as Ben coaxed wave after wave of pleasure from her.

His lips pressed to her ear, and he whispered, "That's my girl," then plunged into her over and over, ramping up the ecstasy each time, leaving her delirious with pleasure. Pressing deep into her, he held tight. His eyes locked with hers as his body tightened and jerked, and a strained groan escaped with his release.

Gasping for air, and drenched in sweat, she rested her head back on the pillow dragging him with her.

Ben pressed his lips to hers, with a kiss that had so much emotion behind it, tears stung her eyes. He gently brushed another to her nose, and his eyes bore into her as he rolled off her. Her body immediately felt the chill of the room, and she tugged at the covers to stave off the cold.

Dragging her to him, his chest still heaving, trying to settle his pulse, Ben wrapped his arm around her, and snuggled her into him. Kissing her shoulder, he said, "Well, that was nice," every word laced with chuckles.

Kaysi playfully swatted him.

"What? It was."

She shot him a "really" look, and he gave in.

"Okay, maybe nice isn't the right word." He tightened his arm and rolled her to him, then placed a tender kiss on her forehead. "Something more like otherworldly?"

She giggled. "Better." Her fingers traced a line up and down his chest and stomach. "Tell me again."

"What? That was some mind-blowing sex. Best I've ever had."

"No."

"What? Yes, it was."

"No. I mean, I agree—"

"Oh good, because I was getting worried."

"Stop. That's not—"

"Oh. You mean the part where I said...I love you, Kaysi?"

"Yeah."

He kissed her softly.

"That part. I like when you say that."

He kissed her again. "I like when you scream." He captured her mouth and took the kiss deeper. His fingers played in her hair, and he pressed his body to hers.

"Can we stay like this all day? It's cold out there."

His finger pushed strands of hair out of Kaysi's eyes again. "I wish we could. The good thing is, Dad is taking care of everything this morning, so we can stay right here for a little while longer."

"What else do you have to do today?"

"I need to go over and check on Poppi, and then I thought we could hook up the trailer and pick up all the junk you found in the house."

"It's not junk." Ben's mouth thinned, and he tipped his head, telling her he didn't believe her. "You'll see. You might even find something you could use. But I don't know that you and I can move everything."

"I'll get Cody or Joe to help us." He scooted up in the bed and grabbed the bottle of aspirin she had set there the night before. He shook out a couple and popped them in his mouth, then drank a swallow of water.

"I thought you said your head was fine."

"I meant I wasn't still drunk. Anyway, you wouldn't have let me have my way with you if I told you my head felt like someone ran over it."

Kaysi giggled, "No, probably not." She scooted up next to him and brushed his lips with hers. "Would it help if I made you some breakfast?"

"I've got some bacon and eggs in there."

"Consider it done." She started to slide off the bed, but he grabbed her.

"Don't leave." The plea in his voice reminded her of the night before. He sounded so wounded when he begged her not to leave.

"I'll never leave you, Ben," she said and leaned in to kiss him. "I don't care what Valerie told you."

"What else did I say last night?"

She sat back and thought. "Well, you said I was beautiful, like a work of art."

"You are." He paused. "Did I say anything else?"

"You definitely didn't want me to leave." A shadow fell over his face, and it again reminded her of the pain in his voice the night before. "It's okay. I didn't mind."

"I'm sorry."

Her hands wrapped his face. "There is nothing to be sorry for. You were adorable."

"I drank quite a bit when my mom died, and Valerie left. It all happened at once, and it was just hard to handle alone."

"I can imagine." Silence took over for a moment then Ben kissed the top of her head and spoke quietly. "I thought about what you said."

Kaysi searched her brain trying to figure out what he might be referring to.

"Honestly, I was kind of relieved when Mom told me to go to the auction. I didn't want to go, but I didn't want to be there when it happened. It was tearing me apart. And when Dad called to tell me she was gone, I was so mad at myself for being such a coward."

"Oh my gosh. How can you say that? No one wants to watch someone they love die. I can't even imagine what it would be like. You weren't a coward. When something like that happens, you do what you can to get through it, because that is all you can do. You were helping your family out by going to the auction. You gave your dad piece of mind, that the financial burden was taken care of, and he wouldn't have to leave her."

"It was just—"

"An impossible situation, that you did the best you could to get through." Kaysi snuggled in next to him, and he draped his arm around her.

"And then Valerie—"

"Was not who you were supposed to be with." She crawled over on top of him and grabbed the sides of his face. "Now. Why don't I go make you some bacon and eggs?" she questioned, trying to get his mind off the depressing stuff.

His eyes twinkled and a smile broke out across his face. "Well—" Their lips met, and she let out a moan, "— I'm not quite finished with you in here yet."

****

It was still early when they got the horses saddled up and Ben made his rounds on Poppi's land. The sky was filled with white puffy clouds and the snow was quickly melting from the warmer temperatures. Ben had called Joe, who planned to meet them at the bunkhouse a little later. They just needed to inform Poppi what their plans were.

The dots of snow across the landscape of pines made a beautiful setting, and Kaysi was enjoying the ride and excited to see Poppi again.

Ben rapped his knuckles on the back door when they arrived. Poppi answered and stopped short with his mouth hanging open. "Do I know you?" His eyes darted to Kaysi, and he winked. "I recognize your partner in crime."

Ben rolled his eyes, but grinned. "She got the sheers after me."

"You don't look like Grizzly Adams anymore. I'm liking this girl more and more. Come on in," Poppi said, moving out of the way as they made their way inside. "Good to see you again, young lady."

"Yeah, I can't seem to get rid of her. She's like a bad cold. Just won't go away." Ben's dimples snuck an appearance, along with a big grin, when he glanced at her. She gave him an elbow and glared at him.

Poppi let out a hearty laugh. "Again, I don't think I would be trying to get rid of her, if it were me." Kaysi scanned Poppi's house. The kitchen and dining room were combined, and the décor was dated. Probably hadn't been updated since his wife died. Tan and green checkered wallpaper covered the dining room walls. A simple, round, wooden table sat in the middle of the room with four matching wooden chairs around it. In the center of the table was a fake floral arrangement with lightly colored, oddly shaped pebbles filling the bottom of a vase. Papers and file folders littered the tabletop. The living room had a fake leather sofa that probably reclined, and a matching chair that had seen better days. Kaysi wondered what April would do in the space.

"We just came by to check on you, and make sure it would be okay if we spent some time at the rock house and took some of the stuff."

"I'm doing just fine," he said patting Ben on the

shoulder, then his eyes darted to Kaysi. "You found something worth keeping in there?"

"Oh my gosh, yes. Tons of stuff. There is a buffet and hutch in the kitchen along with an old iron stove, that I don't know how we are going to get moved, but it will happen. Oh, and upstairs, there's a dresser and some other stuff. We grabbed some smaller items when I came over the other day, kids' toys and a tea kettle and some old bottles. Do you know who lived there?"

"Family relatives. There were two other houses and a big barn on the ridge, that came down years ago. That one was just built sturdier, and we never got around to tearing it down.

"It seems like someone moved out quickly and left their belongings behind. I was curious if you knew what happened." Poppi eyed her, and she knew he had a story to tell.

He scratched the back of his head, "Let's just say the lust for money and treasures can make people do some horrible things."

Kaysi's stomach dropped. "Oh." She knew by the tone of his voice he was referring not only to the house, but also Rick. Libby's comment about possible blood stains on the porch made Kaysi sad, realizing that something tragic probably happened inside the house.

"Wasn't all that stuff in there covered in dirt?" Poppi said, obviously trying to lighten the conversation.

"Oh yes, but nothing that a good scrubbing didn't take care of. I just wish there was some way to save the house. It has so much character. The banister on the stairs is absolutely beautiful."

"Joe might be interested in that."

"He can have what he can haul. No one but the

ghosts have been in that place in years. I'm surprised you didn't run into some wild animals living in there."

"We still may," Ben said quickly. "We may find something hiding in the eight-hundred-pound iron stove that she wants me to move."

Poppi laughed. "Better you than me."

Ben's gaze moved to the pile of papers on the table. "What's all that about?" He nodded his head pointedly.

"Nothing for you to worry about, son. I've got my lawyer and Rick coming by later."

Ben took a deep irritated breath. "Poppi, please tell me you aren't giving in to Rick's demands."

"Ben." Poppi's eyes studied him for a long moment, and Kaysi knew he was torn about sharing something. "This is my affairs. I know what I am doing."

Ben walked over to the papers on the table. "Last Will and Testament?"

"You need to stay out of all of this. I will explain everything in time. Rick might have done some things that I want an explanation for, and I'm—"

Ben pushed around the papers examining them. Police reports, lab results. "What are all these financial pages?"

Poppi put his hands on his hips and gave Ben a long stare. "Randy came to me a few weeks before he died saying he suspected Rick was skimming funds from their company. He didn't want to believe his son would do that to him, but he had evidence to prove it. He loved Rick and was heartbroken. I told him that he needed to sit down and talk to him. I got a call about a week later, and he said they worked out the financial issue. Then, it wasn't a day or so after that, they went hiking and he fell. Rick never knew Randy came to talk to me, but I've been trying to piece this puzzle together ever since. There is a whole lot more involved, and sometimes family issues can get messy. And that's why I can't have you hovering over me, Ben. Please stay out of it. The police have it under control. It's for your own good. Trust me on this."

"Poppi, Valerie said she found some illegal stuff on his computer. She said he is bankrupting the company. He's ruthless, and if you are putting yourself in danger to set some kind of trap—"

"It's not a trap. I just told him I wanted to talk to him; to find out the truth and see if we can come to an agreement. The police are watching this place like a hawk. I've installed some hidden security cameras that send videos to my phone. I know what I am doing. I will be fine. I just don't want you involved."

Kaysi could see how much Ben was struggling. His hands threaded through his hair, then rubbed his face as he let out a frustrated exhale. "Okay. If that's what you want. But you know I'm just a phone call away. If you get into trouble, please call me."

"I know, and I will."

Ben turned to Kaysi. "Well, we better get going if we are going to meet Joe at the bunkhouse." His eyes darted back to Poppi. "We made the rounds, and the horses are in good shape. They have plenty of food."

"Good deal. You kids go have fun and be careful over there."

"You be careful too, Poppi."

****

"Wow! This place is creepy," Joe said, shutting the door to his truck, and joining Ben and Kaysi in front of the rock house.

Kaysi pouted. "It's not that bad. In fact, you won't

believe the inside. I imagine it was beautiful in its heyday."

"Let's get at it then." They carefully ascended the steps, and Kaysi pushed open the front door. Waving her hands like a game show model, Kaysi donned a satisfied smiled when both guys' heads swiveled in all directions taking in the surroundings. Joe immediately nodded in satisfaction.

"There was definitely money spent on this place," Joe said, as his hand skimmed the banister. He dusted some of the dirt in one spot, to get to the wood surface.

"Isn't it amazing?"

"Damn, this is mahogany."

"Poppi said you are free to take anything you want."

"Really? I mean, I'm kind of in agreement with you, Kaysi. I wish this place could be saved. Unfortunately, I think it is too far gone. But yeah, I could salvage a bunch of this stuff. Get my guys out here, and we could tear this place apart in a heartbeat." Joe scrutinized more of the woodwork. "You're serious? He would let us have what we want?"

"I can take you over there and let him tell you himself, if you want me to."

"Not today. You only have me for two hours, then April wants me to help her on her project. She is working on Brant and Bekah's upstairs.

"I can't believe they have another baby on the way."

"Yeah."

"Haven't seen much of him since he started working as a flight medic."

"Says he loves it."

"Guys, are you going to stand there talking, or are we going to get things moving?"

Joe put his hands on his hips. "Okay, miss bossy pants. What do you want moved?"

"In here." She strolled into the kitchen and pointed to the different items."

"Let me get my straps and dolly out of the truck. It will make this much easier. As for the stove, I'm thinking we will probably have to come back for that, with some different equipment."

"That's fine." She moved her hand again, directing them to follow her. Heading upstairs, she went from room to room, pointing out the pieces she wanted."

"Okay, I think we will start here, since we have stairs to contend with, then we can grab the stuff downstairs.

Joe retrieved his dolly and straps and headed upstairs with Ben. Kaysi followed and watched as the two men strapped the dresser and mirror to the dolly. Rocking it forward, to push the foot of the dolly farther under the base, Kaysi was a second too late when the drawer slid out and fell to the floor, allowing dozens of lightly colored pebbles to spill out.

"What is that? Marbles?" Ben asked, trying not to step on any.

She knelt to pick up the rocks. "No, I think it's the decorative pebbles Poppi has at his house."

"Where?"

"In the vase on the dining room table." She stood, after picking up the last one, and held it up to the light. They're pretty. Kind of have a metallic shine."

"That's odd though that Poppi has them in his house. He said no one has been in here in years."

"Who knows. His wife might have snooped around and found them at some point."

Ben shrugged it off. "Could be." His hand brushed over the wood of the dresser. "You know this piece would be really cool stripped, and then carved and charred in just a few spots, with a light stain."

"So, are you telling me you will put your artwork in the store, if I let you have a few pieces to play with?"

He grunted as he lifted the end of the dolly. "Maybe. Oh, speaking of which, I need to show you something in the studio."

They hauled the dresser downstairs, then came back for the beds, before starting on the furniture downstairs. After determining that the stove was too heavy to move with the dolly, and figuring it wouldn't fit in the trailer, with everything else anyway, they decided to call it a day. Kaysi smiled as they shut the trailer. "I can't believe he is letting us take all this stuff. It is going to fit perfectly in the store."

"Are you as excited as April is, about the business?" Joe asked, walking to his truck.

"This is a dream I have had for years. How often do you get to do something you are passionate about, as your job? I can't imagine doing anything else."

"I think April feels the same way."

Kaysi glanced at Ben who'd suddenly become quiet, and she wondered what he was thinking. He turned to Joe and waved him off. "We'll lock up here and meet you at the bunkhouse." Joe hopped in his truck and headed up the dirt path. Ben and Kaysi went back to the house.

A loud gunshot rang out. Ben spun around, searching the area. "Poppi," he breathed. A thundering noise had him stepping in front of Kaysi and backing up, as the wild horses barreled past them in the field just below the ridge. Poppi's saddled horse ran in the mix. Ben took off in a dead sprint in the opposite direction. Kaysi followed close behind. Her heart pounded as she tried to keep up with Ben. Her lungs burned from the cold air. Tears filled her eyes, and she prayed he was okay, but something in her gut told her he wasn't. This would absolutely destroy Ben. "Poppi," Ben yelled, and then they saw him. His battered and broken body was lying on the ground. Ben grabbed his phone, tapped the screen, and set it on the ground.

"Police, fire, or ambulance," the voice on the other end said.

Ben squinted his eyes. "Ambulance. Medivac, please."

"What's your emergency?"

"A man's been trampled by some horses. He's breathing, but he's hurt bad."

"What's your location?"

"Shit, I don't know his house number. It's the address just west of nineteen thirty-eight Springhallow, located just south of highway fifty-one, and east of FM twenty-three eighteen road. There is a large open pasture where the helicopter can land."

"What's your name?"

"Ben Corbett."

Chapter Twenty

Ben sat in the waiting room. The dark cloud of anger was building by the second. There was no way this was an accident. No way. With everything that Poppi told him, this had Rick written all over it, and he wasn't going to get away with it. He dug his phone out of his pocket and tapped the screen.

"Gallagher."

"Hey Mitch, it's Ben. Poppi, I mean, Oren—"

"I'm already on it. How's he doing?"

"Not good. They airlifted him to Mercy."

"Well, I know what you are thinking, Ben, and all I have to say is, let me handle it. You take care of Oren. I'll take care of the rest. There is a lot about this that you don't know. And you don't need to get involved. Oren wanted it that way."

"I can't promise you anything if Rick shows up here." He stood. "What happened, Mitch? I thought you guys were keeping an eye on everything?"

"Initial finding is it was just an accident. I'm trying to get all the paperwork together for an official investigation and search of the property."

Brant exited the heavy metal doors, and Ben didn't like the seriousness of his expression. "I gotta go, Mitch." His eyes locked with Brant's. They had become friends after Ben started working out at the gym. He was one of a small group that hung out together occasionally. Cody and Brant hadn't been on the best of terms, after Brant had assaulted Joe at a bar. And Cody had initially thought Brant had been the one who attacked Jenna. But with the discovery that Cody's dad was the assailant, and Brant's apology for the drunken brawl, a bond developed.

"They took him up for surgery," Brant said. "It may be a while."

"Is he going to make it?"

"I honestly don't know."

Kaysi walked in out of breath. "How is he?" Ben had left her to take his truck and trailer back to the house, while he rode in the medivac chopper with Brant and Poppi.

"He's in surgery," Ben relayed. "Did you get the truck and trailer back to the house okay?"

"Yeah, and I talked to Joe. He will come by later with Cody and get everything unloaded." She put her arm around him, but he backed away. He didn't want to be touched. She hadn't done anything, but he was feeling too much, and couldn't handle it. He was so overwhelmed, and felt like he was about to explode, so he paced.

"I need to get back. I'll let you know if I hear anything," Brant said, before giving Ben a pat on the back, and heading back through the metal doors.

Ben just nodded, then turned to Kaysi. "You don't need to stay. I can handle this. I'm pretty good at handling things on my own," he growled, and turned away from her, but she grabbed his bicep.

"No."

"No what?"

"I'm not leaving. I won't leave you, Ben."

The way she said it, he knew she wasn't just saying it for right now, she was saying it to let him know he didn't have to go through this alone. He was so angry though; so tired of having the rug yanked out from under him. He wanted to let her in, he just didn't know if he could.

Her eyes met his. He tried desperately to hold back all the emotions he was battling. He felt like crying, and screaming, and hitting something, all at once. Again, life had come back to bite him. He broke the stare, turning away, and running his hand through his hair, trying to tamp down everything.

Her arms gently circled him, and he stiffened. She didn't say anything. She didn't have to. Her warmth against him melted him, like the sun on the winter snow. He turned and pulled her close. His fingers dug into her hair, and his nose drew in the floral scent of her shampoo, as he leaned his cheek on her head. He could feel his chest give, ready to release the flood of tears he had been fighting. But he couldn't let go. He couldn't let her see how much pain he was in. He had to be strong.

The heavy metal doors opened and a doctor in green scrubs appeared. "Oren McIntyre family?"

His heart clenched, and he stepped forward, clearing his throat of the knot that had settled there. "I'm not family, but I was with him when he came in. How is he?"

The doctor held out his hand. "I'm Dr. Ellis, and you are?"

"Ben Corbett. I'm Oren's next-door neighbor."

"Yes. He asked for you." The doctor crossed his arms in front of him. "Mr. McIntyre had several injuries. One could have cost him his life, but put together, I have to say, he's in a very precarious situation. To his credit, he's tough. He made it through surgery. But we are having a hard time stabilizing his blood pressure. He had a lacerated liver and spleen, punctured lung, several broken ribs, bruised kidney, swelling around his heart, you name it, he has it. Not to mention a pretty good concussion. We have repaired everything we can. Now, it's just a wait and see if his body can handle all the trauma."

"Can we see him?"

"Yeah. They are getting him settled right now. Does he have family in the area?"

Ben's gut boiled at the thought of Rick. "Yeah, a grandson."

"Please give the nurses at the nurses' station his name. They need to be notified. He's in room twenty-one."

They followed the doctor back and stopped at the nurses' station. "I'm here for Oren McIntyre. Dr. Ellis told me to give you his next of kin. His name is Rick McIntyre.

"Do you have a number for him?" A nurse with glasses and graying hair asked.

"No. ma'am, I don't."

"Do you have Valerie's number?" Kaysi asked.

What would she say if he did? Would it make her mad? "Possibly? I don't know." He retrieved his phone and typed her name. "I don't know if she still has this number since she moved to St. Louis."

"Give it to them anyway. Just in case."

He turned back to the nurse and showed her the number, and she jotted it down.

Dropping his phone back in his pocket, he grabbed

Kaysi's hand and walked to cubicle twenty-one. A young nurse was stationed outside the room and nodded when they stopped at the door.

Kaysi's fingers tightened in Ben's hand as they stepped in the room. Hisses from the oxygen machine echoed. Bags of solution hung on IV trees next to the bed. Ben could feel himself shaking, and he could barely maintain control. Kaysi's other hand wrapped around his bicep steadying him. His phone chimed in his pocket. Checking it, he noticed it was his dad.

"Yeah?" he said softly.

"I just heard what happened. How's he doing?"

"He made it through surgery, but the doc said they are having a hard time keeping his blood pressure up." He paused, swallowing down the rock that had lodged in his throat. "It's bad, Dad. They have him hooked up to everything."

"I'll be up there in about thirty minutes."

"Don't come. They may not let you back here anyway. I think the only reason they let me, was because he asked for me. I can handle it. I will keep you updated."

"You sure, son?"

Ben glanced at Kaysi. "Yeah. Kaysi is here with me."

"Who?"

"Kaysi. Jenna's friend, that's staying in the bunkhouse."

"Okay. I just don't want you to be there by yourself."

"Nah, I'm good." He disconnected the call. A twinge of realization of what his dad had said skirted his thoughts as he walked up closer to Poppi's bed. Poppi's hand reached up and grabbed Ben's, startling him, and giving him a glimmer of hope. Although Poppi had a tube in his throat, keeping him from speaking, his eyes glanced at Kaysi and back to Ben.

"Yeah, she seems to follow me everywhere now." Ben held on to Poppi's hand, not wanting to let go, and Poppi squeezed it. "What happened Poppi?" The old man just shook his head, signaling for Ben to let it go. But he couldn't. "Did Rick do this?" The irritation in his voice was evident. Poppi didn't answer.

Kaysi scooted up a couple of plastic chairs. One contained a white drawstring bag and a pair of boots. When Kaysi lifted everything out of the chair, for Ben to sit down, Poppi released Ben's hand, and pointed to it. "What do you need?" Ben asked. Poppi nodded and pointed again. Releasing the plastic drawstring, Ben sat down and dug inside. Glancing back up at Poppi, he noticed his brows were knitted together, so he started pulling out items. When he reached the phone, Poppi pointed to Ben and nodded. "You want me to take it?" Poppi nodded. "Is there something on it?" Poppi nodded again. "Do you have a passcode?" Poppi held up his hand, and motioned. "Four, one, five, two?" Ben questioned. Poppi nodded again. Ben shoved the phone in his pocket and returned his focus to Poppi. He looked so frail, and Ben's gut tightened as he watched him slowly blinking.

Poppi nodded to the bag again. "There's more?" He pointed with his finger indicating for Ben to continue. He pulled out his wallet and held it up, but Poppi shook his head, so he kept digging. Dragging out a set of keys, Ben held them up, and Poppi nodded. Ben dropped the bag and studied the keys. "I'll keep an eye on your place." Poppi pointed to the keys again. "Is there something else?" Poppi closed his eyes and nodded again. Ben checked the keys again. House key, truck key, trailer key. He knew what all the keys went to, except one. He held it up, and Poppi nodded. "I have no idea what this goes to."

Kaysi grabbed his hand with the keys. "I think it's a safety deposit box key." Poppi nodded again. Kaysi studied it closer. There was nothing on it but a number. "What banks are in Dalton?" she asked.

Ben tapped on his phone and found the list of banks. "Poppi, just give me a thumbs up when I name it." He called off the banks one by one and watched for any reaction. The third one on the list was Dalton Savings and Loan. Poppi immediately gave him the thumbs up. He shoved the keys in his pocket and picked the bag up again. "Is there anything else?" Poppi shook his head with his eyes closed.

Ben grabbed his hand again. "You rest then. I will get everything taken care of. Don't worry. Just get better." Poppi squeezed Ben's hand. Ben leaned over and rested his chin in his other hand. Kaysi scooted up next to him, wrapped her arm around him, and rubbed his back. The room became quiet, except for the constant hiss of the oxygen, and the occasional hum of the blood pressure cuff.

Ben glanced up at the monitor just in time to notice a red light flash a couple of times, before the alarm went off. He immediately stood, but kept his hand wrapped around Poppi's, as the nurse came in, and jogged to the other side of the bed. With her hand in a fist, she rubbed Poppi's chest. "Mr. McIntyre?" Other medical staff entered the room. Dr. Ellis asked them to step out.

The door slowly closed behind them. Panic ripped

through Ben. Poppi couldn't die. He rubbed his hands, down his jeaned legs, and took a deep breath, as he leaned up against the wall. Kaysi wrapped her arms around him, but he stood motionless. His legs felt like they were going to give out. It was taking everything in his power not to let the tears, that had been threatening since they found Poppi, spill from his eyes. He chewed on his upper lip, trying to will them away.

"Ben. It's okay to cry," Kaysi said, putting her hands on his chest. He grabbed her wrists and held her at bay.

"Men aren't supposed to cry. That's how I was raised. I'm supposed to be stronger than that."

She stared at him and backed away. "Crying is natural when you are hurting. It doesn't mean you're weak. It's not good to bottle everything up and stuff it away."

"The only time I saw my dad cry was at my mom's funeral."

"Did you?"

"Did I what?"

"Cry at your mom's funeral." Her words immediately took him back to the day. Back to the pain and anger deep inside him.

"No. I was mad at her," he said under his breath.

Kaysi lifted a critical brow.

Ben glanced away. "You handle things your way. I'll handle them mine. Okay?"

Dr. Ellis stepped through the door with a darkened expression and let out a long sigh. A knot tightened in the pit of Ben's stomach. The news wasn't going to be good. "Mr. McIntyre is not doing well. His blood pressure is dropping. We could take him back to surgery to see if there is more internal bleeding, but he's too weak. Chances are, he wouldn't make it. We have him on every medication we can put him on. He will either stabilize on his own, or not. He's comfortable. We have reached out to his next of kin, but we have not been able to get in contact with anyone."

"So, you don't think he's going to make it?"

"His blood pressure is continuing to drop and at some point—"

Ben swallowed letting the words sink in. "There's nothing else you can do?"

"We can continue to try to resuscitate him, but I think it would only prolong the inevitable. There was just too much trauma for him to handle." Ben felt Kaysi's hand wrap around his. The minute her fingers interlaced with his, he felt a power surge through him, and it calmed him.

"I don't want him to suffer," he managed to rasp as he fought the emotion trying to spill out. "How long do you think he has?"

"Not long."

"Can I stay with him?"

"Sure."

Ben pushed through the door, keeping Kaysi's hand tight in his grasp. His mind was again at war with itself. He didn't want to watch Poppi die, but he'd be damned if he was going to let him die alone. He was so mad that he listened to everyone, including Poppi, telling him to stay away and not get involved. He should have gone with his instincts. But would the outcome have been any different?

Ben wrapped his hand around Poppi's once again and leaned over the bed. "You gotta fight, old man. You hear me? Don't let whoever did this to you, win. You have a lot more good years left in you." He coughed, feeling the tears coming. He couldn't cry. He had to stay strong. Kaysi's hand stroked his back as he leaned over the bed rail, staring at the man in front of him, and fighting like hell to keep his composure. His eyes went to the monitor and watched the numbers dropping one by one, and knew Poppi wasn't going to fight. "God, Poppi. I don't want to lose you, but if you need to go, just know, I'll make sure the horses are taken care of. Don't worry."

The red light started flashing again, and the alarm sounded. The nurse stationed outside the room came in and shut the alarm off. Ben tightened his grip on Poppi, and again felt Kaysi's hands wrap around his other one. His eyes were drawn to the monitor, watching the heartbeat slowly dwindle while his sped up. He stared down at the man, who for years had been the only grandpa to him and one of his best friends. The man who talked to him when he couldn't talk to his folks; the man who took him under his wing and taught him all about the wild horses. He watched as he took his last breath.

The heartbeat on the monitor went flat, and the nurse turned the machines off, and left the room. Ben swallowed hard, squeezed Poppi's hand, and backed away, dropping Kaysi's hand. He put his fist to his mouth, taking deep breaths, trying to steady the anger growing inside him. He suddenly remembered what Mitch said. "They're treating this as an accident." Like hell it's an accident. Ben walked out of the room to the nurses' station. "What needs to be done for Mr. McIntyre?"

"We still haven't reached next of kin. We will be taking his body to the morgue. Would you like us to notify you if we can't reach next of kin?"

"Yes, ma'am."

The nurse handed him a piece of paper. "Please write your name and number down. You are welcome to take his belongings with you."

"Thank you."

He returned to the room. His eyes studied the man before him, who only this morning was full of life. He couldn't quite accept the fact that now he was gone. Picking up the white bag and Poppi's boots, he walked out. Kaysi trailed behind him, but he didn't dare make eye contact, for fear that the concern in her eyes would wreck him.

Ben tried to close his eyes while Kaysi drove them home, but all he could see was Poppi lying on the ground. He wanted to kill Rick. There was nothing that could convince him this was an accident. He pulled out his phone.

"Hello?"

"Mitch?" Ben felt the knot explode in his throat, and he suddenly was incapable of forming words. Clearing his throat didn't help.

"Ben?"

"He's gone, Mitch." The tightness in his chest squeezed to the point that he was unable to suck in a full breath. "What happens now?"

"I'm working on the paperwork, to get my guys out there to search the property."

"Do you know what he was doing today? I went by there to talk to him, and he had a bunch of papers on the table. I think he was trying to set a trap for Rick."

"Ben. Rick didn't have anything to do with his accident."

"How can you say that, Mitch. He's been harassing

Poppi for weeks, if not months."

"I know, because Rick was with me at Tia Lunas. He was getting some breakfast and we got to talking. He left a couple of minutes before the call came in." Mitch paused. "We are going to investigate, but Ben, it might have just been a terrible accident."

"It wasn't, Mitch. I'm sure of it."

"Why are you so sure?"

"We heard a gunshot before we saw the horses."

"We?"

"Kaysi was with me. Oh. And one more thing. Poppi made sure I had the evidence."

"How'd he do that?"

"He gave me his phone and a key."

"Okay. Can you bring them by tomorrow morning?"

"I'll be there bright and early."

Chapter Twenty-One

Ben said he needed some time alone to process everything. He had gone into his studio an hour ago and hadn't come out. At one point, Kaysi heard him talking to someone on the phone, but she couldn't figure out who, since the conversation was one sided. She hated the fact that she wondered who he was talking to. Was he reaching out to someone else? She wanted to be there for him.

After talking to Mitch on the phone, he had called his dad and let him know, but he didn't utter a word to her the whole trip home, except to say, he needed to be alone. Life had suddenly taken a sad turn, and Ben had crawled back behind his protective walls.

Sitting in the living room sipping on some tea and scrolling through her blog on her phone, she caught sight of the little red album.

Still amazed at the fact he truly was her knight in shining armor, she opened the album and stared at the photos.

A couple of pages were full of photos that Robin had secretly taken with her camera, and it brought a smile to her face. She laughed at a close up of her making a funny face. One was set at a diagonal with just a bunch of legs. One was of a guy swinging off a rope into the river. *Must have been the guy Robin thought was cute.* There were people sitting on the balcony railing, waiting for the dining hall to open, and kids playing volleyball with a beach ball. She didn't remember any of the faces, but they were glimpses that served to remind her that not all the time spent at the camp was bad.

Kaysi glanced at another photo with her sitting on Bandit. Ben said no one could ride Bandit except him, but he let her ride him one day around the corral, after they had been on a trail ride. She could remember how jealous some of the older girls were when Ben helped her up on him, and then proceeded to barely acknowledge the girls as he helped put away the saddles and send them on their way.

Turning the page, there was only one photo. It was another one that Robin took, but this one had been burned into her memory and had her returning to the camp year after year. The photo was of her sitting on a log, at a campfire, with an Indian print blanket wrapped around her. The glow from the flames lit up her face. She was facing Ben, who was also wrapped in the blanket, sitting next to her. She had her head turned, talking to him, and he was smiling back at her. She remembered that day so well. It was the day her life changed. The day she decided to live.

Her phone chimed on the table, and she picked it up. "Hello?"

"Hey, Kaysi, it's Joe. You doing okay?"

"Could be better. I just can't believe what happened." She shut the album and set it aside. "I don't exactly know what to do with myself." Turning toward the studio, her heart pinched, thinking of the pain in Ben's eyes when they left the hospital. "Ben is holed up in the studio. He said he needed to be alone. I figured he would have come out by now, but he hasn't."

"I talked to him a little bit ago. He doesn't sound good. You might want to go check on him."

"Yeah. I think I will."

"I thought I would let you know the loft is ready. The appliances that you wanted came in today, and I went ahead and got them installed, so you should be good to go."

The last thing she needed to do right now was leave. Ben needed her, whether he thought he did, or not. He needed to know she wasn't going anywhere, although she did need to come up with a way to use the loft, since they put so much work into getting it ready so fast. The furniture had already been ordered. It was just on hold until the space was ready. "Okay."

"Are you sure you're okay?"

"Yeah. I'm just a little numb. Poppi was a good man, and Ben loved him. This is killing him. He doesn't need to be alone right now. I think I will go ahead and release the furniture to be delivered. We can set everything up and use the loft as a model for April's designs, and I will stay here. At least for now."

"Whatever. We are still a couple of weeks out on the store being ready."

"That's good. We still have a bunch of vendors we are working on getting contracts with anyway."

"All right. Well, let me know if you need anything."

"I will."

Placing the phone back on the table, she picked up the album again and turned to the photo of her and Ben. Kaysi remembered the pain she felt, the thoughts that were playing in her mind, and every word of the conversation with Ben that made her rethink her entire life. How could one person, who she only knew for a few days, change her life so drastically? How could she have trusted what he said? And yet, he had done it again. They had a connection. She felt it from the first time they spoke.

Running her finger over the photo one more time, she shut the album and stood. Strolling to the kitchen, she knew she needed to talk to him, and tried to come up with exactly what to say. Filling a glass with tea, she headed down the hall to the large double doors concealing the studio. She paused for a beat, feeling her heart race.

Ben had been so despondent at the hospital, returning to his hiding place inside his head. She tried to comfort him, but it was met with mixed signals. The pain in his eyes was evident, and even though he hadn't cried when Poppi died, she knew he wanted to. Although she thought she had finally broken through his walls, within a matter of hours he had built them even higher, and she didn't know if he was going to let her inside them again.

Slowly, she pushed the doors open. Ben was on the other side of the room with his back to her. He was using his sander and had his noise cancelling earmuffs on, so he didn't hear her enter. On the table she noticed a couple of drawings, and wondered what he was working on. One drawing was of a compass, with the words Rare Finds written in the center face, and a spyglass as the pointer. The sign for the store. It was so detailed. When did he do this? She had been in the studio with him most of the time the past few days. Her eyes landed on the other drawing, and she reached over to pick it up. This one was even more intricate, more detailed. In the background was an old map with a magnifying glass in the center. Coming out of the magnifying glass was a diamond, with the words Rare Finds. Both were amazing in their own right, and she couldn't wait to see what April thought.

As she lifted her eyes from the table, she saw Ben glaring at her. He turned off the sander, removed his earmuffs and headphones, then his protective glasses. "I need to be alone."

"I know what you told me Ben, I was getting worried about you, though. I came to check on you and bring you some tea. Holding it out to him, he reluctantly took it, and drank down half. Her eyes went back to the drawings on the table. "These are amazing. I think I like the one with the map the best." He threw her a grunt, then walked away.

Not wanting to lose his attention, she said, "I wanted to run something by you." He turned back to her with an exasperated glance. "Joe called. The loft is ready."

"I know. I talked to him earlier."

"Well, I was thinking—"

"I think you should go." The words felt like he'd stabbed her directly in the chest.

She stepped back, hoping she just misunderstood. "Wait. What do you mean, go?"

"This is what you wanted. Your dream. It's ready. So, go."

"No, hear me out—"

"Kaysi, this isn't going to work. You know it. I know it. I'm not what you need. I'm not college educated. The ranch is my life. I was stupid to believe any of this was real. I lost sight of the fact we'd agreed it was fake. The only real thing is my shitty life. I forgot for a minute, but it damn sure came back with a vengeance, and slapped me right in the face. So, go."

"But I want to stay. You *need* me right now."

Ben snickered. "I don't *need* you, Kaysi. You only want to be with me right now because you are enamored with something different from your bright and shiny life. Like Valerie said, you will get tired of it. Walk away now, because you know you will. This life is not where you belong. You belong with those rich folks. I don't."

"Ben, you're wrong. I thought I made that clear to you the other night, when I told you I was falling in love with you."

Ben scoffed. "You're not in love with me. This whole thing was fake." His eyes narrowed and locked on her, and he snickered sarcastically. "I keep forgetting what people are capable of. They're all liars. They're out for themselves, with no regard for anyone else getting hurt in their wake." He pointed at her and shook his finger. "You were good at messing with my head, I give you that. You had me believing things could change. But I remember now, they don't." He took another sip of the tea and slammed it down.

Her body began to shake at the venom he was spewing. Tears burned in her eyes. "Don't say that. You don't mean it."

"What do you want from me, Kaysi? I'm not your dream. You want to be a successful businesswoman and make a name for yourself. I can't give you that. I don't have money. All I have is the ranch, and I'm happy here. You won't be though. You don't want to be a wife to some old rancher."

"You don't have to make it happen for me. I can do that myself, and I am. Why can't I have everything? Why can't I be a rancher's wife, and have a business?"

"Because you don't want that. That's not your dream. Hell, you were perfectly happy with the idea of living in a cool loft above the store, until someone set fire to it."

"You have no idea what my dreams are. Dreams can change, Ben. Remember this week? Remember touching me, and me touching you. Remember kissing me, like I was your last hope for happiness? Remember the feelings you had, and how happy you felt? That's love, Ben. I know you felt it. Remember how happy we were together. I remember, and that's why I told you I loved you. It wasn't a lie."

His eyes softened, and a glimmer of hope rushed through her.

"How the hell do you know I love you?"

"You told me you did. And I believed you."

"They're just words."

"Remember what you told Valerie? You said you finally knew what love felt like." She knew he was just letting Valerie's words get in his head, but she wanted him to remember how he stood up to her. "It's simple, Ben. You know the feeling. Don't overthink it. Do you love me? Do I make you happy?"

"I honestly don't think I can love anyone anymore."

"Everyone has the ability to love. It doesn't matter what you've been through. The ability to love never goes away. It's a choice you make."

"Well, evidently you're wrong."

"Ben, stop it. You are just upset because of what happened to Poppi." The tears were coming hard. She could feel the pain growing in her gut and ripping at every portion of her body. Anger was starting to bubble up, but she didn't want to be angry at him. She didn't want to believe any of his hurtful words. He was just acting out of his pain. He had been hurt so many times before.

"No Kaysi, I'm not just upset."

"You are too afraid to let yourself be happy, too afraid to love, because of your past."

"Happiness means feeling something, and I don't want to feel. Every time I let my guard down, shit happens. Every time I love, shit happens. I don't know why. But it does. You seem to think life is all rainbows and unicorns, and things will get better, but sometimes life just sucks, and it just keeps sucking." The growl in his voice told her she was getting under his skin. "I, honest to God, don't know how you do it."

"Do what?"

"You just seem to go through life, like the queen of sunshine, flitting around, throwing sunshine everywhere. But why not, you've got nothing to worry about."

She could feel the hot stinging tears wetting her cheeks and the pain crawling up her throat. "You don't have the corner on a shitty life. Everybody gets their time in the limelight. I've cried until I thought I didn't have anything left. Yes, I want everything to be rosy all the time, and I know that's unrealistic. But I can choose to wallow in the painful times and let it ruin my life, or I can choose to find the beauty on the other side."

"Oh. Right. Did you have a bad manicure? Or no, wait, you broke the heel on your favorite six-hundred-dollar pair of shoes."

His words were like knives being thrown at her now, lancing her open. Anger was seeping into the pain filling her heart at the mocking tone in his voice. Memories of her past life invaded. If he thought she was the queen of sunshine, she would set him straight. "No, Ben, because you know what? Sometimes money creates a shitty life. This 'queen of sunshine' " she said, making air quotes, "spent all her early teens at expensive schools being teased and bullied by the beautiful people, because she was chubby, and she wore glasses. Oh, and on top of that, she had braces.

"I was constantly reminded of how inferior I was. You wanna know what happened? I wound up in the hospital with bulimia. I was thirteen freaking years old, Ben, and I was throwing up to lose weight. And you know what resulted from that? Not only was I still fat, but people also thought I was crazy. My family didn't trust me. So, I had that going for me." Ben leaned up against the table. Kaysi paced, letting all the memories and hurt return as she shared something she hadn't shared with anyone.

"It was just teenage shit. But being rich, I felt like I was supposed to be this Barbie doll that my parents could parade around. I never felt like I fit in with the rich crowd. I was awkward and felt like a constant embarrassment." Tears streamed down her face. She glanced at Ben, and realized she now had his undivided attention.

"My mom wanted to help. And because we had money, she offered me every fix in the book. But I didn't want her to think she had to fix me. I wanted her to tell me she loved me the way I was, and she didn't. Or at least I couldn't hear her when she did. She told me I was beautiful all the time, and so did Dad, but I didn't believe them. I was too far into my own head.

"Plus, there was Kaleb. He was the golden child of brains and beauty. He never went through an awkward stage. He was always popular, always brilliant, and always talented.

"I stopped going out. Stayed in my room. My parents got worried and thought it would be a good idea for me to go to camp and make new friends. I always wanted to learn how to ride horses, so I found a dude ranch not too far from Fayetteville and it changed my life.

She lifted her eyes, to see if Ben had possibly made the connection, but he remained silent. She figured she'd shared enough of her dark past, so she tried to steer the conversation in a different direction. "So, see, money doesn't keep you from a life of pain. Everyone has shitty lives once in a while, but you have choices. You can dig in and let all the past pains continue to tear you apart, or you can let it go. You won't be able to move on until you let your wounds heal. Quit picking at them and opening them up. This can't be how you want to live the rest of your life."

"Oh, you don't know me very well. I stopped living a long time ago. I'm empty inside."

"You are empty because nothing can penetrate those walls. You are never going to find true happiness until you drop them, forgive whoever you need to forgive, accept what has happened, and move forward."

"The problem is, you think you can figure me out, when I don't know who I am myself."

No, Ben. All I was trying to do was make you happy. That's all. To show you the world through a different perspective. No one knows who they are. But at some point, you have to choose what you want out of life. Most will say they just want to be happy."

"I would love to be happy, but like I said earlier, I

can't. I know how it goes. I open up, try to be happy, then the shit show happens just like today. So, it's just better to leave the walls up. Saves me from the heartache."

"God, and you think I'm stubborn. I thought I was breaking through, that you felt the same as I do, but I guess I was just wishful thinking. You are standing right here in front of me, but you aren't here. How do I fight with that? You aren't listening to what I'm saying. You've just completely given up.

"I thought we had something special. I thought I made you happy. Why you would choose to live this way, when you know what we could have, is beyond me. And it's making me mad. I love you, Ben. Can't you see that? I can't believe you are willing to throw it all away."

Ben turned and picked up a piece of wood and brought it back to where he was working, turning his back on Kaysi. She was ready to explode.

"My mom was like yours. She also had her sayings, and she always told me 'If you can't say something nice, don't say anything at all.'" She turned to leave, feeling the heat from anger burning her up inside. Then his taunting voice pushed her over the edge.

"Oh, go ahead, darling, by all means let me have it. I probably deserve it."

She whirled around to find his icy glare ready to go to war.

"You are a coward," she shrieked through her tears.

"I already knew that. That's nothing new."

Frustration taking over, she slammed her hand on the table. "No, you idiot. Not because you didn't want to watch your mom die. It's natural not to want to watch someone you love, die. No. You are a coward because you are too scared to forgive, because you don't know what you will feel when you do, and because then you will realize that you are partly to blame for your shitty life. You blame everyone else for your pain, but it's not all their fault. You have allowed it. You have to own your part of the pain. You can't just keep blaming everyone else."

"You don't think I blame myself?"

"You blame all women for the guilt and shame you feel. You aren't owning your part, because you won't take the blame for your life. You blame me for your art sales blowing up, you blame Valerie for your relationship falling apart, and you blame your mom for the guilt and anger you feel over her death. But the fact is, you were partially to blame too. And you are to blame for the pain still being there, because you are allowing it."

"But I-I—"

"You immediately think the worst of people. You should try believing and trusting those who really love you and want to make you happy, and not those who have already tried to ruin your life. I've tried everything to show you how I feel about you, but you chose to believe Valerie. You are too afraid to let yourself be happy because of your past, but I know there is someone in there that wants to live life again."

"If you think you know so much about me, why don't you let me in on who you think I am."

"Here's a clue. I know you a lot better than you think, and I hate that you lost yourself. You used to be so different. You had hopes and dreams for your life. You had an easy smile, and such a huge heart. Now all you have is anger and distrust for everyone, because you refuse to allow yourself to see how good life could be."

"What the hell are you talking about?"

"I knew you when you were eighteen."

"That was a thousand years ago, Kaysi. I'm a man now. I've seen what life is really like. I'm not that boy full of dreams anymore. You can't save me from the man I've become. I'm a lost cause."

"You're wrong. I know he's still inside of you. I saw him, and you know it. But you are just too afraid of being happy because you might be disappointed again. A happy life comes with a little sadness sometimes, that's what makes it rich. That's what makes the happy times even better."

"Why are you so hell bent on saving me, Kaysi? Haven't you figured out I can't be saved?

"God Ben, you really want to know why?"

"Yeah."

"Because you saved a thirteen-year-old girl from killing herself."

Chapter Twenty-Two

Ben stood, with his arms crossed over his chest, earmuffs wrapped around his neck, and thoroughly confused. "What are you talking about?" He asked, his tone much softer.

She grabbed his phone. "What's your passcode?"

"Thirteen twenty-eight."

She tapped on the screen and handed it back to him, then walked out of the studio. He stared at the contact screen with her name and phone number and didn't understand, until he read what it said below it. The words "I'm Ray."

His heart stopped. The air in his lungs rushed out like someone had punched him. It all made sense now. All her strange comments, why she was captivated by his photo of Bandit. Everything came back to him. *He* taught her how to ride. But what did she mean that he saved her?

Kaysi walked back into the room with the red album. There were no tears, only a storm of pain brewing in her eyes. She threw the album on the table, and he realized the storm had already hit, and it was probably too late to turn things around. She opened the album. He took a hesitant step forward and scanned the photos, glancing back at her from time to time to study her face. Of course, it was her. He remembered her so well. Remembered how protective she was of Robin, remembered her bright smile and infectious laugh. Why didn't it click before?

"I went to Sterling Springs hanging by the thinnest of threads. I never told my parents I had contemplated suicide, and honestly, I was scared of the thoughts I was having. I figured camp might help me get my mind off the constant barrage of negativity. When I met you, a spark of hope took hold. I couldn't understand why you were being so nice to me, but for some reason I accepted it, because I felt this odd connection to you. It was like you were the only one who could see me. Something in your eyes made me feel like you understood how fragile I was."

Ben swallowed, trying to wet his throat, which had gone dry. "When I was in school there was a kid my age named Chance, who had Down Syndrome. He was the manager for our baseball team, so we all hung out with him. He was always happy, and every time I saw him, he gave me a high five. So, when I saw you hanging out with Robin, it reminded me of hanging out with Chance. You and Robin always seemed so happy. You were my ray of sunshine."

"Julie and Cheryl didn't make it easy. I had a huge crush on you, and when you came to Robin's rescue, it was like you were this superhero, who came in to save the day. You made the two weeks at that camp, bearable." She paused. "Well, you and Robin."

He couldn't help but smile, remembering.

"The night before camp ended, everyone was crowded around the campfire. I was actually sad it was ending. Then I saw Julie and Cheryl sitting across from me, with their tongues down some random guys' throats, and I just couldn't understand why guys fawned over them, even though they were horrible people. I couldn't ever imagine someone wanting to do that to me.

"The dark thoughts, the venom I kept spewing at myself, that I was ugly, and fat, and a disappointment and embarrassment to my family, crept back in. Then, you sat down by me, wrapped a blanket around my shoulders, and when you looked at me, it was like you saw inside me. A place no one else could see. Even though I never said a word to you about what I was thinking, you saw what I was wanting, and you told me I was beautiful. And in that moment, I believed.

"I will never forget it. You pointed over at Julie and Cheryl, and said your mom told you anyone could make themselves attractive, with enough money. Then you stared at me and said, 'but true beauty isn't just outward appearance, it's a gift, given to those with good hearts. It shines from within, to bring beauty to the world.' And then you said, 'I know you can't see what I see, but from my view, you are well on your way to being absolutely beautiful, and don't let anyone tell you different.'

"You told me that if I were older, you would be honored to have me as your girlfriend. It was like you crawled in my head and found every bad thought and threw it in the campfire. I tied those words to the end of my rope and held on. Year after year, I went back to the ranch, praying you would be there.

"You said you weren't part of my life's dreams. But, Ben, you were. It's just, after so many years of you not being there when I went, I gave up on that dream, thinking it wasn't going to come true." She paused and harshly wiped her cheeks then her eyes met his. "But you know what? You were right. Everyone lies. What you said to me were just pretty words to cheer me up, and that's okay. I was a broken, naive thirteen-year-old girl, who fell in love with a handsome older boy at camp. It happens all the time, right?"

His knees felt like they were about to give way. He remembered that night, remembered the sadness on her face, remembered that all he wanted to do was see her sweet smile, and make her happy. He never knew she had been so close to taking her life. "Kaysi, I—"

He watched her heart breaking in front of him. She couldn't really be in love with him, could she?

"No, don't. I'm not going to beg you to let me stay. I know, better than anyone, that you can't make people love you if they don't, no matter how hard you try. I'll give up the fight. But understand one thing. You say everybody leaves you, but make no mistake, it's you who's pushing me away. I told you I loved you, and I wanted to stay, and I meant every word. I really thought you felt it too. If you want it to be over, fine. But it's over because you want it to be, not me. I'll have my stuff out by tomorrow."

She turned, without another word, and disappeared, and he knew as the doors shut, he had made the biggest mistake of his life. He sat down on the stool at the table, because his legs wouldn't hold him, and stared at the photos. He couldn't believe she could have ever thought she was ugly. Her hair was cut into a style, that was shorter, and parted to one side, with long bangs hanging over her eye. Her glasses were large for her face, and had a silvery blue tint, that brought out her blue eyes. He realized now why he kept thinking she looked familiar. How could he have forgotten those big blue eyes.

He was torn. He needed to talk to her, but he didn't even know where to start. After the things he'd said to her, would it even do any good. She was right about everything. He did push her away, and he was dredging up old hurts, and letting them cloud his judgement. His eyes returned to the photos. He flipped through all the pictures, including those when she went back year after year. He noticed more photos of her and Robin.

He heard her voice in the next room, but he couldn't tell if she was on the phone or talking to someone else. What would he say? When she walked out of the studio it was like she took the air with her. He picked his phone up.

"Hello?"

"Joe?"

"What did you do to my sister?"

"Did she call you?"

"No. Well, yes. Earlier. She said she was going to talk to you. I'm guessing by this call, something happened."

"We had a fight."

"And?" Joe grumbled.

"She was right about everything, but I had already dug my grave, and she left."

"What did you say?"

"Basically, everything I shouldn't have." He tipped his eyes to the ceiling and dug his fingers in his hair, and immediately remembered her hands in his hair, and her body pressed up against him. "God, Joe. I am such an idiot, and I'm horrible at this relationship shit. I was pissed at what happened to Poppi, and I started taking it out on her. She told me I was doing it, too. And then some shit Valerie said at the dinner kept playing over and over in my head, that Kaysi would get tired of me and my life, and leave, because she is from a rich family. So,

I told her to go."

"What the ever-loving hell does that have to do with it? The Grayeagles are some of the most down to earth people I've ever met."

"I know. Like I said, I'm an idiot. I have just had so much shit dumped on me, I didn't believe it when she said she loved me, and she didn't want to leave."

"Wait. She said she loved you?"

"Oh. Uh. Yeah."

"You guys have barely known each other a couple of weeks."

"Actually, that isn't true. That was something else I found out during the fight. We met several years ago, when she went to camp. I was there teaching horseback riding."

"I don't care about that. I want to know how you feel about her."

"God, Joe. I don't know." His eyes closed as every moment they spent together raced through his head. Her beautiful blue eyes, wide with excitement, when he told her she could ride with him. Her big smile, when he agreed to let her help him with his art. The pain in her expression, when he shared about his mom. "We have this weird connection. I feel comfortable around her. I don't have to worry about anything. She has this—"

"Stop. Just tell me if she makes you happy." Her voice echoed in his head. "I just wanted to make you happy." She did. So much.

"Yes, God yes, and I don't have to pretend to be. I just am. If that makes sense. And I just screwed it all up." He let out a shaky breath.

"You love her."

"I think I do. But it doesn't matter now." His voice

broke as the words came out. "I pissed her off, if you can believe that. I have never seen the girl mad. She always has this sweet smile on her face. But leave it to me to break her spirit. I have a feeling it's over."

"It's not over until it's over."

Ben remembered her saying it was only over if he wanted it to be.

"I don't want it to be."

"Then go after her." His feet were already moving. Pushing open the doors, he wandered out into the kitchen and dining area and noticed the front door open.

"Kaysi?" he said, jogging toward the door. Her car was still parked in front of the house and the interior light was on. He could see she had already moved some boxes into the back, but he she was nowhere in sight.

"What's wrong?"

"Her car is here, the hatch is open, but she isn't here." Dread filled his gut.

"Hang on, let me ask April if she heard from her." Ben walked back into the house and called for her, but when there was no answer, he went back outside. There was no sign of her. "April said she hasn't heard from her. Maybe one of her friends came over and took her out to console her."

"Maybe so." His thoughts went back to the threatening messages and then the fire. "Did she tell you about the messages she got on her blog?"

"No, but April did. But, Ben, don't go there, man. The simplest answer is usually correct." The chilled breeze brushed across his skin, and after taking one more glance around, he reluctantly started back up the stairs to head inside. "She probably was upset, and she called one of her friends to go talk about it. Again, girls talk."

"Probably so. I'll try calling her."

"Good idea. Anyway, we have a meeting at Grayeagle tomorrow morning at eight, so I'm sure I will see her there."

"Okay."

"If I hear from her before that, I will tell her you are worried about her."

"All right." Ben hung up with Joe and called Kaysi. He heard her phone quietly chime, and his heart dropped into his stomach. Yanking open the front door, he saw the light of her phone glowing next to her car. He ran down the steps and grabbed it, then lowered his phone from his ear. Tapping the screen, it read ten fifteen. It was late. His fingers pressed against his temples, and he realized he was shaking. His mind raced with thoughts of what could have happened to her. He had to do something. Tapping the screen again, he took a deep breath.

"Hello?"

"Mitch. Hey, it's Ben Corbett. I think someone took Kaysi."

"Wanna tell me why?" His voice was gravelly.

Shit. Did I wake the man up? "We had an argument, and she stormed out of the studio. I called Joe to talk to him, and when I came out of the studio to talk to her, the front door was open. Her car was still here, with the hatch open, and I just found her phone on the ground by it."

"Have you tried calling her friends? Maybe one of them came and got her, and she dropped her phone."

"That's what Joe said, but why would she have left the hatch to her car open?"

"Maybe she thought she shut it, and it didn't latch."

"Mitch, I'm worried."

"I can tell but—"

"I keep thinking about the threatening posts, and the fire."

"I understand, but if you had a fight, and she was upset, she might have just left, and didn't realize she dropped her phone. You need to check with her friends and see if she is with them. That's probably where she is."

"I know she isn't with April. I already talked to Joe."

"Who else could she be with?"

"She and Libby had a fight, so I doubt she is with her."

"Check her phone. See if she called her."

He fished for her phone in his pocket and then tapped the screen. "I can't get into her phone."

"We had Miss Janaway up at the station today, questioning her about the fire, so I can get her number off of the computer."

"So, she's not the one who started the fire?"

"Don't know yet. She could be, but everything is circumstantial right now. It is her bracelet, but it could have just fallen off, while she was helping Kaysi move, like Kaysi said."

"She just has a bit of a temper. I'm not really a fan of her. I don't like the way she treats Kaysi."

"Really? She was acting like she and Kaysi were best buddies."

"No. She was pissed at Kaysi for going into business with April, and then she threw a fit at the charity dinner and stormed out."

"What was that about?"

"Apparently, Libby has a crush on Kaysi's ex, and he doesn't want to have anything to do with her, and she blames Kaysi."

"Interesting. Well, let me see if I can get her number, and I'll call you back."

He let out a deep breath. "Okay."

"Ben. Settle down. She probably just left because you were there, and she was pissed."

"I hope so, Mitch. But my gut says something happened."

After hanging up with Mitch, he went back to the studio, grabbed the album and his glass of iced tea, and took them to the living room, to wait for Mitch to call back. His phone buzzed a few minutes later. Mitch.

The number for Elizabeth Janaway is 697-352-9682. You might try calling her. If Kaysi isn't with her, give her until midnight, and give me a call back.

All right.

Staring at the room, after dialing Libby's number, he decided he would spend all night searching for her if he had to.

"Hello?" A groggy voice answered.

"Libby?" Ben said hesitantly.

"Yeah. Who's this?"

"This is Ben. Ben Corbett. Have you seen Kaysi?"

"No. She called me earlier, but I haven't seen her."

"I'm sorry if I woke you, I'm just worried about her. I can't find her."

"She was upset when she called, and asked if I would help her move tomorrow."

"Okay. I'm sorry to bother you."

"Have you talked to April?" Her voice suddenly had an echo and there was a strange thumping noise in the background. Libby cleared her throat and continued. "She might know where she is."

"Yeah. Never mind. I'm sorry to bother you."

He hung the phone up, and dropped his phone on the table, as another thought raced through his head. What if the argument sent her over the edge? What if all her demons came back? Ben leaned forward on the sofa rubbing his face with his hands. His chest tightened and his nose burned. "God, Kaysi, please don't hurt yourself." He started imagining different scenarios of what might have happened, each one more gruesome than the last. Throwing on his jacket, he stepped outside and walked out to her car again. Something out of the corner of his eye caught his attention. There was a red glow in the distance.

Brake lights? Who was driving around on his property? Hopping into his truck, he peeled out and raced up the trail to see if he could catch them, but when he reached the road, there was nothing. Slamming his head on the headrest, he felt like he was going crazy. Seeing things that weren't there. Maybe it was just a reflection or something. He sat at the entrance to their property, trying to decide what to do.

Picking up his phone from the cupholder, he tapped the screen.

"Hello?"

"Dad? Hey. You haven't seen any cars coming on the property in the past couple of hours, have you?"

"No. But I've been in bed since about nine thirty. Why?"

"Kaysi and I had a fight, and now I can't find her. Her car is here, and I found her phone lying beside it. I'm worried about her."

"She probably just called a friend, and they came and got her."

"That's what everyone is saying, but I have a bad feeling."

"Ben. You are letting your imagination run wild, because you are stressed from everything today."

He had a point. After finding Poppi this morning, everything had been a big, angry, blur. "I can't help it. Everything has turned into a big, steaming, pile of—"

"Just go home and get some rest. She will probably turn up fine. She just needed some space."

Leaning his head against the steering wheel, he closed his eyes and took a deep breath, and suddenly realized how tired he was. "Okay. Maybe you're right." He threw his truck in reverse and headed back to the bunkhouse. There was no way he was going to be able to sleep at his place, so he decided to sack out on the sofa, in case she came back.

****

His phone chimed, jarring him from his sleep. He lifted his head and looked around, not remembering he had lain down on the sofa, hoping to catch her when she came in. Pain shot from his head down his spine. Shoving his hand into his pocket, he pulled out his phone, and his eyes popped open, when he noticed it was after eight in the morning.

"Hello?

"Ben, it's Joe. Did you talk to Kaysi last night?"

"No. I fell asleep on the sofa waiting on her. I didn't hear her come in."

"She missed our meeting this morning."

Ben shot up from the sofa and ran into her bedroom. It was empty. "Joe, she didn't come home. She's not here."

Obviously hearing the panic in Ben's voice, Joe

said, "She may have just not wanted to stay there last night. Do you think she's with one of her other friends? Or could she have stayed at the loft?"

"I doubt it. There is no furniture there, and she's not with Libby. Something happened to her, Joe. I know it. I'm calling Mitch."

"Okay. Meet me at the loft. I'll call Cody and Kaleb."

Ten minutes later Ben drove into the shop parking lot. Checking the store, his stomach dropped, finding it, and the loft empty. As he exited the store, Joe showed up. April bailed out of the passenger side of Joe's truck. "What the hell did you do to my friend," she screamed, fire almost leaping from her eyes, mixing with her tears. Joe grabbed her, before she could throw the first punch. Ben had nothing. His neck was still throbbing, from sleeping sitting halfway up on the sofa, and he was exhausted.

"She's not in the loft," Ben mumbled. Cody drove up in his jeep, then Kaleb, who was on the phone as he approached.

"What do you have for me? Kaleb paused. "I'll let you know if I get anything."

"Who's that?"

"I'm calling in reinforcements," he said, in a voice that Ben had never heard.

Mitch was the last to arrive, and Ben closed the distance between them as he got out of his car.

"I told you something was wrong. She didn't come home last night. Something happened to her, Mitch," he said, before Mitch could open his mouth.

"Are you sure she isn't staying with someone?"

Firetrucks raced by, and Ben waited until they had

passed to answer. "No." Mitch rolled his eyes. "But she had an important meeting at Grayeagle this morning, and she didn't show up."

"She's upset. Could she have just forgotten it?"

"Well, to Ben's credit, she is very punctual, and she normally doesn't just blow off meetings." Joe stepped up, obviously hearing the conversation.

"Have you called her friends to see if she is with them?"

"Yeah. I called Libby, after you texted me her number. She said Kaysi called her and asked her to help her move." A small, white sedan pulled into the parking lot. "Speak of the devil." Ben nodded toward the car. Libby hopped out all smiles, with her hair curled, dressed in tight jeans, and a loose sweater, looking like she was going on a date, not moving boxes. When she locked eyes with him, her smile disappeared.

"What's wrong?" she said in a soft, breathy voice.

"Kaysi didn't come home last night."

"Seriously? Well, she did seem pretty upset when she called me."

Something about the tone of her voice was off. Ben noticed, from Mitch's narrowed eyes, he was suspicious too.

"Why exactly did she call you, Libby? You seemed mad at her at the dinner."

"Oh, that didn't last long. We made up."

"When?"

Libby's demeanor quickly changed. Her eyes darted around the group, who were now all staring at her. "Yesterday."

"When yesterday? I don't remember her getting a phone call, and she spent the day with me."

"I don't know. What's with the interrogation. I called her and apologized. She called me last night crying. She said you guys had a fight, and asked if I would help her move this morning, so I'm here."

"What else did she say?"

"Nothing. Malcolm called and told her he was going to bring by some of her things."

Mitch's forehead creased. "I thought you said she called you."

"She did."

"How could you have known what Malcolm told her, if he called her?"

The blood drained from Libby's face. "No. He, he called her before me."

Mitch took a couple of steps closer to Libby, who now resembled a trapped, wild animal.

Ben's phone chimed.

"Hello?"

"Ben. Get home now. Oren's house is on fire, and with the wind today, it's heading straight for us. You need to get the gates open."

"Wait. Poppi's land is on fire?" Cody's head popped up, and Ben nodded. "I'll…" he scanned the faces, remembering why they were there, and his stomach bottomed out. "I'll be right there," he said, completely broken.

His finger tapped the screen. "Poppi's land is on fire, and it's heading our way," he announced to everyone within ear shot.

Libby yanked her arm away from Mitch, who was escorting her back to the patrol car, and turned to Ben. "Is that the guy next door?" she questioned, her voice filled with alarm. "The rock house?"

"Yeah. Why?"

"No, no, no." Libby burst into tears. "She's there."

Ben's heart stopped. "What do you mean, she's there?"

"Kaysi. She's at the rock house."

His legs started moving before Libby finished. He hopped in his truck. Cody followed him in his jeep. His phone chimed again. "Ben, grab Dash when you get here. You are going to have to round up the horses, and get them to the far pasture," his dad instructed.

"I have to save Kaysi first. She's in the rock house."

"What the hell is she doing there? The fire is nearly on top of it."

"I can't talk about it right now. Cody is following me, and I don't know who else. I'll put Cody on it. Can you help?"

"Yeah. I'll get the horses saddled. Just get here."

He hung up with his dad and called Cody. When he heard the click, he started talking. "I'm getting the gate open. Get Poppi's horses to the far pasture by the highway. Dad is at the stables. He's going to help." He glanced up in the rearview mirror to see a stream of vehicles. He wasn't alone. Things were changing.

Ben pulled up to the stable. Barely waiting to shove the truck in park, he hopped out, grabbed Dash, and was racing through his pasture as thick smoke enveloped him, taking away the sunlight. He only hoped Cody and his dad were following.

Quickly unlocking the gate, he headed toward the abandoned house. Riding along the ridge, he could see the fire already surrounding it, as he approached. The roof was starting to smoke. He stopped momentarily, trying to figure out the best way in.

Lifting the bandana around his neck, he raced through the flames, up the backside, toward the house, and watched, as his dad and Cody came through the flames behind him and headed down the ridge, in search of the horses. Jumping from Dash, he tried to go through the back door, but it was locked. The window next to it was busted in one spot, so he slammed his elbow into it, tearing the rest of the glass and framing out. Stepping through the hole, he hollered. "Kaysi!" The smoke was thick, and the licks of the flames were the only things lighting up the interior enough for him to see anything. Coughing from the acrid fog, he brought his arm up, covering his nose and mouth, hoping to add another layer from the smoke. His eyes blinked and squinted as he tried to see through the haze, passing from the living room to the kitchen, then the dining room, but he didn't see her.

Chapter Twenty-Three

Even the slightest movement sent a sharp pain through her, making her dizzy. Her lungs burned from the smoke, pouring into the dark room. Kaysi had tried to stay awake throughout the night, knowing that the lump on her head, along with the cold, could kill her, but everything was starting to blur around her, and her body felt so heavy.

Libby surprised her when she showed up at the bunkhouse. She immediately started yelling at her for telling the sergeant the bracelet was hers, saying she betrayed her. Kaysi had had enough of people yelling at her, and was already bawling from the fight with Ben, so it was nothing for her to bite back at Libby, saying she probably was the one who set the fire. The yelling continued until her phone chimed, and Malcolm was added to the mix. Putting him on speaker, so she could continue to load boxes into her car, he said he wanted to drop off the stuff she had left at his place. She told him to drop it by the loft in the morning.

Obviously hearing the pain in her voice, he asked about her, and she confessed that she and Ben were over. He had asked if there was anything he could do, and that's all she remembered. The next thing she knew, she was waking up with a ferocious headache in pitch black darkness, with her hands and feet taped together, and tape over her mouth.

The cold quickly wrapped around her, and her body began to shake uncontrollably. Letting her eyes adjust to the darkness, she scanned the room. Bookshelves and peeling wallpaper slowly appeared, and she realized she was in the rock house. Her hands felt something fuzzy beneath her. She wasn't lying on the wood floor. The rug. Feeling for the edge, she grasped it, and rolled over until it wrapped around her, which helped a little with the cold. She was thankful that the weather had warmed up from the frigid temperatures that came in with the snow, but the wind that had whipped up in the past few hours had sent bursts of chilly air into the house.

When the sunlight finally broke through the darkness, she was encouraged. Something within her knew Ben was out there, searching for her. She could feel it. He would find her. Daylight peeked through the windows, and her eyes caught wisps of smoke curling through the air. *Oh God, Libby set the house on fire.* Panic surged through her as the sunlight was slowly taken over by the thick clouds of smoke.

Dread set in. She was going to die in the beautiful old house that yesterday, provided her with such happiness. Was it just yesterday that she and Ben were there with Joe? Tears stung her eyes, but she tried to stifle them, because she needed to conserve her breaths. She couldn't afford to cry, although the pain in her chest was unbearable.

How could things have gone so wrong? How could Ben ever think she didn't love him? She could tell, by the shock on his face, how surprised he was when she revealed who she was, but by that time, she knew there was nothing she could say to him that would change his mind. It had to be his decision. She wasn't so much angry at him, as frustrated that he had given up on being happy. He had resolved to live his life angry at the world.

God I'm so tired. She needed to close her eyes, for just a minute, and slowly they fluttered shut. The smell of smoke was now making it hard to breathe. She tried to conserve her breaths and breathe shallower. Darkness started to take over.

A loud bang drew her from her groggy state. Her eyes slowly open, and her heart pounded. She tried to scream, but all that came out was a muffled growl. Glass shattered. Was someone coming in, or was the fire consuming the house? She coughed, as the smoke continued to billow into the room.

"Kaysi!" His scream echoed through the house.

Ben! Her heart leaped out of her chest. She could hear him running through the house. She tried to scream again but it was still just a muffled groan. Mustering all her energy, she lifted her feet and banged them against the floor. Coughing hard from the exertion, she didn't care, and did it again. Tears streamed from her eyes partly from him being there, and partly from the smoke.

A shadowy figure appeared through the haze. She banged her feet once more and he was there. He was really there, leaning over her. Even with the bandana across his face, she could tell it was him. He quickly removed the tape from her mouth.

"You came," she wheezed and choked. Tears spilled from her eyes. The fire roared and a crash came from a nearby room.

"Don't talk. Let me get you out of here." He lifted her into his arms, holding her close as he quickly made his way through the burning structure, while it collapsed around them. Flashes of lights spun around them from the fire trucks arriving, as they stepped outside.

Every part of her body felt like it had stopped working, and her head was spinning, but her heart was soaring. He laid her on the ground next to Dash and cut the tape off with his knife. "How'd you know where I was?" she asked around fits of coughs.

"Libby confessed when she heard about the fire," Ben said quickly.

She took in a small gasp of air and tried to clear her head. "Wait. She didn't set it?"

"I don't think so. She was too surprised when she heard about it, and that's what made her confess." After freeing her feet, he wrapped his arm around her, and climbed into the saddle, then threw her leg over, so she faced him, with her arms wrapped around him. "We are going to go through some heat, so cover your head with your coat, and hang on." He leaned her against him and took off. She could feel the flames licking at their bodies, and it immediately became harder for her to breathe. She tried to take shallow breaths, but the heat was stifling. Her head was spinning. Her body felt heavy. Swaying with Dash's rhythm, she blinked, trying to focus, but the heat…she was so dizzy…darkness engulfed her.

****

"Kaysi?" A panicked voice pierced the fog in her head. She tried to respond but couldn't. Her lungs clamped down when she tried to cough. "Kaysi?" Her body shook, and then it was moving through the air, finally settling on something soft. Voices surrounded her, but they all sounded like distant echoes. Hands grabbed her, and something was on her face. She tried to swat at it, but her arms were still too heavy. "Kaysi, please. Stay with me," the panicked voice said. She wanted to open her eyes, but it took too much effort. Hands lifted her head and she felt them wrap something around it. Finally, her lungs released, and she breathed, then coughed. Her head began to clear, and she slowly peeled her eyes open. Everything was blurry, and she blinked, trying to focus. A deep growling noise surrounded her, causing her headache to return with a vengeance, and she closed her eyes again. A warm hand pressed into hers, and she wrapped her fingers around it. Again, she was moving. The roaring noise grew louder, and with a jolt, she was thrust into a bright light. She could feel a hand on her face gently brushing her forehead. "Open your eyes, baby."

They felt so heavy. She wanted to sleep, but she wanted to know what was happening, so she squinted, and tried to open her eyes again. Blinking to focus, she realized she was on a gurney in the back of an ambulance, and Ben was sitting next to her, covered in soot and blood. His hand was wrapped around hers and his eyes glistened. Must have been from the smoke. He said he never cried. When she turned her head and his eyes captured hers, she wondered, by the streaks on his cheeks, if she was wrong. Where did the blood come from? He dropped to the floor of the ambulance, burying his head in her chest. "There you are," Ben said softly. He lifted her hand to his lips and gently kissed it." God, I thought I lost you, Kaysi." His voice was thick with emotion. Brushing the hair from her face, his eyes met hers, and she could see the fear etched in his expression. "You scared the shit out of me."

"I'm sorry," she said, then slowly pointed at his jacket. "Are you hurt?"

He glanced down. "No, babe. That's you."

"Kaysi, I'm going to start an I.V. and get some fluids in you."

She carefully turned her head to see a guy in a blue uniform and nodded. Lifting her other hand to her head, she touched it gently where the pain was, and felt the gauze. "That's why I have a headache," she said, and another coughing fit hit.

Brant appeared at the back of the ambulance. "We're about ready to head out." Kaysi tried to sit up, but Ben shot her a glare.

Brant locked eyes with Kaysi. "This is my buddy, Jeff. He'll take good care of you." He sat down next to Ben after getting the I.V. started.

"You riding with us?" Jeff asked.

Ben looked at Kaysi, then back at Brant, who was still standing at the back of the ambulance. "Is that okay?"

"Yeah." Brant and Jeff said in unison.

He returned his focus to Jeff. "Yeah. I want to stay with her."

Jeff nodded at Brant, and he slammed the doors.

****

Kaysi faded in and out on the ride to the hospital. She couldn't tell if it was just sheer exhaustion, or something else. Everything hurt and felt like someone had added ten pounds of weight to all her extremities. Ben kept her hand in his, while Jeff took her blood pressure, and asked her a few questions. Every time her eyes landed on Ben, he was leaned over with his eyes closed like he was praying.

Once they were at the hospital, she was wheeled into a curtained area where a doctor was waiting to examine her. Ben went with her when they wheeled her into x-ray, and when she glanced over at him, torment filled his expression. As her head continue to clear, she became more confused. He'd made himself clear when she left him. He didn't want her. Why did he save her?

"Well, young lady, looks like you got lucky." The doctor pointed to the monitor. "I don't see any fractures. I think maybe you got out of this with a little smoke inhalation, and a pretty good concussion. You got a good bump on your head, but I think we can close the wound with a couple of staples, and in a couple of days, you will be good as new. How's your breathing, now that we have removed the oxygen?"

"Okay. My throat just feels a bit raw."

"Yeah. You'll probably be coughing quite a bit for the next couple of days. Just make sure and stay hydrated. The doctor turned to Ben. "You will need to keep an eye on her for the next day. We'll give her some pain medicine, and something for the nausea, but if she loses consciousness again, or she starts having trouble breathing, you will need to bring her back in."

"All right."

The doctor turned back to Kaysi. "Sit tight. I'll have someone come in and get you fixed up, and then you can go home."

When the doctor disappeared on the other side of the curtain, Kaysi slowly sat up on the gurney and Ben moved to her side. "Ben, you don't have to take care—"

He wrapped his arms around her and buried his face in her shoulder. Her heart fluttered with his touch, and she lifted her hands to respond, but the words he had thrown at her the night before, making her heart tear in two, suddenly came rushing back. And the pain returned.

Every angry word carried a jagged edge, that pierced her heart again. She loved him, but she didn't want his pity.

"I can call my…" Her hands moved to push him away, but she stopped, when she heard him sniff, and his body started to quake with sobs.

The floodgate opened. Years of pent-up emotions were finally released. "God, Kaysi, I thought I lost you," he said into her shoulder, each word laced with pain.

She could feel his fingers digging into her back and his arms squeezing tighter.

"You were like a rag doll when I lifted you off Dash," he said through the tears. "I kept calling your name, but you wouldn't wake up." He coughed and his body shuddered as the sobs came harder.

Tears stung her eyes, feeling the wave of emotion hit, knowing exactly how close she was to losing her life. She remembered smelling the smoke, and realizing that she might die, and no one would ever find her. But he did. Ben risked his life and came after her. Tears streamed down her cheeks.

"I love you so much. It would have ended me if I lost you, Kaysi."

Slowly, she wrapped her arms around him, holding him without saying anything. Her fingers massaged his head as his wheezy sobs softened. He leaned back pinching his nose and mouth. Seeing his eyes red rimmed, and face covered in tears, took her breath away.

His hands cupped hers. "You were right about everything, and I am so sorry. When you left, I knew immediately I had screwed up the best thing that has ever happened in my life. God, Kaysi, you have done nothing to deserve the way I treated you. You are so amazing, and so beautiful, and so far out of my league, I got scared.

"And your family—"

"Is just another family, Ben. We all have our faults. We all screw up."

"My screw up was of epic proportion, and I'm such an idiot."

"Ben—"

"I understand completely if you don't ever want to have anything to do with me—"

"Ben!" His eyes lifted to hers. "I love you. I told you that, and I meant it." Tears welled in Ben's eyes again, and he looked away.

His chin quivered as he spoke. "I knew when I couldn't find you at the house, something was wrong. Everyone told me you probably had someone come get you so you could get away from me. But I knew something was wrong."

"Libby showed up as I was packing boxes in the back of the car. She was pissed that I talked to Sergeant Gallagher and told him the bracelet was hers. I told her I didn't know he was trying to pin the fire on her when he asked, but she didn't care to hear it. Then, Malcolm called, wanting to know if he could bring by the stuff I left at his place. He realized something was wrong, and I told him you and I broke up. I'm guessing Libby didn't want me getting my claws into him again, because that is all I remember until I woke up in the house."

"I called her last night to see if you were with her. She acted like I woke her up." Kaysi turned away, again feeling the weight of the moment. She took a deep breath and closed her eyes and felt Ben's arms around her again. This time his lips pressed up against her neck and he whispered, "I don't know how I would have lived if I lost you." Tears filled her eyes, and her hand flew to her face as the tears slid down her cheeks. His fingers turned her face to his, and their eyes met. "I love you."

"I love you so much, Ben."

He leaned down and kissed her gently.

The clinking of the curtain being moved had them both jerking their gaze to a young guy in scrubs, with a big grin on his face. "Sorry for the interruption, but I understand someone needs their head put back together."

Kaysi raised her hand as heat flooded her face. Ben moved off the gurney, back into his chair. "That would be me," she said, wiping the tears from her cheeks.

The scrubs-clad gentleman stepped forward to her bedside and held out his hand. "My name is Charley." She shook his hand, before he slid on some gloves. "I'm going to have you lean forward for me. It might make you a little woozy, but don't worry, I got you." He pressed around on her scalp, then cleaned up the injury. "Okay, we can do this one of two ways. I can deaden your scalp, by sticking a needle into it, and putting some numbing juice in there, then throw a couple of staples in. Or I can pop the staples in there and send you on your way. Either way it's going to sting."

Kaysi glanced at Ben, who gave her an "I don't know" shrug.

"Let's go with number two and get it over with."

"Yeah. You're tough. Good choice." He smiled. Ben rolled his eyes at the guy's cheery disposition. Kaysi couldn't help but smirk.

Charley unwrapped the staple gun and got Kaysi into position. "Okay, here we go. Stay still, and it will be done before you know it." She scrunched her face, feeling the pressure of the gun against her head, and heard a pop, followed by another. "There. All done," he said, backing away. "That wasn't so bad, was it?" Dropping the equipment onto the tray, he shucked his gloves and disposed of them.

Surprised, Kaysi turned to him. "Actually no, it wasn't." Her eyes drifted to Ben, who was noticeably pale.

Apparently seeing her concern, he said, "I've broken bones, and not gotten as nauseous as I am right now, watching him do that to you. Geez. And that didn't hurt?"

"Stung a little, but not bad."

Ben let out a long breath.

"You okay there, man?" Charley questioned with his eyes locked on Ben. "You aren't going to pass out on me, are you?"

"I'll be fine. Just used to being the patient, not so much watching."

"Gotcha." Charley grabbed a clipboard off the counter and jotted some info down then ripped the papers off. "Staples need to come out in seven days. You can wash your hair, but don't scrub the area. This little bottle of pills is for pain," he held it up, and then set it right back down and picked up another, "and this one is for nausea. Rest the next couple of days. No exertion. You may feel a little dizzy and nauseous for a few hours. That's normal. Any blurred vision, severe headache that won't go away, loss of consciousness, or trouble breathing, come back in." He smiled and handed the papers to Kaysi.

"Am I done?" she asked, swinging her legs to the side of the gurney, and then regretting it.

"You are done, my dear, and may resume whatever you guys were doing. But preferably, somewhere else other than here." He yanked the curtain open. "But take it easy on the exertion, if you know what I mean." Charley smirked, and nodded to them both before shutting the curtain, leaving them alone.

Ben stood, grabbed her shoes, and helped her put them on. "Cody should be here in a minute. I texted him earlier."

"He knows?"

"Yeah, he and Dad moved the horses. He said there is quite a bit of damage on Poppi's land, but our land is fine."

Kaysi stood and wobbled.

"Do you want me to get a wheelchair?"

"No, I would rather just lean on you."

Ben tucked his lips in between his teeth but wasn't quick enough to hide his smile from Kaysi and wrapped his arm around her.

****

Kaysi still felt completely drained as Cody parked at the bunkhouse. Although they had given her something for the headache, her brain still was a bit foggy. Ben helped her out of the jeep and into the house. She could smell the faint stench of smoke, and wondered if it was her, or the result of the fire. "Why don't we get cleaned up, and I will put a fire in the fireplace, and make us some dinner."

"That sounds fabulous." She followed him to the walk-in shower in the master bedroom. He got a T-shirt, and another pair of fuzzy pajama bottoms he had stashed in case he worked late in the studio, then grabbed a couple of towels. Turning on the water, he helped her undress, then got himself undressed. Kaysi eyed Ben. She felt so drained, that even though she wanted nothing more than to feel his body against hers, she knew it would have to wait. Ben obviously saw the expression on her face, because he stepped closer to her, and ran his hands along her shoulders. "Don't worry, I'll be a good boy." She smiled and stepped into the shower and let the hot water stream over her sore muscles. Ben grabbed the soap, squeezed some on a rag, and rubbed it together, turning it into a thick lather. He slowly rubbed the rag over her body letting the bubbles wash over her. Wringing it out, he brought the warm rag to her face, and tenderly wiped her cheeks of the soot and blood, then brushed a sweet kiss to her forehead. She grabbed the shampoo, and he took it from her. Rolling her eyes at his obvious need to take care of her, she grabbed the rag and soap, and started soaping up his body.

"You're treading into some dangerous territory, I hope you know," he said with one side of his mouth tipping up. She moved the rag over his belly and up his side. His fingers gently massaged her head. "Where's the staples?" he asked working her hair into a lather.

Wrapping her fingers around his, she moved his fingers to the spot, and he tenderly worked his way around it. His hand wrapped around her jaw as he threaded his fingers down the long tendrils, and a zing shot through her. She closed her eyes while he leaned her into the stream of water and rinsed her hair. Slowly lifting her head, her eyes met his, and a lump formed in her throat. Ben was biting the corner of his mouth, and his eyes were filling with tears again. "I can't believe I was dumb enough to push you out of my life, and it nearly got you killed. Everything you said to me, it was like you were reading my mind. Everything."

"I told you. We have a connection. You did the same

thing to me at camp. It was so strange how you crawled into my head and knew everything I was thinking. I never forgot it. And last night, you knew I was in trouble."

Ben turned off the shower and grabbed the towels. "Did you really go back to camp just to see if I would be there?"

"Yes. But I also went back, because I knew Robin would be there. We stayed in touch, and it became our yearly get together, until I got an internship with a marketing firm in California one summer."

"Did you stay in touch with her after that?"

"Yeah. I went to see her about a year ago. She lives up near Springfield, Missouri, and works at a donut shop there. I surprised her. She's doing great. Has a boyfriend named Anthony, who works with her."

"That's good to hear." After Kaysi got settled on the sofa, Ben got the fire started, made them some sandwiches, and curled up with her. He gently kissed the top of her head. "How are you feeling now?"

"Better. Still dizzy." The warmth of his body against hers, helped her relax. "You didn't have to give me your fuzzy pajama pants, you know."

"I aim to please," he said, with a smile that she knew she would never tire of, because she knew she was the reason it was there. He loved her. She tugged the blanket, at the end of the sofa, over her legs, and Ben's smile disappeared. "Are you cold?"

"No. I'm fine. I just like fuzzy blankets." She smiled but the smile on Ben's face didn't return.

He stared at the fire for a long moment. "When I realized you had been in that house overnight, I was so scared you would have succumbed to the cold, and I would be too late."

"But you weren't. You came for me."

"I'd walk through fire for you. Well, technically I rode through the fire…" he chuckled at his joke. Then the smile disappeared. "You wouldn't have been there, if it weren't for me." He let out a long breath. "Kaysi, I can't tell you how sorry I am. I don't know why you have put up with me and all my shit. I've been nothing but trouble for you." She stared up at him as he studied her. "What is it about me?"

"What do you mean?"

"Why me?"

"Why?" She sat up, slid her plate on the coffee table, and turned to face him. Her fingers gently skimmed over his cheek. "Because I know your heart. I mean, yeah, you lost your way a little. But I saw it when you were eighteen. And I've seen it since. It's in the way you protected Poppi, and how you talked about your mom," her fingers threaded through his hair, "and the way you treat me. You take charge of situations; you don't back down, and you speak your mind. I love the way you put everything into your art." She raised up on her knees, and leaned in, placing both hands on either side of his face. "You're so hard, yet so tender. I love everything about you."

He set his plate on the table next to him and Kaysi straddled him. "Every time I have loved someone they left, and I got hurt. But with you, even though I kept telling myself I couldn't fall in love with you, because you were Joe's sister, because you just needed a fake boyfriend, because love always turned out bad for me, I couldn't stop myself. Every excuse went out the window when I was with you. Every day, I kept falling more and more in love with you." Kaysi could feel how fast Ben's heart was pounding when her hand pressed against his chest. A smile lifted the corners of his mouth, and she leaned in brushing her lips gently over his, and his hand quickly wrapped around her waist, dragging her closer, and deepening the kiss.

Chapter Twenty-Four

She was home. With him. He had to keep telling himself that. Flashes of her tear-stained face as he threw venomous words at her, echoes of the truth she shared, about how close she came to taking her life, and the feeling of her lifeless body in his arms, was almost too much for him to handle. The thought of how close he came to losing her forever, still singed his heart, and made him drop soft kisses to her forehead. His chest tightened, and his eyes burned.

She was as close as he would ever come, he figured, to meeting an angel on earth, and having her snuggled in his arms, fast asleep, took every ounce of breath in his lungs away. He could feel the rise and fall of her chest, and he still couldn't believe she was his. The words he spoke to Valerie came back to him. He did know what love was now. Kaysi had shown it to him over and over, and he was so captivated by her, he couldn't imagine his life without her in it. He never felt that way with Valerie. That all-consuming need to be with her.

His thoughts drifted to her, and Rick, and he wondered if anyone had gotten ahold of them about Poppi. A pang of anger stabbed him, thinking about the fact that they probably already knew, since they caused his accident.

The hurt, of his loss, penetrated his chest, and the

anger bubbled up, but glancing down at his beautiful ray of sunshine, with her hair scattered across his chest, he remembered her words. Love doesn't mean there isn't pain. The pain makes you appreciate what you have even more. And he did. He knew now he could handle the pain, if she was with him. She knew how to take the ache away with just a whisper.

His thoughts went back to the hospital room and Poppi. He was so glad she was with him when he died. Ben thought about the moments before it happened. He knew Poppi wanted to make sure he had the phone and the key. It was obvious. It meant something. But what? Mitch said Rick couldn't have been the reason for Poppi's death, because he was with him, but it couldn't have been an accident. He carefully picked up the phone off the table, trying not to wake Kaysi with his movement, and typed in the passcode.

Thumbing through his screens, he felt like he was invading Poppi's privacy. Nothing seemed odd. Photos, e-mail, games. He had hotel apps and maps, and apps for restaurants. *What do you want me to find Poppi?* He skimmed through his photos, all twenty of them and nothing seemed off or out of the ordinary. Checking through his e-mail, he found some e-mails with his lawyer but nothing revealing, just appointments. Scanning the apps again, he noticed a folder labeled extra, with several icons. Most were likely apps he didn't use. A compass, voice memos, a music app, then he noticed one that said Kloaked, and remembered Poppi talking about the security system he put in, that notified him when there was activity. He clicked on the app and the page opened. Six squares popped up. Three were black, and three were hazy. Ben figured it was the cameras at his house. At the top of the screen on the right, it said activity, with a picture of an eye. Clicking on it, several posts of videos filled the page. Ben clicked on one, that was a still shot of Kaysi and him, when they stopped by. There was a short video of their chat with Poppi. The next one in the time progression, was a still shot of an SUV in the driveway. Tapping on it, he immediately recognized the person at the house, and his heart dropped in his stomach. Mitch needed to know, but it would have to wait. He slid out from under Kaysi, and carefully picked her up. She stirred enough to giggle and wrap her arms around his neck as he carried her to bed.

****

Ben barely got any sleep the past few days, worrying about Kaysi, and thinking about what his meeting with Mitch might mean. With the sunlight breaking through the window, and Kaysi's warm body stirring next to him, he opened his eyes and took a deep breath, then coughed, still feeling the residuals of the fire. Kaysi's lips dusted kisses over his chest, and he glanced down at her and groaned, as a smile danced across his lips, and hers continued down his stomach. "This is a very nice way to wake up," he said with a rasp. She scooted in between his legs, and continued down in the covers, to where all he could see was her big blue eyes, and a bright smile. Her tongue pressed against her teeth as she giggled. *God, how could I have tried to send this woman away.* The sound of her giggle, and the mischievous glint in her eye, made him laugh. What was she up to? Then he felt the tug of his pajama bottoms, and he knew. She popped up from under the covers, with his bottoms held in her hand like a prize. He gave her a playful smirk, and she pounced on him, kissing him all over his face, and down his neck, before his hands gently captured her, and their eyes locked. "I'm guessing you are feeling better?" Her nod was exaggerated. "But you heard the doctor, you shouldn't exert yourself."

"It's been two days. I'm feeling much better," she said wiggling her brows. "But I'll stop if you want—"

"No, no. Don't stop on my account. I'm just making sure you are okay," he said, already feeling his body responding to her touch. She nodded again, with the same exuberance as before. "Hmm…whatever shall we do with all that energy?" He pressed her to him and brought her lips to his. He was happy to let her release her energy on him.

She dragged her lips away far too soon for him. But his body stiffened as she yanked her T-shirt over her head and pushed his up until he sat up and tugged his off. His hands wrapped around her back, and his mouth captured her breast. A gasp escaped, and her fingers dug into his hair. Her mouth lowered, dropping a kiss to the top of his head, then she slowly pushed back and kissed his cheek and neck. Her hips rocked against him, and with a deep moan, she descended on his body again, grazing his neck with her teeth and lips, and traveling over his chest. His hands skimmed down her silky skin and pushed at the last tiny piece of fabric separating them.

Her lips continued to dust his torso with lush kisses as she slipped out of her panties. His brows lifted, and a smile rose on his lips when she held them up and tossed them over her shoulder. Then her eyes closed, and her mouth captured his, as their bodies connected. With a whimper she pushed herself up. Ben watched as the moment took her, and her body moved fluidly against him. She leaned forward, letting her hair fall around her face. Her fingers dug into the pillow, and her lips met his.

The feel of her body moving against his washed over him, and he let out a low growl. Their tongues slid against each other, and he could feel the intensity pulsating through her. His hands slowly slid down her side to her butt. She pulled her lips from his, and he opened his eyes wanting more. With her thick lashes pressed against her cheeks and her fresh-kissed lips parted, Ben couldn't stop staring at the stunning creature in front of him.

Raising up slightly, she slowly opened her eyes, and he knew he had been caught, as a bright smile filled her face. She pulled him up, placed her hand on his cheek and captured his mouth. Her hair fell against his shoulder, and he brushed it back, before he let his lips travel down her neck to her breast again.

A groan crept up his throat as pin pricks fired throughout his body. His hands rested on her hips, pressing her to him, and her body started to tremble. He filled his hand with her silky raven hair, and tugged her head to the side, allowing him access to the soft part between her neck and shoulder. His teeth dragged against her velvet skin, and he nipped and sucked, marking her as his, forever.

Her moans grew louder, driving him to the brink of ecstasy. His body shuddered trying to stave off the sensation threatening to overtake him. She leaned against him, pressing him into the bed, her hand quickly tucking her hair over one shoulder.

Their slick bodies moved in sync. Capturing her mouth, he fed on her plump lips. His eyes opened, and he watched as her head fell back, and her chest heave with jagged breaths. He wrapped his hands around her hips and gazed in amazement at her as her body shuddered in his arms.

His spine exploded when his release hit with such force a strained groan escaped. The intensity took his breath, and his eyes slammed shut. His entire body surged with pleasure. Wrapping his arms around her, he held tight as their bodies satisfied each other.

Slowly Ben rolled to his side, letting her move off him. Her hair flew into her face, and he pushed it behind her ear then tugged her to him. Her face glistened with sweat, but her eyes were sparkling. A smile spread across his face. "How are you feeling now?"

"A bit dizzy actually." The overwhelming feeling of euphoria, popped like a bubble, and concern filled him. Kaysi giggled, evidently seeing his expression change. "Not from the concussion, silly." Her lips pressed against his.

"Ooohhh," he said, with his lips still being assaulted by hers. "In that case…" he deepened the kiss and wrapped his hand over her hip.

****

Ben was quiet on the way to the station, anxiously mulling over everything he wanted to discuss with Mitch. His thoughts went back to Poppi, and the papers he had on his table. What exactly was his plan? Every time he thought about it, anger simmered, But Kaysi's warm touch was like a ground wire to the impulses surging through his body. She kept him steady, able to focus, and not let his emotions get the best of him. He glanced over at her. The sunlight hit her face just right, as she watched the scenery go by, and made her face shimmer. He was convinced, she really was an angel. She had cleansed him of demons that had possessed him for too long.

Her dark brown hair was down today, skimming her face and dusting against a ruby red, loosely fitted, cotton top. Ben didn't realize he was staring, until her eyes widened with fear, and she gasped. He quickly steered the truck back onto the road. Embarrassed, he smirked, "Sorry, I kind of got distracted."

Parking outside the police station, Ben took a deep breath before getting out. He quickly draped his arm over Kaysi's shoulder, letting her ground him again, and kissed the top of her head. Grabbing the door, he let Kaysi go in before him. Mitch stood in the foyer and offered a pleasant smile to her. He shook Ben's hand, before his focus went back to Kaysi. "How are you feeling today, young lady?" They passed through the metal door and headed up the musty hallway.

"Much better. My head is still tender, but my headache finally went away."

"I figured we could kill two birds with one stone, with both of you here. Ben can give me his information, and I can get your statement. Does that work for you guys?"

"Sure," Kaysi said. Pausing for a moment, she softened her voice. "What happened to Libby?"

As they entered Mitch's office, Ben scooted up a couple of metal chairs in front of Mitch's desk. Mitch kicked back in his chair and chunked his sunglasses on his desk. "Well, Miss Janaway's family posted her bail about an hour ago. She was fairly cooperative, and confessed to the loft fire, assaulting you, and leaving you at the abandoned house. I don't feel, at this time, that she set the fire at the McIntyre property though. She said she was just getting you out of the way to meet someone."

"Malcolm," Kaysi quickly said.

"Yes. We will be giving him a call to get his statement and see where he fits into this matter.

"He's an innocent bystander. I doubt he even knows what happened, unless someone was at the loft when he showed up."

Mitch's focus moved to Ben. "You were right. Miss Janaway's tune was much different this go round. She had quite a bit of animosity towards Miss Grayeagle." Mitch turned to Kaysi, pointing his finger in her direction. "We also feel sure that the threatening messages, you were getting on your website, were generated by her."

"Really?" Kaysi's mouth formed a thin line of distress. "I just never thought—"

"Most never do." Mitch sat forward. "So, are you ready to give your statement?"

"Sure. What do I need to do?"

"What I will do first, is take your verbal statement." He retrieved a recorder, from his desk drawer, and set it in front of her. "Start with when she showed up. Try to remember everything you can, about the conversation, and anything else, that stands out. Use all your senses. I may stop you, and ask you questions along the way. Then we will move on to your written statement."

"Okay." The apprehension in her voice stabbed at Ben's chest, and he laced his fingers with hers. As Kaysi recounted the incident, Ben could feel his temper flaring, imagining what she went through, imagining what would have happened, if Libby hadn't had her conscience get the better of her, imagining if he hadn't gotten to her in time. His jaw pulsed, trying to stave off the lump filling his throat. But just as his imagination was carrying him away, Kaysi's delicate hand squeezed his, and calmed him. Even though she was having to recount her terrifying experience, she calmed him. His eyes glanced at her and found her staring at him with a slight smirk. Her eyes were sparkling. Goosebumps sent electric pricks across his skin in waves.

"...And I heard this banging noise, and Ben called out my name. I couldn't see him, but just his voice, sent this overwhelming relief through me. He saved me," Kaysi said, as she finished. Ben tried hard not to smile, but it spread across his face before he could tamp it down.

"You were extremely lucky, Miss Grayeagle."

"Please, call me Kaysi. Anytime anyone calls me Miss Grayeagle, I think they are talking about my mom."

"As long as you call me Mitch," he countered. He pushed a clipboard forward. "All right. Just take your time and give us your written statement recounting the incident. Again, use all your senses." Kaysi's hand slid from Ben's as she picked up the clipboard. Mitch turned his attention to Ben. "While she is doing that, tell me what you have for me."

Ben dug out Poppi's phone and tapped in the passcode. "Did you know Poppi put in security cameras at his house?"

"Good. I told him to."

"Before he died, he made it apparent he wanted me to take his phone and keys. Specifically, a security box key. I didn't understand why, but last night I started snooping around on his phone and found this." He pressed the screen and handed the phone to Mitch. Mitch stared into the phone, watching the footage. Setting the phone down, once the video was done, Mitch locked his fingers together and flexed them.

Ben leaned forward. "I only watched the one, but there are others, and if you check footage before that one, it's of Kaysi and me. The time stamp shows, there wasn't much time between the two videos. We went by there while I was checking on the horses. He had all kinds of paperwork sitting on the table. He said he needed to confront Rick about something. His will was sitting out. I think he might have been trying to trap Rick, Mitch."

"I know what he was doing. Oren wanted to clear the air. He suspected Rick of causing some of the problems that had happened on the ranch, and he also wanted to know what had happened at Randy's company. He said Randy had come to him, just before he died, saying he thought Rick was embezzling funds. He was worried Rick was going to ruin the company and didn't know what to do.

"Oren didn't want to believe Rick was capable of embezzlement." Mitch leaned back in his chair, grasped one wrist with the other, and rested them on his head. "Not that he was incapable of doing it, but he just didn't think Rick would want to hurt his dad's company. And after Randy left that weekend, he called Oren later, and said they had talked, and worked things out.

"Oren said when he heard Rick was later suspected in Randy's death, he didn't believe it. Randy had a good relationship with Rick, and he didn't see why he would do something like that, especially since Randy said they'd worked things out. Right after the memorial service was over, Rick came to him saying the company was in trouble, and he needed money. He didn't give him the details, but said he was trying to make it right. Oren believed him.

"I guess later, Rick came back bad-mouthing his dad, after he didn't leave him the company, blaming him for the financial issue, not knowing Randy had already talked to Oren. Rick said he was trying to fix his dad's mistakes, and he needed more money, which of course pissed Oren off. He wasn't sure what the partner was doing, or what he was aware of, so he forked over more money. And that's when Oren started wondering, if Rick did have something to do with Randy's death. He asked me to find out what evidence the police had.

"Then, I guess about a year ago Rick started talking to Oren about turning the land over to him. When he refused, that's when things started happening, like the cattle that went missing, and the gate being open."

"Yeah, Oren told me Randy and Rick worked the financial issues out, that it was a misunderstanding. But then a few days later, Randy died. Valerie said she thinks he might have killed him. That's why she's back in Dalton."

"Really?" Mitch questioned lifting a brow. "But I thought—"

"She says they're separated."

"Oh. I heard she was here, because her dad had fallen at the butcher shop." Mitch paused. "Anyway, there is no evidence that Randy's death was anything other than an accident. But Oren decided he'd had enough of Rick's silly little games. He said he was going to sit down with him and lay the cards on the table. He had the financial statements Randy had shown him, the police report from Randy's accident, and he got Rick to agree to meet with him at noon on the day he died.

"When I saw Rick at Tia Luna, we talked about him meeting Oren for lunch. Oren's lawyer was going to be there too, and we had planned to have patrol in place for the meeting, but we got pre-empted." He tapped the phone. "The problem with this is, all we have is the exterior video. We don't know what happened inside." Mitch rubbed his face. "Okay what else did you say he gave you?"

Ben brought out the set of keys. "His keys. But specifically," he held up the long gold key, "this one." Ben passed the set of keys to Mitch. "We figured out it goes to a security box at Dalton Savings and Loan."

"Have you been by there yet?"

"No. We were going to go by there after leaving here."

"Go, get back to me on what you find. I'm going to work on a plan moving forward."

Chapter Twenty-Five

"Are you ready?" Mitch asked, as Ben shut his truck door and approached him, nervously wondering what was in store for the day.

"I guess. I'm still not sure why I need to be here."

"Evidently, Oren had his reasons." Mitch wiped his mouth. "When I talked to the lawyer, he said you needed to be here, as per Oren's wishes."

"But you know why. Don't you?"

Obviously avoiding the question, Mitch patted him on the shoulder as he entered the building. "We will be listening in on the meeting, so if anything starts to go awry, don't worry."

Ben let out a nervous laugh at Mitch's evasive tactics, then followed it with a long breath, still feeling a bit confused. "Okay." Mitch handed him the thick, brown, clasped envelope.

Adjusting his untucked, white, button-down shirt, he then ran his fingers through his hair, and gazed to the ceiling of the lobby of the law office of Hill and Farrell, muttering, "Poppi, what have you done?" With one last glance to Mitch, he strolled into the conference room.

It was mid-morning, and although Kaysi offered to make him some waffles, he refused. His stomach was rolling like the surf with an approaching hurricane. An older gray-haired man, in a nice navy suit, was standing in the corner of the dark wood paneled room, staring out the window.

The corner of his mouth turned up, when he noticed Ben, and he held his hand out, as he closed the distance between them. "Frank Hill. And you are?"

"Ben Corbett," he said, letting out a gush of air.

Frank's half smile turned into a full grin. "Pleasure to meet you, Ben. Thank you for coming." He adjusted his gold watch and said, "We have a few more minutes." His eyes returned to Ben. "Would you like a bottle of water?"

"Yes. That would be great." His nerves felt like a swarm of hornets had invaded his body, and his mouth felt like a drought had set in. When he and Kaysi stopped by the savings and loan, he found an old, thick, brown envelope, wrapped with twine, inside the deposit box. He immediately dropped it off with Mitch, in case he needed it for the investigation, without finding out what was inside. Later, he was called with instructions to be present for the reading of the will.

He wished Kaysi was there to help steady him, but Mitch advised against it, and she was helping April stage the loft a block away, anyway.

It had been a week since Poppi's death, and the fire. The incident was still listed as under investigation, and Mitch had been somewhat tight lipped about what all was going on, but said he hoped that today's meeting would put everything to rest. The fact that he had officers hidden away around the building, had Ben wondering what they expected would happen.

His heart dropped to his stomach, when he heard familiar voices. Rick and Valerie entered the room hand and hand. He didn't turn his head, just saw them out of the corner of his eye, but he wondered why Valerie seemed so comfortable next to Rick. What kind of game was she playing? She glanced at him, and a spark of fear danced across her face, before she turned away.

"What the hell are you doing here?" Rick immediately asked as he entered the room.

Frank turned with a smile on his face. "Ah, you must be Rick. Frank Hill." He held his hand out. Rick begrudgingly offered a handshake. "And you must be Valerie. Frank Hill." Valerie pasted on a fake smile and delicately shook his hand. She was dressed in a hunter green, long-sleeved dress. Her hair was twisted on the back of her head. Gold earrings dangled from her ears, and she had a matching necklace around her neck. She had changed so much from the farm girl he'd met years ago. She'd gotten her degree in something to do with finance, and he knew her dad was hoping she would stick around, and help with the business, but she wanted out. She was tired of the tiny town and was always wanting to take day trips to the city, for concerts and shows.

He glanced up at her, as she shook Frank's hand. "Yes. It's nice to meet you," she said in a breathy, high-pitched voice, that Ben had to force himself not to react to, since he'd never heard her use it. *Where the hell did that come from?* He'd always felt like she put on airs when they were dating, like she didn't want people to know the real her, the girl born to a butcher and a schoolteacher.

"Mr. Hill?" Rick interrupted, as Frank turned and headed to the front of the conference table, where piles of papers sat. Frank offered another toothy smile, and his eyes darted to Rick. "Can you tell me why he's here?" Rick's finger stabbed the air toward Ben.

Frank's eyes landed on Ben, then back at Rick. "Would you and Valerie like a bottle of water, before we get started?"

Rick shook his head, and glanced at Valerie, who did the same, and Ben wondered again if Valerie's comment about being separated from Rick was a ruse, by the look he gave her. The rock sitting on her finger, raised his suspicions considerably. Was it there when they talked before?

Frank motioned for everyone to sit down, and Ben took a seat across from Rick and Valerie, with his eyes on the door. Ben had wondered what Mitch had cooked up, and where exactly he had placed the microphone, since they were listening in. He peered from under his brow, glimpsing at Valerie, still unsure if she was part of Poppi's death, or if Rick was abusing her. Seeing her on the security feed sent a rock to his stomach, and even thinking about it made him shudder. It was hard for him to believe she could be cold-blooded enough to kill Poppi. There had to be an explanation.

"All right. We are here—"

"Before we get started, does he need to be here?" Rick pointed again to Ben, and Ben stifled a chuckle, amused at the fact that Frank basically ignored him the last two times he asked.

"Yes. Your grandfather requested that he be present." Frank opened a briefcase and lifted out a small tape recorder, and Ben suddenly noticed the recorder looked oddly familiar.

"Now as I was saying, we are here for the reading of the Last Will and Testament of Oren Patrick McIntyre."

Ben suddenly stilled, realizing Rick was named after his grandfather. All this time he had assumed Rick stood for Richard, but after hearing Oren's full name, it was obvious Rick was also a Patrick. Randy was always close to his dad. He just wasn't cut out to be a rancher. His heart stumbled at the fact that Oren knew his namesake was, quite possibly, responsible for killing his only son.

Frank pressed the button on the small recorder. "This meeting will be recorded for legal purposes. If you agree to this, please answer by saying yes."

Frank nodded, and once each person at the table had agreed, he began.

"I, Frank Hill, have been retained by Oren Patrick McIntyre as executor of his last Will and Testament."

Ben's heart rate ticked up, as his nerves started to eat at him. He rubbed his hands together under the table, trying to steady his pulse, wishing Kaysi was there. The way she gently played in his hair and ran the back of her fingers along his chin and neck, always made him relax. She was the only one who knew how to calm him.

"Mr. McIntyre's assets include one residence, and contents therein, that sits upon approximately two hundred acres. Value of this property is yet to be determined, due to the recent fire. All land, mineral rights, outbuildings, equipment, and livestock on this property, will be deemed property of the benefactor, or benefactors, named in this will. Mr. McIntyre also holds real financial assets at Dalton Savings and Loan, as well as a life insurance policy, that will pay out to the benefactor, or benefactors, within the next thirty days." Frank turned and leveled his eyes at Ben. "Mr. Corbett, do you have the envelope you were given?"

Ben picked up the worn, brown envelope, sitting in front of him, stood slightly, and handed it to Frank, wondering what was inside.

"Thank you." Frank nodded, then turned to Rick and Valerie, and sat back down. Unwinding the string tying the envelope closed, he slid out a pile of papers, unfolded them, then turned to Rick and Valerie. "Among these papers, are signed court documents showing your grandfather to be of sound mind as of approximately two weeks ago, his burial requests, and his signed and notarized will."

Frank pressed the creases out of the folded papers. "I, Oren Patrick McIntyre…" Frank started, and Ben's heart felt like it was going to pound right out of his chest. His mind spun out of control, revisiting the last time he really talked to Poppi; seeing him lying on the ground, blood spilling from his body; watching the monitor as the heartbeats separated farther and farther apart, until it was just a flatline.

His eyes stung. As Frank's voice echoed in his ear, stating that Poppi wanted to be buried next to his wife in the Dalton Memorial Gardens Cemetery, Ben felt the room closing in. That's where his mom was buried, and he avoided that place like the plague. The last time he was out there, was for the graveside service for Randy, Poppi's son, and now it would be for Poppi.

He didn't want to hear any more and felt the overwhelming urge to get up and leave. He didn't want Poppi to be gone, and he damn sure didn't want to be sitting across from the people, who probably were responsible for his death. Responsible for taking Poppi away from him.

Mitch had made him promise he would keep his cool, when they had spoken on the phone, but listening to Frank, as he moved on to the will, and slowly read through the legal jargon, it was absolutely killing him knowing they were going to get their hands on the land after all.

He knew Rick had something to do with Poppi's death, even if Mitch said he was with him when it happened. Poppi didn't want to give up his land. He had said so, but he knew Rick was desperate to get his hands on it, and now he would get it, and probably sell it off for the money, or dig it up for some stupid legend.

A pain shot through every cell of his body, just thinking about what was to come. Everything would be Rick's, including the horses. He had to find a way to get Rick to at least sell him the horses. After helping out with them for so long, he had come to love every one of them. The more he thought about it, the more the storm built in him.

"…I hereby leave all my assets and possessions, both financial and real personal property, to Benjamin Wade Corbett."

Hearing his name, Ben's head jerked up. He was absolutely certain he didn't hear right. "Wait. Come again?" But he wasn't the only one wanting a repeat. Rick and Valerie both stood.

"What did you just say?" Rick raged.

"That isn't right? It says Rick is the benefactor," Valerie blurted.

Rick's eyes shot to Valerie. "Let me handle this, babe."

"What does?" Frank responded.

"He left everything to Ben?" Rick questioned. "That son of a bitch."

Valerie put her hand on Rick's shoulder. "He's mistaken," Valerie said, letting her hand wander down Rick's arm. "The will specifically says you are the benefactor."

Frank leaned back in his chair with one brow raised. "Where did you see this will? And when?" Valerie hesitated, and Frank continued. "I mean, Oren might have made a last-minute change, that I wasn't aware of."

"At his house," she breathed, "a-a couple of days before he died."

"And you are sure it showed Rick as the benefactor?" Frank leaned forward, clasping his hands together on the table.

Ben followed suit, and put his elbows on the table, trying to hold himself up long enough to watch, what was undoubtedly, something Mitch had put together, to finish what Poppi had started.

"Yes." She reached down retrieving her purse. "I have it." She yanked out a pile of folded papers.

Rick's eyes widened. "Valerie? Where'd you get that?" His voice raised an octave, letting Ben know that Rick knew something wasn't right.

She gave him a cheerful glance and shoved them at Frank. "It's just a mistake. He needs the correct paperwork."

"And Oren gave you these papers?" Frank prodded.

The color drained from Valerie's face, and matched Rick's, who was now staring with his mouth gaped open. She glanced at Ben, her eyes pleading for help. "I-I—"

Frank continued to question. "Mrs. McIntyre, how did you manage to get your hands on this will?"

"I-I told you I went by there a couple of days before he died."

"And why did you go by there?"

"I-I wanted to talk to him."

Ben watched her as her eyes darted back and forth

searching for an explanation, that she knew wasn't there. His mind played back the security video. He couldn't bring himself to watch the footage past seeing her on Poppi's doorstep, after he and Kaysi left his house. What was she doing there? He already knew she had lied, saying she was there a couple of days before he died. Why were there two different wills?

"Talk to him about what?" Frank continued to prod.

Ben saw Mitch enter the room from the corner of his eye. He stepped to the table with his arms crossed. Valerie jerked her head quickly. Her eyes narrowed, and Ben could tell she suddenly was aware, that this was more than a reading of the will. She glanced around the room, and her eyes landed on Rick. Ben's blood ran cold from the calculated look that crossed her face.

"I needed to find out how much he knew, and what Rick did." Rick jerked his head, surprised at her comment, and grabbed her arm.

"What the hell, Valerie?"

Mitch moved toward her, but she yanked away from him, and sat back down in her chair. Mitch stepped between them. Ben's eyes bounced between the two of them as confusion filled his head.

"What did Rick do?"

Valerie glanced around the room. "He stole money from his dad's company, and in the process set it into a tailspin."

"I did not."

She rolled her eyes. "He has a gambling problem, and to support it, he skimmed money from the company. The problem though, was he wasn't very good at it, so when he was trying to cover his tracks, he set the entire company into a downward spiral. His dad found out about it, and I'm sure that was the reason his dad didn't leave him the company.

"Rick said he tried to fix it with the money Randy left him, but it wasn't enough. Oren knew the company was in trouble, but I had to find out, if he knew it was because of Rick. If he did, and knew about Rick's other little secret, there was a good chance he wouldn't give us the land, so I had to try to persuade him. All our own money was tied up in the company, so if it went under, we were going with it, and would probably have to file for bankruptcy.

"Even though Randy's partner took over, I don't think he was truly aware of the magnitude of the problem. He handled a different group of clients and wasn't that familiar with Randy's clients. He knew the company was in trouble, however there was no way he could fix it by himself, and knew Rick had a much better chance at correcting the situation.

"Oren's land was the only way we figured we could save the company. He was so adamant though about wanting to keep the land, when he finally said he wanted to talk about turning it over to Rick, I had a feeling something was up, so I decided to go over there. I realized when I got there, he knew what Rick had done. He had financial papers strewn across the dining room table, and other paperwork. It was obvious he was going to confront Rick."

"And what happened?" Mitch questioned, now leaning, with his backside against the table, between Rick and Valerie.

"Nothing. I noticed the will, figured he was going to tell Rick he was going to change it, because of what he did, so I grabbed the papers and left."

"And why did you grab the papers?"

"I-I—" tears welled in her eyes, and Ben felt a pang of sympathy for her. Was she just Rick's pawn? The plea in her eyes at the restaurant, the first night he saw her, made him wonder, but he also knew, from experience, how manipulative she could be. Her lips quivered. "I did it because of Rick."

"Did what Mrs. McIntyre?" Mitch continued to question.

"Don't you dare blame me, Valerie. I had nothing to do with this. I didn't even know you went over there."

"He killed his dad, and when Oren wouldn't give up the land, I was scared he was going to kill him too. I went over there to try to talk to him. Make him realize he was in danger."

"That is bullshit, Valerie, and you know it." Rick barked. "Dad's death was an accident. The rocks gave way, and he fell. I got help as fast as I could. It was just too late. And as far as I'm concerned, Oren's death was an accident, too."

Ben's head was spinning. He remembered Poppi telling the story. He said Randy and Rick had gone up into the mountains to hike and camp, and Randy slipped and fell. It took Rick several hours to get help, because there was no cell service, but it was all Rick's account, so anything could have happened to him.

"He's lying. He killed him, because Randy found out he was embezzling funds from the company."

"That's not true. I made an honest mistake and Dad knew it. Heck, Tetterman even knows it. Otherwise, do you think he would have kept me around?" Rick turned to Mitch. "Dad came to me asking about the discrepancy, and I explained what had happened. It was a rookie mistake. I asked one of my colleagues for help on something, when Dad was out of the office. I misunderstood what he said and entered some wrong data. When I noticed the mistake, I tried to fix it. When Dad questioned me about it, I owned up to it.

"Yes, I kept it from him, but just because I wanted to fix it myself. I didn't want him thinking I couldn't handle the business, or feeling like he had to come behind me, fixing my mistakes. I was learning the business, and I wanted to be a good partner. I wanted to prove myself. We were good after we talked. He's the one who brought up hiking. We were both under a lot of stress, and we hadn't been out in a while. Hell, why would I kill him before the problem was fixed? That's stupid. You can even ask his partner, Bill Tetterman. He was there when Dad brought up going hiking."

"You're lying. Oren found out about you stealing from the company, and your mom's little secret, and you knew he would never give you the land. That's why you killed him."

"Wait. What secret?"

"You know."

Rick stared at her blankly, evidently confused by her statement, then threw himself in the chair, put his hands flat on the table, and laid his head on them. "I have no idea what she's talking about." Breathing hard he lifted his head and continued. "Sergeant, you know I didn't kill him. I was with you when the call came in. He got trampled by his horses."

Ben sat, watching the circus unfold, wondering who was lying, and who was telling the truth. Rick's explanation was plausible. His dad's death could have been an accident. But he could have also used the invitation to get rid of him, so he wouldn't find out what he really did to the books. And if Poppi found out, Rick could have somehow staged the accident with the horses, to save his butt, and gain the estate.

His thoughts went back to the security video which left no questions, Valerie was at the house right after he and Kaysi left, just after eight. By the time they found Poppi it was after eleven. What happened in those hours? Could she have gone there to warn him like she said, or did she want to make sure she got what she wanted.

But if Valerie did kill him, how was she able to do it? Poppi was a decent sized man. He could have easily fought her off. Did Rick somehow help her?

"So, Mrs. McIntyre, how did you find out that Rick might have embezzled funds from the company? His dad died before you guys met, right?"

"I have an accounting degree," Valerie said haughtily. Ben nodded. *Accounting, that was it.* "He left his work computer open one evening, when he was on a call. It wasn't hard to figure out something was off. What he was doing was illegal."

Rick raised up on his elbows, and his head fell into his hands, and he sighed. "She knew, because I told her I screwed up." Dropping his hands from his face, he continued. "When we started dating, right after Dad died, I wanted to be upfront with her. I had gotten it almost completely corrected with the money from Dad's estate, and from Oren, but then the taxes hit, and they were quite a bit more than I expected, and I panicked. She said she would help me fix it. Oh, she fixed it all right. If anyone was doing anything illegal, it was her."

Tears streamed down her face. "He's lying."

Rick slammed his hands on the table making

everyone jump. "Bullshit, Valerie. You did it because you were scared we wouldn't be able to afford your cute little Porsche, and your Jimmy Choo shoes, and your Coach bags."

Ben's conversation with her at the charity event popped into his head. Her comment about doing just about anything to keep your money once you have it, made his stomach churn. Could she really be greedy enough to murder someone?

Mitch piped in, "So, you are saying *she* was the reason behind you going to Oren for money, and then the land?"

"I went to him *one* time for help, right after Dad died, when I realized I couldn't fix the problem I had created, with the money he left me. Dad started to show me how, but he died before we were able to get it done. I went to Oren for help, and he gave me some money. I was trying to fix it, I swear. That, coupled with the money Dad left me in the estate, gave me enough to almost get back on track, but then the taxes hit.

I asked Darren, the guy I'd worked with before, to help. He came over, and we started working on it together. We thought we had it worked out, but something was still off. Money was still missing. Then Valerie got into the mix, and things spiraled out of control, and that's when the company really started to go haywire. She told me to go back to Oren. I'll admit I was pissed that dad didn't leave me the business, and was tempted to say screw it, and walk away, and let them deal with it. But ultimately, it was Dad's company, and I couldn't just let it die, no matter how mad I was."

"I had nothing to do with the mess you were in."

"You may not have started it, but you damn sure

made it worse."

"You were gambling it all away."

"Bullshit. Everything I did, I did for you. I wanted to give you what you wanted. At first, I thought everything she was telling me was legal. I mean, hell, she did have an accounting degree. Mine was in business, so I figured she knew some tricks of the trade, that I didn't, and she was just trying to help me get my ass out of trouble. But then Tetterman said something about someone in the company stealing funds, and when he brought me some of the paperwork, I could tell it was way beyond my screw up. It was then I figured out what she had done, but by then I was in too deep. I kept jacking with the books hoping to reverse what she did, but money kept disappearing, and things went from bad to worse.

"I did gamble some, hoping I could get some of it back. When that didn't work either, Valerie told me to go back to Oren, and talk him out of his land. I remembered some of the older folks talking about the rumors, that diamonds had been found on it. I started researching the land in the area, and then went to the county developers. That's when I realized the rumors might be true. There are old mines all around this area, and I figured if I could get the land, maybe just maybe, I would get lucky. I knew the land by itself would only help so much, and I was grasping for straws. But hell, I was willing to try just about anything to get my ass out of trouble."

Ben's blood boiled, as he listened to Rick's words. "I knew you were full of shit when you were after him about the land. I knew you weren't looking out for his well-being; you piece of shit. How could you do that to him, knowing how much he loved those horses? He was your grandfather."

"No, he wasn't." Valerie popped off. "That was the other reason he killed him."

Rick jerked his gaze to her. "What the hell are you talking about?"

"You know exactly what I'm talking about. Your mom's little secret. I found the paperwork in your dad's chest of drawers, when we were cleaning everything out. And Poppi knew, because I saw the same envelope in that stack of papers. That's why you killed him."

"I. Didn't. Kill. Him. And I damn sure don't know what the hell you are talking about."

"Don't play that game with me."

"No. Seriously Valerie, I have no idea."

"You aren't a McIntyre." Rick's body deflated like a pricked balloon. Disbelief filled his face. "Don't pretend you didn't know, Rick. The papers were twenty years old."

"No. I didn't," Rick responded, his voice barely audible. He stared down at the table. "That's why they divorced. Mom said he was never home. Always doing something with the company. She had an affair, and he found out. But if I wasn't his, why did he keep me? Why didn't he…" His voice trailed off as his eyes stayed locked on the woodgrain of the table.

Ben could hear the distress in his voice. Rick finally lifted his eyes to the sergeant. "He never said a word. Neither did Oren." Rick stood. His eyes still searched for the truth. "I swear, sergeant, I didn't kill my dad, and I didn't kill Oren, nor was I planning on killing him. Yes, I wanted the land, and I may have done a few things to make him more likely to turn it over to me. But I never was going to hurt him. God no. He was a stubborn ole geezer, but he was my granddad. Or at least I thought he was."

From Rick's distressed expression, Ben actually felt sympathy for him. He was starting to believe he might be telling the truth.

"You had no idea about the paternity test?"

"None. I swear."

"Well, how did she know, and you didn't?"

Valerie was now leaned up against the dark paneled wall. "When we were cleaning out Randy's house, I found a brown envelope in the chest of drawers that said 'Lab results.' I figured whatever was in it, was important, so I looked to see what it was."

"And you didn't tell Rick?"

"No. I figured he knew. Actually, that's when I started really wondering if Rick killed Randy. I mean, it stands to reason. If you knew you weren't his and screwed your dear old dad over in his company, and he found out about it, you might get a little worried about your gravy train ending and getting kicked to the curb."

The sergeant crossed his arms and turned back to Rick. "If you didn't know, then why were you trying to get Oren to turn the land over to you on conservatorship? Because that to me screams that you knew, and you were trying to jump the gun on getting your inheritance."

"Yes. I was trying to jump the gun on my inheritance. But the only reason I had, was because I needed the money yesterday, and there were no other resources. Look, the land was valuable, and he didn't need all of it, even with the horses. I figured I could start by selling some of it off, while I did some tests to see if there were any diamonds. I thought I could also make some money on the crops. It all wouldn't add up to what I needed, but it would keep us afloat while I tried to undo what Valerie managed to screw up."

"And if he didn't agree to turn over the conservatorship?"

"I had already filed papers for diminished capacity, and I didn't know the results until a minute ago. But honestly, when he called to meet me for lunch, I was hoping we could work things out somehow. He said he wanted us to lay our cards on the table and I was planning on doing just that. I told Valerie I was ready to tell him everything."

"No, you weren't, Rick. You had been talking about killing him and getting him out of the way."

Rick's eyes flared with anger as he leveled his gaze with Valerie, and Frank cleared his throat. "So, getting back to the matter at hand," he said, before Rick could respond. "Mrs. McIntyre, why exactly did you take the will? It would do you no good while Mr. McIntyre was alive."

Valerie lifted her eyes level with Mitch's, and the cold calculated expression reappeared.

Mitch, still standing next to Valerie, rubbed his chin. "I would think long and hard about what you are about to say Mrs. McIntyre, because there is no reason you would have taken that will unless Oren McIntyre was out of the picture."

Chapter Twenty-Six

Ben took a deep breath and swallowed, trying to digest what had transpired in the last hour. His emotions were a jumbled mess, and he didn't know whether to laugh or cry. Watching Mitch tighten the handcuffs around Valerie's wrists was surreal. It was still hard for him to believe that she would be capable of murder. But the evidence was pretty damning.

His eyes landed on Rick, who still was seated across from him, and shook his head. Though he never liked the guy, he truly felt sorry for him. He either was a damn good actor, or he was telling the truth, and didn't have anything to do with his dad's or Poppi's deaths.

Apparently, he really did love Valerie, and her actions completely devastated him. Frank had explained to him that Poppi had hoped they could work things out. That was the reason the will was there. But it had not been completed. There was no signature or notary, so the will in the safety deposit box was the final will. The land was his. The house, what was left of it, was his. The horses were his. He was officially overwhelmed. Frank's voice barely registered as he set a pile of papers before him.

"This is the information you will need for the accounts at the bank, and the life insurance policies." The only thing Ben could manage was a nod. Each page he thumbed through, caused his heart rate to escalate a little more, until he was about ready to crawl out of his skin. Then suddenly, delicate fingers were dancing around his neck, followed by a sweet smell, as Kaysi wrapped her arms around him from behind, and whispered in his ear. His mind was so preoccupied, he didn't even notice when she came in.

"I came to check and see if you guys were done." He laced his fingers in hers and lifted her hand to his lips. The anxiety, that was threatening to consume him only moments before, had completely dissipated with her touch.

He lifted his eyes but not his head, glancing at everyone around the room. Frank was snapping his briefcase. Mitch was talking to another officer, who had his hand wrapped around Valerie's bicep, and Rick had his elbows resting on the table, with his head in his hands. "Yeah. I think we are done." His eyes finally made it to hers, just as her mouth dropped open.

"What hap—"

"I'll tell you in a little bit," he said, keeping his voice barely above a whisper. "Let's get some lunch." He stood, and made eye contact with Frank, who turned and shook his hand.

"You have my number if you have any questions."

"Thank you for everything."

"I didn't do anything, son. I just relayed the information," he said, patting Ben on the shoulder.

Ben hesitantly nodded, and then his attention shifted to Mitch.

"You good?"

A laugh unexpectedly escaped. "Nope. Not even close."

Mitch smirked. "Yeah, well, I think you came out all right."

Ben let out a long breath. "I think I'm still in shock. It will probably hit me in a few hours." His eyes drifted to Rick. "What's going to happen to him?"

Mitch darted his eyes over his shoulder. "Not sure yet. I don't know that we have the whole story, but right now we don't have enough evidence to arrest him. Hell, I'm his alibi. He's agreed to come to the station and give his statement, so we will see. Currently, at best, he's committed some misdemeanor crimes. They investigated his dad's death, and came up with nothing that stuck to him, so the truth to that story may have died with Randy."

"After what happened today, I hate to say it, but I kind of feel sorry for him."

"You and me both." They both watched as Rick stood. His eyes followed, as the officer escorted Valerie out of the room. "I don't know that he's completely innocent of everything, but from the shock on his face, that man was seriously blindsided."

"Yep."

"Corbett." Ben's eyes met Rick's, then darted back to Mitch, then Kaysi.

"Give me a minute," Ben said to Kaysi, and he lightly grabbed her hand. She nodded.

"I'm heading out," Mitch said, and patted Ben on the shoulder as Ben made his way around the table, to where Rick was standing.

Rick's eyes met Ben's, and he let out an audible breath as he donned a frustrated expression. "Look, I don't know what's—"

"I hope you don't think I had anything to do with

this."

Shaking his head, Rick barked a laugh. "Nah, I saw your expression when the lawyer said your name. I think the old man pretty much surprised the shit out of both of us." He folded his arms across his chest and his eyes drifted.

"What are you going to do?" Ben asked hesitantly, rolling the papers into a tube in his hands.

Still not making eye contact, Rick responded. "I don't know. I guess I will talk to Tetterman, and explain what happened, and beg him not to fire me from my dad's company.

"Tetterman?"

"My dad's partner. Well, was his partner. He now owns the company."

"You think he will let you stay on?"

"Who knows. I mean, he knew what happened when I messed up the first time. But I need to come clean about the rest of it." His eyes made it back to Ben. "He's a decent guy, and he knows the business. So, maybe?"

"Do you like doing all that financial trading stuff?"

"Yeah, I do. Well, did. But I'm apparently not that good at it." Rick rested his head on the wall and averted his eyes, and Ben thought he saw them glistening. "Funny thing is, I really thought I had figured things out. Even beyond what Valerie screwed up. It was going to take some work, and I would still need some money from somewhere, but I thought I could fix it. And not illegally either."

"Well, that's—"

"But it won't matter anyway. Tetterman won't go for—"

"Maybe we can work something out."

"Don't do me any favors, Corbett."

"Just let me see what all is in this paperwork, okay?"

"Don't bother. I seriously doubt I'm going to have a job next week. Hell, I may be going to prison. Who knows." He leaned forward and put his hands on the back of the chair like his legs were about to give way. "Anyway, that's not what I wanted to talk to you about."

"Oh?" Ben mimicked Rick's position, leaning on the chair. "What then?"

"I was going to ask if you might let me help with Oren's service and burial."

Ben didn't know how to respond. "You aren't in any position to help with the cost, and I think Poppi—"

"I didn't mean money. I just thought…" He took a deep breath. "Never mind—"

"Ohhh. Sure. I'm good with us working together on it."

"I mean, that's if I'm not in jail."

"Yeah. Let me get your phone number, and once I sort through all this," he held up the pile of papers in his hand, "I'll call you, and we can handle it together. Does that sound okay?"

"Yeah."

****

Ben pressed his hand to the small of Kaysi's back and guided her to their booth. She was still snickering at Arnie's sidewalk sign when she slid in. "What did it say? I didn't see it," Ben asked, as he slid in on his side, and took one of the menus the hostess handed him.

"Soup of the day. Tears of our competitors. We also have loaded baked potato."

"That actually sounds really good. I think I might get that, and the Orange You Jealous, club."

"That sounds perfect."

Ben let his attention drift out the window. A couple, bundled in their coats and hats, strolled down the sidewalk, walking a tiny ball of white fur on a leash. He couldn't help snickering to himself, clicking through the possibilities of what it was. All he could see were four tiny legs, and a massive ball of fur. Dog? Guinea pig? Rat?

Like Kaysi knew where his mind was, she said, "Those dogs are just too small for me. I would be terrified I would trip over it and squash it. If we ever get a dog, I want one that at least will break my fall, without me hurting it. Like a Weimaraner."

Ben loved the fact that she used the word "we." but he wasn't sure what she was talking about. "A what?"

"A Weimaraner. They are big silver dogs with these gray eyes." She immediately retrieved her phone and started tapping. Ben watched her until he heard a voice.

"Are you guys ready to order?"

Kaysi let her eyes settle on the young waitress for a moment. "I'll have the potato soup and the Orange You Jealous club, with an unsweetened iced tea."

"Make that two," Ben added.

The waitress smiled and collected the menus. "My name is Brooke," she said, while she scrawled her name on a smaller version of the sign from outside. "If you need anything just hang the sign on the hook at the end of the table and I'll be right over." She handed the sign to Ben and walked away, with her blonde ponytail bouncing with each step.

Kaysi cleared her throat in an exaggerated fashion, and Ben's eyes darted back to her, to see her holding up her phone to him. "Sorry."

"Well, she is cute."

"No. It's not that. She looked like a younger version of Valerie." Kaysi winced, and Ben knew he needed to explain everything that had happened earlier, but he didn't quite know where to begin. He glanced at the phone she was still holding in her hand. Several photos were displayed of a silver haired dog with light eyes. He scrolled through the photos, already knowing that they would own one, if he could find it. His heart skipped, when one photo showed a dog with a pheasant in its mouth. "They're hunting dogs?"

"I have no idea. I've just wanted one since the first time I saw it. I'd love to have a longhaired one, but they are harder to find, and more expensive."

"Well, let me get past all this estate stuff, and we can do some research." The way Kaysi's eyes lit up made him wish he could make it magically appear right then and there. She nodded and gave him that easy smile, that pierced his heart with her special light, and sent a warmth through him, calming the thoughts that kept parading through his head. His eyes met hers again, and he returned the smile.

With a tip of her head, she leaned in and asked, "What happened today? Why was Valerie in handcuffs? And what kind of deal was Rick trying to cut with—"

Her rapid-fire questions had Ben shaking his head and holding up his hand. He took a deep breath, and his eyes settled on her. Glimpsing outside, another person, bundled against the winter chill, passed by, and as they waited for their food, Ben began filling her in.

Minutes passed. The waitress arrived with their drinks and plates and slid them into place. She asked if there was anything else they needed, and when they both shook their heads, she smiled and disappeared. Ben took a drink of his tea and noticed Kaysi still staring at him.

"Why didn't Randy leave the company to Rick? Was he just concerned he couldn't handle it?"

"From what the lawyer said, the company was founded by Randy and his buddy, before families came into the picture. They were equal partners, and in their initial partnership they had put each other down as benefactors, in case something happened, and the contract never got changed."

Ben gazed out the window for a moment. "You know what's sad?" His eyes slowly reconnected with Kaysi's. "The lawyer said that Poppi had planned on trying to work things out with Rick. That's why he had the will there. He was going to put him back in the will, if he could get the truth out of Rick, and they could come to some kind of agreement."

"Wait. He's not the benefactor? Then who is? I didn't think he had other family around here."

"He doesn't."

"Then who…"

Ben's mind immediately replayed the moment when Frank called out his name. He still couldn't come to terms with that part. It was surreal. He really didn't think he heard right. The thoughts must have played out in his expression, because Kaysi's lips parted in surprise.

"You. He left everything…" She didn't even finish her sentence, before Ben hesitantly nodded his head, and the sting of tears made him bark out a laugh.

"Dammit Kaysi. What kind of switch did you flip in me? Every time I turn around now, I get the waterworks." He swiped at his eyes with the pads of his hands. Kaysi jumped up from her seat and moved to his.

Turning his face to her, she wiped more tears away.

"Are you okay?" Her fingers threaded through his hair as she studied him.

"Do I look okay?" He chuckled again, feeling a bit embarrassed. Her lip popped out, concern filled her face, but she quickly moved in, planting a gentle kiss on his lips. That was her go-to move now. Every time he seemed to be getting upset, she would kiss him. And damned if it didn't work like a charm. Her fingers moved to his beard, and as she backed away, her eyes glinted, and she gave him a playful wink, then grabbed a chip from his plate. *Damn. This woman.* Sliding her plate closer to her, she took another bite of her sandwich, still angled toward him.

"So that's what all the paperwork was for?"

"Yeah. Insurance policies and bank accounts. I don't know what all is in there, but I'm not messing with any of it until after the funeral. I need to figure out what to do."

"About what?"

"Everything. I am not a big fan of Rick, and I still don't know if he was completely innocent in everything, but from what Frank said, Poppi was considering giving him at least some of the land, until Valerie jumped the gun. And if I'm being honest, I feel like I need to do something. She kind of screwed him over good."

"So, the will she grabbed—"

"Wasn't completed. It wasn't signed or notarized."

Chapter Twenty-Seven

"Ray, you are going to have to be quick about this, because this thing weighs a thousand pounds. Think about where you want it, before we haul it out of the trailer, because you are not getting a second, or third option on this one. This is a one and done." Ben stood at the back of the trailer, that was backed up to the front of the store. Kaysi couldn't stop the smile from spreading across her face at his nickname for her, from their days at camp. Cody and Ben, along with Joe and Kaleb, had been working all morning, unloading different pieces of furniture, that had been carefully restored, and now held a place in the new store. The last piece was the antique cast iron stove, that Ben rescued from the rock house, before Joe and his crew started demolition. Although the house was damaged from the fire, Joe managed to salvage quite a bit of material, to use for future projects.

The old stove was a rusted piece of junk, until Ben worked his magic on it, and now it was a conversation piece.

"No, I've got a place already marked off for it. It might be a tight squeeze though."

"Please, tell me it isn't going upstairs, because—"

"No, of course not. It is going in the front window."

"Great. Where?"

Kaysi pointed to the corner window. "Right there."

This was the last push, to get everything set up, before the grand opening. Ben had finished the sign, and got it hung on the corner of the building, which instantly gave Kaysi the realization, that the business was becoming a reality. She had been through the dream stage, the planning stage, and with the sign now in place, and the building completely remodeled, her heart hadn't stopped racing with the thought of opening day.

In the weeks since Poppi's death, Ben had worked with the lawyer to get all the paperwork to the ranch and accounts switched over. Everything was officially his. He stayed true to his word, and worked with Rick, to help plan the funeral. And after the graveside service, he visited his mom's grave. Through it all, Kaysi never left his side. It wasn't easy for him. Kaysi could see the pain in his eyes, but he had weathered the storm, and come out on the other side.

Still, she knew he was bothered by the fact that Poppi hadn't really gotten the resolution he'd hoped for with Rick. The case still wasn't closed, but Ben had a long talk with Rick, and he told Kaysi he wished there was some way they could find some sort of compromise.

She eyed him in his flannel, button-down shirt, with his hair hanging in his eyes, straining against the cast iron behemoth, trying to load it onto the cart, and her whole body shivered. He was all man, and all hers.

As they rolled the stove into place, Mitch arrived at the store. Though Ben had spoken to the sergeant a few times during the investigation, he had mostly left the team of investigators alone, other than allowing them onto the land when necessary.

Kaysi smiled at Mitch when he entered the store, removing his gloves. He had a box tucked under his arm.

His head bobbed as he scanned his surroundings. "You guys look like you are about ready to open."

"We're getting there." Her head tilted. "Did you bring us a grand opening gift?"

Mitch glanced at the box as he shoved his gloves in his pocket. "Not exactly." He reached for the box with one hand and pushed his sunglasses up with the other. His eyes drifted to Ben. Kaysi had a feeling this wasn't exactly a social call by the tone of his voice. "I went by your place, but you weren't there. While I was heading back to the office, I noticed your truck, so I decided to stop. When will you be available?"

"Is this about the investigation?"

"Yeah."

"We're just finishing up. Is it confidential?"

"That's up to you."

"They pretty much know everything."

"Bar-b-que has arrived." A cheery voice crooned, and all eyes were aimed at the door again, where Jenna stood, with her hands full of plastic bags. Cody grabbed a couple of the bags from her.

"Ya hungry?" Ben asked, bringing his focus back to Mitch.

"I won't ever pass up bar-b-que."

"Good. There will be plenty." Jenna passed by them, and Ben twitched his head. "There's a table and chairs upstairs."

"Wow! This place looks pretty good." Mitch commented, as the stairs opened to the fully decorated loft.

"Gee, Mitch. Thanks for the vote of confidence," April said sarcastically with a snicker.

Kaysi lifted out the containers of food and prepared

them buffet style. A deliciously smokey scent wafted through the room.

Mitch set the box on a bean shaped coffee table and grabbed a paper plate. Kaysi stared at the box, wondering what was inside.

Setting her plate down at the table, she scooted out the chair next to Ben.

"So, what did you find out, Mitch?" Ben questioned, filling his fork with some of the potato salad.

"From everything we have gathered so far in the investigation, we think Valerie instigated this on her own."

"You don't think Rick had any part of it?"

"He owned up to letting the horses out and stealing the feed and cattle."

"How did he get the fence open?"

"Found a key in Randy's stuff."

"But that was it? You didn't get the sense that Valerie was being coerced?"

"Not at all. If anything, it was the other way around. Why?"

"It's nothing. After the reading of the will, I kind of figured that was the case. She had just tried to drag me into her web of lies a couple of times. She said he'd verbally abused her, and they were separated."

"Yeah, you mentioned that before. They had been living apart off and on, but it was because her father was hurt. I haven't seen anything leading me to believe they were legally separated. She was probably trying to manipulate you into believing her story and using you as a shield. So far, we haven't been able to connect Rick to much. Just a few misdemeanor charges. In fact, as far as the embezzlement charges, evidence is showing that

Rick was an unwilling participant in a much bigger scheme."

"You've gotta be kidding me."

"Remember Rick talking about seeking the help of one of his colleagues?"

"Yeah."

"Turns out that guy, Darren Adler, was already skimming money from the company, and took the opportunity to use Rick's limited knowledge to his advantage. With a few keystrokes it threw the blame on Rick, yet still funneled the money into his account. And later, when Rick asked for his help again, Darren got well acquainted with Valerie, and they became partners."

"Oh shit. Seriously?"

"Yep. I think, she figured out what he was doing and called him on it. But instead of turning him in, she saw it as her path to fame and fortune. He knew she held the cards, so he became her accomplice. They cooked the whole thing up regarding Poppi. He was the guy you saw her with at the charity dinner.

"On the security video you could see her on the phone when she left the first time. We traced the number back to him. From the information we have gathered, we are pretty sure Poppi was attacked in the stables. We found traces of blood in there, and on his saddle. So, he was definitely injured before falling from his horse and being trampled."

Kaysi slowly lowered her hand to Ben's leg and gently rubbed it. He eyed her, and gave her a wink, letting her know he was okay.

Ben's focus returned to Mitch. "And the fire?"

"We found traces of accelerant in Mr. Adler's car."

"It sounds like she had him do all the dirty work.

Are you going to make anything stick to her?"

"Granted we were grasping at straws, until one piece of evidence reared it's oh so expensive head." Mitch smirked, and Kaysi wondered what bomb he was about to drop. "Remember Rick talking about having to have money to pay for Mrs. McIntyre's caviar taste?" Ben raised his brows and nodded. "Turns out those expensive shoes, that she just couldn't part with, were her undoing. We found traces of blood on them." Ben sat back in his chair, crossed his arms, and let out a long sigh."

"I don't get it though. She and Adler killed Poppi for the land she thought was going to Rick."

"Yeah. Kind of need Rick out of the picture, don't you think? You said she told you they were separated, and Rick was being verbally abusive. We are thinking she might have been setting the stage for an alibi for his death."

"Damn. I never would have thought—"

"So that's it, then. Go. To. Jail. Don't pass go. Do not collect two hundred dollars," April teased, and all eyes landed on her. "Oh. Sorry." A red hue crept up her neck. Kaysi busted out laughing, watching April turn the shade of a ripe strawberry.

"She's not wrong. With the evidence we have on both of them, we have a decent case against them."

"And you really feel like Rick was completely innocent?"

"The investigation isn't closed yet. But so far, we have found no connection with him to the incident, other than what I've told you already. As far as the death of his dad, I honestly have no idea. The actual embezzlement issue is now linked to Mr. Adler and Mrs. McIntyre. His boss has already stated that he is comfortable with letting

Rick remain at the company, since he uncovered Adler's embezzlement."

Ben tipped his head back, ran his fingers through his hair, and chewed on the side of his lip.

"Why are you so hell bent on pinning something on Rick?"

"I'm not, actually. I just want to make sure he deserves me trying to help him."

"What do you mean, help him?"

"Well, if Valerie wouldn't have jumped in and screwed things up, Poppi would have likely given Rick at least some of the land or helped him out of his financial issue. I think Poppi would have wanted me to work something out with Rick. I just don't know what to do exactly. He was wanting to dig up the land for some legend about diamonds, and I'm not going to let him do that, just to come up empty."

"About that." Mitch pushed his chair out, and walked over to the coffee table, to retrieve the box. "When we were collecting evidence at the house, after the fire, we found this." He dropped the box on the table and nodded to Ben. Ben eyed Kaysi, then his focus traveled around the table.

"What is it?"

"Open it."

Ben stood, and lifted the flaps, and found a box of oddly shaped shiny rocks, in hues of yellow and brown. "What? These are the rocks he had in the bottom of a vase on his table."

"There were some in the abandoned house too," Kaysi added.

"Guys. Those aren't rocks. They are raw diamonds."

"Oh, you gotta be shittin' me."

Kaysi couldn't keep the smile from spreading across her face.

"Let me see." Jenna said, motioning for them to push the box to her."

"These are diamonds?" she questioned, after peeking in the box and passing it to Cody.

"That's what I've been told," Mitch responded.

"I've found stuff like this in our stream. I just thought it was a weird type of quartz." Jenna picked one of the stones out, and examined it closely, as the box made its way to everyone at the table.

"Apparently not. The vase was shattered, so it was confiscated along with the rocks, and beads, and flowers, to check for blood. And I guess one of the guys examining the material knew a little about gemstones."

"We found jars of these in the cellar, under the house, when we were tearing it down," Joe added. "I have them at the office."

"Well damn. Rick was right," Ben growled. "I guess I have no excuse to help him now." His hand rubbed the back of his neck. "Somehow, I think Poppi had a hand in this."

"You could be right."

As the box made its way back to Ben, Kaysi peeked inside, then dipped her hand in, letting the stones glide through her fingers. She palmed a handful and examined them closely. Picking out one, she spun it in between her thumb and finger. It was the size of a jellybean and yellow, but a soft yellow, like the color of jasmine. As she twirled it between her fingers, Ben could see colors of green and orange glinting from it. It was exquisite, even in its raw form. From the corner of her eye, she saw Ben staring at her. She turned her head to glare at him.

"What?" she questioned.

"Nothing."

"It's such a soft yellow, but there are so many colors within it. It's beautiful. Can I keep this one?" Kaysi asked, as her eyes made it back to Mitch.

"They're Ben's. You need to ask him."

Her head jerked to Ben, and he quirked his mouth, making a face like he was pondering the question, then opened his hand, requesting her to hand it over.

Wondering what he was up to, she slowly dropped the rock in his hand.

Ben took the stone and held it up to the light, rotating it from one side to the other. His eyes slowly slid to her, and his lips pursed. She could tell he was holding back a smile.

"Well?" She held her hand out, hoping he would return the stone, but his fingers closed around it.

"I think I might have plans for this one."

A word about the author...

DeDe Ramey is a multi-award-winning author. She's a Texas girl transplanted in the heart of Oklahoma. She is a wife. mom to two grown kids, Drew and Leah, and Nina to one grandson, Jude.

Growing up in the beautiful historic town of Georgetown Texas, her crazy life experiences help fuel her rich colorful stories.

She began writing lyrics to songs at an early age hoping one day to become a country and western recording artist. Although that dream didn't transpire, she never lost her love of the written word.

But it wasn't until after her children were raised that she went in search of something else that gave her joy. She found it in the pages of books.

With the encouragement of her husband, she wrote her first novel in 2018 and never looked back.

Her vivid imagination and love for people watching gave her a passion to write romance novels filled with swoon worthy heroes, smart, sassy heroines, unexpected, nail-biting suspense, and a good helping of steamy, heart melting romance.

When she is not reading or writing, she enjoys working out at the gym, going to concerts of old rock bands, and exploring new cities and national parks and forests with her husband, Keith, her very own devastatingly handsome hero of 40 years.

Thank you for purchasing
this publication of The Wild Rose Press, Inc.

For questions or more information
contact us at
info@thewildrosepress.com.

The Wild Rose Press, Inc.
www.thewildrosepress.com